Asda Tickled Pink

45p from the sale of this book will be donated to Tickled Pink.

Asda Tickled Pink wants to ensure all breast cancer is diagnosed early and help improve people's many different experiences of the disease. Working with our charity partners, Breast Cancer Now and CoppaFeel!, we're on a mission to make checking your boobs, pecs and chests, whoever you are, as normal as your Asda shop. And with your help, we're raising funds for new treatments, vital education and life-changing support, for anyone who needs it. Together, we're putting breast cancer awareness on everyone's list.

Since the partnership began in 1996, Asda Tickled Pink has raised over £82 million for its charity partners. Through the campaign, Asda has been committed to raising funds and breast-check awareness via in-store fundraising, disruptive awareness campaigns, and products turning pink to support the campaign. The funds have been vital for Breast Cancer Now's world-class research and life-changing support services, such as their Helpline, there for anyone affected by breast cancer to cope with the emotional impact of the disease. Asda Tickled Pink's educational and outreach work with CoppaFeel! aims to empower 1 million 18–24 year olds to adopt a regular boob-checking behaviour by 2025. Together we will continue to make a tangible difference to breast cancer in the UK.

Asda Tickled Pink and Penguin Random House have teamed up to bring you Tickled Pink Books. By buying this book and supporting the partnership, you ensure that 45p goes directly to Breast Cancer Now and CoppaFeel!.

Breast cancer is the most common cancer in women in the UK, with one in seven women facing it in their lifetime.

Around 55,000 women and 370 men are diagnosed with breast cancer every year in the UK and nearly 1,000 people still lose their life to the disease each month. This is one person every 45 minutes and this is why your support and the support from Asda Tickled Pink is so important.

A new Tickled Pink Book will go on sale in Asda stores every two weeks – we aim to bring you the best stories of friendship, love, heartbreak and laughter.

*To find out more about the Tickled Pink partnership
visit www.asda.com/tickled-pink*

Penguin
Random House
UK

STAY BREAST AWARE AND CHECK YOURSELF REGULARLY

One in seven women in the UK will be diagnosed with breast cancer in their lifetime

'TOUCH, LOOK, KNOW YOUR NORMAL, REPEAT REGULARLY'

Make sure you stay breast aware
- Get to know what's normal for you
- Look and feel to notice any unusual changes early
- The earlier breast cancer is diagnosed, the better the chance of successful treatment
- Check your boobs regularly and see a GP if you notice a change

PENGUIN BOOKS

the
love
of
my
afterlife

Kirsty Greenwood is a bestselling author of funny, fearless romantic comedies about extraordinary love. When she's not writing books she composes musicals and explores London where she lives with her husband.

Also by Kirsty Greenwood

Novels

Yours Truly

Jessica Beam is a Hot Mess

Big Sexy Love

The Movie Star and Me

Novellas

It Happened on Christmas Eve

Love Will Save the Day

the
love
of
my
afterlife

KIRSTY GREENWOOD

PENGUIN BOOKS

PENGUIN BOOKS

UK | USA | Canada | Ireland | Australia
India | New Zealand | South Africa

Penguin Books is part of the Penguin Random House group
of companies whose addresses can be found at
global.penguinrandomhouse.com

Penguin
Random House
UK

Published in Penguin Books 2024
001

Typeset in 10.4/15pt Palatino LT Pro by Jouve (UK), Milton Keynes
Printed and bound in Great Britain by Clays Ltd, Elcograf S.p.A.

The authorised representative in the EEA is Penguin Random House Ireland,
Morrison Chambers, 32 Nassau Street, Dublin D02 YH68

A CIP catalogue record for this book is available from the British Library

ISBN: 978–1–804–94911–5

www.greenpenguin.co.uk

MIX
Paper | Supporting
responsible forestry
FSC
www.fsc.org   FSC® C018179

Penguin Random House is committed to a
sustainable future for our business, our readers
and our planet. This book is made from Forest
Stewardship Council® certified paper.

For my little sister Nic. A true ride or die friend and the most fearless and mischievous accomplice I will ever know.

the
love
of
my
afterlife

Chapter One

This cannot be how I die.

It really, *really* can't.

Naturally, I know not everyone is blessed with the whole old-lady-from-*Titanic* option, drifting off into a toasty sleep, memories of making love to a peak Leonardo DiCaprio there to soften the blow of perishing. But choking to death at the age of twenty-seven? Delphie, *no*.

As I gasp for air, my brain seems unable to compute how I might save myself from this horror show and instead fixates entirely on the mortifying circumstances via which it's playing out.

For a start, I'm choking on a burger. Not even a premium or homemade burger but a cheap microwaveable one I grabbed from the corner shop after work. And then there are the clothes I'm wearing as I choke: pickle-green socks paired with the worst of all my nightwear – an over-washed oversized atrocity with a cartoon of a grinning star above the slogan HONEY, IT'S TIME TO SPARKLE AND SHINE! My TV is paused a quarter of the way through *The Tinder Swindler* and my laptop is lit with one solitary tab: a Google page on which I have enquired are microwaveable burgers real meat?

Who's going to find me in this state? My despicable

downstairs neighbour Cooper (who will definitely sneer when he sees my nightie)? The police? Rummaging through my private belongings, hunting for evidence of possible foul play? They'd have a tricky time finding anyone with motive, considering I only know three people in all of London – Leanne and her mum, Jan, from the pharmacy where I work, plus old Mr Yoon from next door.

Oh God, what if it's old Mr Yoon who discovers me? That must not happen – his heart is way too fragile to handle something as grim as this. Sweet Mr Yoon! If I'm gone there won't be anyone to check he's properly extinguished his cigarettes before he goes to sleep. And who will make him a breakfast that isn't just a bowl of boring old cardboardy All-Bran?

At the thought of Mr Yoon gazing sorrowfully into his cereal cupboard, I fling myself over to a rickety kitchen chair and slam my body over the top in a bid to self-Heimlich. I once saw Miranda on *Sex and the City* do this and she survived, shaken but emotionally wiser for the experience.

I bash my diaphragm down onto the chair over and over again. Then I clasp my hands together and thump myself in the stomach. Ow. Nothing. Am I punching myself in the correct place? I do it again, this time a little lower down. And then again, higher up. It's not working! This chunk of bun and possibly-not-real-meat is lodged in my gullet and I believe it intends to stay there. Shit.

I race from one side of my tiny living room to the other, searching for something, anything at all that might help me. My beloved *Broad City* baseball cap hanging from the hook on my front door? Useless! Box of unopened Blackwing pencils on the kitchen table? Come *on*, Delphie! My eyes zero in on my phone, peeking out from beneath a sofa cushion. I grab it to call an ambulance but my hands are trembling so much that I can't get a grip. The phone tumbles to the floor, skidding under the edge of my TV stand to live in an entire habitat of dust plus an antidepressant I dropped last month and never quite got around to retrieving.

Argh. Everything's going dark around the edges. My tongue feels weird, heavy, like it's lolling. Is my tongue *lolling*? My knees collapse and I flail theatrically to the ground, head landing with a thud on the lovely soft stripy rug I've spent the last three months saving up for.

Oh God.

I think . . . I think this is actually *it*?

My grand finale.

My expiration date.

The End.

Here lies Delphie Denise Bookham.

She died just as she lived: alone, perplexed, wearing something a bit shit.

'Open your eyes . . . That's it. Time to come to . . . Time to awaken . . . Aha, there you are! Hey, darling girl.'

The stranger's voice is female, a wisp of melodic Irish cadence softening the edges. My eyes fly open. A woman smiles maniacally, small up-turned nose barely an inch from mine. I take her in: springy butter-blonde curls drawn into a high ponytail, voguish gold specs making the earnest green

3

eyes she's using to openly gawk at me look twice the size. She's wearing orange lipstick that's bled onto her large teeth, both rows fully exposed to form said maniacal smile. I squeeze my eyes shut. Then I open them again, try desperately to get my bearings. My insides immediately make a fuss when I realise that I'm not in my flat where I pretty much always am, but sitting in a strange plastic chair, legs propped up on a floral upholstered buffet like a nana.

Where am I right now?

Bobby McFerrin's 'Don't Worry, Be Happy' echoes from some unknown direction, the reverberation of it eerie and dreamlike. Wide-eyed, I scan the room: pale blue painted walls, a row of aqua-green washing machines lined up in front of me, spinning and gurgling and puffing out warm lavender-scented air at even intervals. Hold up. Is this a launderette? What the hell am I doing in a *launderette*? How did I get here? *When* did I get here?

Above the washers I spot a large framed photo of the bespectacled woman. She's doing a double thumbs-up, her smile at pageant winner wattage. My gaze slides from the picture on the wall, back to the real-life version crouched beside my chair. She beams like she could not be more delighted to see me. Then she gives me a double thumbs-up exactly like the one in the photo.

Who is this? Where am I? 'Uh . . . uh . . .'

My panicked brain refuses to assist me in delivering the questions aloud.

'Clever, right?' The woman grins. 'No one ever gets scared in a launderette! Seemed smart to offset such an objectively terrifying moment with the most calming environment I could imagine. And this is it – a lobby that looks and feels like a cosy little launderette! When I was younger and things got a little *Argh, life is so hard, wah-wah-wah*, I'd take myself off to the local outfit and watch all the machines spinning around and around and around for hours. All those blossomy smells, all those sloshy sounds? *So* comforting, don't you think?'

I flinch as the woman jumps up from her squat, proudly flinging her arms around the room like she's a gameshow host about to reveal the grand prize.

'The blue on the walls is identical to the colour of the sky just before the sun sets in the last week of June. Took me an age to find the exact right chromaticity. It's this paint shade called Dehydrated Goose, discontinued in 'ninety-two. But I knew a guy who knew a gal who knew a guy who knew the right guy and yeah, I eventually pulled it off.' She presses her lips together and thrusts her hands into the pockets of her mustard dungarees, swinging lightly from side to side. 'The Higher-Ups made it *quite* clear they wanted a cleaner, more "professional" aesthetic but I said to them, I said, "Guys, you can't expect me to be a top-tier Afterlife Therapist without allowing me full autonomy over the environment in which I therapise the deceased. I mean, *come on*, guys . . ." Idiots. Idiots everywhere! It's a gorgeous shade though, isn't it?' She gazes up at the walls, sighs happily, and runs her teeth over her bottom lip, dragging off a bunch more lipstick in the process. 'It almost changes hue with the light. Sometimes a chalky lilac grey. Sometimes denim blue. Like the eyes of Jamie Fraser. You know Jamie Fraser? From the *Out-lander* books? What a ride. He's in my top ten fictional romantic leads. Maybe actually top five. Maybe even top—'

'The deceased?' I manage to cut in.

'Oh, yeah . . . You're dead, sweetie. I'm sorry.' She rubs my shoulder gamely.

'What? No . . . I . . . Is this a dream?'

I urge my brain to wake itself up. This is the oddest dream I've ever had, and I once dreamed I ran a struggling hair salon with Tramp from *Lady and the Tramp*.

'You choked, remember?' the chatty woman tells me. 'On a microwave burger? They *are* real meat, by the way. One hundred per cent beef, or as I like to call it, *bœuf*. I recently started learning French in between client arrivals. Not that I'm bored or anything. Not really. Could things pick up a little around here?' She shrugs a smooth, tanned shoulder, mouth bunching up to the side. 'Sure. But better a steady trickle of Deads than an ambush, I guess.'

Deads?

My gut spirals as I suddenly remember what happened in my flat. The choking. I press a hand to my throat and start gasping for air.

'Oh, it's okay. You're totally fine,' the woman soothes, crouching back down so that she's eye level with me. 'All corporeal physical ailments are eliminated as soon as you arrive here. But the emotional transition period from living to not-living can be . . . tricky. That's where I come in. I'm Merritt, twenty-eight years old – always will be – and my absolute favourite things are curry and romance novels, the

6

hotter the better on both accounts. I'm your assigned After-life Therapist.'

She shoves out her hand to shake mine and I notice that she's wearing a different statement ring on every finger. One of them is a vintage-looking diamond rose, another is thick black enamel with a skull and crossbones dotted out in rubies. On her thumb is a silver band that says HALF AGONY/ HALF HOPE. It's like she dipped her digits in a lost property box and didn't much care what came out. I can only stare so she picks my limp hand up from where it dangles off the armrest and yanks it so enthusiastically that I sort of wobble back and forth in the chair.

'It's my job to make sure you get settled in, don't freak out too much, answer any questions you may have, etc., etc. I will be your main point of contact going forward. Sound good? *Oui?*'

No. No, it does not sound good at all. *Non.*

'I'm amazing at my job, don't worry,' Merritt continues breezily. 'I started at Evermore – that's what we call it here – about six months after I died. I'm now the youngest woman to be made a full Afterlife Therapist. Most of the other thera-pists are old cronies in their sixties and seventies, but I guess I just showed a natural affinity for the role. Plus I'm ambi-tious as fuck.'

'Help,' I whisper.

'The other therapists don't like it one bit – a hot young woman making waves. They steal all the incoming Deads away before I can get my hands on them.' She looks down at her feet for a second, which I notice are shoeless, toenails

7

painted Coca-Cola red. 'I could run circles around everyone here if I was just given a fair chance,' she mutters grimly. 'Anyway, I won't bore you with all that. The point is that two of those old gobshites are on annual leave right now so they didn't get a chance to steal you! You're my first arrival in a whole week! Yay for me. Boo-hoo for you, obviously. But for me? Brilliant.'

I watch dumbly as Merritt marches towards a door on the opposite side of the room, a flick of her forefinger indicating that I should follow her.

'Where . . . where are we going?' I ask, my entire body now trembling so much that the words come out with a vibrato so rapid I sound like Jessie J.

'My office, of course. I can't conduct the enrolment here in the lobby, can I? What if another Dead arrives while you're in the middle of answering an intimate question? Awkward. If there's one thing people always said about me back on earth it was that I was a very professional person. Privacy first. Don't fret. I got you, babe.' She sings the last bit in a Cher voice.

Merritt opens the door and I'm somewhat comforted to discover that it leads to a very nice, relatively normal-looking office. There are candles everywhere, the flames a warm shimmering pink colour. In the middle of the room stands a glass desk, covered with knick-knacks including three absolutely thriving plants, a Japanese waving lucky cat and a desk-tidy, which is empty because the pens it's supposed to be holding are scattered haphazardly across the

8

desk. On the far wall, there's a floor-to-ceiling bookcase totally stuffed with books, their spines all the colours of the rainbow. Every single one seems to be a romance novel. Titles like *The Proposal*, *A Match Made in Devon* and *The Bride Test*. Merritt sees me looking and selects one of them – a pretty cloth-covered hardback of *Persuasion* by Jane Austen. She presses it to her chest and closes her eyes blissfully like she's cuddling a puppy. 'You can totally borrow anything you like,' she says, sliding the book back onto the shelf and dancing her fingers lovingly across the surrounding spines.

'Um, thanks.'

Merritt sniffs the air, exhaling audibly. 'Roses and black-currants. My signature scent.' She points to a flickering white candle on a little wooden table. 'Gorgeous, right? We have a Diptyque shop at Evermore. *C'est magnifique*. Ooh, we must find you a signature scent too. I bet you're a honey-suckle girl, am I right? Prone to introspection, sensitive heart but with a rich inner world. Plenty of passion bubbling beneath the surface.'

I blink. What the fuck is happening right now? What is this place?

Merritt throws me a benevolent smile. 'Okay. I can see you're perturbed, which . . . absolutely. This situation is bat-shit, I know. When I first arrived here, I literally spewed. Why don't you take a seat, rest your bones a moment.'

She indicates a white leather spinny chair in front of her desk and then, before I can rest, bones or otherwise, she claps her hands decisively.

'Right! Excellent. Okay.' She plucks a clipboard from her desk and scans the paper atop it. 'First question is . . . Would you like to see your life flash before your eyes?'

'Ex-excuse me?' My teeth have started to chatter.

'I *said*, "Would you like to see your life flash before your eyes?" We never used to offer the service, but of course Hollywood gave humans the impression that they got to see their lives pass before their eyes when they expire. And while I love me a well-trodden trope, that one is simply not based in reality. We had a few complaints from disgruntled Deads on arrival so now we offer it, if you want it. Totally up to you, no presh.'

I feel cold. Why is it so cold? I spot a furry blanket draped on one of the other chairs. I grab it and wrap it tightly around my shoulders, bunching it beneath my chin.

'So . . . do you want it or not?' Merritt repeats, fingernail tapping on the back of the clipboard.

'Uh . . . um . . .' I bleat, fingering the corner of the blanket. 'Can I go home now?'

Merritt sighs lightly. 'Shall we just say yes about the life flashing before your eyes bit? This is the only chance you'll get to see it. If I don't show you now and you change your mind later then you'll probably be in a mood with me and that's no way for us to start an everlasting friendship.'

I watch open-mouthed as Merritt disappears into a cupboard before wheeling out a white metal trolley on which there is a big grey nineties TV and a DVD player. 'It doesn't last for too long,' she says. 'We show what we feel are the most relevant clips, otherwise it would be a massive snoozefest, and while technically we have eternity at our disposal, ain't nobody got time for that kind of navel-gazing. Like, what's done is done, you know?'

I can only stare as Merritt presses play. Is the DVD already in? Is the player just for show? I'm so confused.

'Here we go!' Merritt says. 'Delphie Denise Bookham. This . . . was . . . YOUR LIFE!'

Chapter Two

To a soundtrack of Stevie Wonder's 'Isn't She Lovely?' Merritt's video fades in on an adorable montage of moments from my idyllic childhood. Way before Dad got bored of us and left. Before Mum got a new boyfriend and ran away to join an artists' commune in Texas. This was back when life was as close to perfect as it could be.

I drink in the clips, suddenly terrified to miss a single detail. Look how the three of us cartwheel and roly-poly through long daisy-dotted grass, snuggle together on a Sunday morning, draw pictures of made-up sea creatures, or dance on the bed to Aretha Franklin. There's Mum letting me try out her shiny cherry-flavoured lip gloss and laughing as I immediately lick the gloss off and ask for more. There I am hanging out at various birthday parties, surrounded by other children, laughing, bright-eyed, cheeky-faced and chattering non-stop. In a few of the clips I see Gen, my childhood best friend, our arms flung around each other, the pair of us giggling naughtily at some now-forgotten mischief. I look away from the screen, a flicker of shame and sadness sparking in my chest.

'My God,' Merritt says, pressing a hand to her chest. 'I thought *I* was a nerd but you are something else! Adorable.'

12

The Love of My Afterlife

Celine Dion's 'All By Myself' starts to play as the video transitions into a clip of me sitting alone at the dining table of our home – the flat I still live in – in West London. I'm carefully cutting out pictures from the *TV Times* and arranging them into collages. At the time I thought my collages were super cool and artistic. I see now they were actually rather odd.

I have all the accoutrements of an awkward teen: the rashy face, the thick glasses, the braces, and a wad of cotton wool poking out of one ear on account of the chronic ear infections I couldn't seem to shake off. The clips fade into each other – me at the kitchen table making my collages, drawing soap stars, wincing as I put in my eardrops, tucking myself into bed. Night after night.

'Sad.' Merritt shakes her head.

She's right. It does look sad. It didn't feel sad at the time, when I was drawing and collaging alone. Did it?

The video melts into my time at Bayswater High School. I shrug off the furry blanket as my entire body immediately goes hot. The back of my head starts to thump.

'Can we fast-forward this bit, please?' I ask, knowing that every single memory of that time is a bad one. Those same memories still keep me awake at night.

''Fraid not,' Merritt says. 'Once it's on it's on.'

My chest tightens as the screen flickers onto an image of fifteen-year-old me. My skin has cleared up now. The thick jam-jar glasses have been swapped for something lighter and the braces have successfully straightened out my wonky teeth. My wavy red hair fans out over my

13

shoulders, pretty against the bottle green of Bayswater High's uniform.

I'm pencil-sketching in an empty classroom, occasionally taking bites of the cheese sandwich I'd made myself that morning. And then, there she is. Gen Hartley. My childhood best friend. The girl I loved the most. The primary architect of pretty much all my trauma. She slams into the classroom accompanied by her boyfriend, Ryan Sweeting. It's almost comedic how on-the-nose they look: Gen with her shiny curtain of golden hair, thick layers of blue mascara, tiny skirt. Ryan, handsome and tall for his age, wearing the school rugby kit, his blond hair shaved close to his scalp. If this were a teen movie, you'd immediately identify them as the mean kids. Although they look smaller on the video than they did back then. Back then they seemed like giants.

'Hey, Delphie!' Gen says sweetly, wandering over to me and pressing both her hands onto my desk. Ryan follows her and swings both arms around her waist. Gen smiles at me. 'Me and Ryan had a question and we were hoping you'd help us to answer it?'

'Sure,' I say eagerly, putting down my pencil and pushing my glasses up my nose with a grin. 'Is it about the chemistry test? It's gonna be a tricky one, but I'm happy to help you if you need it? Do you want to borrow my revision notes?'

Gen laughs, a bright xylophone of a laugh, tinkling a melody that belies its intention. 'Nah, Delphie. Our question is . . . why is your hair so . . . GROSS.' She grabs a handful of it. You can see the shock on my face. 'Honestly, it feels like wire wool. Don't you even use conditioner?'

My eyes fill with tears as Ryan comes around to the other side of the desk and musses his hand roughly through my hair. 'You're right!' he grunts, wiping his hands on his jeans like they're covered in dirt. 'It's like pubes.'

Gen shrieks with mirth. I jump up from the desk, the motion making my drawing slide onto the floor. I hurry to pick it up but Ryan gets there before me. He glances at the picture, his mouth curling up into a nasty grin. 'Oh. My. God.'

'Give that back to me.' I reach out to snatch it, but Ryan dangles it in the air.

Gen gasps, grabbing it from Ryan. 'Is that Mr Taylor?' she squeals. 'You've drawn Mr Taylor? Do you fancy him?'

I remember wishing at the time that I was a better liar, but my red cheeks gave it away. Of course I fancied our art teacher. All the girls did. He was gorgeous, with his bright blue eyes and spiky hair the colour of toffee. He was kind too, never too busy to talk to me about composition and light and the importance of daily creative practice – a concept I'd never heard of before.

'She does! She's gone beetroot red. She wants to fuck Mr Taylor. She wants to fuck him and then afterwards she'll draw him naked with his willy flopping out.'

I watch from Merritt's desk chair, my heart pounding thickly the exact same way it did back then.

'Ha! No one will ever fuck Delphie,' Ryan snickers. 'Jesus, they'd have to be *desperate*.'

'Yeah, she'll probably be a virgin forever,' Gen adds.

'Can . . . can I have my drawing back now?'

'You can have it back tomorrow,' Gen says as she and Ryan saunter out of the room.

'Please don't show it to anyone!' I call after her as she leaves, the tears in my eyes now plopping onto my cheeks.

'Promise I won't!' she sing-songs, folding up the paper so that there would be a crease right across Mr Taylor's forehead.

Merritt gasps and presses pause on the tape.

'Oh no. She totally showed everyone, didn't she?'

I nod, the memory of my Mr Taylor drawing photocopied and plastered all over the school halls. The shame of everyone laughing at me. Sadness that the whole thing had made Mr Taylor so uncomfortable that, beyond what was in the curriculum, he'd stopped talking to me about art at all.

'What a piece of shit,' Merritt gasps before eagerly pressing play again, like this is just some TV drama she's binge-watching.

The video blurs into even more clips of Gen and Ryan – who had started to become known across the school as The Sweethearts – tormenting me with increasing regularity: pressing chewing gum into my hair; calling me a suck-up; getting the other students to turn their backs on me whenever I walked by. Making sure that everyone knew that being friends with me was pretty much a death knell for their future popularity.

There's me, hiding in the top-floor toilets, munching on an apple and staring at the door, alert for the sound of anyone approaching. I swallow hard. 'I've seen enough,' I say firmly. 'Turn it off.' I've not cried since the age of sixteen and I don't intend to start now. 'Seriously. I've had enough. Turn it fucking off.'

'Surely it gets better?' Merritt asks gently. 'There's only a few minutes left!'

I chew on my lip as I watch myself become an adult, the video swimming into a loop of days working quietly at the pharmacy and nights watching television or surfing the internet from my sofa. Each day looks so alike that you can't tell the difference between one month and the next. The video ends with a highly unflattering jump scare in which I'm opening my mouth extra wide to take a bite of the murderous burger.

'Yikes,' Merritt mutters, flicking off the TV and rolling the trolley back into the cupboard. 'Reader, it did *not* get better. All your days looked exactly the same as each other. You were so alone.'

I lift my chin. 'Well. That was out of choice. I was alone, yeah, but not lonely. Not at all. I'm like a giant panda. We *thrive* alone.'

'Oh, that didn't look like thriving, doll.'

'And you didn't even show Mr Yoon on that video,' I protest. 'I see him practically every day for breakfast. He might not have ever spoken to me out loud, but that's only because he literally cannot speak out loud. Sometimes he writes me notes, though, so . . .'

Merritt takes a seat behind her desk, steepling her fingers beneath her chin thoughtfully. 'We didn't see a boyfriend or a girlfriend in there, Delphie. Or even a brief dalliance of any kind. Did you never . . . ?' She trails off and raises her eyebrow.

I tut. This woman is really starting to get on my nerves.

'If you mean "Did I have sex?" then no. No, I didn't. People can have fulfilling lives without sex.' I cross my arms. Yes, my life didn't look very fulfilling on that video but it was clearly a bad edit. They missed out my nice times with Mr Yoon, and my solo trip to Greece which was truly delightful. They completely neglected to include how gorgeous the view is from my living-room window, the joy I feel looking out of it and watching the seasons change.

'I wouldn't have a clue what the satisfaction levels of a sexless person would be because I was a huge slut while alive. It was glorious. I'm sad for you.'

The spark of irritation I often feel when encountering other humans flames into a quick blaze of anger. 'I don't need your pity. Certainly not for that reason.'

Merritt stands up and comes round to sit on the edge of her desk so that our knees are almost touching.

'Have you ever even kissed anyone before?'

'Yes. Course I have! At uni. I kissed a guy called Jonny Terry.'

What I neglect to say out loud is that it was an absolutely horrendous kiss. It was sloppy and awkward, our teeth clashed, and he breathed noisily through his nose the whole time. Then afterwards he wiped his mouth with the sleeve of his woolly jumper. Funnily enough, I've not been keen to repeat the experience since then.

'So . . . you're a virgin,' Merritt says, almost to herself. 'At the age of twenty-seven. Niche. Oh, wait . . . Oh my God, Delphie, you're a virgin . . .' She looks down at her clipboard. 'Who can't drive. Literally a virgin who can't drive. Like in the seminal teen romance movie *Clueless*!'

It seems bonkers that I'm about to say these words, but I really feel like I have no choice at this point because this is just highly inappropriate. 'Can I speak to a manager?'

Merritt grimaces. 'Eek, yeah, the Higher-Ups have said I should try to work on my tact. I'm sorry, babe.'

'Manager,' I repeat.

'Oh, you *really* don't want me to get Eric. He's the colleague who's subbing in while my actual manager is on annual leave. He's awful, trust me. A full-scale prick. Hot as hell too, which makes it all the more annoying, but I promise you, I'll get him and you will regret it and wish you had stuck with me.' She lowers her voice. 'You know, I once heard him say he didn't like bread.'

I pull a face. This Eric *does* sound like a moron.

'Look, I'm sorry for upsetting you, okay? I'll try to do better. I'm a little out of practice, you know? But I promise I'm way, *way* better than Eric. Do you want a cookie? To say sorry.'

I sigh. Of course I want a cookie. And I *would* rather avoid having to meet a whole new person.

Merritt pulls open her desk drawer and hands me a foil-wrapped biscuit. I unwrap it and take a bite. She has one too, shoving the whole thing in her mouth so that her cheeks are all puffed up like a squirrel.

'Okay,' she says, when she's eventually finished crunching. 'Would you be open to meeting someone at our in-house dating service? I'll be honest, it's still in beta so it's a leeettle glitchy, but I'm one of the team behind it so I'd be happy to get you in there. We could do with a few more willing participants. It's called Eternity 4U. Isn't that cute?'

I swallow my biscuit. 'The afterlife has a dating service?'

'Dead people gotta get laid too. And hey, maybe we can get to work on showing you what you've been missing? So can I sign you up? What's your type? Tall, piercing blue eyes – like Mr Taylor the art teacher, right?'

I think it's the nonchalance with which she says 'dead people'.

I'm dead.

I'm dead?

I'm stuck here? With this woman and her *energy*? Eternity 4 me?

My body starts to tremble again.

Nope.

All the way nope.

I have to get out of here. This is a mistake. I can't stay in this place. I can't do this!

Heartbeat pulsing in my cheeks, I jump out of the chair and run towards the door of Merritt's office. There has to be someone else I can talk to. Someone normal. Someone who can actually help me figure out what's going on right now.

'Delphie, wait! Don't go! Ah, jeez, not again.'

I heave open the door and run out into the psychotic launderette waiting room, crashing immediately into the solid chest of a beautiful stranger.

Chapter Three

'Woah! Easy!' The beautiful stranger grabs me by the arms, peering at me with concern, light brown eyebrows furrowed over frankly dazzling blue eyes.

'God, I'm so sorry,' I mutter, panting a little. 'I need to find a doctor, or, like, the boss or something. I can't stay in this place. Do you know where I can find someone who can get me out of here?'

The man shakes his head, hands still on my arms. The sensation of his warm human skin against mine immediately calms my rapid breathing. I break out into goosebumps.

'I'm afraid I only just . . . I just woke up here,' the man explains, squinting curiously at the row of washing machines. 'The last thing I remember is being given sedatives for dental surgery. Now I'm here, so either this is a really unusual dream or . . . I'm dead?'

I nod emphatically. 'That's what I was trying to work out – dream or dead? Worst trivia game ever.'

The man's mouth quirks upwards with surprised amusement. 'What is this place?' He eyes the framed picture of Merritt on the wall. 'Who's that?'

'That's Merritt, the crazy woman who works here. She's

decorated it to look like a launderette. She thinks it's sooth-ing or something.'

'It's so creepy, though.' The man leans down and peers at the machines. 'All the clothes are the same colour.'

He's right. They're all the same mustard colour as Mer-ritt's dungarees.

'That *is* creepy.' I shudder.

He tilts his head to the side. 'Is that 'Don't Worry, Be Happy'?'

'It's playing on repeat.'

'Of course it is. And the ominous vibes intensify.'

'Right? Even the best song sounds a bit menacing if it's played over and over again.'

'I listened to nothing but My Chemical Romance for the whole of 2007. Can't hear their music now without feeling a bit sick.'

'My Chemical Romance?' I raise an eyebrow.

He winces. 'They were cool once upon a time.'

'Were they, though?'

He blushes a little. 'Fine. But my parents had just got divorced and I was in a full emo phase. Dyed my hair black, had the asymmetrical fringe cut in, the whole thing.'

'Wow. And I thought my parents' divorce fucked me up.'

His eyes soften a little. 'How old were you?'

'Fifteen. Mum's much happier now, but I haven't spoken to Dad since. I wrote him a letter a few years ago, to see if he wanted to meet up. He never wrote back, but he sends me a Christmas card once every few years.'

'Brutal.'

I shrug. 'How old were you?'

'I was sixteen.'

'Still no excuse for an asymmetrical fringe.'

He laughs out loud again. 'You're funny.'

You're nice, I think to myself. In fact, this is the longest I've ever talked to such an aesthetically superior man. To my surprise, my usual nerves and irritation have softened a little. And this conversation feels easy. No stutters, no awkward pauses, no me melting into a puddle of cringe because he's so ridiculously attractive.

I notice then that his hair is the exact colour of Winsor & Newton's Burnt Umber oil paint, but with little glimmers of bronze here and there, like he spends most of his time outside in the sun.

'Dead, huh?' he grimaces, reminding us both of the shit circumstances in which we find ourselves. My shoulders slump again. It had been a relief to forget reality for a couple of minutes.

'Dead,' I repeat gently. 'I'm so sorry.'

'Fuck. I had so many plans this August. I'll be gutted to miss London during the summer. It really is something magical.' He bites his objectively juicy-looking bottom lip. 'The best city on earth.'

I immediately think of how the piles of bin bags on the street start to stink in the heat of the summer sun. How the rats become bold enough to emerge in the daylight and look you right in the eye. How the onslaught of tourists arriving into Paddington station wheel their gigantic suitcases down my road at midnight, waking me up. I think of the chewy smog that feels unbearable when it's warmed up in rush hour. Like pollution stew.

'Definitely.' I nod. 'Magical.'

I glance down at the man's tanned hands on my arms. It feels quite lovely, his skin on my skin. Usually when people touch me I get sweaty and anxious, the urge to either run away or kick them in the shin intensifying with each second of contact. But this? It feels . . . pleasing. Steady and soft and sensual all at the same time. Like a warm bubble bath on a brittle February day.

The man sees me staring at his hands on my arms and quickly removes them, shoving them into the pockets of his blue jeans.

'Yikes. Sorry. I didn't realise I was totally grabbing you. Bit weird. Promise I'm not a perv.'

'It's okay.' I tuck my hair behind my ears and giggle. I don't think I've giggled since 2011.

'This is strange,' his eyes narrow. 'And it probably sounds totally like a *line* but . . . I . . . feel like I've met you before. Like I know you . . . Does that sound nuts? It does, right?'

I nod quickly because I realise I feel the exact same way. I mean, I know I've never met this man before. I *know* that. But, right now, I'm experiencing a sort of peaceful sensation that I haven't felt around anyone else, ever. It's like this man knows me. Like he already knows all my foibles and bad habits and stressy thoughts and he couldn't give a hoot. Like he likes me despite, well, *me*. Like I've been missing him my whole life. It's a strange feeling. A good feeling. I scan his face. His teeth, his strong straight nose and the exact cornflower blue of his eyes remind me an awful lot of Mr Taylor, which is odd because I was just talking about him. The man's gaze runs over my face and lingers on my lips for a moment. My whole body starts to tingle and fizz in response, like I'm a glittery snow globe that's just been shaken. Everything surrounding me fades in comparison to the brightness of his presence. Who the hell *is* this man?

He laughs self-consciously and runs a hand across his jaw. 'So, er, do you come here often?' He leans against the wall and does a silly over-the-top face. I grin, once more forgetting where I am or that I am, in fact, dead. This beautiful stranger is looking at me like no one has ever looked at me my entire life. Like I'm fascinating and pretty, and not in any way a loser.

'You're so young.' He frowns. 'Too young to die.'

'You too.'

'Sucks.'

'Blows.'

'At least we'll always be hot, I guess? Preserved.'

He said it. He thinks I'm hot. With my hair one day past acceptably unwashed and my weird nightdress. My cheeks flame. What is happening right now?

'Preserved,' I murmur. 'Like lemon curd.'

He laughs out loud. 'Lemon curd?' He takes a step closer to me, his voice suddenly low and intimate. 'Tell me your name.'

I notice that his pupils are almost fully dilated. I . . . I think this is chemistry! This must be what it feels like to have instant chemistry with someone. Wow.

'My name is Delphie. Delphie Bookham.'

'It's good to meet you, Delphie Bookham.' He holds out his hand and I take it. But we don't shake. We just hold hands. If this were a film there'd be sweeping orchestral music playing, a camera circling us as we stare at each other, maybe a cacophony of fireworks popping off overhead.

'What's *your* name?' I return.

'I'm Jonah. Jonah T—'

I don't get to hear the rest of his name because the door to Merritt's office slams open and she runs in, goggling at Jonah and me. We jump apart and Merritt, who appears to be holding a piece of fax paper, strides over, blonde curls bouncing with each step.

'Hi!' she says through a gritted sort of smile, wide eyes blinking rapidly. 'Jonah, right?'

'Um, yeah?' his voice breaks a little with shock at the interruption. He clears his throat and tries again. 'Yes. That's me.'

'Hello, Jonah! Sooooo, I'm afraid there's been a tiny little mix-up – it sometimes happens, but nothing to worry about.'

'What is it?' Jonah asks. He is no longer relaxed. His face has turned a ghostly white.

'Yeah,' Merritt blows out the air from her cheeks. 'So, good news, as it turns out! You are not actually dead, Jonah. Thing is, you're just what we term an "unconscious visitor". Our systems can get a bit screwy and deliver us people who are not ready to be here.' Her eyes snag on the fax in her hand. 'Not for a very long time as it happens. So . . .'

And then, before Jonah or I can say or do anything, Merritt steps forward and presses her thumb right into the middle of Jonah's forehead. I scream as his whole body starts to shimmer before sort of bursting like a wet bubble that's just been popped.

I look down at my hand, the one that was just holding his.

It's empty.

No, no, no!

I think . . . I think I might have just met the only person I was ever truly supposed to meet.

And now he's gone.

Chapter Four

I stare at the space where Jonah just was, blinking dumbly, my brain trying and failing to process what the hell just happened.

'Well, well, well!' Merritt drawls, brushing off her hands. She wiggles her eyebrows, a know-it-all smile on her face. 'Even the mighty Nora Roberts herself would sell a kidney to get that kind of chemistry on the page.'

'That . . . that was. Who was that? He was . . . And now he's . . .'

'He's gone, sweet girl. Back in the land of the living once more. Admin glitch – it happens. Such a shame. You would have had a much nicer time at Evermore if he'd been hanging around. From what I saw from his file he's a genuinely great guy. I'm so sorry, Delphie. Hate to see it.'

I gasp and look directly into Merritt's big green eyes. 'Wait a minute . . . you just sent him back. Send me back too! You have the power to do it. I just saw it!'

Frantically, I grab her thumb and press it against my head. 'Come on, just do it! Do that thumb thing! I really don't want to be here. I can't stay here! Mr Yoon needs me. I . . . I have a job! You just sent Jonah back. Send me!'

Merritt snatches her thumb away from my head, holding it protectively to her chest.

'Anyone can send accidental unconscious visitors back to earth – they're just an admin error.' She shrugs as if it's no big deal that she literally just disappeared a whole entire beautiful and interested-in-me human. 'But for people who are *actually* supposed to be here? No can do.'

I sink down onto one of the plastic chairs.

'I'm sorry,' Merritt grimaces. 'You two really did have some kind of spark, right? Were you holding hands? Even though you'd only just met? That's bonkers. What a shame he had to go. For you, I mean. He's a very popular man on earth so I'm sure he'll be fine.'

I bury my head in my hands and let out a low groan. This is what eternity looks like? Stuck with this woman?

'Oh, wait a hot sec . . .' Merritt says thoughtfully. 'What if I . . . ? Maybe I could . . . And then you would go back and . . . No . . . it wouldn't work . . . Hmmmm, unless . . .'

I lift my head, ears pricked up like a dog's. 'What did you just say? Maybe I could go back what? What wouldn't work? What are you thinking?'

Merritt plops down onto a chair opposite me and taps her beringed hands against her thighs. 'Well, I guess there is the Franklin Bellamy Clause. Maybe that could work . . .'

'The Franklin Bellamy Clause? What's the Franklin Bellamy Clause?'

Merritt pushes her glasses up her nose and sits forward in her seat. '*So*. There's a clause in the Evermore handbook, written by this Higher-Up called Franklin Bellamy. It was back in the 1990s, I think. He introduced a rule stating that within three hours of arrival – provided they're not yet

29

known to be deceased – a Dead can be sent back to earth by an Afterlife Therapist. Under certain conditions, of course.'

'What conditions?'

'They can return to carry out an important favour for a staff member. If they do it, the Dead gets to remain on earth.'

'They get to stay alive?'

'If they successfully complete the given task, yes. Franklin Bellamy created the clause so that he could have someone return to earth and tell the woman set to cure IBS in 2028 that she had a carbon monoxide leak in her flat. He prevented her death and in 2028, the world will become a happier and more comfortable place for many.'

'Why didn't he just go back himself? If he had that kind of power? Why did he need to send someone else to go?'

Merritt rolls her eyes. 'Did you not hear me, babe? There has to be a provision of the returning Dead not yet being recognised as deceased. Can you imagine? Me rocking up on earth after being gone for five years? As careful as I might be, there's always the chance that someone who knew me might see me wandering about. It would be a potential disaster in the very fabric of space and time, not to mention highly embarrassing.' She shudders at the thought.

'So you can only get new Deads – I mean, arrivals – to do the "favour".'

'Yeah. The rules are that it can only be done once, it needs to be for something important, and it can never directly involve someone you knew on earth.'

'Why not?'

Merritt's eyes widen. 'Oh, if we were able to manipulate

the outcomes of those we knew and loved on earth it would send us crazy. Everyone would break the rules and risk revealing the existence of Evermore. Nightmare!'

'Do you still have your send-back?' I ask, almost breathless.

Merritt nods. 'Yeah, I've been saving it.'

'For what?'

'For bargaining power – what else?' She raises an eyebrow. 'We can gift our send-backs to other staff members, trade them for promotions or perks. As long as I hold on to mine then I have a little something in my back pocket, should I ever need it.'

I stand up. 'Don't save your send-back! Use it on me!' I glance at a pink digital clock on the wall. I've only been here about two hours, right? There's still time for me to go back! You must be able to think of a favour I can do for you? Anything. I want to live! I'll do anything at all!'

Merritt bunches her mouth up for a moment and then lifts her chin, her eyes lit up. 'You'll do anything?'

'Yes!' I shout. 'Anything you want!'

Merritt glances towards another door before scooching right to the edge of her chair, her face close enough that I can smell the cookie on her breath.

'Okay, I might have a little idea, but . . .' she trails off and lowers her voice. 'But the other therapists would not like it . . .'

'I thought you said you could run rings around those old guys?'

Merritt nods quickly, her curls bouncing in time. She

31

presses her teeth over her bottom lip. 'I did. I did say that. And I totally can. Evermore is very much like earth: a bunch of old men in charge, all so stuck in their ways. Heaven help anyone who actually tries to *innovate*, to bring a little modernity to this place.'

'Tell me your idea.'

'Ah yes, my idea. It sounds nuts but . . . I think, Delphie, that Jonah might have been your soulmate.' She grabs my hands in hers. 'I mean, technically, humans have five soulmates wandering the earth at any one time, but I think Jonah might be one of yours . . . The way you were looking at each other.' She sighs dreamily. 'Like Laurie and Jack in Josie Silver's *One Day in December.* Like all you wanted to do was touch each other. I mean, what are the chances that this guy accidentally turns up here at the same time as you? In *my* lobby, no less.' She gasps, jumping up from the chair and pacing around the room. 'What if it was fate, and I just have to, you know, give it a little nudge?'

I blink. A soulmate. Soulmates are real? I get a sudden vision of walking hand-in-hand with Jonah down a snowy Oxford Street. Which is mad because I despise the busy-ness of Oxford Street and I usually avoid the snow whenever possible. In the fantasy Jonah and I are wearing matching mittens and giggling. And I don't feel irritated or scared or sad. I don't feel like me at all. It's funny, I've never even pondered the possibility of a soulmate before . . . But what if this is real and Merritt is right and Jonah was *it*? What if I actually have a way to feel something better than everything I've been feeling up until now?

'I'll give you ten days,' Merritt says decisively.

'Ten days?'

'Ten days back on earth to find Jonah. If he kisses you then you can stay.'

'I can stay alive? Like this never even happened? Like I'd never choked at all?'

'Yeah. But *he* has to kiss *you*. Of his own free will.'

I narrow my eyes. 'Why only ten days?'

Merritt folds her arms. 'Those therapists I told you about? The ones who keep stealing new Deads away from me, who don't think I've got what it takes to make a difference round here? Those two rodent droppings are on holiday for the next ten days. So we could get this all done and dusted before they return . . . and no one would ever have to know!'

'Wait . . . you're not actually allowed to do this?'

Merritt shakes her head quickly. 'Of course I am! I would *never* break the rules of Evermore.' She tuts. 'It would just be better to, you know, keep this between us. Jeez. Anyone would think you haven't just been offered the chance of a lifetime.'

I screw up my face. 'How would this be a "favour" to you?'

Merritt laughs and wiggles her eyebrows slightly. 'Well, I would get to watch it all play out.'

'I don't understand.'

'Look, you don't even know this man's full name. You don't know where the hell in London he is. You have a ticking clock provided by *moi*, and God knows how many obstacles keeping you apart. It's like a real-life romance

novel! That I get to watch unfold in real time! The *dream*.'
She claps her hands together, bouncing on her heels.

'You won't even tell me his full name?' I goggle.

'Where's the fun in that? Ooh, and his memory will have
been wiped too so he won't remember your little dalliance
here today.' Merritt wanders over to the framed picture of
herself and straightens it tenderly. 'I want to see fate in
action. See if you can pull it off. Like I said, Deads are being
stolen away from me left, right and centre. A girl needs to
get her kicks somewhere.'

I stand up and start to pace the room. 'What if I can't find
him? What if he doesn't kiss me? Do I have to come back
here? 'Cos I really, really don't want to.'

Merritt rubs her hands together and stares into the distance for a moment. Then a huge smile spreads across her
face.

'Yes. You have to come back here *and* work with me on
the dating service I'm setting up. Eternity 4U. We need
guinea pigs. Volunteers to go on test dates and feed back
about how they can be improved. You would have to agree
to be a guinea pig for as long as I need you . . . Also, you
have to sign this contract agreeing to my terms.' Seemingly
from nowhere she whips out a piece of paper and places it
onto my lap. Then she reaches into her dungaree pocket and
takes out a gold pen topped with a burgundy feather.

Being a date tester for a load of people I've never met
before sounds like my actual nightmare. I've never even
talked to the shopkeeper of the corner shop, even though
I see her almost every day. I don't *do* people. But . . . then

I think of how Jonah just looked at me. Like he would definitely kiss me of his own free will. In a heartbeat, in fact. All I'd have to do is find him. I already know that he lives in London. And that his first name is Jonah, second name something beginning with the letter T. How many Jonah Ts can there be in one city?

I picture my cosy flat with my new stripy rug. All the TV series I've yet to finish. Old Mr Yoon, who has been getting more forgetful of late and has no one else but me to check in on him. This would be a chance to make sure he's okay, to make sure he has everything he needs in case I do end up snuffing it for good. My heart starts to beat desperately with the innate human instinct to save one's own life. To keep breathing and living and being, no matter what it takes.

Before I can second-guess myself, I grab the pen from Merritt and scribble my signature across the bottom of the paper. The wet ink is purple, shimmering like oil in a puddle.

'Ten days,' Merritt repeats. 'And *he* has to kiss *you*.'

'But what about if—'

I don't get to finish my question because Merritt snatches the paper out of my hand and then, with a manic laugh, reaches out her thumb, pressing it resolutely onto my forehead.

I gasp and look down at my arms as they turn iridescent and then into a silver sort of liquid, and then . . .

Chapter Five

'Delphie? For fuck's sake. Delphie? Wake up.'

I frown, opening my eyes to see a pair of eyes so dark they're almost black. The man's face is so close to mine that I can smell the soap on his skin, something clean and expensive. He's saying my name and he seems really pissed off. It takes me a few seconds to recognise the patrician tones, and when I do I feel a sharp spike of dislike in my belly. I sit bolt upright and push the man's face away from mine.

'Christ,' a brief look of relief crosses his despicable face. 'You're alive, at least.'

I wipe multiple beads of sweat from my forehead and mash my lips together, mouth dry. I look around. I'm on the floor of my flat. I'm alive? I gasp for air and take a huge gulp of it in when I realise there's no restriction. Beautiful air. Wonderful, beautiful, life-giving air.

'Holy shit,' I stand up with a wobble, noticing as I do that my phone is right there on the side table. There is zero sign of a microwave burger anywhere in the vicinity. My TV is switched off and my laptop is closed. 'What the fuck?'

Cooper from downstairs towers over me, his tree-like frame making my living room look even tinier than it is. He holds his hands up as if he wants no part in answering my question. 'I came to bring you that,' he says stiffly, pointing to a cardboard parcel on my kitchen table. 'They delivered it to me *again*. Your door was ajar and I came in to find you passed out on the floor. But you're clearly not dead. Hurrah. I should go.'

'Wait!' I say, pulling down my nightie. 'How long was I passed out? What time is it? Where's my burger gone? I don't . . .' I look towards my window. The sun is setting. I squint at my clock: 8 p.m. 'Two hours have passed?'

Cooper regards me coolly. 'Are you drunk?'

I grab my throat. 'No. No . . . The beefburger is gone,' I mutter. 'Completely vanished. Was that a dream? The launderette . . . Was it not real?' I shuffle over to my coffee table and scan it. 'If there's no burger, that means . . . What does that mean?'

Cooper steps towards me and uses two fingers to push my shoulder so that I plop down onto the sofa. 'Starting to feel like I should telephone a doctor . . .' he says, mouth settling into its usual grim line.

'No. No . . . I'm fine.' I wave him away. 'I think . . . I think I just had a really weird dream.'

Cooper glances around my little living room, a single eyebrow raised. I suddenly see the place through his eyes – faded old floral wallpaper I never got around to changing after Mum moved out, unopened boxes of oil paint stacked high on the teak side table, a row of second-tier knickers drying into cardboard on the radiator.

His eyes snag on the underwear for a moment before sliding back to me with an expression that rests somewhere

37

between mild boredom and outright scorn. Ugh. This guy thinks he's so much better than everyone else. He's dressed, as usual, like some wounded yet enigmatic French guy. The kind of guy who reads sun-burnished paperbacks at a bar because he wouldn't dream of being tethered to an iPhone. The kind of guy who smokes just for the aesthetic. Like if Timothée Chalamet had an extremely tall, extremely brooding arsehole of an older brother. Black leather jacket, plain black T-shirt, black jeans, black boots neatly and tightly laced. Thick stubble because he's just too clever and mysterious to shave.

When Cooper first moved into the building five years ago he looked totally different – dark hair much shorter than the jumble of curls it is now. He was clean-shaven then, strutting about in obnoxiously loud Hawaiian shirts and board shorts, a pencil tucked behind his ear. There was far, far less scowling. In fact, the day he moved in I remember thinking his eyes were the most glittering, cheerful eyes I'd ever seen, which goes to show that first impressions are mostly bullshit.

That was all way back, before I'd frequently bump into him in the hallway waving off yet another beautiful woman he'd clearly entertained for one night only. Back before he told me to fuck off the morning I politely asked him to turn down the music he was blasting at 6 a.m. After that interaction his eyes looked significantly less glittery to me. I'd studiously ignore him if I passed him in the hallway. He stopped wearing a pencil behind his ear and would snipe at me every time one of my parcels got accidentally delivered to his place on the ground floor. People say I'm prickly, but I am rainbow-stuffed sunshine compared to this guy.

'Right.' He rolls his eyes. 'All very normal. And you're sure I don't need to telephone for help?'

'*Telephone*? Alright, Downton Abbey. No. You don't need to telephone anyone. You don't need to be here at all, in fact.'

'Good.' His eyes travel down to my nightie and then back up to meet mine. 'I'll let you get back to sparkling and shining, shall I?'

'I'll let you get back to Rydell High. The other T-Birds are wondering where their shittest member is.'

'I sincerely hope you find that missing beefburger.'

'I sincerely hope you don't get heat rash from wearing leather *on the hottest day of the year*.'

I smile but it's not real.

He glares and it's very real.

He turns on the heel of his dumb boot and strides out of my flat, not shutting the door behind him, which I know is on purpose. Grumbling, I go and close it, locking all three locks and double-checking them.

'And stay out!' I call after him, although my door is already closed and Cooper is probably back in his own flat now. God. Irritation might be my default setting most of the time, but my goodness does that idiot know how to conjure it.

As soon as he's gone I scan my flat once more for evidence of the burger, or the plant I knocked over on my frantic run to the kitchen chair to Heimlich myself. I find nothing.

I pick up my phone. No notifications, no calls, which

isn't a rare occurrence. No notifications and no calls is exactly how I like it.

Hearing the sound of Mrs Ernestine from downstairs giving grief to someone on the street, and the hum of my fridge, and smelling the scent of roast chicken coming through my windows – the things I encounter every day – it occurs to me that what just happened was almost certainly the world's most disturbing dream.

There's an unexpected roll of disappointment in my gut. I mean, of course I'm delighted I'm not dead. Obviously. But if none of that was real then that means Jonah T wasn't real either. Just a figment of my clearly outrageous imagination. Huh.

Lying on the floor in the setting sun has made my skin gross and sticky, so I strip off my nightie and dive under a tepid shower. I soap my body and stare blankly at the pale pink wall tiles. How did I end up passed out on the floor? Am I unwell? Am I dehydrated? Jan at work told me I needed to drink more water to account for the buckets we're all sweating in this heatwave.

I think of Jonah T as I wash my hair with my favourite sweet apple shampoo. About how my body felt in that dream. How just for a moment I was excited about the possibility of . . . I don't know what. Something better. I think about his eyes and his hair and the way his hand felt in mine. My chest aches with longing.

'Get a grip, Delphie,' I say out loud. 'It was just a weird dream.'

Climbing out of the shower, I pad about from room to

room feeling desperately uneasy. My flat feels too hot and too small. The sun is still too bright for 8 p.m. I stare at the spot on my new striped rug where I collapsed. Where I'm certain the air left my lungs. God, it felt so real.

Inspecting the fridge, I spot the offending burger. It's unopened. I quickly grab it and dump it straight in the bin.

Then, at a loss for what else to do and with absolutely no one to talk to about this strange occurrence, I switch the TV back onto Netflix and turn on *The Tinder Swindler*, picking right up where I left off.

Chapter Six

After slipping into a sleeping Mr Yoon's flat to make sure his cigarettes are stubbed out and his oven is turned off, I climb into bed. It takes me ages to get to sleep on account of my brand-new fear of having horrifyingly vivid dreams featuring pushy dungareed women. But eventually I drift off.

When my alarm blares in the morning the whole thing is still right at the front of my thoughts. I kick off my summer quilt and Jonah's face flashes brightly into my mind. I recall the exact shade of his irises: cobalt blue, speckled with shiny touches of hazelnut brown. But more than that, the absolute warmth of them. The kindness. How calm I felt when they were on me.

I sit up, sigh, and briefly wonder if I have a brain tumour. In *Grey's Anatomy* Izzie started a full sexual affair with a hallucination. Is that what's happening to me? Or have I seen some hot guy in a movie at some point and his face has somehow imprinted into my subconscious?

'My God,' I mutter as I remember that whole video Merritt played. Those memories were crystal clear. The Sweethearts' mocking laughs. Me sitting alone on my sofa watching TV on an endless loop. Mum, before Gerard and the artists' commune.

My heart lurches and I pull out my phone.

Hey Mum! How's it going? Do you have time for a call later today or tomorrow? Would be nice to catch up.

I scroll up through the last few messages she's sent me, photos of big abstract paintings she's been working on, which, by all accounts, are set to sell out before they're even shown publicly. I studiously ignore my own stack of unused oil paints and head to the bathroom where I create my usual hairstyle of two braids pinned up tightly across the top of my head. Then I get dressed into my work uniform of black trousers and white short-sleeved shirt.

'Merritt! Ha!' I snort. How the hell did my brain come up with that name? I've never even heard it before. So weird. Maybe I should see Dr Lane, get my fluoxetine dosage increased. I make a note to call her, but then remember how much she was pushing for me to start talk therapy. I'll call another time.

My phone buzzes with Mum's reply.

Darling! Today/tomorrow is manic. We have a New York art curator staying at the commune and I'm doing the welcome dinner party. Isn't that exciting? Glad to hear you're doing well. Gerard sends his love.

Rolling my eyes, I pick up the box of Blackwing pencils from my side table, a pack of bagels from the bread bin and, opening my fridge, grab a carton of eggs, a slab of butter and a packet of smoked salmon. I leave my flat and knock on Mr Yoon's door.

Mr Yoon and I have an understanding. I always give him a chance to answer the door before I use the keys I had cut. He rarely does but I don't want to burst in and see something that could forever change the simple, relaxed nature of our relationship.

After two minutes of knocking with no response, I unlock the door and head in.

Mr Yoon's flat is twice the size of mine and while mine has the same nice high ceilings, his has a huge bay window and a little balcony overlooking the shops on our street. The August sun streams into the large living room and I notice with a slump that the house has fallen into disarray again. The dishes are washed, precariously stacked on top of Mr Yoon's favourite tea towel (red, covered with little musical notes), but the kitchen tops are mucky and the sun illuminates a haze of stagnant dust in the air. This wouldn't be such a big deal if Mr Yoon weren't usually so fastidious about keeping his house immaculate. I've caught him looking spacey recently, forgetting things, not combing his hair or cleaning up the way he usually does. I make a mental note to call his GP. It's probably normal for an eighty-something to get a little scatterbrained from time to time, but it's probably best to double-check.

'Hello, hello, Mr Yoon,' I grin, approaching my neighbour as he sits at his circular table by the window, smoking a cigarette and puzzling over one of the crossword books he's obsessed with. I plonk the box of pencils at his side. 'Only the best for you.' He gives me a small smile and a distracted wave before returning to his puzzle book.

Mr Yoon is non-verbal. He's recently started to write little notes to me every so often – which is how I learned he had a vocal cord injury as a baby and has never spoken – but mostly we just sit together in silence. I think this is largely one of the reasons I like hanging out with him so much. That and the fact that he's not fake. He doesn't pretend to like me or dislike me. The problem with so many people you encounter in life is that they're being the version of themselves they think they *should* be rather than the person they actually are. Which is almost always judgy and superior and – if it serves them – willing to break your heart without a second thought. If there's one thing I know for certain it's that people are mostly shit. Not Mr Yoon though. He's good and true, not an ulterior motive to be seen.

It's funny. I remember being scared of him as a child. The grumpy-faced silent man who was forever gesturing with his finger over his lips that I should hush if I was being too loud in the hallway with Gen. Mum always said he was just a lonely old man who wanted to be left alone so I never tried to interact with him. And then, a couple of years ago, it was my birthday. Mum had forgotten to call so in a burst of self-pity I went to the nearest bakery and bought myself a whole cake. I bumped into Mr Yoon in the hallway. He looked at me and then down to the cake and then back up to me.

'It's my birthday and I'm eating all of it,' I muttered, pushing into my flat with a sigh. About an hour later, an envelope slid under my door, skidding across the floor-boards with speed. I opened it to find a piece of thick A4 paper folded in half. On the front was a little pencil drawing of a birthday cake. Inside, in neat handwriting it said: 'Happy birthday to you, Delphie. From Mr Yoon.'

It was the only birthday card I got that year. I pressed it to my nose for some reason, immediately sneezing at the scent of cigarette ash. Now I keep it carefully tucked inside my folder of important documents, alongside my tax forms and degree certificate.

Heading to the open-plan kitchen, I prepare a pot of coffee in Mr Yoon's old copper cafetière. Then I grab a mixing bowl and crack the eggs into it, whisking them up with sea salt, pepper and a pinch of chilli flakes before adding them to a hot pan and stirring as quickly as I can. I lightly toast and butter two bagels, top them with the eggs and add the smoked salmon. I set our plates down on the table with a flourish.

'Order up!'

Mr Yoon closes his puzzle book and hungrily tucks into the food. He seems ravenous. Did he forget to eat last night? I notice his wrists are looking bonier, his old silver watch looser than usual.

I pour us both a glass of orange juice from the open carton on the table and spoon some of my eggs onto his plate. 'I don't know about you, Mr Yoon, but I had the most crackpot dream last night,' I say, taking a bite of my bagel. 'I dreamed I died and ended up in some afterlife place that looked like a launderette. Oh, and there was this totally

46

over-the-top woman there. She was supposed to be a therapist of some sort, but she was shit at it.'

Mr Yoon takes a sip of his coffee, making a small sigh of pleasure. It took me months to elicit this from him. The first few weeks of my making coffee he scowled upon tasting it. I soon realised, via trial and error, that he liked his coffee strong, the beans freshly ground, and with almond milk. The whole thing was like a science experiment. I even kept a little notebook with scores out of ten based on his reactions.

'And there was this guy,' I continue. At this Mr Yoon looks directly at me. He raises his eyebrows as if to say, *Oh, really?* I laugh. 'Yeah. A very handsome guy with a stellar set of teeth. His name is – *was* – Jonah. And he was *lovely*. Just sweet and kind.' I put down my knife and fork. 'And now I miss him, lunatic that I am. So stupid, right? Missing a stranger from a dream ...' I laugh darkly. 'It was nice, though. For a moment. To feel that way. Honestly, I wasn't sure I had it in me.'

Mr Yoon carries on chewing, eyes back down on his plate.

'I should probably get one of those *What Your Dreams Mean* books ...' I muse, taking a sip of my own coffee. 'Although I doubt they'd have a chapter on "Waking Up Dead in a Launderette and Meeting a Beautiful Man".'

Mr Yoon chuckles silently, his breath coming out in little gasps, the crinkles at the corners of his eyes deepening.

'You may laugh but I am perturbed, Mr Yoon.' I say, picking up our empty plates and taking them over to the dishwasher. '*Perturbed*. What if I'm going mad?'

Mr Yoon grabs a pencil and scratches something out at the top of his puzzle page.

Delphie, you cannot go mad if you are already mad.

'Oi!' I scold. 'Although you're probably right. And on that note off I go to the pharmacy, where I will spend my whole day hearing mournful tales of dry skin and gunky eyes and itchy bits. You have a good day, hey? I'll pop in later probably, wipe those countertops down, if you haven't managed it.'

Mr Yoon gives me a thumbs-up before picking up his box of cigarettes and lighting a fresh one with shaky hands. I once mentioned to him that maybe he should cut down, to which he gave me a scowl so forceful I ended up buying him a new ashtray to apologise for interfering.

As I leave his flat and head back to my own, my phone makes a weird noise. It's the opening notes of the song 'Jump Around' by House of Pain, playing over and over again. What the hell? I dig my phone out of my pocket. There's a text. Wait, I don't have sound notifications on for texts.

I open the message and my heart jolts.

Yo Delphie, this is Merritt. From Evermore. I'm getting the impression that you think what happened between us yesterday was a dream . . . Because why are you farting around when you only have ten days to find Jonah? Actually nine days now, because last night was technically day one and today is day two . . .

P. S. This text will vanish as soon as you've finished reading it.

48

I gawk at the message and then right before my human eyes it shimmers and pops into nothing, just like Jonah did in my dream.

Which . . . *wasn't* a dream?

I click back into my text folder. Yep. The text has gone.

I look up and down the hall corridor. Is this a prank? No, I don't know enough people for one of them to be a clandestine prankster. Maybe I really am unwell . . . Maybe I should have let Cooper call a doctor last night.

The sound of 'Jump Around' blasts out again.

'Is this a dream?' I whisper, lightly slapping my face in a bid to wake myself up.

> Jeez. Can we get this bit over with, Delphie? This isn't a dream. It's real. It's happening. We agreed on ten days. You have until 6 p.m. on the tenth day to find Jonah and get him to kiss you. Or I will keep you forever . . . Mua-ha-ha-ha.

The message pops and disappears. I feel my knees weaken like I'm some flake in a period drama. I grab the handle of my door as I slide down to the carpeted floor.

> Me again. Seriously though. Can you let me know that you understand? I can't keep texting all day. Eric just walked into my office and said, 'Hmm you look super busy.' What a dick. I just need you to say it out loud. To acknowledge this is real. Say: 'I know this is real!'

49

I gasp as the message floats away once more. 'Uh . . . This is real?' My voice comes out in a whisper. I clear my throat and say it louder. 'This is real.'

It is real! Okay, girly. I'm out for now but we'll speak soon. Good luck, good luck! I'm so excited to see how this goes! Woohoo!

In the midst of the fear and the disbelief and the general pervading worry that I am going crazy, I feel something unexpected. A warm curl of excitement. A glimmer of hope deep in the pit of my belly.

If this is real then that means Jonah is real.

And he's somewhere in London.

Chapter Seven

The bell of Meyer's Pharmacy dings out as I blast the door open. I'm immediately hit with the comforting smell of soap and tinctures that lingers here. Jan, who works the till, jumps in shock, the phone she's been watching dropping onto the glass countertop with a clank. She throws her arms upwards like I'm a burglar and she's planning to take me down. When she realises it's only me, her shoulders soften and she returns to one of the pro-shot musicals she's always watching in between customers.

Jan's daughter, Leanne, pops out from behind the partition, her perfectly microbladed eyebrows drawn into a V, lip gloss shining beneath the artificial lighting. She's the pharmacist here and mine and Jan's boss. She doesn't resemble any pharmacist I've ever met before. She looks like an Instagram influencer – skin poreless, hair balayaged and wavy, eyelashes artificially abundant. And then there's her clothes – she has a side-passion for fashion, which means that she's forever coming into work in designs of her own creation: usually severe, fashiony-coloured fields of neon fabric with huge sleeves that sometimes dangle into her salad at lunchtime.

'What's with the slamming?' Leanne hisses, her eyes

dipping down to the clear Perspex wristwatch she always wears. 'And you're late.'

When I first started working here three years ago Leanne kept trying to get me to go out for after-work drinks with her. I kept putting her off on account of two things:

1. She was suspiciously friendly. No one should be that happy handing out bumhole cream to the general public day after day.

2. If the friendship didn't work out (and experience has taught me that they never do) then it would be awkward at work. And while this job doesn't exactly set my heart alight, it's literally opposite my flat, it's easy enough packaging tablets, and the pay is enough to manage the cost of living. I did not want to muddy those boundaries.

I march up to the counter. 'I need the next nine days off.'

'But you never take days off,' Leanne says, a brief look of concern crossing her face before it settles back into her unimpressed frown. 'And it's really late notice.'

'I know.' I shrug apologetically. 'But I'm desperate and you know I wouldn't ask unless I needed to.'

Jan presses pause on Broadway HD. 'Is everything alright, Delphie? You look a little bit pale.'

I wave her concern away. 'Yeah, totally fine.' *Technically dead, less than ten days to find and kiss the possible man of my dreams or else I die for a second time.* 'I just need . . . you know . . . a break. Um . . . Things are getting on top of me.'

Leanne crosses her arms. Her sleeves are not dangly today but billowy, like someone has puffed them up with air. 'You want to go off sick for that long? Because if that's the case then technically you need a doctor's note. Do you have one?'

I shake my head. 'Oh, come on, Leanne. It's not busy season. You can manage for a few days. I'll do the stock-take when I get back.'

Leanne tuts. 'Your tone is very rude and snippy for someone asking for a favour, Delphie. What if stock runs out before you come back? What if the local residents of Paddington and Bayswater don't receive their life-saving medicine because you couldn't arrange appropriate notice for annual leave?'

'Bloody hell, don't be so dramatic,' Jan pipes up, fiddling with the gold clover pendant that never leaves her neck. 'I can help you, Leanne. Let the girl take some time off. She don't ever ask.'

I squint at Jan. Why is she on my side? What's the catch? She only ever talks to me to ask if I know who Stephen Sondheim is. I always say no, because I do not, and she always says that I'm missing out on the greatest works of art that have ever existed.

Leanne narrows her eyes and I see that her eyeliner is Ultramarine Violet to match her shoes. 'If I give you nine days off without notice, you'll need to do me a favour, too.'

'Fine. What is it?'

Leanne lifts her chin. 'You will come for after-work drinks with me next Friday.'

I gawk. It's been three years since she's stopped asking. Why is she so bothered about this? When have I ever given off friend vibes? I have cultivated the opposite my entire adult life. Maybe it was that one night when we shared a bottle of wine after closing up shortly after I first started here. She just magicked the booze out of her bag, and I'd had a shitty day so I said yes to a glass and she just kept topping it up. I got so tipsy I barely remember it, but she must have had a downright lovely time because she won't let up on trying to get a repeat experience.

'Oi, if you're going out then I'm coming too!' Jan tuts. 'It'd be discrimination otherwise. Leaving me out just 'cos I'm older than you lot.'

'Fine!' I say. 'Jeez. We'll all go out! First round's on me!' I add because on television that's what people who go out for drinks say.

Leanne nods slowly, a smile of satisfaction spreading across her perfectly symmetrical face.

I nip back home to research Jonah on my laptop, but within a few seconds of staring at the stripy rug where I recently died I'm too creeped out and I decide to go to a library instead. Out on the street I check my phone to find out where the nearest library is. Some would say that's definitely something I ought to know after twenty-seven years of living in London, but following school and university I've bought most of my books online.

The nearest one to me is Tyburnia Library, which is within walking distance. I very rarely travel outside of Bayswater – why would I when it has everything I need? – but when I do, I always prefer to walk, preferably with my headphones on full blast so that no one can talk to me. If they do, I can just pretend I didn't hear them because *head-phones*. I may not have it all figured out, but I'm not a complete idiot.

I walk down the bustling Praed Street, dodging and weaving around people in my way, eyes laser-focused on some unknown spot in the distance. My headphones blast out a podcast all about van Gogh and Gauguin's turbulent time in Arles and I wonder if when van Gogh went crazy, he knew it was happening.

The library is large and old-looking, its big dusty windows dotted with colourful cut-outs of children's book characters.

I push open the heavy doors and wander through carpeted rooms filled with yellowing books until I find a huge table with two other people working on laptops. Perfect. I sit down, opening up my own computer and immediately typing into Google Jonah T London.

Twenty-three million results.

At my groan, one of the other people at the desk shushes me. I glare at him. There's a gentle tap on my shoulder.

I spin around in my chair to find a tall, skinny man who looks to be in his early forties peering down at me curiously. He's wearing a satin waistcoat over a white shirt. His face is impish, his hair a wispy ash blond. 'Hello.' He points at a little golden badge on his waistcoat. 'I'm Aled. Can I help you?' His accent is pure warm Yorkshire, round and agreeable. 'I heard you groan from just over there and I thought, *That's the sound of a bookworm in distress.* Can I assist?'

I grimace at my computer screen.

'Actually, yes. Do you have, like, records of people? Addresses and phone numbers and things?'

'For members of the public? You want someone's address? Use a search engine!'

'I just did! But there are millions of results. I'm trying to find someone and there isn't much time.'

'You sound panicked, love!' Aled purses his lips. 'Is . . . is this serious?'

'It's literally life or death,' I mutter distractedly, scrolling down the Google results and then clicking onto the images page. Nothing of use.

'Hmmm, I see, I see,' Aled rubs his hands together. 'I may not have access to private phone numbers, but I think I do have something that can help. A little something called . . . *books*!'

Chapter Eight

Aled is super helpful. Oddly so – like he decided that was his personal brand and he was going to lean the hell into it. Trailing me through the library he calls out to various people perusing the shelves. 'Mrs Marani, I ordered you the new Ottolenghi book. It's at the front desk.' And: 'You don't want that one, Danny – it's not twisty enough for you. Try the Lisa Jewell instead.' And, strangely: 'Mr Timms, don't you have an optician's appointment in five minutes? You'll be late!'

He chuckles, looking back at me excitedly as we enter the true crime section of the library. It's packed with people. Disturbing. Aled announces the most helpful books by actually taking them off the shelf and dumping them in my arms.

'I don't think I need all of these.' I try to unload three books on missing persons back into Aled's skinny arms but he holds his palms out so that I can't.

'This Jonah character you mentioned . . . He's a missing person, isn't he?'

'Well, not officially a "missing person".'

'Can you find him?'

'No, but I don't really know him . . .'

'And you say it's literally life or death?'

'Well, yes. Yes, it is.'

'Sounds like a missing person to me, or, as they say in the biz, a "misper".' He taps the spine of another book. 'Oh, this one is very good. They don't end up finding the victim, but the story is heart-wrenching. Very emotional. I did cry, but then I cry at everything. I once cried at an advertisement for bubble bath.'

He piles another three books into my arms, and while I'm usually excellent at shoving off unwanted interactions, Aled is persistent in a way I have not encountered in a while. I'm not quite sure how to respond.

When we get to the library counter, me with five big-ass books about missing persons and true crime, and one called *Detecting for Dummies*, Aled asks me for my library card.

'I don't have one.'

His face crumples like I've just revealed *he* has ten days to live.

'Did you lose it?'

'Nope. I just don't have one.'

Aled shakes his head in disbelief, handing me a form to fill in with my full name and address. 'Wow. Well, this is an exciting day for you and me both. A library card is a portal, if you will, into any universe you can imagine. Oh, the adventures you will have, eh?'

I scribble down my details and hand the form back to him. 'I'm not sure I'll be coming back any time soon.'

'You have to!' he says tapping my details into the computer and then handing me a little green plastic card, magically printed with my name. 'To return the books! That's the trick, see? And when you do, I'll be here with recommendations galore.' He claps his hands together. 'I'll start a list as soon as you've gone.'

'Okay,' I say vaguely, stacking the books into my arms and heading towards the exit. 'Um, thanks . . .'

'You'll be back,' Aled says in a robotic impression of the Terminator. He holds up a little stuffed owl from his desk and waves its wing as I walk away. I turn back before I leave the front door.

He's still waving.

I schlep through the smoggy heat with my pile of books and by the time I reach home I'm sweating so much my thin white shirt has plastered itself to my skin. I shift the books over to one arm while I fiddle with my key. Getting it into the lock and twisting it the correct way without dropping the books takes every ounce of concentration I can muster. I've almost succeeded when suddenly the door is yanked open from the inside. I jerk forward and the books fall from my arms, tumbling down the dusty front steps of the building.

'Nooo,' I wail gently. I glare at the opening door to see who I should blame.

Of course.

Despicable Cooper stands on the top step. He is now sans leather jacket, though the rest of his clothes are still black. He must be sweltering, but his face looks perfectly cool and calm.

'Are you going to apologise?' I hiss, heading down the steps to pick up the books I didn't even want.

His stubbled jaw tenses a smidge. 'I didn't know you'd be on the other side of the door, did I?' He reaches down to pick up one of the books, something called *Geographic Profiling – The Essential Guide*.

'Why would you yank the door open like that?'

'Like what?'

'Like you're angry at it!'

'It's a heavy door so you really have to pull it. I can't help my natural strength.'

Is he joking right now? Seeing as I've never witnessed him joking, I'm gonna go with not.

'Natural strength? Wow. Congratulations to you on that. Can I get past now, please?'

Cooper's frame blocks my entrance to the doorway. He doesn't move, but frowns, picking up the top book from the pile again.

'You're searching for someone?'

'Maybe.'

He bends his knees to squint at the spines of the other books in my pile. 'That's some hefty reading for a maybe.' He taps the bottom book with his forefinger. 'That one's not bad. The rest of them are unhelpful.'

Now it's my turn to frown. 'You've read them?'

'Yeah.'

'Why?'

He avoids the question. 'Are you really trying to find someone? Who? Why?'

'Would you like me to make a written statement down at the station, Detective Cooper?'

His eyes harden again, hands up in the air. 'Fine. Jesus. Good luck with it.'

I think about what Leanne said this morning. About me being rude and snippy sometimes. I didn't think I was but the way I just spoke to Cooper echoes back at me. Yeah. Little bit rude, definitely snippy.

'I'm trying to find my uh, ex-hook-up,' I blurt. I almost said 'boyfriend' but Cooper would know that was a massive lie on account of me never having any visitors.

'Oh?' The pitch of his voice rises and it rankles me that he seems surprised. I could hypothetically have had a hook-up. Yes, not a single man apart from Jonah has ever shown an interest in me, but Cooper doesn't know that. For all *he* knows I could be hooking up all over this town.

I huff. 'You're not the only one having, you know, saucy liaisons in this building!'

'Saucy liaisons?'

'Yeah. But unlike you, I just stuck with one. He's called Jonah and he is *great*. Very good-looking, super smart. Dreamy eyes . . .' I smile to myself, getting lost for a moment.

Cooper arches a single brow. 'Is that so?'

'Yeah, it is so. We, er, we hooked up all over this town.'

Oh, God. My cheeks flame.

'And now he's ghosting you?' Cooper nods slowly, as if to say *Of course that's what would be happening.* 'And you want to find out why he's ghosting you?'

God, this guy is insufferable. 'Actually, Columbo . . .' I trail off. I have no idea how to complete that sentence. I can't exactly say I'm trying to find the potential love of my life who I met for five minutes during death, and who I now have to kiss in order to avoid death once more. I spot Leanne waving at me from the window of the pharmacy over the road. The poster in the window beside her is advertising STD medication. 'I . . . I gave him chlamydia,' I finish.

Why did I say that? Why did that come out of my mouth? To his credit, Cooper's expression remains neutral.

'I've not got it anymore, obviously,' I add quickly. 'I've been treated. I'm fully in the clear as far as my . . . you know . . . is concerned. Clean as a whistle, in fact. But . . . you know. I have a duty to inform Jonah.'

Cooper nods. 'Quite.'

'Yes. *Quite.*'

I want to slide away into a puddle, slip into an underground drain never to be seen or heard from again. Take me now, Merritt.

As soon as I get upstairs to my flat I run into the bathroom to see if I am indeed as red-faced as I suspect. I truly am. I am a highly pigmented cadmium red. *Jeez, Delphie.*

I head to my bedroom, completely strip off and sit cross-legged on the floor in front of my tower fan. I take a deep breath and open the first of the books that Aled gave me.

I push away the surge of mortification that runs through me each time I think of what I just said to Cooper.

It's time to focus.

Two hours later and while I am versed in every possible method of hiding a body, and even how one might evade police capture, I am even more clueless about how to locate Jonah than I was this morning.

I open up my laptop and google Jonah T London again. The sheer volume of results is just as overwhelming as the last five times I searched Jonah T London. I click onto a LinkedIn profile for a Jonah Tanner. It is a man in his fifties who lives in Tucson, Arizona, and is passionate about microfinance. Not my soulmate. Then I click onto a Jonah Tyburn, who *is* in London. He is not the man I'm looking for because he is, in fact, a fifteen-year-old boy looking for someone to play Fortnite with. Not my soulmate. I click through a bunch of other Jonahs but there are so many of them and none of them are the perfect man I met in Evermore.

I shove my laptop away and knead my temples. Then I close my eyes and allow myself to picture Jonah's face again. How bright and twinkling his blue eyes were. How he looked at me as though he saw what I've sometimes suspected is there when I've examined my reflection with kindness: pale but reasonably unblemished skin and honest hazel eyes. A nose that's a little big, but straight and classical looking in the right light. A soft and welcoming body, with thighs that are strong and thick and hips that curve outwards in a way that could be considered sexy.

I'm jolted out of my thoughts by my TV, which suddenly switches itself on. I gasp and search for the remote, only to see it lying innocently on my bedside table. An episode of *Schitt's Creek* starts to play with subtitles. My jaw drops: the subtitles on the screen are written in a hot-pink cursive font, displayed bang in the middle of the screen, obscuring the actors' faces. I read.

> Whatever you're doing doesn't seem to be bearing much fruit, Delpherina. You might want to get a little help.

'I'm fine. I don't need help,' I call into the air as the subtitles fizz into a brand-new paragraph.

> If you say so. Just trying to be useful. It's quiet around here today and I've read the whole of Emily Henry's backlist plus re-read the entire Bridgerton series. I had a spare moment, so I thought I'd offer assistance. No probs if it's not needed! No skin off my nose!

'You could tell me where Jonah lives,' I try.

I stare at the screen and wait for a reply. But instead of a new set of subtitles, the TV simply switches itself back off. Of course. Merritt handing me an address would be no fun for her real-life romance novel and that's clearly all that interests her.

'Where are you, Jonah?' I mutter to myself. I picture him in Evermore and try hard to remember if there were any useful clues from our brief interaction. His T-shirt was plain, no logo. He mentioned London in general, but no specifics besides how magical he thought it was. I didn't really get the measure of what kind of job he had but I wouldn't be surprised if he was something impressive, like a doctor, or a fireman or something . . . And while the thought of that is pleasing on a base aesthetic level, it does not transfer into an actionable plan.

I spend another hour dashing off online messages to every photoless Jonah T I can find on the internet before concluding that Merritt was right.

I totally need help.

Chapter Nine

When Cooper answers his door his brows are already furrowed, like he's pre-empting the disappointment of our interaction. I think I've only ever seen him smile once. Back when he first moved in, he walked by me in the hallway. He was on the phone to someone, absolutely beaming. I remember him doing a little bow of greeting as I passed, his eyes lingering on mine for an amount of time that was frankly a little awkward.

His body mostly blocks the doorway but I can tell from the light behind him that his blinds are closed, only the blue hue of computer screens illuminating the room.

'What now?' he sighs.

His attitude stinks.

'Just checking to see if the rumours were true,' I say extra breezily. 'That you *do* sit alone in a darkened room all day, trolling strangers on Twitter for kicks. Biiiig incel energy.'

His eyebrows shoot up. 'My house is darkened because it's thirty-three degrees outside and this is an old building with thick walls. And I don't use Twitter.' He fake-smiles and moves to close his door but I put my foot in the doorway before he can.

'Hold up . . . Can I come in?'

'No.'

'I . . . I need some help as soon as possible,' I say – a sentence I've only ever said twice in my life: once to a cashier when I couldn't find the ripe and ready avocados in the corner shop, and the other time when I saw a pigeon and a rat having a fight outside Ladbroke Grove Tube station.

I can see that Cooper really doesn't want to let me in, but posh-boy politeness gets the better of him and he steps back, opening the door with a barely concealed grumble.

I step into his flat and notice that it's much bigger than mine. In fact, it's even bigger than Mr Yoon's. I take a look around. It looks like the home of someone much warmer and more interesting than Cooper. The walls are crammed with bookcases and art and framed pictures of vintage paperback covers. The sofa is a stripy cream fabric, covered with plump velvet scatter cushions in a dense Prussian blue. I gasp as I spot an original fireplace, the black cast iron almost pewter with age.

'Lucky!' I breathe. 'Does it work?'

'I think so.'

'You think so? If I had a fireplace like that it would be lit the whole time.'

'Even in a heatwave?'

'I'd have a cold bath first and not get dressed so that I could feel the benefits.'

His eyebrow quirks upwards a smidge.

Above the fireplace, there's a large black-framed line drawing hanging in pride of place. It's an ink drawing of a naked woman, posing with her back turned. It's beautiful and more erotic than I would expect to be hanging in the living room of someone like sour-faced Cooper. I stand in front of the picture and admire it.

'Is there something I can help you with or did you come by to inspect my belongings?'

I spin around and point at the desk to the left of the fireplace, the one with three computer screens lighting the room with a neon glow. These computers are lit up every time I come to collect a parcel from Cooper's flat. 'You're a computer guy, right?'

'I . . . Yes, I suppose I am these days. Are you having trouble with your laptop? There's a repair shop over on Queensway.'

'No . . .' I wander over to the computer and squint at the biggest screen in the middle. It's covered in rows of numbers and symbols I don't understand. 'I'm here about the man I'm looking for . . . The . . .'

'The gentleman with whom you hooked up all over this town?'

I flush red. 'Yes, him. I've been reading through the books I got from the library. The first one said that I should do a public directory search. But there were so many Jonahs in London that I got overwhelmed and didn't know where to begin. So I wondered if you, with your computer whizzery, knew how I could hurry up the process?'

Cooper shakes his head. 'I'm afraid now is not a good time. I'm busy. Perhaps in a day or two I can have a look.'

'Why did you let me in if you weren't going to help me?'

'I didn't know the nature of the request. Now I do.'

'I don't have time to wait a day or two!'

Cooper folds his arms, his shirt straining across unreasonably large shoulders. 'Why?'

'Um, well. I think with, uh, chlamydia, time is of the essence. I mean, I, of course, was treated immediately and am now—'

'Clean as a whistle. You mentioned.'

God. 'Yes, but Jonah. He doesn't know. And he should definitely know. It's the *responsible* thing to do. I mean, you would hate it if Little Cooper was in peril and you had zero clue!'

I clamp my mouth shut, the words 'Little Cooper' hanging horrifyingly in the air.

'Great.' Big Cooper narrows his eyes for a moment. 'Okay. I think perhaps you should go. I'm sorry Delphie, but I really do have work to do.'

He strides over to the door and opens it.

'Please help me today. I'll owe you. Anything you want.'

'I don't need anything.'

'You might. One day.'

He smirks. 'What do you think I might ever possibly need from you?'

I shrug. 'A cup of sugar? Some candles if there's a blackout?' I look around his living room. 'You don't seem to have any candles. I have loads of them.'

'I don't take sugar because I'm not twelve years old, and London hasn't had a blackout in twenty years.'

Good lord, he is horrible. The worst. Is his rudeness towards me personal, or is he like this with everyone? No.

That can't be it. If he was this dreadful all the time he wouldn't have so many women hanging about. I huff loudly. 'Fine. Thanks for nothing, Cooper. Don't you dare come knocking on my door when your washing machine breaks and you need somewhere to wash your intimates.'

Why did I say 'intimates'? Why am I saying anything? There are many reasons I keep myself to myself and this verbal malfunction has got to be in the top five of them.

'An excruciating prospect but somehow I think I'll manage.' His phone buzzes with a text and he pulls it out of his pocket, reading the screen. His other hand points at the door. We're clearly done here.

'You're the most obnoxious man I've ever encountered,' I hiss, irritation and frustration sending a lump right to my throat.

What the hell am I supposed to do next?

I spin around and march towards the door, hoping to myself that one day Cooper has a terrible urge for a hot cup of tea at daft o'clock and simply must borrow some milk at which point I will say no. Or even better, fill a cup with gone-off milk and give him that. I have a little chuckle at the thought. I'm about to slam the door behind me when Cooper calls my name.

'Delphie, wait . . .'

I turn to face him, give him my best withering glare. 'What?'

'There, uh, is actually something you can do for me.' He peers at his phone and frowns.

'What is it?'

Cooper closes his eyes for a brief moment. 'I . . . Would you take a photo with me?'

I screw up my face. 'You want to take my picture?'

'Um, yes. A . . . a selfie.'

The word 'selfie' sounds odd coming out of his mouth and I would bet everything I own – which admittedly is not much – that this is the first time he's said it. His ears turn slightly pink.

'Why do you want a selfie?' I narrow my eyes. 'Is this some kind of trick?' I get a vision of him pasting my face onto a photo of a naked body and posting it all across the internet just to be an arsehole.

'It's not for anything nefarious, I promise. It'll be quick. Do you want my help or not?'

I do want his help. I need his help. 'Fine. I am a bit sweaty, though.'

'What, you want to freshen up or something?'

'Um. Okay? I mean, I can do?'

'The bathroom is that way.' He thumbs behind him to a door that's ajar.'

Slightly befuddled, I shuffle into Cooper's bathroom, which is as bare as his living room is busy. There's no way I'm using his bar of soap because God knows what he's washed with it. Instead I run some cool water into my cupped hands and splash it onto my face. I open the cupboard beneath the sink to see a set of fresh towels in an elegant charcoal colour, a small cream box with REAL FEEL CONDOMS printed on the side in a chic serif font, and an unopened bottle of Kiehl's handwash.

I grab a towel, pat my face dry and head back out.

I point at my clean cheeks. 'Sweat eliminated.'

Cooper doesn't reply, just positions himself beside me so that we're shoulder-to-shoulder. I shuffle uncomfortably.

He holds up his camera. 'You have to smile,' he says.

I show all my teeth in response.

'A real smile, Delphie. Are you capable?'

'Are you?'

'It has to look genuine. I don't know, think of your happy place.'

My happy place. I hear Jonah's voice saying he felt like he'd met me before. I grin at the memory as Cooper takes a burst of pictures.

'You won't put them on the internet, will you?' I ask, leaning over to try to get a look at the snaps.

'Why on earth would I?' he scoffs, slipping his phone back into his pocket. 'These will be deleted by this evening I can assure you. Now . . .' He eyes the clock on his phone. 'I have around thirty minutes before I have to be somewhere else. How can I help you?'

Chapter Ten

I've never been to East London before and I do not like it. I don't know my way around the unfamiliar streets and every person I see looks like they're on their way to audition for some wanky indie band with a name like Radiator Conspiracy or Breakfast With Carl. There is, however, a huge chance that Jonah is here tonight so I battle through the discomfort.

As suspected, Cooper was a whizz on the computer. To my surprise he had access to some sort of private police database, though he annoyingly refused to tell me how or why. He used the database to quickly generate a list of Jonah Ts under the age of thirty in London, and while a social media search showed that most of them were not *my* Jonah, there was one man who was a definite maybe. Jonah Thompson. His social media profiles were mostly private or lapsed, but the display image showed a man of the right age, with the same Burnt Umber hair. His face was obscured by sunglasses so I couldn't be 100 per cent sure. We saw on Instagram that Jonah Thompson had been tagged in a photo at a weekly musical theatre night in East London – which happens to be on tonight. And so it seemed the next logical step to show up here in the hopes that it's a regular hang-out of his. I mean, my Jonah didn't exactly seem like the kind of man to attend a musical theatre piano bar, but he did say he was anticipating a magical summer in London and maybe this is what he considers magical? Either way, at the thought of seeing him again my heart starts to beat a little faster, a warm flush spreading across my neck and chest.

I spot a neon sign directing me to THE ORCHESTRA PIT and head down some rusty-looking stairs to a basement.

I open the door and am hit with a wall of noise, synthetic vape smells, disco-ball lights, and tinkly music coming from an upright piano standing right in the centre of the room.

'Eek,' I mutter to myself. 'What hellscape is this and why would someone as wonderful as Jonah come here?'

I shuffle to the bar, grimacing as a group of women wearing feather boas shove past me, saying something disparaging about Andrew Lloyd Webber.

The man behind the bar is dressed in a T-shirt made entirely of red sequins.

'Uh, hi there.' I give an awkward little wave.

'Your hair! Very *Sound of Music*!' The man presses a hand to his chest in delight.

I pat my braids self-consciously. 'I've not seen that one,' I say. 'I don't like musicals.'

The man laughs out loud as if I'm joking. When I don't laugh back his smile falters. 'Shit. You're definitely gonna need a drink then.'

I nod. 'Agreed. A glass of white wine would be lovely. Pinot Grigio, please.'

'We have cocktails for half-price on our happy hour

menu – they're delicious. I know because I make them. They're a lot cheaper than the wine. And a ton more potent.'

He hands me a paper menu, on which there is a list of complicated-looking drinks: the Liza, the Patti, the Barbra, the Idina and the Bernadette.

I've never had a cocktail before. But half the price is half the price.

'Cool.' I run my finger down the list. 'I'll have a Liza.'

'Nice choice.' The man selects a fancy-looking glass like something out of a James Bond movie and gathers ingredients to prepare my cocktail. 'You're new here,' he says as he pours an obscene amount of vodka into a metal shaker. 'And you hate musicals. So . . . why?'

'I'm looking for a man,' I tell him distractedly, scanning the room for any sign of Jonah.

'Yeah, not sure this is the best place for that,' he laughs, sliding over my drink. It's decorated with a curly silver straw, a sticky maraschino cherry and a cocktail umbrella. I fight my way through all the accoutrements and take a tentative sip. I immediately take another.

'Holy shit.'

'Right? I put in a dash of apple sour to give it that extra zazz.' He wiggles his fingers when he says 'zazz'.

I take another gulp of the drink and feel soothed by a mellow sensation loosening my limbs. At the piano, a woman starts to sing a song about someone not being able to pay their rent. She's terrible but no one seems to care, instead they just gather around the piano and join in. This is such a weird place. I order another drink and start to make my way around the basement bar, eyes on stalks for a sighting of Jonah. Every toffee-haired man catches my eye, but not one of them is him. I wander across the bar, trying unsuccessfully to tune out the wail of terrible singing. I peek my head into each seating booth as I pass by. Jonah isn't in any of them.

My phone vibrates in my purse. I pull it out. A text from Merritt.

Bonjour, belle! I LOVE this place! I used to go all the time. You have to sing 'All That Jazz' for me.

'No way,' I hiss. 'I'm here to find Jonah.'

PLEASE. If I was there I would do it myself. But I can't. Because I'm dead. So tragic. Taken away in my prime.

I turn to face the wall so that the surrounding revellers don't think I'm talking to myself as I answer her.

'I don't even know that song. And even if I did there's no way I would ever get up and sing in front of other people.'

I spot a tall man with Jonah-coloured hair on the other side of the piano. I speed-walk in his direction, but he disappears into the men's toilets before I can reach him.

'Dammit!'

As I stand outside the men's room and wait for him to finish his business, my phone continues to vibrate in a frenzied way.

76

'All That Jazz'! I demand it. If you don't I will take off
a day.

'What the fuck? You can't do that!'

A man coming out of the loo gives me a cocky look. 'I just
did, honey,' he drawls.

'Not you!' I call after him, but he's already disappeared
into the crowd.

'I don't need another day,' I say to Merritt. 'I think I might
have found him.'

At that moment, the tall Jonah-haired guy exits the toilets. My heart sinks. While this man is roughly the same
height as Jonah, with identical hair, his face is less sharp, his
eyes much closer together and not at all cobalt blue.

'Is your name Jonah Thompson?' I ask.

'Nope, not me.'

'You looking for Australian Jonah?' a woman asks,
sidling up to the man from the loos and swinging an arm
around his waist. 'He moved back to Sydney six months
ago. Visa ran out. We miss him. He did a mean Jean
Valjean.'

'Wait . . . Jonah Thompson is Australian? With an Australian accent?'

Toilet guy grins. 'That's how it tends to work.'

My Jonah had a British accent. And he currently lives in
London. So my Jonah is not Jonah Thompson. Dammit. I
thought I at least had a name.

As the man and woman wander off towards the group
wearing feather boas, my phone buzzes again and I hear the

faint sounds of 'Jump Around' beneath the jangling piano music.

Looks like losing a day would be terrible right about now!

'Why are you insisting on this? I thought you were trying to help me? Look, my Jonah isn't here. Has probably never been here. Just let me go home so I can make a new plan.' I lift my phone to my ear so it looks like I'm talking into it, lest any passers-by think I'm fully insane.

If I cannot live, let me live vicariously. 'All That Jazz' or you lose a day.

'I don't know "All That Jazz".'

Everyone knows 'All That Jazz'.

She's right. Somehow, everyone does know 'All That Jazz'. Via osmosis or something.

Come on. Be brave, Delphie. Don't you at least want to live a little, while you've got the chance?

'Aaaaargh.'
I slump back to the bar. 'One shot of tequila and another Liza, please.'
'Did you find your man?'
I nod, knocking back the tequila. 'It was the wrong one.'

'Been there.' The barman expertly mixes the cocktail and nudges it over to me. 'This one's on the house.'

My eyebrows shoot up. 'What's the catch?'

'No catch.' He shrugs. 'You just look like you need it.'

I nod my thanks, leave a £5 tip on the bar and head over to the piano man who is just finishing up a song that even I – with very little theatre experience – know is from *Hamilton*.

I nudge my way through the crowd surrounding the piano man and lean in close.

'Can I . . . can I put in a request for "All That Jazz", please?'

He rolls his eyes. 'No Sondheim? A little Tesori? Or God, at least any other Kander and Ebb song would make a nice change . . .'

I have no clue what he's talking about.

'Name?' he eventually says with a little huff.

'Delphie Denise Bookham.'

'Only need your first one, but fine!' He hands me the mic. I take it from him with a trembling hand, and down the cocktail that's in my other.

The piano man starts to play the opening vamp of the song. Shaking, I lift the microphone to my lips.

I open my mouth. Nothing comes out.

'You have to actually sing!' the piano man hisses, playing the same opening vamp once again.

The surrounding crowd looks at me blank-faced, but then the sequin-topped bar guy walks over to stand next to me and quietly starts singing the song, his voice unreasonably beautiful. He gives me a nod of encouragement. But despite that and the tequila and the threat of Merritt taking a day away from me, I can't do it. I think my ears are sweating. Just yesterday my life involved interacting with as few people as I could get away with. And now, somehow, I'm standing in front of a bunch of total strangers being forced to sing a song I only half sort of know for a pushy Afterlife Therapist who wants to laugh at me before she kills me.

Just when I think things can't get any worse I spot a woman towards the back of the room. She's with the group wearing the feather boas and is clearly the leader – her alpha energy creating a sort of aura around her.

My breath catches in my throat as it dawns on me that the woman is Gen. Best-friend-turned-evil-tormentor Gen. She's pointing at me and saying something to her friends, smirking.

Bile jets into my throat. How is she here? *Why* is she here? My stomach swoops and I worry I'm going to be sick. I drop the microphone onto the piano where it makes a discordant jangle on the keys.

'Hey!' the piano man scolds. 'That's a premium Sennheiser 430!'

'S-sorry,' I call back as I dart away from the piano.

My jaw tightens as Gen starts to walk towards me. And it's only then that I realise that the woman is not Gen at all. Just a skinny, confident-looking woman with blonde hair but, actually, a completely different face. I wait for my heart to stop pounding, but it doesn't. The very notion that it might have been Gen has set waves of cortisol off in my bloodstream. My heart pounds.

'Are you alright?' I hear the sequinned barman ask, though his voice sounds like it's coming from underwater.

'Sorry,' I mutter again.

Then I whirl around and race as fast as I can out of the basement bar and onto the crowded street.

I don't stop running until I reach the bus stop.

Chapter Eleven

I get off the bus at Paddington and as the summer-evening breeze hits me I realise that I am drunk. I don't drink often so the cocktails have really hit me and I find myself stumbling down past the library tripping over thin air every thirty seconds or so.

'Delphie? Delphie Bookham? Goodness, is that you?'

I look behind me to see a lanky man jogging over to me. How does he know my name? And why is he running after me?

I speed up my walk, managing about two metres before my lack of co-ordination means I go tumbling onto the pavement.

'Nooooo!'

The chaser catches up while I'm still splayed on the ground. Relief softens my shoulders as the glow of a street-lamp reveals that my 'assailant' is actually just the man I met this morning at the library. The one who helped me out with all the books.

'You silly goose!' he says, holding out a hand to help me up.

I ignore the hand because I can get up myself. Except that everything seems to be swaying the wrong way.

'It's me, Aled!' the man says, holding out his hand again.

I have no choice but to take it. He yanks me upright, surprisingly strong for someone so skinny.

'I'm fine now!' I say brightly to Aled. 'Thanks for the help. All the best to you and yours!'

As I make my way down the street, I immediately careen into the wall, bouncing off it right into a bollard. This walking straight thing is not working out for me at all. Aled catches me up and steadies me.

'How far have you to go? Let me walk you. Unless it's more than a ten-minute trek, in which case I'll call us a taxi. I'm returning from my Crime Lovers book club at the library' – he thumbs backwards towards the old library building – 'and, frankly, I'm shattered. People are bloody exhausting.'

I give him a sideways glance and point over the road. 'I only live down there. And I agree. People are exhausting.'

'Exhausting but necessary.'

Not necessarily necessary is what I intend to say, but it comes out more like, 'Not nesha neshararraaa.'

Somehow Aled seems to understand. 'Come on. Let's get you back, you enormous pisshead.'

I let him angle me towards my house and only half listen as he tells me more about the books he gave me today along with a few others he could recommend. '*How Do They Sleep at Night?* isn't in stock but I could order it in and it'll be at the library within seven to ten days.'

'Probably won't be here in seven to ten days,' I mutter, uncertain of anything after tonight's disaster.

'Off on your holidays, are you?'

'Something like that,' I say realising that we're now right outside my front door.

'Bye then!' I call out, but Aled doesn't leave.

'Wait. Do you have stairs, Delphie?'

'Just a single flight. I'll be fine.' I wave him off.

He pulls a face. 'In the book we discussed tonight, the first murder victim was pushed down the stairs and the police didn't even investigate it because she was an enormous pisshead like you.'

I muffle a tiny burp. 'If I let you in, you could murder me.'

Aled laughs at the idea and I notice that when he laughs he does so with his whole body. 'Imagine. I'm not the type. I'm a vegan.'

I'm not sure how that reasoning adds up, but I agree that he doesn't look the type. And even if he did murder me, Merritt would probably send me back down to earth again to humiliate me for her own amusement.

I knock on the front door before remembering that I have some keys because I live here.

'Give me your keys, love,' Aled chuckles. I root around in my purse and hand them over.

He unlocks the door and I bumble into the hallway. We must be making an almighty racket because Cooper pops his head out of his door. His hair is wet from the shower and he's wearing a dazzling white towelling robe, like someone from a spa. How does he keep his robe so white? Mine stays grey no matter how much Daz I use. Cooper steps out into the hallway.

I wave my hand vaguely. 'Sorry! Sorry for the disturbance, despicable Cooper!'

'Hello there,' he says, moving at a weirdly speedy pace out into the corridor. He manoeuvres himself in front of Aled. 'We haven't met.' His voice sounds deeper than usual.

'I'm Aled. Your local enormous pisshead delivery service,' Aled tells Cooper cheerily, dropping my keys back into my hands.

'Do you know this man?' Cooper squats down and locks onto my eyes in a strangely intense way.

It dawns on me that he thinks I'm so drunk that Aled might be about to take advantage of me in some way. It needles me that he thinks I can't look after myself just because I've had a few very potent cocktails.

I lift my chin. 'Actually, yes. This is Aled, my best friend and confidant,' I tell Cooper, a huge hiccup punctuating the end of my sentence. 'I know him very well. Very well indeed.'

'Oh, blimey!' Aled says. 'Well, this is unexpected. I have many friends but not a best one at the moment.' He appears to consider something briefly. 'Okay . . . I accept. Best friends it is. We'll confirm tomorrow when you're not so sozzled. You might have changed your mind by then. That's happened to me once before, sadly. But if you still feel the same way tomorrow then I accept.'

Cooper looks incredulously at Aled and then at me and then back at Aled again.

'You didn't find Jonah?' Cooper takes my arm and steadies me up the stairs to my flat, while Aled watches us from the bottom step.

85

'Nope. It was the wrong guy. His eyes were too close together.'

'Ooh, who is Jonah?' Aled calls up.

'You didn't tell your best friend about Jonah?' Cooper asks as I, after two failed attempts, eventually manage to slot the key into my door lock.

'Jonah is the missing person I was telling you about,' I hiss to Aled.

'Oh yes, you poor love. No wonder you've been drinking like a fish. The stress of a missing loved one is so much to bear.'

'Loved one?' Cooper makes a face. 'I thought Jonah was—'

Yikes. 'Yes, yes,' I interrupt. 'Here we are! Home at last. Aah, it's good to be back. Lovely indeed – home is where the heart is!'

I turn to say goodnight when I see Aled staring up at Cooper through narrowed eyes. 'You look very familiar,' he muses. 'Do I know you?'

'I'm certain you don't,' Cooper replies curtly. Then without so much as a goodbye or a backward glance, he spins on his heel and hurries back down the stairs, whizzing past Aled and back to his own flat.

'Maybe he just has one of those faces,' Aled remarks.

'A despicable one, you mean.'

'Oh, I'd say it was quite delightful. Brooding, like if Timothée Chalamet—'

'Had an arsehole brother!' I finish with a giggle.

'Exactly!' Aled grins and leans against the banister.

'You'll be okay from here, yes? Because I really am exhausted. But I will contact you tomorrow about the best friends thing. To see if you still feel the same way.'

I nod, safe in the knowledge that Aled does not have my phone number and that there is a drop-off box outside the library so I needn't ever see him again. 'Absolutely. Thanks very much for the assist.'

'Of course.'

I shut the door behind me and take five steps through the open bedroom door towards my bed where I sort of splat down, my face in between two pillows. I fall asleep in less than a minute.

Chapter Twelve

It's already day three. I wake up sweating after a terrible dream in which Gen and Ryan beat me up with a pair of Sennheiser microphones and livestream the whole thing on YouTube.

'That's so dark, Delphie,' I mutter to myself, sitting up and thus initiating the horrendous sensation of my brain trying to escape my skull via my eyeballs. I pick up my phone to check the time. Five a.m.? Gross.

A wave of horror immediately worms its way through my body. Usually I don't have specific reasons to feel bad – it's more just what my GP refers to as 'general malaise that will be improved by a good diet, regular exercise, talking therapy and 20mg of daily fluoxetine', but now I have a great big bunch of reasons.

'Uuuuuggggh.' I bury my head in my hands. Then it dawns on me. 'Mr Yoon!' Shit. I was so drunk last night, I forgot to check on his gas and cigarettes. The fact that I'm not dead of fire bodes well, but still, anything could have happened.

I gingerly crawl out of bed and take my copy of Mr Yoon's key from where it hangs by the front door. As quietly as I can, I enter his flat, the sound of him lightly snoring away a balm to my anxieties. The living room is bright but still cool. I check the oven and his ashtray. Both fine. Good. That's good.

Mr Yoon's cigarettes are extinguished but the ashtray is almost overflowing with cigarette butts. It would wake him up if I tried to wash it now, so I take it over to the kitchen, tip the ends into the bin, and then crouch down to the left-hand cupboard to look for a fresh ashtray, so that he has a clean one when he wakes up.

The cupboard is crammed with *stuff* and I make a mental note to organise it when I get a spare moment. I spot an ashtray behind a picture frame. As quietly as I can, I slide out the picture frame so I can get to the ashtray. I plop down on the floor and turn the frame in the direction of the morning light filtering through the curtains. Gosh! Is this a picture of a young Mr Yoon? Yes. It's definitely him. He's standing on a grand-looking stage, holding a violin and a bow in one hand and a trophy in the other. I try to make out what the words on the trophy say, but it's an old photo and the quality is pretty low. Either way, Mr Yoon plays the violin! And he is so good at it that he was once given some sort of award. I wonder why he's never told me about this in his notes.

'Very cool, Mr Yoon,' I whisper to myself, sliding the frame back into the cupboard. I take the clean ashtray over to his table. Beside the bunch of sweet peas I brought him last week lies a massive bag of the fizzy cola bottles I've been trying to get him to stop snacking on. How the hell did he get his hands on those? Does he have a dealer? A shady sweet-shop man lurking about the building and exchanging baggies of sours for cash?

Tutting, I let myself out of Mr Yoon's and creep back over to my flat. As I step inside, my foot skids slightly on an envelope that's been slipped under my door.

I pick it up, open it, and take out two pieces of paper. I unfold the first piece of paper, my heart immediately lifting when I see that it's a black-and-white print-out of a photo of Jonah. The actual Jonah! He's even more beautiful than I remembered, his eyes twinkling brightly, his smile welcoming and confident. I shake my head. Who sent this?

I unfold the other piece of paper – it's a note scribbled in black ink, the writing looped and precise.

Delphie,

I did a little more hunting and this sounds like the man you described? Unfortunately, due to the resolution of the image, I cannot ascertain whether his eyes could be deemed 'dreamy', but otherwise I believe it might be him. His name is Jonah Truman. His social profiles are private and he doesn't accept messages, but after some investigating I found that he is a member of Kensington Gardens running club. They run every morning at 7 a.m. I hope you are able to catch him, if it is indeed the Jonah you hooked up with all over this town.

Regards,
Cooper

Oh my gosh! Jonah has been found! And Kensington Gardens? That's so close. Does he live in Paddington? Notting Hill? Was he nearby all this time and I never knew?

Wow.

'Jonah,' I whisper to myself. I close my eyes and imagine his lips pressed against mine. In Evermore he looked at me like all I'd have to do is ask him. Just like that. Like someone in a movie from the 1940s. *Now kiss me, you fool!* But this is the real world. Surely I'll need to prep things. Ask him for a drink first at the very least.

A surge of adrenaline pulses through me at the thought of being sat in a bar, across the table from Jonah, his dazzling blue eyes lit by candlelight.

'Ahahaha!' I shout into the air in case Merritt is watching. 'In less than two days! Bet you feel silly for gloating now.' The excitement at getting to see Jonah again, not to mention the huge relief that I have managed to save my own life, propels me straight past my headache and into the shower where I perform an intense toothbrush, because, while Jonah is unlikely to kiss me immediately, it seems that, in this particular scenario, it's best to be prepared for absolutely anything to happen.

While I have plenty of clothes just fine for a hot day outdoors, I don't have much to choose from that is a) suitable for running (assuming that Jonah is going to be jogging), and b) alluring enough to move a man to ask me to coffee or to dinner or to go for a walk that will – hopefully quite quickly – lead to a life-saving kiss. My clothes are built for practicality and he's hardly going to be enticed if I'm wearing my oversized V&A T-shirt and denim shorts.

I open my wardrobe and rifle frantically through all the

clothes I have. As expected, nothing that could be considered at all enticing. And then I get a brainwave. The bag full of stuff Mum didn't take with her to the artists' commune! Maybe there's something in there? Everyone found Mum alluring. Well, everyone except for Dad, in the end.

I drag a kitchen chair over to the tall cupboard by my front door and, standing on my tiptoes, yank the plastic bag out. It's much heavier than I anticipated and it bounces off my head before plopping onto to the ground with a crinkly thud, me following swiftly behind.

I get my bearings and eagerly untie the yellow plastic strings at the top of the bag. As it opens, I'm hit with a scent that triggers a heady rush of emotion. Sadness and longing and nostalgia and anger tumble around my stomach. I pull out a cotton dress, the fabric a red-and-white love-heart print. How can these clothes still smell like Chanel N°5 and Lenor and Nivea sun cream? Like Mum? I made sure to wash them all before I packed them away – I'd meant to take them to the charity shop but somehow I'd never got round to it.

I press the dress to my nose for a millisecond. I'm rewarded for my idiocy with a surge of recollections about Mum. In my memories she is never still. Always zipping from one room to the other, racing through chores, arranging parties, chatting to her pals on the phone, helping me and Gen with homework because Gen's own mum was at work all the time. Mum treated home life like a project, giving it her all in an effort to make it a total success. After Dad broke her heart it's like she suddenly saw the whole project as a failure. Not just the marriage, but her entire life, including me.

She spent the next six months barely functioning, sleeping in until 5 p.m., having cocktail hour at 11 a.m., crying loudly in the bath. After Gen and I got home after school one day to find Mum passed out on the sofa, an empty saucepan burning away on the hob, I stopped inviting Gen over. I couldn't bear the embarrassment of Gen knowing that since Dad had gone, life at home had become so bleak. By the time Mum came through the other side, Gen had decided she hated me. And then, of course, Mum met Gerard and moved to the artists' commune in Texas, deciding to pick back up on the art she used to make before she got pregnant with me.

The dust layered over the old clothes makes me sneeze four times in a row before I recover enough to search through the bag for anything that might be suitable for a momentous kiss in the park.

Aha! There it is! I unearth the outfit Mum used to wear to go running. It's much skimpier than I remember, though. A cool grey sports bra with orange stripes down the side and a pair of matching leggings. Mum was much smaller than my size 12, but that might be a good thing. If TV shows are anything to go by then tight clothes could do the trick. I quickly pull the clothes on. I don't have a full-length mirror to check that the bottom half looks good, but it seems to fit quite well. I check my top half in the bathroom mirror. The tightness makes my boobs splodge out at the top. Other than that it's fine. Way better for running than anything else I have.

I blast my hair with the cool setting of the hairdryer and

tie it up into my usual braids, fastening them securely at the top of my head with ten bobby pins and a shit-ton of hairspray. Then I dab some concealer under my eyes in what turns out to be a futile attempt to cover the grey circles caused by last night's cocktails.

I slip my feet into my good old Nikes and leave the building.

Chapter Thirteen

I'm not sure I've ever been out of the house this early before. The four streets surrounding my building are much quieter without the arrivals and departures of the tourists from the station and surrounding hotels. Despite the hour the temperature is already blazing, the scent of hot tarmac heavy in the air. I feel grateful to be wearing something so light. As I cross the road, the woman who runs the little florist's hut by the estate agents gives a wave. I glance behind me to see who she's waving at then realise that *I* am who she's waving at. I tentatively wave back but as I get closer to her she gives me the strangest look. A cross between horror and amusement. That's the exact way Gen and her gang used to look at me whenever I'd raise my hand to answer a question in class. Usually followed by a chorus of giggles and sometimes a wad of chewing gum somehow finding its way into my hair (hence the beginning of my daily extra-tight braids ritual).

I scowl at the woman and chastise myself for not knowing better than to wave at people. I march past the gleaming white rows of buildings, taking a shortcut through a pretty cobbled mews. It's less than a five-minute walk to the Italian Gardens in Kensington Gardens and when I get there, I'm immediately taken by how serene it is. The ornate fountains send out a light mist that forms a miniature rainbow in the sunlight. There's a heron perched on one of the statues. Up the hill to the left there's a man setting up stripy green deckchairs in haphazard rows. A lone woman in a wide-brimmed hat lounges on a wooden bench, breakfasting on an icy Solero.

No wonder Mum used to come here every morning. It's peaceful and open, just a gentle buzz of dog-walkers and joggers passing by every so often.

Okay. Cooper's note says that Jonah runs here with his group every morning at 7 a.m. I pull my phone from where it's tucked into the waistband of my Lycra trousers. It's 6.59.

I have no idea which entrance of Kensington Gardens Jonah will be coming from, so I decide my best bet is to power-walk around as fast as I can and save the jogging for once I've spotted him. I'm pretty sure that I only have around five min-utes of full-on speed-running available in my body and I don't want to use it up before I absolutely need to.

I pass a slick-looking jogger who stares at my chest.

'Keep your eyes on your own business, pal,' I spit at him. I'm aware that my boobs splodging like this might be attract-ive to some people, but that gives them no right to gawk. The man flushes red and runs past me, briefly looking back as he does.

I shake my head and continue on, but then a woman jog-ging with a stroller runs past me and also stares, not at my chest but at my whole body, her eyes running up and down and then back again.

'Keep your eyes on your own business!' I say again, slightly outraged that people feel so bold as to openly rubberneck, but also starting to wonder if this running outfit . . . Does this running outfit make me look hot?

When three more park-frequenters seem unable to take their eyes off me, I conclude that this get-up might have somehow transformed me into someone undeniably sexy.

I feel an unusual rush of power in my gut. The only person who has ever looked at me like I was a sexual being was Jonah. And now five people in a row can't take their eyes away. Woah. This must be how Gal Gadot feels every day of her life.

I steel myself, and with the swell of outraged/pleased energy that comes from all the sudden attention, I break into a light jog. Which is useful because ahead of me, turning out from a path on the right and sprinting towards the Serpentine is a group of about eight people running in sets of two down the narrow path.

One of the runners turns to say something to the other. I catch the shape of his chin and I know immediately that it is him! It's Jonah! That's my Jonah, running with his group just like Cooper said he would be!

'Jonah!' I call out, but I'm forty metres away and he doesn't hear me. I speed up my run. I'm not exactly slow but he is actively fast. It certainly doesn't help my focus that almost every person I pass stares at me with buggy eyes. It crosses my mind that if I wore this outfit on the regular I could probably have my pick of first-ever sexual partners. But of course, I want Jonah. The sweetest, most handsome man I've ever laid eyes on. My literal soulmate! It's funny. I was quite settled with the idea of never having sex, until I met Jonah. But the moment he put his hands on my arms I haven't been able to stop imagining what it might be like. And then, of course, immediately following that pleasantness comes the swirl of anxiety about how I'm supposed to be any good at something I've never done before. What if I do it wrong?

I think I'm gaining ground, the gap between me and Jonah closing with each pound of the pathway. But just when I get close enough to call out Jonah's name again, a group of dogs runs right in front of me, leads of various colours trailing behind them. My foot gets looped in one of the leads and I trip forward.

'Oof.' I pitch to the ground, grazing my knee and the heel of my hand.

Dazed, I sit upright, only able to watch in horror as Jonah runs further and further away from me. I struggle to my feet and attempt to extricate myself from the dog leads, but all five dogs are scrambling over me, jumping up at my chest and licking my face with their stinky tongues.

'Get off, gremlins!' I shoo away the dogs. They ignore my request, becoming even more pumped up now that I'm speaking to them. I want to chase after Jonah, see if I can somehow catch him up, but I can hardly leave these dogs on their own. A harassed hippy-looking woman runs over to me from the side-path. I pick up the jumble of leads and try to remain upright while the biggest of the dogs, a large fluffy bear of a thing tries its best to take me down again.

'I don't know what happened!' the woman pants as she reaches me. She's a little younger than me, with dark blonde hair in waves all the way down to her waist. She's wearing a long violet chiffony dress and flip-flops. Her accent is Eastern European, I think. 'I'm a professional,' she continues, wiping the sweat from her brow. 'I walk these five pups every morning and I've never dropped their leads! My hand just went like this.' She dangles her wrist. 'I lost my grip and off they went. I'm sorry!'

'It's okay,' I say, my shoulders sagging as I watch Jonah round the final bend towards the Serpentine Lido. 'They're all safe, at least.'

The woman has tears in her eyes, although from the red rims around them it looks like she's been crying long before our encounter. 'I'm betrayed, once again.' She side-eyes the dogs and shakes her head. 'Five years I've been walking them and the first chance they get, it's *Goodbye, I'm outta here.*'

'They were probably just excited.'

'Ian, I am especially the most disappointed in you,' she scolds the smallest of the bunch – a grey teacup Chihuahua. 'You are supposed to be the sensible one. The pack leader! Anyway.' She sighs, her eyes returning to me. 'Thanks for catching them. Everyone seems to be running away from me these days. Ha-ha.'

She laughs, although there's no cheer in it and I understand the reason for her tear-stained face. Even I know that this is the facial expression of the recently dumped.

I tentatively reach a hand out to pat her arm but then,

wondering if that's too much, bail at the last minute and just sort of skim the surface of her sleeve instead. I glance down to see that one of the dogs is peeing on the path, the flow getting way too close to my trainers. I yelp and jump away, shielding myself behind the park noticeboard that overlooks the lake. My eyes skim up to the noticeboard. Blu-Tacked right in the centre there's a poster; a group of happy people proudly holding up charcoal drawings.

Oh my God.

I squeak.

One of the happy people on the poster is Jonah.

Chapter Fourteen

How can this be? I peer closer. Yes! Jonah is right there, beaming into the camera along with six other people. Some cynics would call this a coincidence. And just a few days ago I would have been one of those cynics. But now, knowing what I know about soulmates, I can see that it's clearly a sign that Jonah and I are fated to meet, just like Merritt said. I scan the text – it's advertising a weekly art class called Drawing From Life. Jonah draws? *I* draw! I mean, I used to. But still. Jonah is interested in art too? I suddenly see us together, wandering the cavernous rooms of the National Gallery, gently disagreeing about who the real star of the Post-Impressionist movement is. He would eventually acquiesce to my superior opinion, take me in his arms by a Cézanne, and kiss me on the nose.

I feel the press of paws against my calves and turn to find the dog-walking woman and her rambunctious group of hounds are still there.

'I walk past this sign every single day,' the woman says, scanning the poster. 'And I think, *Oh my! That guy is really something.*' I expect her to point at Jonah but she doesn't. She points at the man next to him. The one with the bald head and the black turtleneck. 'I think to myself, *I'd like to go to this class*. But I'm terrible at drawing.'

I shrug. 'I don't think that matters. Drawing is mostly about the act of it, I reckon. The act of creating something from nothing and the way that feels. In the beginning, it doesn't much matter if it's good or not because—'

I cut myself off. What right have I got to talk about drawing? I haven't done it in over ten years.

'Do you think you'll go?'

The class is held in Notting Hill once a week – and it's on tomorrow night! And while waiting a whole day isn't ideal, at least Jonah will be there and he'll be standing still. Plus, I won't be so sweaty, no matter how hot I look in this retro running outfit.

I nod, holding my phone up to take a picture of the poster and the address of the class.

The woman's eyes widen. 'If you will go, I will go. We could go together! For support. I always find these new situations to be nerve-wracking.'

I shake my head quickly. 'Oh, no . . . No, that's alright. I can go on my own. I won't be staying for the whole class anyway. I just need to speak to someone there.' *And get him to kiss me as soon as possible.*

'Let's go together. Let's "buddy up".'

This has now become uncomfortable. 'I . . . I don't do that,' I say, as her dogs continue to jump up at me, the smaller one attempting to climb my leg.

'Why not?' The woman tilts her head to the side.

'Well . . . I'm not exactly a "buddy" kind of a person.'

The woman screws up her face. 'What?'

'I don't just *hang around* with people. Especially strangers.'

The woman pulls another face. 'Then they will always be strangers if you never hang out with them. Never friends.'

'Exactly.'

The woman sighs, using a plastic bag to pick up one of the dogs' poos and speedily twisting the bag closed into an efficient knot. 'I would love to have more friends, but it's hard in London, you see? All of my friends are dogs. And sometimes they're not great friends. Like Ian, who, as you now know, is Machiavelli in a cute dog suit. I did have Gant – he was my lover. But now he's gone.' She bows her head solemnly.

'Oh God. He *died*?'

'No. He got caught under the spell of another lover.'

The expression on her face reminds me of something, but I can't quite tell what. And then it comes to me. She looks like I did in Merritt's *This Was Your Life* video. Entirely deflated.

'Fine.' I blow the air out from my cheeks. 'Let's just go together.'

'Buddy up?'

'No. No buddying up. We'll go into the class together if you want. But I won't be staying to draw so don't expect me to, like, wait around for you or anything.'

'That's okay with me!' The woman grins and holds out her hand. 'I'm Frida.'

'My name's Delphie,' I say giving her hand a quick shake.

Frida hesitates for a moment before leaning in and lowering her voice.

'If we were buddies I'd probably have to tell you. Those pants, they give you ... What's the correct expression in England? A caramel slice?'

A caramel slice? What? I follow her gaze down to my crotch and it becomes very clear that she means 'camel toe'. That's why everyone has been staring at me. Good God. Once again I use the noticeboard as a shield while I try to yank the fabric out, but it's extremely elastic and snaps right back into its previous X-rated position.

'They never looked this way on my mum,' I complain, pulling at the fabric again.

'You probably just have a fatter labia. You know, some labia are just hungry. It's all natural and human, don't be upset.'

Absolutely mortified, I back away from Frida before turning and immediately jogging off down the path towards home, hands placed firmly over my private parts.

'I'll meet you there at seven twenty-five tomorrow!' Frida calls after me. 'Because you're now running away without telling me your phone number!'

'Yeah, okay!' I call, running back past the fountains, and out onto Bayswater Road. I run as fast as I possibly can because if I stop, the business I was telling everyone to keep their eyes off will be on full display for anyone who wants to have a gander.

I eventually slow down as I reach Westbourne Hyde Road, placing my hands over my crotch again. I spot Leanne from work looking out of the huge pharmacy window. She gives me a little wave, then frowns as she notices the position of my hands. I nod a brief hello and frantically open my front door.

I step inside the hallway only to be faced with the disconcerting image of a dark-haired woman in yoga pants wrapped all the way around Cooper. They're pressed up against the doorway to his flat, a morning goodbye that appears to be lingering. The woman kisses Cooper's neck. He nuzzles into her with a groan and scrapes his teeth lightly against her earlobe. His eyes open and latch briefly onto mine. I immediately blush and shuffle towards the stairs, hands still covering my modesty. The sound of the outer door slamming behind me yanks the woman away from her nibbling. She tinkles her fingers at Cooper in a reluctant goodbye. When she passes by me I see that her eyes are all floaty looking, pupils fully dilated.

Cooper is still lingering in his doorway. I definitely do not want him to witness the fit of these running pants, so I side-step like a crab across the corridor and then up the stairs.

'Delphie.'

Ah jeez.

Cooper strolls to the bottom step. 'My extra research this morning. Did it help? Was it the right man?'

I continue up the stairs, angling myself completely away from him so that he is faced with a view of my butt as I ascend. Not ideal but better than the alternative. 'Oh, yeah!' I call over my shoulder. 'His name is definitely Jonah

Truman. Thanks so, so much for that. Really nice of you. I'm going to meet him tomorrow night and finally get all of this figured out. Okay! Bye then!'

I hop up a couple more steps.

'Wait. I need to ask you something.'

I pause, twisting my head as far round as I can without moving the rest of my body. Like in *The Exorcist*. 'What is it?' I ask, wishing he would just bugger off. 'I already updated my grocery delivery instructions online. They won't ring your buzzer again.'

Cooper scoots up two of the stairs. Yikes. If he nudges past he'll see *everything*. I drop down, sitting myself onto the top stair and hunching my knees up so that the area between my waist and knees is covered. Cooper looks tired, his curls fluffy and wayward, the circles beneath his eyes darker than usual. It irritates me that this makes him look like a cooler version of himself. Like a drummer in a band. If I pulled sexual all-nighters at the rate he did, my face would look all baggy and my eyes would constantly have those gross crusty bits in the corners.

To his credit, Cooper doesn't seem to notice my boobs spilling out of the crop top, and even if he does he manages to refrain from making a snide remark.

'It's not about the groceries.' He shifts onto his other foot. 'Remember how you said you would do anything for my help?'

'Of course I remember, it was literally yesterday. And I already did your weird selfie thing so we're even.'

'The selfie was in return for the help I gave you finding

106

every Jonah T in London. I did extra research this morning and told you about Jonah Truman and the running club, ergo you *technically* owe me again.'

'Ergo? Christ.'

'Ergo.'

I sigh. 'What do you want?'

Cooper studies me for a moment. 'Are you free this evening?'

I cross my arms over my chest. 'Tell me why and then I'll tell you if I'm free.'

Cooper runs his finger up and down the banister. 'So . . . I may have told my parents we were dating. And now they want to meet you.' He grimaces. 'Tonight.'

'Yikes. Why? Is this something to do with why you wanted that selfie?'

He shrugs a shoulder. I feel a small flicker of pride that he thought I looked like someone who could feasibly be his girlfriend: for all his dickheadedness there is no denying that Cooper is objectively attractive, if you're into the whole French-poet-meets-Cool-Rider vibe. The parade of women he has on rotation are all way, way better looking than me.

My face must be doing something because Cooper quickly clears his throat. 'My parents are trying to set me up with our old neighbour, Veronica. I needed someone to quickly take a picture with so they would hold off playing Cupid. I was desperate and you were right there, already in my flat. You wouldn't have been my first choice, of course, but—'

'Fuck you!' I jump up and then immediately sit back

down for fear of exposing my caramel slice. 'No, I'm not free this evening. Ask one of the others.'

'The others?'

'Your other women? The one-night stands? There's a whole buffet to choose from. Why didn't you ask the woman who just left?'

Cooper shakes his head. 'Because I sent my mum and dad *your* photograph. Now they've invited us for games night, and if I say no they will invite Veronica. Frankly I can't bear her, but my parents think she's the bee's knees.'

'The bee's knees, eh? Still no.'

I start to drag myself along the corridor towards my flat. I traverse the whole distance on my bottom so that I don't have to stand up and risk revealing anything to Cooper.

'Why are you scooching like that?' His brows dip in confusion, creating a little rivet above his nose.

'I . . . I like to mix it up. Walking all the time is no fun.'

Cooper shakes his head like he can't quite figure me out. He leans back against the banister. 'You really don't care what people think of you, do you?' he says.

I shrug. 'Mostly no.'

'How do you do that?' He narrows his eyes. 'My sister used to tell me I cared entirely too much what people thought of me. That it was stunting me.'

'You obviously don't care what I think of you, though. Otherwise you wouldn't be so rude to me all the time.'

Cooper shrugs. 'I'm only rude to you because you're rude to me.'

'Well, that's because you were rude to me first.'

'Your memory is skewed, Delphie. You were definitely the instigator of' – he gestures between us – 'this.'

I scoff. 'I don't have time for *this*! I have to get back to looking for Jonah.'

Cooper runs a hand through his hair, the front lick of it dropping to obscure one eye. 'Well, I very much care what my parents think of me. What am I supposed to tell them?'

I throw my hands up. 'I don't know. Tell them you have other plans tonight, moping about or playing your shit music, or whatever it is you do in your personal leisure time.'

'I'd already told them I was free because I actually *wanted* to attend games night. Just me. But then they invited you and I couldn't come up with an excuse that they would accept, so . . . Come on. I thought we were in a quid-pro-quo agreement here.'

'I'm not exactly the meet-the-parents type,' I try. Which is to say I've never had a boyfriend whose parents I could possibly meet.

'Clearly, I know that, but—'

'Start that sentence again.'

'Apologies.' Cooper's mouth twitches upwards a little. 'That *was* rude of me. But it would just be this once. Just to get them off my back. And also, if it wasn't for me, you wouldn't even know Jonah's surname.'

That's true. In that sense, Cooper may have literally saved my life. And if I get my life back from Merritt I rather like the idea of Cooper owing me one. Maybe I could use his fireplace whenever I wanted to in the winter. Or have him deliver my packages directly to me so I don't have to traipse downstairs and risk running into scary Mrs Ernestine. Ooh, maybe he could do a couple of shifts for me at the pharmacy? I'd like to see how well he maintains that arrogance after being forced to inspect Mrs Wren's antibiotic-resistant toenail infection bi-weekly.

'Fine,' I say with a cool smile. 'I'll do it. What time do you need me?'

He pulls his phone out of his tight jeans pocket. 'Give me your number. I'll double-check with my parents and text you once I know the definite time.'

I recite my number with an eye-roll before Cooper leaves me be. Twenty minutes later my phone vibrates with a text.

I'll be waiting in the hallway at 7 p.m. Are you allergic to anything? Best, Cooper

Just you, I type out, sniggering. Then I delete it and write No allergies instead.

Chapter Fifteen

I'm running late for Mr Yoon so I speed through my shower and change into my faithful old T-shirt and extra-roomy shorts. While I'm getting dressed, my phone dings with a non-Merritt text.

> Delphie, did you mean what you said last night? It is me, Aled, by the way.

I screw my face up because all memories of what I said last night and to whom have already squirrelled themselves away into the corners of my brain. And how does Aled even have my number? I puzzle for a moment before remembering that I had to input it onto the form to get my library card. Rolling my eyes, I shove my phone back into my shorts pocket and head next door.

Mr Yoon is tucked in at his kitchen table, beavering away at the crossword. The bright sun lights up his coarse grey hair making it look silver. The fresh ashtray I laid out earlier is already three cigarettes deep.

I think of the morning after I got a birthday card from Mr Yoon. Despite my best efforts I hadn't managed to eat the entire cake myself, so I took a slice over to his house to say thank you. He cut the cake slice into two, sharing half with me, and we sat at his kitchen table, not saying a word but somehow knowing that what was happening was needed by the both of us.

'Morning,' I trill, opening the fridge to get some milk. It's almost bare. Mr Yoon is usually good at keeping himself well stocked with groceries. But it seems like he's completely forgotten to make his order. I catch sight of the red circular emergency button he had installed on his kitchen wall a few years ago. It's from a company called London Home Team. If he's ever in any trouble or becomes unwell he can press the red button and someone will turn up to help him. I don't know if it's a private or council service, but either way I make a note to call the number on the laminated card beside the button. Maybe they offer grocery-shopping services? Or perhaps someone could come in and help Mr Yoon in general? If all of this goes tits-up and I'm gone, then things should be set up so that he's got the help he's clearly starting to need.

After we've finished the avocado on toast I made us, I go to his cupboard and pull out the framed photo I saw earlier. I want to let Mr Yoon know that I think it's super cool that he played the violin so brilliantly that he won an award for it.

'This is awesome.' I place the frame on the table in front of him. 'I love the sound of the violin. I can't believe you won a prize. And look at the size of that stage! You must have been epic.'

Mr Yoon stares at the photograph for a moment and then his face crumples, first into sadness and then a sort of wide-eyed anger. He opens his mouth a few times but of course nothing comes out. I've clearly done something very wrong, because while I might catch a huff or a scowl from Mr Yoon, he's never been openly annoyed at me. I move to grab the frame and take it back to the cupboard, but before I can Mr Yoon swipes it off the table with an energy that contradicts his age. The photograph crashes onto the wooden floor, the glass shattering.

'I'm so sorry!' I stutter, not quite sure what I've done to provoke this reaction. 'I'll clean this up.'

Mr Yoon shakes his head furiously, his lips pressed in on themselves. With a shaking hand he points to his door, then at me, and then back towards his door.

'You . . . you want me to leave?'

He nods three times, his mouth downturned like a child's picture of a sad face.

'But . . . who will clean the . . . you might step on the glass and—'

I don't get a chance to finish because Mr Yoon stamps his foot and points again at the door, his face red with upset.

I hold my hands up. 'Okay, okay, I'm going. Just sit down and breathe. I'm going – jeez!' I back away until I'm out of his flat, and dive straight into mine. My own hands shake with the shock of Mr Yoon's anger.

I walk slowly over to my sofa and perch on the end of it.

And then I do something I've not done in a very long time.

I cry.

It takes about twenty whole minutes for me to get a hold of myself. I wipe my eyes and take a deep shaky breath. It's fine. Everything is *fine*. That was just an outburst. Mr Yoon is pissed off at me, maybe for being nosy, maybe because I never really explicitly asked him if it was okay for me to go there every morning to make his breakfast and snoop around and interfere.

I shuffle into the bathroom to get some loo roll on which to blow my nose, only to find that Merritt is sitting on the edge of my bath staring at herself in the mirror and smiling. It's the creepiest thing I've ever seen.

'For fuck's sake!' I yell.

Merritt pivots to face me.

'We don't have proper mirrors at Evermore,' she says, smoothing down her T-shirt which is emblazoned with the slogan RESPECT ROMANTIC FICTION! 'Some people lose their reflections when they arrive, and mirrors would create massive jealousy amongst the Deads, which of course we don't want. But God, it's nice to see myself again. I had forgotten how enchanting my eyes were. Woah. Look at them – look at my beautiful eyes!'

She widens her eyes, glances down for a moment and then looks back up at me from beneath her lashes.

'What are you doing here?' I shake my head, reaching around her to grab the toilet paper and blow my nose.

Merritt takes my arm and drags me out into the living room. She looks around shiftily and lowers her voice.

'The thing is . . . we have heat on us, baby girl.'

'Excuse me?'

'Heat. On us. I have to lie low on the texting for a little while. That son-of-a-bitch Eric saw me checking my phone and asked me why I was on it so much. I lied and told him I was playing Tetris. But I was never a good liar, my heart is too pure for it. Anyway, he got altogether suspicious, started asking a bunch of questions. I'll try to communicate when I can but—'

'I don't understand. Why is you contacting me even a problem?'

Merritt bites her lip and starts to fiddle with the neckline of her T-shirt. 'You know when we first met and I said, "I would *never* break the rules of Evermore"? Yeah, that was a teeny, tiny fib. Sending you back here for ten days . . . It wasn't exactly, you know . . . sanctioned.'

'I don't get it. The Franklin Bellamy Clause?'

Merritt blows out the air from her cheeks. 'Okay. So, technically, the clause is supposed to be used for something very important. Like saving lives, or preventing disaster. I kind of sort of maybe slightly fudged it so that you could come here for my entertainment. I mean, ordinarily I'm not allowed to communicate with people on earth under any circumstances. But I've been so very bored lately and, as I told you, my direct bosses are on annual leave, and you're such a mess and it was funny and romantic, like a juicy Sophie Kinsella novel and—'

'Oi! I'm not a mess! That's a horrid thing to say.'

'Not, like, physically, Delphie. You're hella cute. But emotionally? YIKES. Come on. *Quelle horreur*. You can't see it? It's exactly the kind of narrative arc I go nuts for. Total fish out of water. I can't believe you don't see that.'

I fold my arms. 'No. I don't.'

115

'Hmm. The point is, the Higher-Ups absolutely cannot find out about any of this, because . . .' She trails off, her eyes widening in what looks to be genuine fear.

'What?'

'They'll fire me for sure. If that happens Eternity 4U will never get off the ground, and it has so much potential. And then there's you . . .'

'WHAT ABOUT ME?'

'If they find out and Jonah *doesn't* plant his lips on yours, well, they might not let you back in.'

'To Evermore?'

'Yep.'

'So? Where would I go?'

Merritt shrugs. 'Who the fuck knows? They keep that shit under lock and key. But I have heard rumours of a place called Nevermore. Apparently acoustic song circles and making their own pea houmous are big over there. Word on the street is that it's a completely screen-free environment too. Not even televisions.'

'That sounds terrible.'

'I know. And I heard Eric once mention a place called Clevermore, where they communicate entirely in Ancient Greek and sit exams for fun.'

'My God.'

'And for all I know those might be the best-case scenarios. *So*, the point is that I will no longer be in touch as much, and frankly, the quicker you can get things going with Jonah the better. That way I can cut contact and we'll be in the clear.'

I shake my head. 'Is Jonah even my soulmate or did you lie about that too, just to have me put on some sort of show because you were bored at work?'

'Oh, he totally is!' Merritt says, breezily waving my question away. 'So you really do need to get on with it.'

Totally my soulmate. My stomach warms at the thought. A person completely *meant* for me.

'Wait . . .' I say. 'Are you still going to take away a day because I didn't sing "All That Jazz"?'

Merritt shakes her head. 'I did consider it, but then I figured you tried, at least. And, you know, trying to do the scary thing is almost as good as actually doing the scary thing. But I'd appreciate if you tried to hurry things along as much as you can.'

'I'm seeing Jonah tomorrow night. At the life-drawing class.'

She wiggles her eyebrows. 'Yeaaah, you are. Hey, maybe you could take the braids out? You have such gorgeous red hair. Let it be free! The braids are so severe on you. Miss-Trunchbull-meets-Russian-ballerina-dancing-through-the-pain. *Très rigide.*'

I tut. 'You were saying you shouldn't even be here?'

'Yes! Right.' Merritt claps her hands together. 'I'll be in touch when I can, and in the meantime good luck with Jonah. And seriously, doll. Think about the braids. You need him to want to kiss you as soon as possible or . . .'

She does a horrifying throat-cutting motion before turning into an iridescent shimmer and then popping into nothing.

Chapter Sixteen

I call up the GP's surgery and the London Home Team, both of whom seem reluctant to engage with me because I'm not a family member of Mr Yoon. I consider going round to his house and asking him to sign a declaration registering me as a point of contact and dropping it off at both offices. But then I remember that a) Mr Yoon currently hates me, and b) I may have been inserting myself into his life a little too much and should probably scale it back.

I hate it when people get up in my business and Mr Yoon has a very similar personality type to me, so I can understand why he's pissed off at my nosing about. Either way, he's the closest thing I have to family in London – almost a surrogate grandpa – and the thought of having upset him made me cry the hardest I've cried since, well, since I didn't wear plaits on top of my head. In the end, I make a decision to get in touch with the local council and see if there's someone there to co-ordinate Mr Yoon's care so that he can have a bit of space from me when he wants it.

In my bedroom, I switch on my fan and google Gen Hartley. Since thinking I saw her last night, her face has been buzzing annoyingly around my brain and I find myself curious about what her situation is these days. Unlike Jonah, she is right there at the top of Google. It's a newspaper article. Gen Hartley and Ryan Sweeting holding one of those obnoxious gigantic charity cheques, smiling graciously into the camera. I scan the text. 'Gen and Ryan Hartley' – he took her name? – 'hand over their cheque for the fundraising night of their new party-planning business, Sweethearts Events.'

I roll my eyes and look up at the date of the article. It's only from a year ago. I carry on reading.

> Gen and Ryan have recently returned to Gen's childhood home in West London with their two children (Freya, 9, and George, 6), after spending ten years in New York. They finally set up the business they had always dreamed of running when they met at Bayswater High School as teenagers.

I frown. She's back in London after living in New York?

> Since launching their business, The Sweethearts – as they're known by their friends – have planned charity events for celebrities as illustrious as Benedict Cumberbatch, Niall Horan from One Direction and *The Great British Bake Off*'s Paul Hollywood.
>
> About the fundraiser, Gen says:
>
> 'Since Ryan and I met we always wanted to run a business where people could have fun and experience joy, while also giving back to the causes that mean so much to us. We are delighted to be based in West London once more, and hope to plan many more fundraising parties in our corner of London and beyond.'

Ugh. If this were a real newspaper I would light it on fire. But it's just the internet, so instead I give the screen the middle finger and a hard stare. How are Gen and Ryan still managing to scam people? They want to give back to the causes that mean something to them? They only ever cared about how they could best humiliate me for cachet with the other pupils. Kids who never actually liked them but were too scared to do anything about their reign of terror over me.

I click the link to Gen's Instagram page. She looks shiny and happy on every picture, surrounded by her friends and admittedly very cute children. She's having days out in the country, visiting literary festivals, going horse-riding with Ryan. Her house, which was slightly run-down when we were kids, now has underfloor heating and a set of Le Creuset pans.

A small, faraway place inside my heart feels happy that my nerdy little pal from the neighbourhood got everything she ever wanted. It is immediately taken over by a swell of rage at the unfairness that Gen and Ryan have all of this when I have . . .

Exactly what *I* wanted.

Right?

The relentless heat means that I take my third shower of the day at 6.15 p.m. and get dressed in a light sleeveless cotton shirt and baggy white trousers. I add some concealer to my now slightly sunburned face, and a few coats of waterproof mascara to my lashes. I can't bring myself to remove my braids, but I do take a butterfly hair pin that belonged to my mum and clip my already-dampening fringe to one side.

When I reach the bottom of the stairs I see that Cooper is wearing a black shirt, as usual, but this time with pale jeans instead of black ones. He doesn't seem to notice that I've made any effort at all, which makes me feel slightly embarrassed about the butterfly hairclip. Instead, he hands me a paper bag that I recognise as coming from Meyer's Pharmacy.

I peek inside and see a pill box. It is for Canesten. Also in there is a leaflet about thrush. On the back of the leaflet there's a scribble of words written in blue ink.

Dear Delphie,

I saw you were having some difficulties with your vulval area earlier today while you were walking by the shop. My first instinct was thrush so I have included a medicine that will knock it out right away. I will dock the cost from your wage. If you are having any burning while peeing I would suggest booking in with the GP as you may have something that needs a prescription, like cystitis or a UTI.

Hope you continue to have a good week off work.

With all best wishes,
Leanne (from Meyer's Pharmacy)

My cheeks go hot. I shove the note back in the paper bag and then the whole thing into my tote.

I side-eye Cooper.

'Did you look in the pharmacy bag?'

'Of course I didn't look in your pharmacy bag.'

'Did you read the note?'

'Delphie, your medical concerns couldn't be of less interest to me.' He glances down at the serious black leather watch strapped to his wrist. 'We ought to go or we'll be late.'

I lean back and narrow my eyes, examining his face for some indication that he's lying. Finding none, I nod slowly.

'Okay, good. Let's get this over with.'

Chapter Seventeen

Cooper's car is messier than one would expect for someone with such a stick up his bottom. There are piles of papers and books in the backseat, Bic biros and water bottles scattered in the footwell.

Cooper's parents live in North London and as we set off it becomes clear that neither one of us is keen to initiate a chat. Instead, I lean forward and press the dial for the radio. It's pre-programmed to a station called Jazz Noir because of course it is.

Cooper immediately flicks it off.

I flick it back on.

He flicks it back off.

We both reach for the button at the same time, our fingers brushing. I tut and snatch my hand back like I've been burned. He clears his throat.

When his hands are safely back on the steering wheel and out of the way of my hands, I press play on the CD deck, snorting when I realise that the song that was just playing on the radio is also playing on the CD.

'Not much of an eclectic musical taste then?' I say breezily.

'Eclectic taste is what people who don't understand music describe themselves as having.'

'Oh, sorry, *Rolling Stone* magazine.'

I start rifling through a stack of CDs on a little shelf above the stereo, but Cooper blocks me with his arm.

'We have to establish some exposition.'

Jesus. Who on earth talks like that?

'My parents are Amy and Malcolm. They are very nice and very nosy. I . . . Well, I told them that we met three weeks ago at a . . .' He murmurs the end of the sentence and I don't quite catch it.

'What was that?'

'A Charlie Parker tribute concert.'

'Sorry, say again? I couldn't hear.'

'You heard perfectly well.'

I feel a little flicker of delight at his discomfort but remain innocent of face.

'They won't expect us to know everything about each other because we've only been . . . *dating* . . . for a few weeks. But let's get the basics established so that there are no major errors.'

'You go first.'

Cooper turns onto the North Circular and immediately pulls into the fast lane. I wind my window up so I can hear him properly.

'Fine,' he says. 'I work from home as a computer programmer. Writing code, testing code, that sort of thing. I'm thirty-three years old. I like to listen to music, drink delicious wine, read novels, explore London and—'

'Did you copy-and-paste that from Guardian Soul-mates?'

'How about you?' he asks, side-stepping my dig.

'I work at Meyer's Pharmacy as an assistant and I'm twenty-seven.'

'And?'

'And . . . that's it.'

'Now is not the time to be facetious. I can hardly intro-duce you to my parents like that: "This is Delphie, who works as a pharmacy assistant, is twenty-seven, and – ah yes! – has hooked up all over this town with a man named Jonah, now missing.'

I wiggle uncomfortably and dart him a dirty look for once again bringing up my unfortunate phrasing about sleeping with Jonah.

'Seriously,' he says. 'Tell me something real about you.'

The truth is – there isn't much more than that. I don't really have any hobbies. I'm not a hobby person. What else do I do apart from work and hang out with Mr Yoon and watch TV? I suppose I love drawing. Well, loved, at least.

'I like art,' I tell him.

Cooper glances over with interest. 'Nice. Who's your favourite painter?'

I smile to myself. 'Modigliani. For definite. He's got such a specific point of view. All those elongated lines, all that melancholy.'

'Did you copy-and-paste that from the National Gallery website?'

'Did you copy-and-paste your comebacks from me?'

'Ha! I like Modigliani too. *Woman with Red Hair* is my favourite.'

'Artists and red hair. They're obsessed.'

'I mean, I get it.' He shrugs a shoulder.

I give him a sideways glance. Is he . . . is he flirting with me? His eyes remain on the road, face straight. No. Of course he's not. The very thought is absurd.

I tut and pat my own red hair self-consciously.

We disappear into our own thoughts for a while, and eventually turn onto a road that looks like pure suburbia. Cooper stops the car. 'Dammit. I thought we'd have a little time out here to discuss backstory, but that's my mother at the window. Watching us.'

I look up to see a smiling woman, her face squashed between two window blinds. I'm not sure but I think she wiggles her eyebrows at us.

I'd thought, judging by Cooper's plummy accent and general demeanour that his parents would live in a big townhouse somewhere in Hampstead or Richmond. But we're in the much less fancy Barnet parked on a street that looks the epitome of middle class.

'Just follow my lead,' Cooper instructs, sounding slightly nervous, which makes me feel nervous. Hmm, this actually seems like a big deal to him. He really does care what people think and is now probably shitting himself that I was his only option for the ruse.

I lift my chin and decide to use this games night as practice for when I meet Jonah and hopefully, maybe one day, meet his parents. I am going to be the opposite of what everyone thinks I can be. I am going to be fucking *lovely*.

I'm doing a great job. I have complimented Cooper's mum Amy's dress, as well as the prosecco she gave me. His father, Malcolm, told me I had a handshake firm enough to rival his old friend Doug, who is legendary for his impactful handshakes. Also in attendance at the games night is Cooper's Uncle Lester, who is a lot older than Malcolm and has already knocked back three proseccos in the fifteen minutes since we've arrived.

The five of us are sitting at a large rectangular table by the front window. There are a couple of bowls of crisps and a bowl of chocolate truffles, as well as a stack of board games including Operation and Pictionary. A flicker of excitement unfurls in my belly. I used to love playing Pictionary when I was a kid.

Sipping my prosecco – being careful to go slowly because last night was more booze than I usually have in a year – I take a peek around the living room. It's crammed wall-to-wall with stacks of books and newspapers, the sofa big and cosy looking, a worn pink Persian rug on the floor. I like it.

'You're not Cooper's usual type!' Amy remarks, nudging the bowl of crisps over to me. I take one and nibble it delicately around the edge which makes it crack into two pieces, one of which drops onto the table. I quickly pick up the broken piece and shove it into my mouth. 'Beautiful, of course. They're always beautiful, but yeah, his other girlfriends were all very different to you.'

'What's his usual type?'

'Well, there hasn't been anyone in rather a while, but when there was, they were one after the other and they all looked the same.'

Cooper rolls his eyes and his dad chuckles.

'How was it that Em used to describe them?' his dad asks.

Amy laughs. 'Like a rotation of Wednesday Addamses walking for Chanel.'

I laugh and think of the dark-haired woman in Cooper's doorway. The description fits. 'Who's Em?'

Amy's face crumples. She gives Cooper a wounded glance. 'You haven't told Delphie about Em?'

Cooper's nostrils flare. He drains his glass of water as if it's the prosecco he was offered but turned down on account of driving. 'It's fine,' I say to the table. 'You absolutely don't need to tell me anything! I've only known Cooper a few weeks, after all.'

'Em is Cooper's twin sister,' Malcolm says softly. '*Was*. She passed away in 2018.'

My heart sinks for Cooper. For all of them. 'It sounds like she had a great sense of humour.'

'Oh, she did. She was absolutely crackers.' Amy's eyes water slightly. 'Smart as all heck, too. Top of her class in grammar school, just like her brother, and then a full scholarship to Trinity College. This one here went to Oxford.' She thumbs at Cooper.

'As I'm sure he mentioned within two seconds of meeting you,' Lester adds.

'When I say I was a proud mother . . .' Amy raises her voice to drown out Lester.

Cooper went to grammar school and Oxford? That explains the blue-blooded tones of a man whose family is pure North London.

'I'm sorry you lost her,' I say directly to Cooper.

I've lost a few people over the years, but never anyone to death. I can't begin to imagine how painful that would be.

'Thick as thieves, they were,' Malcolm sighs, putting a hand on his son's arm. 'Em and Cooper, Cooper and Em.'

Cooper clears his throat, gently moving his arm away from Malcolm's touch. 'Let's not talk about Em,' he says brightly. 'We're here for you to meet Delphie.'

'Of course, you're right, love. Delphie. Tell us all about yourself!' Amy rubs my shoulder. I flinch because I'm not used to people touching me. But flinching looks bonkers so I style it out with a little shimmy.

Cooper's eyes widen. He's clearly nervous about me taking centre stage.

Screw him. I can be delightful. I set my jaw.

'I work at a pharmacy in West London. I love running in Kensington Gardens. I'm part of a club there in fact. I also like . . .' What else do delightful women do? I get a vision of period dramas in which all the women are trained to be cultured and well rounded. It's a stupid outdated reference but it's all my mind can glom on to in the moment. 'I read poetry and, um, often partake in . . . crochet?'

'You don't sound so sure about that,' Lester grunts, his words already melting into one another.

Malcolm, though, seems delighted with my answer and leans forward, his chin in his hands.

'I adore poetry. Lester read Byron's 'She Walks in Beauty' at mine and Amy's wedding. Oh, do recite us something, won't you, Delphie?'

Ah, shit. Why did I say poetry? I know no poems. None. I'm going to be immediately outed as a fraud. Cooper was right to worry about me.

He clears his throat. 'Ah, let's not put Delphie on the spot!' he says, faux cheerily.

'Delphie doesn't mind!' Amy says, patting me again. 'I too would love to hear a poem. It's so romantic. A poetry reading in our living room!'

I can't feel my face. I slurp down the rest of my prosecco and then, in a state of acute panic, stand up onto suddenly trembling legs. I take a deep breath.

A poem. A poem . . . Think of something that rhymes at least, for fuck's sake, Delphie.

'Lo, back up now and give a woman room. The fuse is . . . alit and I'm about to go boom.'

I have started. I have started this way and now I cannot stop.

'Mercy, mercy – oh, mercy me, my whole life feels like a cage. Yet on stage . . . I am free.'

I hear a snort. Cooper's eyes are wide and he's covering his mouth, though I can see that his shoulders are shaking. His parents and Lester throw him a curious look, but don't seem to have realised that I am on the spot adapting 'Boom! Shake the Room' so that it sounds less like a bop and more poet-y.

When I'm done, they give a slightly bewildered round of

applause. Cooper joins in. He's managed to stop laughing, but his face is still a little flushed from it, his eyes glittering in a way I haven't seen since the first few weeks he lived in the building.

'How interesting,' Amy says. 'That's a new one to me.'

'Who's the poet?'

'I believe he's called William Smith,' Cooper answers, expression serious. 'A modern poet with a very important œuvre. 'Wild Wild West' is a favourite of mine.'

'Gosh,' Malcolm says. 'Thank you for introducing him to us, Delphie.'

'Most of Cooper's old girlfriends wouldn't know Keats if he bit them on the behind.'

I laugh heartily, also not knowing anything about Keats.

'I didn't come here to get bloody read to.' Uncle Lester pours himself another glass from the bottle. 'Let's play, dammit.'

'You can choose the game, Delphie,' Cooper says, to which his mum 'awww's as if he just offered me a kidney.

I nod and look up and down the pile, eventually pointing at my selection. 'I choose Pictionary.'

It may have been many years since I last played Pictionary, but I'm as competitive about it as I ever was. Amy has set up an easel in the middle of the room and, of course, I've been paired with Cooper who, as it happens, is shite at Pictionary. We're getting annihilated by Amy, Lester and Malcolm. It doesn't help that Cooper's sketches are thoughtless, the lines lax and unfocused.

When it's my turn to draw, Cooper gets so frustrated that his voice pitches an octave deeper – an unsuccessful attempt to conceal the frustration.

'You're shading? You're shading right now? Delphie? The clock is ticking.'

'The reason I haven't correctly guessed your drawings, Cooper, is because your drawings lack basic information,' I reply through gritted teeth. If he is managing to keep his shit together then I will not be the one who gets visibly angry.

'It's Pictionary, Delphie. We don't need bloody chiaroscuro. Just draw what it says on the card.'

'I *am* drawing what it says on the card, Cooper.' I speed up my rendering of 'surprise party' because we only have fifteen seconds left.

'Come on, come on!' Cooper stands up from the sofa, the top of his curls almost touching the ceiling.

'Please refrain from speaking unless you have a reasonable guess, Cooper.'

'Well, clearly the sex is dynamite,' a now-sozzled Lester says grinning from ear to ear. The rest of us studiously ignore him.

I finish my final flourish – the object of the surprise party – her mouth open in a scream. 'There. Come on! Surely you can see . . .'

'Oh . . . Oh! It's a surprise . . . Surprise party!' Cooper yells, hands on his knees.

'Yes!' I squeal, fist pumping the air.

Cooper crosses the room and pulls me into a celebratory hug. I immediately stiffen. Not overtly, but enough for him to realise. He immediately steps back. He doesn't say sorry because that would look totally weird in front of his family, but he gives me a small apologetic shrug.

'Don't know why you're getting excited,' Lester says. 'You still lost.'

'Thanks, Uncle Lester.'

'Congratulations to you all,' I say with a little bow. 'You were worthy winners. Good game.'

'I rather think we are the winners for having met you tonight!' Amy says, also pulling me into a hug. This time I'm prepared and don't corpse on her. I sort of melt into the hug, the soft cottony smell of her blouse sending a soothing, comforting sensation swimming right through me. She pats the back of my head softly. To my mortification my eyes fill with tears. Great. I don't cry in over ten years and now twice in the same day?

Amy leans back and beams at me, her hands on my shoulders. 'You look after him, won't you? He could do with a little happiness.'

'Mother,' Cooper barks. 'Christ. Delphie and I . . . It's been three weeks.'

Amy shrugs. 'I just . . . It's nice to see you smiling is all.'

'He so rarely smiles,' I nod, stealthily dabbing a tear from my eye before it falls.

Cooper is stony-faced. He runs his hand through his curls and looks at his wristwatch. 'Perhaps time for us to go.'

'And it's such a lovely smile,' Amy continues as if Cooper hasn't spoken. 'Go on, Coop. Show us all that lovely smile.'

'Yeah, come on, son,' Malcolm adds. 'Show your mum

that killer smile. It'll sustain her for a week and then I won't have to hear her go on about how you never smile anymore.'

Amy turns back to Cooper, a hopeful, slightly desperate look on her face.

Cooper closes his eyes briefly, like he would rather be anywhere else right now. I think of how he told me to fuck off that cold morning when I asked him to turn down his music. 'Yeah, Cooper, show us those beautiful white teeth.' I lean in to Malcolm. 'His teeth are my favourite thing about him.'

'Really?' Malcolm snorts. 'His *teeth*?'

I nod. 'They're so straight. It's mesmerising.'

'Years of orthodontics,' Amy says. 'I took him to all his appointments.'

'Fine!' Cooper growls. He produces a massively over-the-top smile, like Wallace of Wallace and Gromit. He holds the smile for a second before his face drops back into its usual sternness, although his eyes have softened slightly.

'It's a start, I suppose,' Amy chuckles as she walks us to the door. 'It was lovely to meet you, Delphie.'

'I've loved meeting you too,' I say, a flood of confusion swishing up my insides as I realise that I'm not just being polite. I'm telling the truth.

On the way home I think of Mum and text her to let her know that I'm going to a life-drawing class tomorrow. Not that I intend to do any drawing when I'm there, but seeing Amy with Cooper made me remember how much Mum and I used to like drawing together. When we get back to West-bourne Hyde Road, Cooper opens the car door for me.

'Thanks,' I say. 'Your key or mine?'

I trail off as Cooper slides his own key out of his jeans pocket and slots it into the lock.

He strides across the hallway towards his flat, turning to me when he's at the door. 'Thank you for your help this evening.' His eyes soften a little. 'I enjoyed it more than expected. And it should call off the Veronica set-up for the foreseeable.'

I shrug a shoulder. 'It was fine. Your parents are nice.'

He makes no move to open his door.

I step forward. 'I . . . I was sorry to hear about your sister,' I say.

He swallows and unlocks his door. 'Let's not, eh? I assume we're even now, Delphie. I did you a favour, you did me one. Quid pro quo.'

His demeanour cools the temperature of the hallway by at least a degree.

'All squared up,' I say brightly.

'I hope things go well with Jonah.'

'I hope things go well with . . . your delicious fine wine,' I finish in the absence of a smarter response. 'See you around, Cooper.'

He doesn't answer, just dips into his flat and closes the door respectfully quietly behind him.

Chapter Eighteen

It's day four. Day four of ten and I've yet to even speak to Jonah on earth, let alone charm him into kissing me. My stomach swirls with anxiety at Merritt's ticking clock and the thought of what lies in store for me if I don't pull this off. I *have* to make a connection with him at the life-drawing class tonight.

I sit up in bed, hair damp with sweat. I check my phone and groan when it tells me that today is going to be even hotter than yesterday. The first few days of the heatwave were pleasant enough – it was nice to see the sun after months of grey sky. But now it's getting uncomfortable and I long for rain. I notice a text from Mum and eagerly open it up, wondering what her response will be to the news that I'm going to a life-drawing class.

> Here is a pic of me with Larry the NYC art curator. He has a gallery in Brooklyn and just adores my work!

She must just be busy.

I'm not sure if Mr Yoon wants to see me, but it would be the responsible neighbour thing to at least check. Not because I care. Not that much, anyway. I'm just checking on the very old man next door is all. I grab some eggs and bacon from my fridge and take them across, knocking first and then peeking my head around the door. Mr Yoon is sitting at his table, looking at the crossword, pencil in his mouth, cigarette in his hand.

'Give me a sign if you want me to leave,' I shout into the room. 'Wave, or stamp your feet – I know you're good at that.'

Mr Yoon gives me a blank look but his expression is no longer furious so I take it as a good sign. I head straight to the kitchen and notice that he hasn't managed to clean the dishes. I give them a quick wash then put some eggs on to boil.

I almost jump out my skin when I feel a warm dry hand on my bare shoulder. It's Mr Yoon. He pats me twice. His eyes soften as he gives me a small apologetic smile. To my surprise my instinct is to hug him but I don't want to overwhelm him again. Instead I just nod. 'Don't worry, it's fine. I get on my own nerves sometimes too.'

As Mr Yoon returns to his crossword, I sniff the air. Not good. I think . . . I think that's Mr Yoon. He is ripe. Is he forgetting to bathe now too? How long has that been happening for?

It's scorching today. He can't sit all day in his own stale sweat.

I prepare our breakfast first and as we sit and eat it, I casually say to him, 'You're gonna want a cool bath in this heat. It's gnarly out there.'

He nods his agreement and so when we've finished

breakfast I lead Mr Yoon over to the bathroom, instructing him to get undressed and telling him that I will close my eyes as he steps into the bath. I close the walk-in bath door and once he's sitting down – privacy intact – I turn on the taps, pouring in a heathy glug of bubbles for extra cover-up.

I position myself on the corner of the bath, grab the shower head and run it over Mr Yoon's hair. When I shampoo it he sighs and I hope it's because it feels pleasant and not because I'm scrubbing too hard. I mean, I've only ever washed my own hair.

If Mr Yoon feels uncomfortable in any way he doesn't show it, but I feel uncomfortable lots of times in life and don't show it either. So I try to keep up a breezy conversation and tell him about last night.

'And then Cooper told me I was spending too long on the shading so I—'

As I say Cooper's name, Mr Yoon glances round at me, head full of fluffy suds.

'You know Cooper?' I ask him. 'You've seen him about the building?'

Mr Yoon nods once.

I lower my voice. 'He's a bit obnoxious, right?'

Mr Yoon nods twice, which send me into a huge peal of laughter. 'You agree. Anyway, I think he was just jealous of my superior artistic skills. We lost the game. But it was his fault. If I'd have been paired with Amy or Malcolm I would definitely have won.'

Once Mr Yoon's hair is rinsed, I grab a flannel and soap from the little wooden shelf above the bath taps.

'I'll leave you to wash your . . . you know. Ain't no way I'm doing that and I'm pretty sure you wouldn't want me to.' I hand Mr Yoon the flannel and he nods his understanding.

Once Mr Yoon is out of the bath and wrapped in a clean bathrobe, I dry his hair using my hairdryer from next door and then comb it into a perfect side parting. When I bring him a mirror to take a look, he smiles at his reflection and gives a little laugh. I bring his deodorant spray out of his bedroom and mime spraying it on myself. 'You're gonna need a whole bunch of this today,' I tell him. He takes the deodorant from me and pats me on the arm once more. I smile and pat him back. Then he pats *me* back again because he must have forgotten the first time he patted me. I pat him back and say, 'Whoever stops patting first is a loser.' Mr Yoon pats me back, his mouth opening into a silent breathy laugh. He clutches his stomach with it, causing me to dissolve into a fit of giggles.

There's something about laughing – it makes any awkwardness disappear because you're both in on the same thing. I'd forgotten that.

When I get back to my own flat I take another look through my mother's bag of clothes to find a wealth of skimpy dresses as well as some shiny nylon shirts straight from the nineties. I unearth a tan skirt made from suede. It's soft and pretty and would have me melting into a puddle of sweat in under thirty seconds. I put it back.

Eventually I find a thigh-skimming button-up white dress dotted with tiny silver daisies. Perfect.

I imagine Jonah kissing me, running his hands through my hair. No one can run their hands through braids this tight. I think about how Merritt said I might look better with my hair down. I take every bobby pin out so that my hair falls in thick waves across my shoulders.

Hmm. I don't look much different.

Chapter Nineteen

'Your hair! You are Ophelia! You are *Venus Rising from the Sea*!'

It takes me a moment to recognise the voice of the woman from the park. Like me she has also made an effort to look alluring, although her version of that seems to be wearing a flower crown and a pale lace dress with long sleeves that sway as she moves.

I shuffle uncomfortably as a couple of patrons in a nearby cafe turn to look at me, seeing not Ophelia or any other Pre-Raphaelite figure but an embarrassed and sweaty ginger woman in a too-short dress and tatty trainers.

'Shush!' I admonish. Then: 'I'm so sorry – I think you told me your name at the park but I can't remember it.'

'It's Frida.'

I hold out my hand. 'Ah, yes. I'm Delphie.'

'Our hands together, it's like soup.'

'Sorry?'

'Our sweating hands, all smooshed together. Feels like soup.'

'Hmm, yeah.'

Ew. I wipe my hands on the back of my dress. She does the same, grinning at me as though that was a pleasant interaction. She pats her bag, a patchwork, tasselly affair. 'I've brought pencils and pens for drawing. Have you got yours?'

I shake my head. 'Oh, no, no, no. I'm not here to do any drawing. I'm here to meet Jonah off the poster. The one with the blue eyes.'

'Ah, I thought he was the model.'

I blink. Somehow that possibility has not occurred to me. I'd only considered the notion that Jonah was a participant, or maybe even the instructor. But the *model?* How will this work? How am I supposed to even introduce myself with his junk on full display? There is so much to worry about right now.

I follow Frida into the pub, climbing a staircase that leads to a function room. Every window is all the way open, but the room remains as hot as Hades. There's a circle of chairs, easels set up in front of each one. In the middle of the circle is a rug, upon which is an absolutely beautiful short-haired woman sitting cross-legged in a kimono.

'Welcome, welcome!' It's the bald man from the poster. The one that Frida fancied. I hear her make a little excited noise beside me.

'Hallo!' She waves at the other attendees, a varied selection – some who look like they've come straight from the office, one in a supermarket uniform, a teenager with dyed black hair in a severe bob and a stud on each side of her nose.

Frida takes a seat and nods at me to do the same. 'Come on, Delphie. Sit by me so we can buddy up.'

'Where's Jonah?' I ask the bald man, who introduces himself as Claude. 'I actually just came to see him.'

Claude looks at his watch. 'Kat is our model for the first session,' he points at the beautiful woman sitting on the rug. 'Jonah models for the second session.'

He *is* a model!

'What time is the second session, please?'

'In an hour.'

I nod. An hour. An hour is nothing when the alternative is eternity in Evermore.

I sit stiffly in front of an easel. While Claude busies about saying hello to his regulars my phone vibrates with a text.

I realise that perhaps I was rude last night. I apologise. Best, Cooper.

'You have no materials with you?' Claude asks, distracting me before I can reply. I shove my phone back in my bag.

'Oh. No. Sorry. I didn't think I was . . . I was just coming to see . . . Um . . . no. I don't.'

'What's your medium? Charcoal? Pencil? Ink? I think we have some acrylics somewhere if you want to paint, but the sink isn't working so probably not a great idea in terms of mess.'

'Charcoal?' I say. I'm not quite sure why because I've never drawn in charcoal. Maybe that's why. I remember my pencil drawing of Mr Taylor, the speckled photocopies pinned up all over school. I push the memory back into the locked box of doom in my brain and smile my thanks as

Claude hands me a few sheets of thin paper and a long stick of charcoal.

'Okay, guys.' Claude claps his hands together like a flamenco dancer. 'We will do a series of ten-minute speed sessions in which Kat will switch poses each time. Then we will do a longer thirty-minute pose. Following that will be a short break before Jonah arrives and we begin session two.'

I cannot believe I'm going to see Jonah again in one hour. I grin to myself as I imagine us talking again. Having him look at me with those kind, sweet eyes. Touching my arms. Like he was totally fine with being dead just as long as he could be dead with me.

'Delphie?' Frida whispers beside me. I look up to find that everyone has already begun drawing. Kat has stood up and unrobed, her arms upright and in a prayer position. 'You were caught in a daydream,' Frida says.

I pick up my charcoal and press it against the sheet of paper. It immediately snaps in half. Damn. I have no clue what I'm doing. I place one of the broken halves of the charcoal on the easel ledge and look up at Kat. Her skin is so unmarked, like it's been filtered. You can see her ribs, but she is not skinny. She has a narrow strip of pubic hair that is so neat it looks like it's been drawn on. Is that how it's supposed to look? Because I wouldn't know where to begin.

Shit. Jonah has seen Kat naked. Have they slept together? Surely they must have – two people as genetically blessed as them seeing each other in the buff week after week.

'Delphie!' Frida repeats. 'Are you well?'

While I've been worrying, she's done an entire drawing

that's not half bad. A little beeper goes off and Kat changes her pose. She does a sort of splits position on the floor, and holds one hand to her ear as if she can hear something in the distance.

'I'm fine! I'm doing it!' I wave Frida away. Pressing the charcoal to the paper with less tension, I begin sketching the outline of Kat's body.

Before I know it, the timer has beeped again and Kat is now sitting crouched, with her hands across her knees, and then again standing up and doing a ninja posture. I fall into a kind of trance, only the smell of charcoal dust and the sound of scratching on paper making any dent in my consciousness.

'Time is up!' Claude shouts. I blink as if I've just awoken from a long sleep. A flood of emotion spreads through me. It's a good emotion, euphoria almost. My heart is beating fast like I've had a little too much coffee.

That was . . . I haven't drawn anything since the incident at school. God, I've missed it.

'Wow,' Frida says leaning over to look at my drawings. She picks up my papers one by one, making a noise of delight at each new sketch. 'You didn't say you were a professional.' She holds up her hand to high-five me. I studiously ignore it.

'I'm not a professional.'

'She is not,' Claude murmurs from behind me, weirdly close to my neck. 'But perhaps she could be . . . one day.'

Frida hands him the papers which he examines, making comments about lines and compositional choices which I don't quite understand. All I know is that it feels good. Whatever is happening right now feels good.

'You work well on the female form,' Claude drawls. 'And you will get to do more of Kat in session two because alas, dear Jonah has texted to say that he cannot make it.'

I jump up, my papers scattering onto the floor. 'What? No! I thought he was the model for the second session? I came here to see him.'

Claude puts his hands up. 'I'm sorry! Since he modelled for David Hockney last year we have many people show up just to see him.' He rolls his eyes. 'But life-drawing should be about the art, not the model! This is not a pop concert, you know.'

Frida muffles a snort beside me.

'Jonah modelled for Hockney?!' I yelp. I love David Hockney. He's my second favourite artist after Modigliani. And Jonah *modelled* for him? What are the chances?

Claude nods like it's no big deal. 'Jonah is an excellent model. He makes the most wonderful shapes with his body.'

I wonder dazedly about the shapes that Jonah makes with his body. What shapes can I make with my body? Will Jonah like my shapes? I quickly shake my head and force my mind to focus on the more vital issue at hand. I *have* to see Jonah tonight. I'm running out of time. 'You said he texted you, right? I need to get in touch with him about . . . something. Please can I have his number?'

Claude presses a hand to his chest. 'Gosh, no. I can't just hand out the private information of my models to anyone. Their safety is very important to me.'

'Safety? I don't want to hurt him!'

'I wouldn't know that. How would I know that?'

'She would *never* hurt him,' Frida pipes up, full of indignation, as if she's known me for longer than the sum total of sixty-five minutes.

'I'm his . . . *friend*. I wouldn't do anything to hurt him, ever. Please give me his number.'

'If you really are his friend,' Kat calls over, 'surely he would have texted you to tell you about the last-minute gig.' A gig? Doing what? 'Some exclusive dance event at the Shard,' Kat continues. 'That's why he can't come tonight. He was so excited about it. I expect he texted all of his friends. He texted me. But not you. You don't even have his number. Which leads me to believe you are *not* his friend.'

Kat. You gotta love Kat. 'Yes, yes,' I say digging out my phone and pointing at the empty black screen. 'Ah, yes! The Shard! Dance event! There's the text! What time did it say the event was on your text?'

Kat opens her mouth, but Claude tells her to hush. 'Kat! She is clearly lying. Zip it.'

Kat literally mimes zipping her mouth.

I dash over to her. 'Kat, will you give me Jonah's number? Woman to woman. It's important.'

Kat points at the imaginary zip on her mouth.

'Fine,' I say.

And it is fine. It's not ideal, but it's fine. I have a lead. He will be at the Shard tonight.

I roll up my sketches, slip them into my bag, and determinedly march out of the function room.

'We're leaving?' Frida asks. 'But we've paid for the whole two hours!'

'Oh, you can stay!' I say vaguely. 'But I have somewhere to be.'

There's a Tube strike this week so I pull out my phone, flicking onto a ride-sharing app. It shows an available car two minutes away. I should get to the Shard in . . . fifty minutes? That's ages. Frida peeks over my shoulder at the screen. 'Taxi's too expensive. You could take a bus.'

'I don't have time,' I say, pressing the booking button.

'I'll come with you,' Frida announces, bringing me back to the present.

I shake my head quickly. 'Oh, no. No need. Anyway, I thought you wanted to ask Claude out?'

Frida shrugs. 'I feel his personality doesn't match the picture on the poster, you know? On the poster he looks like a dynamo. But in real life it's like he has a stick of charcoal lodged where the sun will not shine.'

When the car pulls up, I dive into the back seat. Frida – ignoring my polite rejection of her company – immediately climbs into the other side, strapping herself in and giving me a thumbs-up. 'It's funny,' she says her eyes shining with excitement. 'All this time I've lived in London and I've never been to the Shard. I always said to Gant we should go and he always said, "Frida, be quiet." I do talk a lot, I suppose.'

'Gant sounds like a dick,' I mutter.

Frida shrugs and nods her head slightly, her gold moon earrings dancing at the movement. 'He wasn't so bad.' Her eyes have welled up again. She seems genuinely heartbroken.

As we slowly pull away from the pavement, Claude jogs out of the pub and over to the car. 'You are crazy and possibly a danger to my most popular model!' he shouts through the open window, his cut-glass voice ringing in my ears. 'But you have much artistic potential!'

Chapter Twenty

A quick Google search tells us that there's only one dance event on at the Shard this evening – a silent disco in an event space called The View. A *silent* disco! I've never heard of such a thing. As we step into the lift, Frida presses a hand to her chest.

'Here I am at last! In the world-famous Shard.'

When we reach level 72, the lift opens with a quiet swoosh.

Frida starts to shimmy her shoulders in anticipation as we walk towards a set of glass doors through which we can see at least 100 people dancing in a room lit up in purple and pink. Everyone is wearing headphones. Aha! They *do* listen to music, but I assume it's music of their own choosing. What a good idea! Not that I've been to any discos recently, but I like the idea of having my own personal soundtrack for such an occasion.

In front of the glass door there's a tall, wide woman wearing a headset and carrying a clipboard. Behind her is a sign that requests all visitors 'please have their tickets ready'. We don't have tickets. Damn. Maybe if I explain to the woman that we only want to dip in and out to find someone she'll just . . . let us in? But judging from the irritated curl of her mouth I am doubtful of her inclination to relax any kind of rule. The woman shakes her head furiously as we approach. She runs her eyes over my little dress and then up towards Frida's flower crown.

'You're late!' she hisses.

'Excuse me?'

'You better not bail early like the last guy. So unprofessional. Left me up shit creek without a paddle. That's the last time I'm hiring from Maurice Alabaster.' She huffs. 'Though I'm glad he sent two of you, at least.'

What is she on about? Who is Maurice Alabaster? Who does this woman think we are?

I open my mouth to ask all of these questions but Frida darts in front of me. 'Yes, he sent two of us,' she echoes, chin lifted, as the woman opens the glass doors and leads us into the event space. I immediately scan the room for signs of Jonah. Nothing yet but it won't take long for me to spot someone so tall and magnetic in this crowd.

'The pair of you are on that one,' the woman points to an uplit pink podium on the left side of the room. In each corner of the space there is a podium, atop which are dancers. Professional dancers. Professional dancers *dancing*. And then I realise that each dancer is wearing flower crowns exactly like Frida's. This woman thinks we're here to *dance*?

'Where's your headdress?' The woman asks me, massive eyeroll indicating that she's edging close to the end of her tether.

'It was stolen!' Frida reveals as I stand there agog at what is unfolding right now. 'On the street – yes. Someone pinched it off her head. A wizened old man, in fact. He had long silver hair and one wayward eye looking to the east. But Delphie is the most beautiful dancer in London. Nobody will care that she isn't wearing the head flowers.'

I side-eye Frida. How is she this good at lying? The stern woman looks me up and down. 'Fine,' she tuts. 'But I will be making a complaint to Maurice. I expect performers to arrive in costume.'

'So sorry,' Frida sing-songs as the woman stalks away back towards the glass doors. 'Come on then!' she says to me, pointing at the podium. 'She's still watching us.' I follow Frida's gaze to see the stern woman – now outside the room – peering at us through the glass doors.'

'I'm not getting up on a podium!'

'It's the only way we're allowed in here without tickets.'

'But I . . . I don't dance.'

'Everybody dances!'

'There's no music!'

Frida takes my hand and places it on my chest. 'The music, it's in here.'

I snatch my hand away. 'How are the other dancers dancing without any music – none of them are wearing headphones!'

'The headphones would crush their flower crowns,' Frida returns, as if this is obvious and I am thick. 'Come on. From the podium you'll see far and wide across the room – it's much better for locating Jonah.'

That's true – I'll be able to see everything from up there.

I glance back towards the stern woman. She's gesturing madly through the glass that we should get a move on.

Fuck.

Following Frida – who seems oddly keen to get going – I climb onto the podium as elegantly as I can and peer out across the sea of bodies dancing before me, eyes peeled for Jonah's soft shiny bronze mane. I'm momentarily distracted by the evening view out of the huge windowed wall. I can see the curves of the Thames, Tower Bridge looking like an expensive golden bracelet, the lights of a thousand buildings all twinkling, showing off like they know someone is watching. As the sun lazily bows out, the sky is a rich crocus purple, streaked with pink. God, it all looks so serene from up here. So *simple*.

I think about what Jonah said about London being magical. I'd immediately discounted it at the time but I have to admit . . . from this angle it looks pretty damn special.

'Dance, Delphie!' I'm brought back to the room by Frida elbowing me in the ribs. She's circling her hips, arms waving about in a delicate way, the floaty sleeves of her dress getting a chance to shine.

For crying out loud. I tentatively start to wiggle my hips from side to side and do the one and only dance I seem able to remember under such enormous pressure, which to my surprise and mortification is the hand jive from *Grease*.

'Don't panic,' I mutter to myself, bumping my fists above one another, then jerking my flattened palms this way and that.

I must be doing quite a good job because the stern woman

nods her approval before marching off, probably to make that complaint to Maurice whatshisname. Shit, what if she finds out that we've not been sent by anyone? That we absolutely do not belong here? What if we get kicked out before I can even say hello to Jonah?

Hang about – some of the people in the crowd are turning to watch Frida and me, like we really are professional dancers here to dance for them. I glance at Frida who has also started to do the hand jive, perhaps in solidarity, or maybe because it just looks good? The attention makes my heart flip nervously and every cell in my body is telling me to run away. But then I realise that the crowd staring at me is actually a very useful thing indeed – if I can see everyone's faces then I can more easily spot Jonah's! I speed up my hand jive to make it look even more impressive – Frida's eyes widen but she keeps up like a champ. It works and more people turn around to watch, some of them even nudging each other with what I think is admiration. Within a minute or so pretty much every eye in the room is on us. I smile brightly at the crowd and continue my hand jive while scanning the room for Jonah's face. But I don't see him anywhere. Dammit. He must be here. Kat said he would be here – that he was *working* here. He *has* to fucking be here.

At a loss for what else to do, I clear my throat and call out across the event space, 'I'm looking for Jonah Truman,' my voice piercing in the otherwise-silent room. 'Jonah Truman!' I yell again, even louder. 'Are you here? I need to speak with you! Jonah Truman?'

Frida stops dancing before taking a deep breath and yelling, 'Jonaaaaaaaaaaah!' out into the room.

This is not the fun, flirty, casual vibe I was going for. But what other options do I have left? I cannot have schlepped all this way for nothing – time is running out!

Now that we're no longer dancing, the crowd starts to turn away. I step down from the podium with a frustrated sigh. Where the hell is he? Kat definitely said the Shard!

My stomach twists at the thought that I'll never find him. I cannot die again. I cannot end up in Evermore, or Nevermore, or bloody Clevermore. I've been given this one chance – how many people get that? I can't blow it.

I'm helping Frida down from the podium so we can decide what to do next when a pixie-haired woman wearing a dress covered in multi-coloured jewels approaches us.

'You know Jonah?' she says excitedly, looking between the two of us. Her accent is northern, her voice slightly gravelly.

'Yes, yes, I do,' I say. 'Do you? Is he here? Where is he?'

The woman sighs. 'I *wish* I knew him! He was here about half an hour ago, dancing right there where you were.' She points up at the podium.

Jonah was right there?

'I was on the balcony having a ciggy,' the woman continues, 'and out he comes, "for a breather" he says. We struck up a conversation, but five minutes later he got a call from the hospital he volunteers at. Someone hadn't shown up so he had to fill in.'

Jonah volunteers at a hospital?

'Which hospital?' I say frantically. 'Did he mention where?'

The woman shakes her head. 'All he said was that he couldn't let the children down!'

Not only does he volunteer at a hospital – but for children? God, Jonah is a far better human than I am. If Merritt wasn't so convinced that he's my soulmate, I'd say he was *too* good for me.

'And he definitely didn't say which hospital? Or a specific area he had to get to?'

'Nope. Just took off into the night like a beautiful and noble superhero.'

'Excuse me, I am not paying you to chat to the guests.' I spin around to see headset woman scowling at us, her cheeks red with fury. She throws her hands up in the air. 'I have never, ever dealt with such unprofessionalism in my life. You are fired. Please leave. And if Maurice Alabaster has any sense he will remove you from his books without a second thought.'

My mouth drops open, pride oddly wounded at being fired from a job I don't actually have.

Frida steps in front of me, arms folded across her chest. 'You can't fire us, because guess what, lady? We QUIT.'

I goggle as Frida grabs my hand and yanks me towards the exit. 'Come on, Delphie. Let's blow this joint.'

Chapter Twenty-One

Outside Frida erupts into giggles. 'I've always wanted to say, "I QUIT!"'' Her eyes shine. 'But you don't have much of a chance when you're a dog-walker. Ha-ha! "Let's blow this joint!"' she repeats to herself. 'I can't believe I said that!'

I can't help but grin at her excitement, despite my rising internal panic that not only have I missed Jonah again, but also the chances of finding him at a random hospital when there are so many in London, and all of them so big, is next to zero.

I need to get home and make a new plan. Maybe convince Merritt to give me a clue. Surely by now she can see that luck is not on my side, despite my very best efforts. We walk to the nearest bus stop, only to find that the queue is at least thirty deep on account of the Tube strike. One jam-packed bus drives straight past the stop without even bothering to stop.

I open my car-sharing app and press the button, despite the surge pricing. Somehow overspending doesn't hold the same fear it once did – I have nothing to lose!

'I'm sorry you didn't find Jonah,' Frida says, once we're neatly in the back of a blissfully air-conditioned taxi. 'I can tell you are very much attracted to him. You made quite the fuss at our drawing class. I wonder if we'll ever be allowed back in?'

'It's much, much more than attraction,' I mutter. 'I wouldn't make such a fuss if it was just about attraction.'

'Ah. I wish I could find much more than attraction.' Frida looks dreamy for a moment, leaning back on the headrest, her arms behind her head. 'But even just attraction is hard enough to find. I thought in London I'd meet lots of people but everyone is always' – she starts to do a sort of robotic impression – 'eyes down to the ground, don't talk to me, no eye contact allowed on the Central line! I thought maybe Claude at the drawing class would be nice. But he was not. I thought Gant was my soulmate. But he left me. So now what am I supposed to do?'

'I once heard that we actually have up to five soulmates,' I say, remembering what Merritt told me in Evermore.

'Who told you that?' Frida removes her arms from behind her head and leans forward. 'Was it Gwyneth Paltrow? Because I do not trust her. Never again will I trust Gwyneth Paltrow or her magazine.'

I laugh. 'I'm going to need to know more about what she did to make you so mad.'

'I'll never share. It's too humiliating.'

'No. It wasn't Gwyneth Paltrow. It was a woman I met recently. She . . . well, she actually introduced me to Jonah. She was the one who saw that there was something special between us. Told me to go after him.'

'She sounds very insightful. I would love to meet her.'

'Trust me, you don't want to meet this woman.'

'I think I'll do whatever it takes to find love. I've even been learning about witchcraft, and though it can help in many ways, it can't bring true love your way. That's up to the fates.'

I decide not to baulk at the bonkersly casual way in which Frida refers to taking up witchcraft, because who am I to question any supernatural inclinations when I am literally a dead person on the earth for a borrowed amount of time? Instead, I ask her to tell me a little more about Gant. She talks about how she was with him for two years and how he broke up with her around once per month because he kept changing his mind about whether he was in love with her.

'I've been single for my whole life,' I tell her as we turn onto my road. 'It's not so bad. It sounds like Gant leaving was a blessing in disguise.'

'My brain knows that, but I think it'll take my heart some time to catch up.'

When we reach my house I realise that Aled is leaning against my front door, looking intently at his phone. We climb out of the car.

'Aled!' I say, a swarm of guilt enveloping me at not replying to his text, and a flicker of alarm that he has turned up to my actual house as a consequence. 'What are you doing here?'

He waves hello. 'You didn't respond to my message. To have gone from being so pally to nothing at all made me worried that you had perhaps drunk too much, or that something terrible had happened to you.'

'I'm sorry,' I say. 'But here I am. Alive!'

For how long, who knows? But for now.

'Who is this?' Frida asks in a weird voice.

'This is Aled who works at Tyburnia Library. Aled, this is Frida, a professional dog-walker in the area.'

'I'm Delphie's friend.' Frida holds her hand out.

'Me too!' Aled gasps as if this is a level of coincidence that ought to be investigated by experts.

'Thanks for the company, Frida,' I say, unlocking my door and heading inside. 'And for . . . you know, dancing with me.'

'My pleasure.' Frida steps into the hallway with me. Aled follows. Are they expecting me to invite them up? I don't invite people up. I've never invited people up. 'LET'S BLOW THIS JOINT!' she yells once more, her hands on her hips. Aled laughs heartily at this although he has no idea what she's referring to.

Within seconds Cooper peers out into the hallway to see what's causing the noise.

He looks at me curiously, as if he doesn't know who I am, and then his eyebrows shoot up, his gaze skimming over my hair. I wait for him to make some disagreeable comment, but instead he looks between Aled and Frida, a puzzled expression on his face.

'Sorry for the hullabaloo,' Frida giggles. 'We've been hunting for a man at the Shard. It was a very fun evening and we're all a little over-excited.'

'Did you find him?' Cooper asks, eyebrows still raised. I

shake my head no and open my mouth to thank him for his apology text, but before I can Aled gasps loudly.

'Hold on a moment!' Aled narrows his eyes at Cooper. 'I *knew* I recognised you!'

Cooper's shoulders slump.

'You're R. L. Cooper!'

I screw up my face. 'Who the hell is R. L. Cooper?'

'Um, only one of the best crime writers of our generation!' Aled's voice rises with excitement. 'Your books are always out on loan at the library. But there's not been a new one in so long. Why is that? Wow. THE R. L. Cooper himself. Tell me, R. L., how did you come up with the bank heist plot in *Money Maims, Money Kills*? It was ingenious. What is your process? Where do you get your inspiration?'

Cooper is a writer? Of crime books? I thought he was a computer programmer. Wait – is that how he had access to the police database? Crime writers usually have people in the police to help them with research – or at least that's what happens on one of my favourite TV shows, *Murder in the Pretty Village*. Is that how he was able to locate Jonah so quickly? I glance at Cooper and see that he's now shuffling from foot to foot, clearly uncomfortable with Aled's line of questioning.

'Okay!' I yawn in such an over-the-top way that it's impossible for Aled to ignore. 'I really do need to go. Frida, will you be okay getting home from here?'

'Of course! It's only a five-minute walk to Edgware Road.'

'Edgware Road is on my way!' Aled beams.

'We'll walk together?' Frida grins amiably. 'I would love to hear all about the library.' I can't help but smile. How Frida doesn't have more friends is beyond me. I've never in my life met someone so comfortable around new people. I feel physical discomfort when I have to make small talk – but she seems to actively enjoy it.

'I'll be back!' Aled says to Cooper as Frida leads him away. 'We must get you booked in for an event at the library. And, Delphie, I will be in touch about the best friendship – do not think I have forgotten!'

As I close the door on Aled and Frida, Cooper clears his throat.

'Thanks for that. Haven't been recognised in a while.'

I yawn again. 'No worries.'

He looks like he's about to say something else when Mrs Ernestine's door creaks open and her head pokes out, her craggy face all pinched. 'It's like bloody King's Cross station out here,' she spits. 'Do none of you have homes to go to? I'm trying to eat my lasagne and watch *Breaking Bad* and all I can hear is ruckus and bloody doors slamming. All and sundry popping in and out like it's a damn thoroughfare.'

Mrs Ernestine terrifies me. Every time I see her, she's arguing with someone. Out on the street or in the hallway. Sometimes when I walk past her door I hear her screeching inside her flat, God only knows at who. Plus, she has a tattoo on her knuckles that says NEVER AGAIN. I often find myself wondering what it means, every conclusion I reach making me even more determined to stay out her way.

'Sorry, Mrs Ernestine,' I say as politely as I can, bowing my head a little.

'Yes. Ever so sorry,' Cooper adds, also bowing his head a little.

Is he making fun of me?

Mrs Ernestine rolls her eyes and backs away into her flat, glaring at the pair of us until her door is closed again.

Cooper reaches his hand out towards me and I'm pretty sure he's going to touch my cheek – the thought of which makes my face flame – but his hand moves swiftly to my hair, slowly plucking something out.

He holds up a yellow petal between finger and thumb. I pat my head self-consciously. It must be from Frida's flower crown.

'Thank you.' I say stiffly, before turning and running up to my flat, slamming the door behind me.

In my flat, I immediately grab my laptop and search Jonah's name plus dancer and the Shard.

Still nothing? Jeez.

'Why are you so fucking elusive, Jonah?' I huff. 'I'm literally depending on you for my life.'

I imagine Jonah grinning at me, running a hand through his lovely caramel hair. *I'm worth the effort*, he says in my imagination. I picture running my own hands through his hair and a little shiver of delight softens the anxiety for a brief, beautiful moment.

'Merritt, you have to help me,' I mutter. 'Can't you see I'm doing everything I can? Please!'

I wait for a text, an appearance, *anything*. But nothing happens. With a sigh, I take my sketches out of my bag and unroll them on the kitchen table, pinning them flat with salt and pepper shakers. I touch a finger lightly to one of them, a close-up of Kat's face drawn in a free, almost loopy style. My heart lifts, despite itself. This *is* good. I glance over at the stack of oil paints I'm forever buying but am too scared to open. I wonder briefly what life would have looked like if I'd never stopped making art. Would I still be in this situation? I push the thought away.

There's a firm knock at the door.

My heart leaps. Merritt? Though surely she would never do anything as pedestrian as *knocking*.

I open up to find Cooper standing there, arms folded across his chest.

I sigh. 'If you're coming to me with anything that could be even slightly considered stressful then I beg of you go back from whence you came. It's been a tricky day.'

'"Whence you came"? Why are you talking like that?'

I narrow my eyes. 'Actually, I'm not sure. I think it's your formal demeanour. The, you know, stiffness. I respond in kind.'

'The stiffness?'

'Oh, come on. You must know that about yourself,' I say, backing into my flat as he takes a large step in and closes the door behind him. 'I'd even go so far as to say you've cultivated it.'

'The same way you have with your "I'm a lone wolf" schtick. And it *is* schtick.'

164

'You must know all about schtick, making things up for a living?'

'I don't do that anymore.' Cooper clears his throat, strides across the room and sits on my sofa without being invited to. His jeans hitch up. His socks are yellow.

I throw my hands up. 'What do you want? I am currently trying to find my way out of a rather large life pickle and I'm short on time.'

'I see. Can I help?'

I narrow my eyes. He'd only be offering to help if ... 'You need another favour?'

He shifts in his seat and runs his hand over his jaw. 'I do. I was going to ask you downstairs but you literally ran away.' His voice dips with disbelief.

I tut. 'Like I say, I'm short on time. Anyway, did you not hear what I just said about bringing chaos to my doorstep?'

'Like you did with me when you barged into my flat and insisted I help you? Look, I really am sorry for being rude the other night. My sister ... It's not something I talk about. Ever. With anyone.'

I soften slightly. 'I understand. I shouldn't have been so nosy. How can I help?'

Cooper's mouth bunches to the side. 'My mother ...'

'Amy. Yes.'

'She wants you to join us at the aquarium. To meet my Aunt Beverley. Tomorrow morning.'

I grimace. 'Sorry, no can do. I need to go to the park again to find Jonah.'

'You still haven't found him?'

165

I huff. 'It's . . . complicated.'

Cooper tilts his head to the side and crosses one leg over the other. 'Have you considered that he may be actively avoiding you?'

I make a face. 'Jonah isn't like that.'

'And yet . . .'

'Are we done here, Cooper? I have things to do.'

Cooper leans forward. 'Surely it would only take you a few minutes to inform Jonah of the . . . issue? And then you'd be free, right?'

I sigh. If only it were as simple as that. But it's not. Not only do I have to locate a man who seems never to stay in one place for long enough, I then have to get him to kiss me with barely any preamble. I can't be dallying around an aquarium in the middle of all this.

'Maybe another time, eh?' I puzzle for a moment, curiosity getting the better of me. 'Anyway, why on earth would your mum want me to meet your aunt?'

Cooper looks at his feet which are booted as usual, although one of the laces is now undone. 'She, well, she, uh, she liked you. For some unknown reason, she liked you very much.'

'Heaven forbid anyone could possibly enjoy my company.'

Cooper sighs. 'My Auntie Bev is flying out to trek across Nepal tomorrow night. As soon as Mum told her how "nice" you are she insisted on meeting you before she goes . . . She's very pushy – Mum's a little terrified of her. We all are, frankly.'

My heart warms at hearing that Amy liked me very much. I liked her very much too. I liked how it felt when she patted the back of my head. I swallow and a weird sensation tugs at my chest.

'Why the aquarium?'

'Bev loves all that touristy stuff,' he says vaguely. 'And, you know. Tropical fish are cool.'

I nod. Tropical fish *are* cool. And seeing Amy again does sound nice. Really nice, in fact. But I can't. I'm in a life-or-death scenario right now, and luck does not appear to be on my side. I can't waste time gawking at sea creatures. 'I'm sorry,' I say with a small shrug. 'I really can't.'

Cooper nods quickly. 'Of course. Yes, of course. Mum asked me to ask, so I, you know, asked. We'll be meeting for coffee at Laurents cafe beforehand, if you change your mind.'

I nod. 'You need to deal with that,' I say, pointing at his undone lace.

He speedily ties the lace, double-knotting it and pulling so hard I wonder how on earth he'll be able to undo it again.

'So,' I say once he's stood back up, 'all this time, I've been living above the best crime writer of our generation?'

'Oh, I was never that. I'm not a writer at all anymore.'

'Seems like a pretty cool job to dump in favour of becoming a computer programmer?'

Cooper gestures towards the door. 'I should get going.'

On his way out he stops by the kitchen table, glancing down at my nude sketches. Shit.

'They're private!' I say sharply, hurrying over.

'They're beautiful,' he murmurs, bending his knees to get a closer look, tilting his head to the side.

167

I wave him away. 'They're not that good. I don't really draw anymore. This was a one-off.'

Cooper stretches back up and looks right at me. 'They're beautiful, Delphie,' he repeats, his voice unnervingly gentle.

I swallow and look down at my feet. 'Well, thanks,' I mumble, a smile tugging at the corner of my mouth.

'Right, then,' Cooper says, voice back to normal plummy confidence. 'Have a good evening.'

I watch him stride out of my flat, an odd prickle of disappointment in my stomach. I peer down at my sketches again, seeing them through Cooper's eyes.

Maybe they are beautiful.

I take out my phone and snap some pictures to send to Mum.

Chapter Twenty-Two

Rather than frantically guessing where in the park Jonah might be, I plonk myself outside the Serpentine Lido in the hopes that his running group takes the same route every morning. I buy myself a bottle of water from the nearby cart and settle myself on a bench with a view of pathways to the left and the right. This way I can get a decent heads-up of his approach no matter what direction he's running in. While I wait, I idly watch the early-morning swimmers and imagine how pleasant it must feel to be in the cool water during this insane heat. I spot an elderly couple splashing about at the far edge of the water, giggling like teenagers. I wonder how they met, and if they knew right away that they were soulmates.

My phone buzzes.

I'm only sending this because my mum insisted but she wants you to know that we're meeting at Laurents at 9 in case you have time to join us for a coffee before we set off to the aquarium. Best, Cooper.

I tap out a response.

I'm waiting to see if Jonah is jogging in the park again but there's no sign of him. I should probably keep waiting, but please thank your mum for the invitation.

I press send.

Then I can't help but type out:

Best? You sign your texts 'best'?

What do you suggest in place of 'best'?

I bite my lip and have a think.

I don't think you have to formally sign off. Maybe just a relevant emoji would work.

A few seconds later . . .

I laugh out loud in surprise. Then, realising that I shouldn't be staring down at my phone when Jonah could run past any minute, I reply with 👎 and shove my phone back into my pocket.

After an hour passes with no sign of Jonah I consider moving to a different spot. But what if that's the exact moment he shows up?

After two hours of waiting I call up Kensington Leisure

Centre, only to be informed that the running club has been cancelled for the remainder of the week on account of the dangerously rising temperatures. When I ask the reception-ist to please, please, *please* give me Jonah's contact details she reacts the same way Claude did at the drawing class – like it's an absolute outrage for me to ask her to do something so unprofessional.

I plod dejectedly back towards my flat, my head spin-ning with panic, my underarms soaked with sweat, my heart squeezing with doubt about what the hell I'm sup-posed to do next.

'Merriiiiiitttttt, help meeeeee!' I whisper, already know-ing that she won't respond from wherever she's hiding. I picture Kat at the drawing class. She seemed like she might have been persuaded to talk if Claude hadn't been there to stop her. Could I track Kat down? But how? I know even less about her than I do Jonah.

'Aaaaargh,' I moan to myself as I walk down Craven Road. I pull out my phone and google Kat nude model London.

Big mistake. Wow, there are so many horny cougars in my area.

'Delphie! You came!'

I'm pulled out of my X-rated online search to see Cooper, his mum, Amy, and a perfectly round, perfectly put together woman drinking iced coffees outside Laurents cafe. Oh, shit. He said they were going to be meeting here. I should have snuck around the back way.

'Hi!' I give them a polite wave. 'I'm actually just on my way to—'

'I'm so glad you're here!' Amy jumps up from her chair and pulls me into a tight hug that somewhat settles my racing heart. 'I was ever so disappointed when Cooper said you couldn't make it. I knew if we just waited here a little longer you might come by!'

'I didn't actually . . .' I go to tell them that I'd forgotten they were even coming to the neighbourhood but Amy softly presses her hand to the back of my head and the words disappear on my tongue.

Once Amy releases me, I'm immediately gathered into a second, more bosomy, hug by the other woman. The scent of her perfume is a lovely subtle cedar. Her bare arms sort of stick to my bare arms. This must be the 'pushy' Aunt Bev. 'Nice to meet you,' I say, my entire face muffled in her neck.

'Darling girl!' Bev exclaims, leaning back and examining me like I'm a dear friend she hasn't seen in years. 'How wonderful! As soon as Amy told me you'd made our eternally sour-faced boy laugh I said, "Good Lord, I have to see this for myself at once!" He's been such a miserable little wretch these last few years. We have all asked him to go to therapy, but of course he thinks he knows better than the older and the much, much *wiser*. But perhaps all he needed this whole time was *love*.'

'We've only been dating a few weeks, Bev,' Cooper sighs, finishing the remainder of his coffee.

Bev tuts. 'Your Uncle Jerry – God rest his soul – and I knew within half a second that we loved each other. Time means nothing. Chemistry is what counts!'

Cooper avoids my wide-eyed glance, horror at his aunt's indiscretion turning his cheeks lightly pink. I can't help but giggle at his discomfort. Nothing strips away the carefully curated cool demeanour of a person faster than being around those who raised them.

'Shall we hail a taxi to the aquarium?'

I grimace. I really should get back home and figure out a new plan. But Amy looks genuinely delighted to see me. And Bev is already bustling about, excitedly telling me about her favourite fish. And then there's Cooper, eyeing me with an expression akin to pleading. He clearly wants to keep his mum smiling. I get that. God knows I tried with my own mum after Dad left.

'We won't stay for long,' Cooper murmurs in my ear. 'And I'll owe you. *Again.*'

I suppose it's not like I'm going to make much headway in the next hour anyway. And when we return Cooper's assistance *would* be helpful. Maybe he could use some of his computer whizzery to track down Kat, who I think might actually give me Jonah's number if I beg her for long enough.

'Okay, then,' I say brightly. 'But I'll have to nip home to shower first. I'm a little sweaty.'

'Oh, you can shower later.' Bev waves away the suggestion. 'We're all friends here.'

'Join the sweaty club!' Amy says, swinging her arm around me.

'Sweaty Bettys unite!' Bev adds, looping her arm through mine and hailing a taxi with a practised flick of her wrist.

'Speak for yourselves,' Cooper says, pinching his nose as the four of us bundle into the taxi.

I've never been to the London Aquarium before. I always imagined it would be serene and empty. All dim lighting and fish nerds talking in hushed voices. I was so wrong. The London Aquarium is noisy as hell, with crowds of people shoving and shouting and pressing their whole faces or their phones up against the glass of the tanks. Bev immediately leads us to an area called the Syngnathidae section and I'm relieved to find it's much quieter than downstairs, the tanks filled with tiny spiky creatures that aren't as flashy as the sharks and the jellyfish, but are magical, nevertheless.

'They're smaller than I thought they'd be,' I say, pointing at the seahorses, ducking my head to get a closer look. 'They're beautiful, though. Like little pieces of jewellery.'

'I can't believe they're alive,' Amy says. 'That they're breathing.'

'Aha,' Bev calls out, pointing at an information board beside the tank. 'The Hippocampus histrix – or thorny seahorse as it's better known – sticks with just one other seahorse for their entire life! Whenever I'd bring Cooper and Em here as youngsters they'd run straight to this area. Used to sit in front of the tank linking pinkies like the seahorses link tails.'

I glance at Cooper who is staring intently at a wall sign that says EXIT THIS WAY.

'Look at those two there! They're linking tails right now!'

Amy points to a far corner of the coral where there are indeed two tiny seahorses, little tails looped into each other.

'We simply must get a photo,' Bev says decisively. 'Cooper, darling. Delphie. Come on. Stand here. Oh, and kiss! Kiss by the seahorses. How romantic!'

Amy nudges Cooper away from the exit sign and towards the front of the tank while Bev drags me over so forcefully I almost trip on my own shoes.

'No, no need to take a photo,' Cooper shakes his head quickly. 'Let's just use our memories, shall we?'

'Yes!' I agree firmly. 'Analogue. Plus, we don't want to get in the way of the other visitors.'

Bev pouts. 'Don't be ridiculous, there's hardly anyone else in here.' She steps back and holds up her phone. 'Come on. Kiss by the seahorses. You'll thank me at your wedding.'

Cooper's mouth is set into a grim line, his shoulders hunched higher than I've ever seen them. I look around in panic. I cannot kiss him, even for a ruse.

Amy giggles. 'Bev, leave them be.'

I exhale. *Thank you, Amy.* But then Amy reconsiders. 'You don't have to kiss if it feels too awkward in front of every-one. But perhaps you could look at each other for the photograph? Into each other's eyes.'

'Yes, and hold hands! Face each other and hold hands!'

Christ.

'Let's just get this over with,' Cooper murmurs out of the side of his mouth.

I sigh and turn towards him in front of the glass.

'Hold hands!' Bev shouts.

'You're right. She is pushy,' I hiss as Cooper reaches to take my hands in his. I snatch my hands away.

Cooper pinches the bridge of his nose. 'You try stopping her once she's got an idea in her head. I've tried my whole life. The only one who could ever out-push her was Em.'

I glance over at Bev. I open my mouth to tell her that this is ridiculous and that she cannot bully us into taking a romantic picture in front of some seahorses. But then I spot Amy beside her. Her hands are clasped to her chest and she's smiling like this is the most fun she's had in ages.

'Take the picture already,' I say as politely as I can manage, pasting a smile onto my face and looking up at Cooper. He takes my hands in his once more. Then, so slowly that I'm not even sure it's happening, he curls his index finger upwards across my palm. I swallow and frown at him slightly. His face is unchanged. He must not know he's doing it. My nostrils flare in alarm at the sensations that Cooper's finger is causing. I'm clearly so unused to human touch that even an accidental tickle from someone I don't fancy is giving me a full body blush.

'Three! Two! One!' Bev counts down.

Cooper and I look at each other and I notice that the light coming from the fish tank makes his eyes look like they're dancing.

'Oh, blast . . . I pressed the wrong thing,' Bev cries. 'Okay, let me try again.'

Cooper continues to look at me, seemingly unphased. Sweat starts to prickle the back of my neck.

'For fuck's sake,' I sing, still fake smiling. It's so hot in here. I wish she'd hurry up.

'Oh, hang on, darlings. I appear to have pressed the button for the calculator application.'

'Is it not that one?' Amy joins in, stabbing a finger to the phone screen. 'Ah, cripes. What have I done?'

The room fills with the tinny sounds of Roberta Flack's 'Killing Me Softly'.

'Amy, you've turned on Spotify. You two, don't move! Keep posing. Oh! Aha! *Here's* the camera thingamajig.'

'Kill *me* softly,' I mutter.

Cooper's lips press together, the edges of them turning pale pink. What a weird smile. I squint. Is he okay?

His shoulders start to shake. Then his mouth opens and he crouches over, a blast of laughter filling the air.

I jump in shock at the sound of it, hands covering my face. And then the sight of this stiff, perennially haughty man laughing so unabashedly catches me and I let out a small laugh of my own. Cooper splutters which makes me laugh even more, and before I know it the pair of us are bent double, shrieking so hard we can barely catch our breath.

I see a flash of light from the corner of my eye.

'Told you she made him laugh,' Amy says.

'I never would have believed it,' Bev chuckles. 'But it's true! And now I have photographic evidence!'

When we've toured the remainder of the aquarium I dash off to the loo. I head towards the line of sinks to wash my hands when I see that one of the mirrors is covered in lipstick so obnoxiously orange it can only belong to Merritt.

Having a nice time at the aquarium, are we? You're going to have to try harder than this, babe. You have five days left to find Jonah or else I have no choice but to bring you back to the land of the Deads! You signed a contract!!!

I wriggle uncomfortably. She's right. I am having a nice time at the aquarium. I've already been here for way too long. Five days left is no time at all.

'So help me out!' I yell frustratedly into the air, much to the befuddlement of a woman exiting one of the cubicles. She gives me a wide berth and throws a pointed look at the mirror. I turn the cold water on full blast and cool my wrists beneath the flow. 'I'm willing to try harder, believe me,' I call out to wherever Merritt is. 'But I'm stuck. I literally don't know what to do next! Cooper's going to help me search for Kat when we get back, but other than that I'm at a loss and I'm, frankly, scared. So throw me a bone.'

I wait for a response.

Nothing. She's dipped again.

'Nice. Really nice. Thanks, Merritt.'

I sigh, patting cold water onto my hot, sticky cheeks. I've searched the internet, The Orchestra Pit, the park, the drawing class and the Shard! I've run into terrible luck and stupid obstacles each and every time. I think about what Cooper

178

said last night, about Jonah actively avoiding me. But that can't be possible. He doesn't know I exist. Does he?

Once the cool water has helped to lower my temperature a tad, I turn off the tap, noticing as I do a little logo on the rim of the sink. LONDON ALABASTER. Something flickers in my brain, a small crackle at first and then a lightning bolt. I get a vision of the irritable woman at the Shard last night. Asking if Maurice Alabaster had sent us there to dance, and how she was going to make a complaint to Maurice Alabaster. Then I remember how the northern girl in the jewelled dress said Jonah had been dancing on the podium just before me. Hmmm. Maurice Alabaster must be Jonah's manager or agent or something?

I speedily dry my hands on a paper towel and open up my phone to search. Aha! The Maurice Alabaster Talent and Casting Agency! I scroll quickly through the list of dance clients and – oh my God – there he is! It's Jonah – a black-and-white headshot of him looking handsome and sweet and kind, just like he was in Evermore. His name is not Jonah Truman here, though. It says Jonah Electric. Huh. Is that a stage name? Is that why he didn't show up in any of my internet sleuthing?

I scan down his bio, my eyes widening as I see that Jonah is an actor and a dancer and just last year appeared in a French Riviera cruise production of *Cats*. I picture him in a furry outfit, whiskers painted onto his face. I immediately shove the image away to the lockbox of doom and scroll back up to the headshot to admire his warm, sparkling eyes. There he is. Jonah – actor, dancer, saver of my life, soulmate.

I glance at the lipstick note on the mirror again, then type out a message.

> Cooper, I have an encouraging lead on Jonah and have to go. Please tell Amy and Bev I'm sorry.

If I find Jonah, I would really like to hang out with them again. But if I don't find Jonah I won't get to hang out with anyone but Merritt and whatever other Deads she sets me up with for her weird dating service.

Cooper replies right away with 👍, the worst but most efficient of all the emojis. An improvement on signing off with 'Best, Cooper' I suppose.

'Maybe I don't need your help after all!' I call out to Merritt. 'Maybe I can figure this out all on my own.'

Then I fly down the stairs of the aquarium, speed past the tourists and the fish nerds, and run out into the sunshine.

Chapter Twenty-Three

Well, all of my Abstract 23 collection has sold out! Every single one bought before the exhibition!

That's great, Mum. Congratulations! Did you see my drawing? Is something wrong with your phone? I keep trying to call but no answer.

I generally avoid most places outside my little corner of West London but nowhere more than Soho. Soho is the grubbiest, seediest, most self-satisfied area in the entire city. The pavements are all too narrow, the people hanging around there are all obnoxious, and there are so many weird noises and smells and colours that you'd need to lie down in a darkened room for an hour afterwards just to decompress.

To my chagrin, the Maurice Alabaster Talent and Casting Agency is located in an office above a bar on Old Compton Street, smack-bang in the middle of the fray. After the disaster of the last few days' attempts to locate Jonah, and Merritt's unwillingness to give me any intel, I don't have a choice but to go there.

I reach the bar and to the left of it there's a shiny black door with a little intercom pad on the brick wall beside it. I trace my finger down the names and the buttons. Aha! There it is. The Maurice Alabaster Talent and Casting Agency. I press the buzzer and am quickly greeted by a female voice.

'Name.'

'Delphie. Delphie Bookham.'

'One moment . . . You're not on my list? Did you confirm attendance for the call-back online? The system's been a little glitchy, I'm afraid.'

'I'm just here to speak to Maurice Alabaster. I'm looking for Jonah Truman – I mean, Jonah Electric, as you might know him – and I hoped Maurice could help.'

The woman sighs. 'Today Maurice is holding the call-back only. He does not have time for anything else. Feel free to send an email. Goodbye.'

I hear a clink through the intercom speaker. Dammit. This is way too urgent for an email.

I'm nudged out of the way by a young brunette woman who leans over me to press the buzzer.

'Name?' comes the intercom voice.

'Here for the call-back. Ellie Damson, three-thirty appointment.'

The buzzer sounds and the young woman is immediately let into the building. I quickly slip in behind her and covertly follow her up the stairs to a shabby-looking office lobby, the walls plastered with framed black-and-white headshots like the one I just saw of Jonah on the website.

'Through there.' The woman at the reception desk thumbs down a brown carpeted corridor, barely looking up at me or Ellie Damson Three-Thirty Appointment.

We shuffle into a tiny waiting room area filled with other young brunette women. A door creaks open and a white-haired moustachioed man pokes his head around it. His face is craggy and tanned, grey eyes slightly bored-looking. I recognise from the website that this man is Maurice Alabaster himself. 'Rachel Calloway?' he calls out with a spiritless sigh, glancing down at a piece of paper in his hand. 'Three-twenty?'

No one responds.

'Rachel Calloway?' the man repeats, a smidge louder. Ellie Damson shakes her head at another of the brunettes. One of them tuts.

'Rachel Calloway, final call?'

I'm on my feet before I can think it through. 'That is me!' I say. 'Yes, Rachel Calloway is my name!'

Maurice Alabaster ushers me into a small triangular office and settles himself behind a desk, an old grey laptop resting upon piles of papers and headshots, bright Post-it notes stuck onto every surface. On the wall behind him there are haphazardly placed photographs of Maurice, arm slung around people I vaguely recognise from old television shows. Each picture is signed with an autograph.

'I don't remember seeing you at the first casting call, Rachel,' Maurice says, sliding on a pair of large square-shaped spectacles and squinting into his laptop. 'Have you dyed your hair since then? The production company specifically asked me for brunettes.'

Ah, yes. Rachel Calloway. He thinks I am Rachel Calloway. I open my mouth to explain to him that I'm actually

Delphie Bookham and that I'm very sorry for slipping in under false pretences but that I'm here to find Jonah Truman/ Electric. And then I remember Claude's reaction from the life-drawing class when I asked after Jonah. He went into immediate protective mode – like I was dangerous or something. Hmm. I definitely don't want that to happen again. Maurice wouldn't still be in business if he gave out the details of his clients willy-nilly, especially to someone who's snuck into his office under a false name.

I really have not thought this through. All I was focused on was getting in here, and now . . .

'I dyed my hair,' I explain, my voice as even as I can get it. 'But I can dye it back.'

Maurice harrumphs and shuffles through his papers. I peer around the room, spotting a filing cabinet in the corner. I bet that's where he keeps his client files. Okay. A plan: I need to get Maurice out of the room somehow. Then I can sneak into the filing cabinet and grab Jonah's file and all of his contact details.

'So, as you know, the part is for the new police constable on *Murder in the Pretty Village*, and . . .'

I zone out for a moment. I love *Murder in the Pretty Village*! It's a stalwart of British programming, been on telly for years. Before Dad left, he and Mum used to watch it every Sunday night.

'And so today, we're just wanting to find out a little more about you, and those of you selected for a third call-back will return for a meeting with the show producers. Sound good?'

I nod quickly. Maurice takes a sip from a half-empty glass of green juice and grimaces. Then he leans back into his well-worn office chair. It squeaks beneath his weight and he gives a little 'ah' of pleasure. Doesn't look like he plans on moving any time soon, but I need him to bog off so I can get into that filing cabinet pronto.

'I see you trained at RADA, very nice,' Maurice reads from what I assume is Rachel Calloway's CV. 'Do you have your monologue prepared?'

My eyes flick from side to side, as if the solution to what the hell I'm supposed to do in this most niche of scenarios is somewhere nearby.

Maurice's face softens. 'A little nervous? It *is* rather a significant role.' He leans forward and lowers his voice. 'Well, dear, here's a tip from me to you. We're looking for someone who can really get *angry*, no holds barred. PC Buttersby has quite the temper, and everyone I've seen so far?' He waves his hands about. 'They're a little too subtle. And I know that's the trend right now on HBO and in American prestige TV and what have you, but this is British Sunday-night drama and I'm looking for someone who isn't afraid to just . . . let rip.' He smiles. 'Does that help?'

No, Maurice. No, it does not. What would help is if you took off so I can get access to your filing cabinet and find the only person on earth who can save my life. I need more time to think of a proper plan. I need to be smarter than this.

'Go ahead.' Maurice nods.

I take a deep breath. 'Errrrr . . . Let's see. Um . . . Na-na,

na, na, na-na-na. Na-na, na, na, na-na. Getting jiggy wit' it,'
I begin before clamping my mouth closed.

*Delphie, why? Why, at times of great stress and pressure, do
you immediately go to Will Smith? Maurice wants a monologue.
Not whatever this is! He's going to kick you out.*

Shit. Okay. Angry. He said he wants angry. I can be angry.
I'm always angry! I transform my face into a frown and fold
my arms across my chest. I think of people who say, 'Wow.
Just . . . wow.' I think of how terrible it is that Mr Yoon has
no family around him. I think of cleaning the cheese grater.
I think of how awful secondary school was. I think of Mum
never calling me back. I think of all my worst things, but to
my dismay, instead of getting angry, a flood of tears journey
to my eyes. I frantically sniff them away. I am ridiculous. I
am fully ridiculous and this is never going to work! I should
just leave, go home, and wait for Merritt. I should just accept
my fate. It's inevitable.

Maurice sighs like maybe this has happened to him
before. 'Let's come back to the monologue a little later.' He
taps at the laptop screen. 'It says here you studied Acting
through Dance under Pauline LaRue Toussaint! Wonderful.
Pauline and I go back a long way. Dear, dear woman.'

I'm about to apologise for wasting his time when I suddenly spot that something outrageous is happening behind
Maurice's head. On a framed photo of Maurice and what
looks to be a very young Judi Dench words start to appear in
the same black handwriting as Judi Dench's autograph. I
gasp. Merritt? I look at the scrawled sentence.

Knock over the green juice!

She's trying to help me! At last! My eyes flick to the glass on Maurice's desk. Of course! If I knock that onto him, he'll leave the room to clean himself off and I can get into the filing cabinet!

'Yes!' I say brightly, focus returning. 'Pauline De La Roo, croissant. She taught me how to do this.'

I start to do the first dance that occurs to me which, based on its being such a hit last night, is once more the hand jive. Maurice sits up in his chair, jaw open as I hand-jive across the office towards him. I do an exuberant shimmy forward and in the midst of a wrist crossing, reach out and knock the green juice onto his chest.

He yelps and jumps up from his chair, glaring down at his striped shirt in dismay.

'I'm so sorry!' I try, but he doesn't hear me. He's already scooting his way out of the office door, muttering something about the shirt being a gift from Sir Anthony Hopkins.

Yes! Yes, yes! I dash over to the filing cabinet. I'll start at the top and work my way down. Only . . . Fuck. The drawer doesn't budge. It's locked. No! Keys. I need the keys to the filing cabinet. I hurry over to Maurice's desk, opening the top desk drawer and rustling through. No keys. I try the bottom two drawers. Nothing.

'Any more help, Merritt?' I mutter, scanning the walls for key-holding hooks.

Nada.

I rifle across the messy desk noticing slight flecks of gloopy green juice spotting the screen of the laptop.

'Shit. Come on, keys!' I growl to myself.

Oh, no. I can hear Maurice talking outside the office door. He's coming back. And then, without me even touching it, a blue cardboard folder flies off the desk and onto the floor. 'Merritt?!' I whisper. I pick up the folder and see a hot-pink Post-it note stuck onto the corner of it. I squint. The Post-it has Jonah's name scrawled across it, along with something else that I don't have time to decipher because the door opens and Maurice flusters in. I swipe the Post-it off the folder and tuck it quickly into my bra. Maurice dabs at his shirt with a huge wad of kitchen towel.

'I really am sorry, Mr Alabaster,' I say, darting past him and making a note to myself to send him some money for the dry-cleaning bill as soon as I can.

Outside on the street I catch my breath and lean my head back against the brick wall of the building next door. Then I reach into my bra and pull out the hot-pink Post-it, eyes greedily taking in the information.

Jonah Electric
Derwent Manor Annual Gala

There's a date scrawled right at the bottom of the Post-it. It's the day after tomorrow.

Bingo.

Chapter Twenty-Four

As soon as I get home, I grab my laptop and look up the Derwent Manor Annual Gala. I'm sent to a website that looks very slick and secretive. I press the ENTER button and am taken to an events page, where a gallery of images shows the most insanely glamorous house I've ever seen. Underneath, in an elegant typeface, there's a description of the event:

> Join Lady Derwent for her annual fundraising gala in the glorious Derwent Manor ballroom. This year's theme is 'Couples Throughout History'. We very much hope to top last year's extravaganza and raise a record sum for this year's charity – Ditch the Bullies.

Wow. Jonah must be an incredible dancer if he's going to be performing at something as swish as this. I close my eyes for a moment and imagine Jonah and I at a gala, in a ballroom, twirling around a polished parquet floor. In this vision there is no hand jive to be seen.

I scroll down the page and gasp when I see that the price of the tickets is £1,500 per head.

'Fuck me.'

I could dip into my savings? Money means nothing if I'm dead. I click on the BUY TICKETS button.

This event is now sold out.

Nooooo. I bury my face in my arms and muffle a scream. I am getting thwarted at every turn and I *need* to get into this gala! I click onto the Facebook event page and tap out a comment.

Hi there! I was wondering if anyone had any spare tickets for the gala? I so want to go and I only need one ticket. I am a solo flyer! Please comment or DM if you can help.

I immediately get three comments. One from a woman called Gloria Montpellier, who says: No solo flyers. It's a couples-themed event so you would need a partner. Then a comment from a guy with a picture of a waterfall as his profile pic – that one is just three laughing emojis in a row. The last response is from the event handler themselves.

My gosh, ever so sorry. We are fully booked out and tickets are non-transferable. Feel free to make a donation via our website and add yourself to the mailing list for news of next year's gala.

'I won't bloody be here for next year's gala!' I cry at the screen, slamming my laptop closed and rubbing my temples. A wave of tiredness flops over me. I don't think I've ever had this much happening in my life at one time. It's exhausting. With a grumble, I open my laptop again and google Jonah's names, both real and stage, narrowing the search to the last twenty-four hours in case anything new has come up. Nothing! For someone who gallivants around London so much, Jonah is a total digital recluse.

'Merritt?' I yell into the air. 'Are you there? I am very clearly flailing here! I don't think I can do this.'

I wait a few minutes, but there's no answer. I try again. 'I really did appreciate you telling me to knock over the juice, by the way! But I've reached another dead end, no pun intended.'

I wait hopefully, padding out into the living room in case she appears in there. And then into the bathroom where the mirror is. Nope. No sign.

I sulk at myself in the mirror. I've developed bit of a tan over the last few days. It makes my eyes look bright and clear and the freckles scattered over my nose have deepened.

'At least when I die a second time I'll look marginally better than I did the first,' I muse grimly. I tut at my reflection. It was a huge stroke of luck getting into the silent disco without a ticket, but a posh gala at a country house? I wouldn't have the faintest clue where to begin.

Unless . . . As swiftly as if the memory has been inserted into my brain, I remember what Aled said about Cooper writing a story about a bank heist. If he can write a story about infiltrating a bank and have it be plausible then surely, *surely* he would know how one might slip uncaught into, say, a fancy charity gala at a country house?

Plus, there's the small matter of needing to be in a couple to get in.

I pull out my phone and write the text.

I NEED YOUR HELP.

The bell on the door of the pharmacy jingles cheerily as I burst in the next morning. Jan jumps up from watching the Broadway filming of *Hamilton*, her face softening when she sees that it's only me and not someone in desperate and immediate need of diarrhoea relief – a customer type more common than any of us would prefer.

'How are you feeling, love?' Jan asks, her voice wobbling with sympathy. 'Leanne told me . . . you know . . .' Her eyes flicker down towards my crotch. She trails off discreetly, for which I am grateful.

'About the possible thrush!' Leanne calls out, her head popping out from the back, her voice resounding. An elderly woman browsing the loofah selection looks me up and down. 'Apple cider vinegar, dear. A gallon of apple cider vinegar.'

'I am . . . fine. Very well,' I say to Leanne, pasting a smile onto my face. 'Thank you so much for your assistance.'

She comes out from behind the counter and puts her hands on her hips. 'You're acting different.'

'Am I?' I shrug. 'I don't think so.'

'You are . . . What is it? Something's off . . .'

'Wait . . .' Jan says curiously. 'She's being *nice*.'

'OMG, that's it. She's being nice,' Leanne adds as if the very notion is absurd. 'What's wrong?' She dashes out from behind the counter and places the back of her hand on my forehead as if to check my temperature.

'Oi!' I shoo her away.

'Seriously, though. What's going on?'

I wonder what would happen if I told them that the reason I'm being nice is because I want help infiltrating a fancy gala so that I can find a man who has to kiss me within the next four days or else I will die once more and be swept up into a possibly unknown afterlife where my eternity could be acting as a guinea pig for a mad woman's Cupid service.

'I'm actually here because, um, I'm going to a costume party and I need your help.'

The words feel entirely foreign coming out of my mouth. This is a sentence I never expected I would say. A sentence I never wanted to say.

'Theme?' Leanne breathes, pressing her neon green nails against her chest.

'Famous couples throughout history.'

'Ah, yes, a classic. What are you thinking?'

'I'm thinking I need something that looks – but is not – expensive. The people going there are fancy as hell and I really need to blend in.'

'Ooh, how about Celine Dion and René Angélil?' Jan suggests excitedly. '*Very* glamorous.'

I shake my head. 'I'm not sure the man I'm going with would be able to pull off René.'

'A man, eh?' Leanne raises an eyebrow.

'Just a friend. Well, not even that, really.'

193

'How about Barbra Streisand and James Brolin?' Jan tries. 'You could wear a lovely updo like Barbra does in *Funny Girl*!'

'Better . . . But . . . I'm not sure they're obvious enough.'

'You *want* obvious?'

'I want to look good, but not too noticeable. Nothing too quirky – I need to look like I fit.'

'Okay so . . . basic. Well, then you want Gatsby and Daisy. You can wear something sparkly and just get your not-so-much-a-friend into a tux. Hey presto.'

I nod. 'That sounds doable.'

I screw my face up and try to remember the last party I went to. I can't, which is fine, because parties I've seen on television seem like a full-on nightmare. All those performatively jolly people, beige food, small talk, *DJs*.

Leanne grabs her phone and pulls up her calendar app. 'How long do I have to design the costume? I can try to do everything at cost, but obviously there's my time and the fittings and you'll definitely want embellishments.'

'Oh no, you don't understand.' I cut in. 'The gala is on Thursday night.'

'This Thursday night? As in tomorrow?'

I nod.

Leanne shakes her head. 'There's just no way. No way in sweet hell that I can pull that off by tomorrow. My God, Delphie. I need warning. You can't just come in here and demand time off and spectacular costumes with zero notice!'

I grimace. That's fair. 'I'm sorry,' I say. 'Do you know of a costume shop where I could hire something?'

Leanne wrinkles her nose. 'Christ, I can't let you hire.

Anything decent will be already booked out, and the fabric they use in those places is lousy. I once hired a mermaid costume from a shop and there was a literal flea in the bra. No, no. You'll spend the evening scratching and pulling and that won't be fitting for something so fancy.'

'Ooh,' Jan says thoughtfully, boxing up a bottle of Buttercup cough syrup for a customer openly disgruntled by the lack of attentive service they're receiving.

'What is it, Mum?'

'Remember that dress you wore for your Grandma Diane's seventieth birthday party? The grey silky one with the . . . thingies.' She points at her shoulders.

'The capped sleeves?' Leanne finishes pressing a finger to her chin.

'You were a bit chunkier then so it would probably fit Delphie now, and you two are about the same height.'

Leanne closes her eyes and starts mumbling to herself. 'It would need fringing, and some sort of sparkle. I could leave the capped sleeves on, yes, and then there's the feathers from . . . And the hair could . . .'

She opens her eyes and then looks me up and down three times, spinning me around with her hand and giving a final nod. 'What time are you leaving tomorrow?'

I think about the plan I've made with Cooper. 'We're going to set off at five in time for the gala to start at seven p.m..'

'In that case you'll have to be here at two.'

'Two? Ha! Are you kidding? I don't need three hours to get ready!'

'I assume you need assistance with your glam?'

'Glam?'

'Hair and make-up,' Jan purses her lips together, a know-all expression on her face. 'Are you not on Instagram, Delphie? All the movie stars get glam. They have glam teams and all sorts.'

I shake my head. 'I'm not on Instagram. Too many videos of people pointing at words.'

I don't mention that I did once sign up to Instagram, posting a selfie that only got one like from a US marine doctor. He later messaged me and asked if I would like to rate his dick. I deleted the app soon after.

Leanne and Jan give each other a look.

'Just . . . leave it with me,' Leanne says. 'Be here at two p.m.'

'Ooh, and before you go, this came for you.' Jan says, handing me a copy of *Money Maims, Money Kills* by R. L. Cooper.

'You opened it?' I tut.

'I thought it was for me. You never have stuff delivered here. I didn't know you were into crime novels!'

'I'm not.'

But I am curious to know why Aled was so excited to meet Cooper, and there was no way I was chancing the package being sent to Cooper's flat by mistake and him knowing I'd ordered his book.

I tuck the novel deep into my tote bag and glance up at the clock on the wall. 'Shit. I've really got to leg it. I've booked myself in for a manicure!'

'A manicure? Who even are you right now?' Leanne calls after me as I run out of the pharmacy.

I've been wondering the same thing myself.

Chapter Twenty-Five

Today is day seven of Merritt's ten days. This *has* to be the day I finally meet my soulmate in person. It *has* to be the day I save Merritt's fate at Evermore and, you know, my entire life. Amidst the panic there's a small, strange feeling that maybe this was exactly how it was supposed to play out. That fate doesn't want me to meet Jonah again in a park or a drawing class or a silent disco. It wants me to meet him somewhere grand and undeniably romantic. And what's more romantic than an opulent ballroom? Granted, there will be loads of other people there, which isn't ideal. But there will be champagne and spectacular lighting and probably some sort of swishy orchestral music.

Last night, before I said goodnight to Mr Yoon, I let him know that I'd arranged a food delivery for that evening and that all he had to do was answer the door. I told him I wouldn't get home until after he'd gone to sleep so would see him for breakfast in the morning. In response, he wrote me a note that said 'Go, be young and have fun!' which made me feel a little sad, though I'm not fully sure why.

As I leave for the pharmacy Cooper pokes his head round his door.

'How did you do that?' I ask. 'Know exactly when I'd be

in the hall? Have you been poking your head out every few minutes just in case? That's insane. Or, wait . . . Do you have a secret camera?' I peer up at the ceiling corners.

'You're not exactly light-footed, Delphie,' Cooper says, his hand pressed against the top of the doorframe. 'It's known across the whole ground floor.'

'Really?'

He nods his head towards the door opposite his. 'Mrs Ernestine says she knows when you're on your way out because it sounds like a herd of elephants making their way across the Serengeti.'

'Was there a point to this interaction?'

Cooper frowns and I immediately feel guilty about my snappishness, making a mental note to really try to address it if I get a chance to stay alive. Cooper was surprisingly willing to help me when I asked him the other night. Even when I told him that he would probably have to come to the gala with me – a pretty massive thing to ask of someone on such short notice. I should try to be nicer.

'Is everything okay?' I ask, softening my tone.

'Just wanted to lend you these,' Cooper says. 'I wasn't sure where in my flat they were but I eventually found them at the back of a cupboard.'

He hands me a large red jewellery box, the word CARTIER printed in silver on the top. Up close the box is worn and faded, marked in patches where it's been handled time and again.

I open the box and gasp. Nestled inside is a pair of huge diamond-and-pearl earrings in a beautifully intricate tri-angular shape.

'They belonged to Em,' Cooper explains. 'She bought them at one of the estate sales she used to love going to. I know this because she wouldn't stop telling everybody how clever she was to have found them at such a bargain price. They were made in 1922, which, as you know, is the exact year *The Great Gatsby* is set.'

I absolutely did not know that. Either way the earrings are incredible, like nothing I've ever seen before. 'You . . . Are you sure?'

This seems like a huge deal. These earrings must have such sentimental value to Cooper, and he doesn't know me well enough to know that I won't lose one (which, let's face it, isn't entirely unlikely).

He waves my question away. 'Nothing more than clever preparation. Nobody will expect you of being an interloper when you're wearing vintage diamond earrings that large.'

'These diamonds are *real*?' I yelp.

'Of course they are. Cartier doesn't do cubic zirconia.'

'Holy shit. They must be worth—'

'Enough that I would appreciate you being careful with them, yes.'

I picture myself wandering around the party, clutching my ears the whole time so that the earrings don't fall out.

'They're so heavy,' I muse, weighing them in my hands, entranced as they glitter beneath the hallway light.

'Your lobes look sturdy enough,' he replies. 'I think you can handle it.'

'I will choose to take that as a compliment.'

'As intended.'

'You know, Cooper, that's the first pleasant thing you've ever said to me.'

Cooper gives a swift shake of his head. 'I told you I liked your cactus the first time I brought a parcel to your flat.'

'You remember that?'

'I remember everything, Delphie.'

His eyes glint as he fixes me with an unsettling look that lasts a second longer than is polite. I think of his finger in the aquarium.

'Anyway!' I sort of shout in response. 'Gotta go!' I hold up the earrings. 'Got to do some ear-strength training if I'm gonna handle these bad boys. Wonder if they make miniature kettlebells for earlobes? Ha-ha.'

Cooper raises an eyebrow.

I give him a half-wave and then spin on my heel and scarper out of the building.

I reach the pharmacy to find Leanne holding aloft a pair of gold spray-painted angel wings, a beam on her lineless face.

'I thought we said Daisy and Gatsby!'

'Do you not trust me? After all these years?'

'No!' I say, eyeing Jan who has three different sets of heated hair implements plugged into the wall.

'Well, well, well. She's got what she wanted, so now the sweetness and light has buggered off. I knew it was too good to last.'

'I'm just not sure about angel wings. I said I wanted to blend in!'

'You're not going to be wearing the wings, you turnip.

I'm plucking from them for the dress. I'll use some of the feathers as embellishments, but I won't know which exact feathers and where to put them until you're in the dress.'

'Oh.'

'Yes,' Leanne echoes. '*Oh*.'

'Right, come on, Mum.' Leanne claps her hands together and looks me up and down. 'We've got some serious heavy lifting to do.'

It has taken three hours and I have felt every one of them deeply. From the shapewear that Leanne insisted she help me squidge myself into (and which she promised had never been used even though she kept glancing at Jan as she said it), to Jan's snail's pace looping of my hair over a metal tong that came perilously close to my eye four separate times. And then there was the whole fifteen minutes in which Leanne absolutely lost her shit because I wasn't keeping my eyelashes still enough for her to stick individual lashes onto my existing lashes and create a 'cat's eye vibe'.'

'Does it even matter?' I asked, to which she had to 'step outside for some air'.

When they're done, Leanne and Jan step back and nudge each other, smiling.

'Go into the blood pressure room and have a look,' Jan urges.

I head into the blood pressure booth and pull back the cupboard door that has one of those wiggly IKEA mirrors glued onto the back of it. It genuinely takes me a moment of staring before I realise that the person in the mirror is me.

Delphie Bookham. I look . . . fucking incredible. The dress hugs my body like it was custom-made for me. The silver fringing swishes when I swing from the left and then to the right. Leanne has glued the golden-tipped angel wing feathers onto the cap sleeves of the dress making it look dramatic and glamorous. My hair has uniform waves the whole long length of it. It's tucked behind my ears and is draped over one shoulder, showing off Em's incredible vintage earrings.

'I didn't have time to do actual finger waves, but I watched a YouTube tutorial on how to get the effect with tongs,' Jan says, holding up her phone and snapping pictures of my hair. 'It's come out pretty stonking! I might have a go on meself. That'll get Dan at the deli to give me a second glance, I bet.'

I lean in to get a closer look at my face. My skin looks clear and glowy, the depth of the freckles on my nose offsetting the severity of the eye make-up. My lips are painted in a glossy burgundy colour, the tone mirrored by the pale plum blush on my cheekbones.

'How did you make my eyes look so big?' I gasp. 'I look like my mum.'

'Just tricks,' Leanne says modestly. 'Your eyes are already massive to begin with.'

Tears well in my massive eyes.

'Don't you fucking dare,' Leanne hisses, jumping in front of me and flapping my face with her hands.

'I . . . I . . .' I swallow the lump in my throat. 'Thank you.' I look at them each in turn. 'You didn't have to do this and . . . you just did? Without any conditions.'

'Well, let's say first *and* second round is on you.'

If this works and I get my life back, every drink Leanne and Jan ever want is on me. Forever. I'll go to the pub with them every single week.

I say this to them and Jan pretends to faint.

'Go on. Get gone, or else you'll be late,' Leanne grins, shooing me out of the door. I give them one more round of grateful thank-yous before leaving the pharmacy.

As I walk across the road back home my face stretches into a huge smile. There is no way that Jonah won't want to kiss me when he sees me looking like this. Absolutely no way.

I think about what kissing him might feel like. Soft, I expect. And sweet. Like chocolate mousse. Then it occurs to me that I've only ever kissed one person before. And that went terribly. Shit, what if it was my fault that it went badly? What if Jonny Terry was actually a great kisser and it was me who made it awkward and sloppy? My stomach lurches at the thought.

What if, after all this, I don't know how to kiss? What if, when the time is right, I make a move towards Jonah and he can immediately spot that I have zero clue what I'm doing? And it scares him off?

I push the thought out of my head and try to focus on the way Jonah looked at me in Evermore. On the feeling of certainty I experienced in his presence.

I can do this. Merritt didn't say it had to be the world's most perfect kiss. Just that he had to kiss me.

It will be fine.

It *has* to be.

Chapter Twenty-Six

I wait for Cooper by his car, pulling my phone out and googling gala etiquette in the hopes of gleaning some tips.

'Delphie.'

I look up to see Cooper in front of me. He's dressed in a perfectly cut black tuxedo, his usually messy hair neat and shiny. He now looks like if Timothée Chalamet had an extremely tall, extremely brooding, *extremely easy-on-the-eye* arsehole of a brother. His eyes widen and flicker across my dress and then slowly over my face. He licks his lips slightly. I think he's about to pay me a compliment but instead he runs a hand over his jaw and says, 'I thought in the 1920s the feathers were worn in the headdress, not on the shoulders?'

'Alright, Miranda Priestly.'

'Who's Miranda Priestly?'

I roll my eyes.

'Nice tuxedo,' I say, ignoring his question. 'I'm surprised and impressed you managed to hire one to fit you at such late notice.' We climb into the car and I see that the pens and bottles that littered the car the other night have now disappeared. There's a brand-new air freshener hanging from the rear-view mirror. The scent is called Clean Tuscan Leather. I lean forward to sniff it. Not bad. Rather pleasant, in fact.

Cooper pulls a face. 'I already had a tux,' he says as if *of course* every man has a tuxedo on hand for any occasion.

'Oh, sorry. Forgot you're a fancy writer who probably goes to loads of fancy author events where they all blow smoke up your bum and give you awards.'

'Your entire view of the life of an author is madly skewed. Mostly it was sitting alone in front of a computer, worrying, and occasionally stopping to answer the door or make another hot drink that I didn't really want.'

'So pretty much the life you have now? But without any book to show for it?'

'You have a way of cutting right to the meanest comment you could possibly make in any given situation.'

I shrug, adjusting my shoulder sleeves because one of the feathers is poking into my skin. 'You know how when someone says something horrid to you and at the time you never have the appropriate comeback prepared? Like, you think of something withering in the middle of the night and then fixate on it, getting more and more annoyed at yourself for not saying it in the moment?'

'Of course.'

'Yeah, well, I spent the entirety of my high-school career doing that, pretty much. And soon enough I cultivated the skill of actually being able to respond immediately when someone annoyed me. And you annoy me so much. It's been good to get the field practice in.'

'It's quite a skill,' Cooper says, switching gear as we leave the city behind.

'I should put it on my CV.'

'Ten GCSEs, three A-Levels, diploma in searing on-the-spot ripostes.'

'Masters in being a gigantic bitch.' I chuckle. 'Seriously, though. Aled was so excited to meet you. I think if I'd managed to do something that made other people that giddy about me, I'd never want to stop doing it. Don't you miss it?'

'I miss it very much.'

'So why don't you—'

'Why are all the boxes of paints in your flat unopened?'

He shoots me a look and I get the hint. I clamp my mouth shut.

As we continue to drive I notice that to the left of me there's a field filled with cows and sheep. 'Cows and sheep!' I coo.

'Have you never left the city?'

'I once went to Barnet . . .'

'You mean my parents' house the other night? That's seriously the only time you've left central?'

'I went on a solo trip to Greece once. But other than that, I've never had much desire to venture out. Bayswater has everything I could ever need.'

'You didn't ever go abroad with your family? Travel with your friends?'

'My mum lives in Marfa,' I tell him.

'Marfa? Where's that?'

'It's a desert town in Texas. She lives there with her boyfriend, Gerard.'

'What does she do there?'

'She's an artist.'

'That's cool. Do you visit much?'

I shake my head. When Mum left for Marfa she said that after I'd finished my exams she'd arrange a plane ticket over there so I could see what I thought, maybe consider moving there too. But when I finished school Mum suggested that it might be more useful for me to look after the flat in London, and that anyway, the weather in Marfa was way too hot for me and that all the other residents of the commune were over forty so I would probably feel awkward and out of place.

'I've never been,' I say. 'Far too hot for me.'

There must be something in my voice because Cooper glances over, a flash of sympathy in his eyes.

'No big deal,' I say brightly. 'She's happy and that's a good thing. A really good thing. Anyway! Let's not talk about that. Totally boring.'

Cooper clears his throat. 'Okay. So, you had no gap-year jaunts then? Hen parties? Weddings in Italy?'

'Weddings in Italy? Ha!' I shake my head. 'Was never interested in any of that. I find weddings to be a bit dull and travelling seems like a waste of money.' I don't mention that I've never actually been to a wedding, let alone one in Italy.

I say it with as much conviction as I can but even to my own ears it sounds thin. Which is odd because I actively *planned* a life cocooned in my home with no one else to bother me. So why does disappointment prickle my chest?

'There's so much out there to see,' Cooper murmurs. 'So much experience to be had.'

'Yeah, thanks for the feedback, Michael Palin. Shall we put on some music?'

I don't wait for an answer before switching on London Pop FM and turning it all the way up.

Duckett's Edge looks exactly like one of those picturesque villages in *Murder in the Pretty Village*. The houses are huge with thatched roofs and doors painted in glossy heritage colours. The roads are winding and dotted with plant boxes stuffed with colourful blooms. Cooper pulls into the car park of a pub called the Bee and Bonnet and turns off the engine.

'Have you been here before?' I ask, getting out of the car and stretching my back. The sun is now lower in the sky, casting a soft golden glow over the pair of us. I fuss about with my dress so that it doesn't look quite so crumpled. Then I fluff my feathers and reach into the little silk purse Leanne has leant me, taking out a powder compact and dabbing extra carefully at my forehead and the sides of my nose.

'No.' Cooper locks the car door and brushes down his tux trousers. 'But I did do an online map search and that pub is conveniently located only a fifteen-minute walk from Derwent Manor.'

'Fifteen minutes?' I screw up my face, eyeing the slightly too small heels that Leanne has smushed me into. 'I'm not sure you've noticed but I don't ever wear heels. Never. And it's boiling. And I look as close to perfect as it's possible for me to be right now. If I get sweaty I will not look perfect anymore.'

'It's fifteen minutes, not fifteen miles. And you have that little powder thingy for the sweat.'

He doesn't say anything about me looking perfect or otherwise. In fact, when I met him by his car earlier he said absolutely zero about how I looked, even though I know that I have never, ever looked better than this.

I take my phone from my purse. There's a text from the Italian restaurant on Kensington Park Road letting me know that Mr Yoon's order has been delivered. Fab. Then I notice the time.

'Wait – another fifteen minutes and we'll be late! I thought you said we'd be inconspicuous? The two of us rocking up after it's all started will totally draw attention to our lack of invitation!'

'My plan involves us being fifteen minutes late.'

'Oh?'

'While you got much wrong about the life of an author earlier on, you did not stray too far from the truth when it came to awards. I have won two Daggers.'

'I have no idea what that means.'

'It means I write books about heists that have won respect and admiration from my peers. Getting into a charity gala without a ticket is not going to be a problem for me.'

Hmm. I'm not sure I believe him.

'We'll be there in no time,' he says confidently as we set off across the pub car park.

The back of my heel is bleeding. We're on what looks to be a never-ending country lane being followed by a lone sheep who *baa*s at us every so often as if to tell us we are going totally the wrong way.

'Are you sure this is the right direction?' I ask, not for the first time.

Cooper stops walking and rubs his hand across his jaw. 'I beg you to stop asking. I have checked and double-checked. Christ, I spent almost the entirety of yesterday making sure that this would work.'

'You did?' I ask in surprise. 'The entirety of yesterday?'

'I did,' he returns, exasperated. 'I said I would. *This* is the only way to get to the back of Derwent Manor without being seen. And then I will tell you the remainder of the plan.'

'I don't understand why you won't tell me now, though? What if it's not a good plan and I need to make adjustments? I need you to understand how important it is that this works!'

He takes a step towards me, his nose a mere inch from mine. I notice that his dark green eyes are flecked with tiny splashes of olive green. They glint, making me think of a flinted emerald. 'Because, Delphie,' he says, his voice low, 'you make cynical remarks at every possible opportunity and ask far, far too many questions.' His eyes travel over my face. 'Have *you* ever planned a heist?'

'Well, no,' I say, noticing then that he has shaved, the usual scruffy stubble shorter and neater.

'I have planned many.' He tugs at his bowtie.

'Fictional, though. Not real ones.'

'Can't you have a little fucking faith?'

I blink.

Faith. Huh.

In the absence of a suitably cynical response, I nod my head.

'Fine.'

'Fine.'

'Fine.' His eyes linger on mine for a moment longer before he turns on his heel and continues to stride down the country lane, me hobbling after him, the errant sheep trotting after me.

Soon enough we turn a corner and the rear of Derwent Manor comes into view. It is vast, and even grander than it looks in the pictures online.

'Woah,' I breathe. 'It's blummin' gorgeous. And so old! I wonder if it's haunted. I wonder if Lady Derwent sleeps in a four-poster bed. Ooh, do you think there's a scullery?'

Cooper ignores me, purposefully striding towards a tall black cast-iron fence enclosing the whole back of the building. I'm about to ask Cooper how the hell he figures we're going to get over the fence, but before I can he starts quietly counting the iron bars. 'There should be a small lock about one hundred and fifty railings to the left,' he murmurs to himself.

We start counting the bars together and, just as he said, there's a lock at number 150. The railings here are slightly thicker, and in the middle of one of them is a small rusting space for a key.

'A secret gate!' I breathe, straight-up enchanted. I think this is what having fun feels like.

Cooper reaches into his inside jacket pocket and pulls out a Swiss Army knife, inserting one of the fittings deftly into the keyhole and wiggling it from side to side, his tongue poking slightly between his teeth.

'Picking a lock!' I exclaim, impressed despite myself.

'You going to narrate this whole thing?' He flashes me a look before giving the lock one last firm yank. The hinges squeak open with a noise that suggests it's not been touched in perhaps a century.

'We have to leave you here,' I say to the sheep lingering behind us. 'We'd take you with us but it's too dangerous.'

Cooper turns to the sheep. 'Thank you for helping us to get this far,' he adds straight-faced and earnest. 'But your stench would arouse too much suspicion.'

'We will never forget you.' I reach out to pat the sheep on the head but decide against it, because Cooper is right about the stench, and *sheep* is not a good bouquet on anyone trying to attract the man of their dreams.

'Goodbye, Special Agent Balthazar,' Cooper says with a solemn bow of his head.

Special Agent Balthazar? I bark out a laugh so loud it shocks me and makes the sheep literally shit on the grass beneath him.

'Come on, Delphie,' Cooper scolds, as if he wasn't the one just fooling about. 'This ruse is a long way from over.' His eyes glint excitedly, cheeks lightly flushed. Is . . . is he enjoying himself?

We clamber up to a small grass verge until we reach some sort of outhouse connected to the main building.

Cooper reaches into his inside pocket and pulls out a folded piece of paper, opening it up to reveal a print-out of what looks like a blueprint.

'Is that Derwent Manor?' I gasp. 'You printed out *plans*?'

'Of course. How else would I know there was an outhouse?'

He hands me the paper and hops up a step to peer through the window of the outhouse. 'I need a rock.'

A task for me at last. I search for the best rock I can find. I pick up two and discard them, settling on a large round one that's heavier than the others.

'Good rock.' Cooper nods his approval, bounding back down off the step and passing it between both of his hands. 'Next, I'm going to throw this through that window.' He points at the outhouse window. 'According to the most recent fire safety report of Derwent Manor there's a fire alarm just to the left of the window. I'm going to set it off. Everyone will be brought outside for a count, at which point we will slip into the crowd. I'm betting that guests will be irritated enough by the interruption that no one will ask to see tickets for a second time. And you and I? We will smoothly saunter in with everyone else. Just like we'd always been there.'

I grin. 'I'm impressed, Cooper.'

'We can't rest until we have that first glass of champagne in our hands. That's when we'll know we have successfully infiltrated the event.'

'And I can finally, *finally* find Jonah!'

He nods, face suddenly serious again. Then he steps back and with much more force than I personally believe is necessary, he chucks the rock through the outhouse window.

Chapter Twenty-Seven

The window shatters so loudly I'm afraid the whole party must have heard it.

'Shit, Cooper! That was bonkers loud. What if—'

'There's a ten-piece swing band playing in the hall,' Cooper assures me, hopping back up to the outhouse and carefully reaching his arm into the window. 'No one heard.' He squints for a moment, feeling around the inner wall before his eyes light up. 'Got it! Okay. When this goes off, we'll go round to the front and melt in with the others. Are you ready?'

I nod furiously, my heart starting to thud. 'I'm ready!'

Cooper wrenches the fire alarm and a high-pitched siren sounds out so loudly the strength of the vibration makes my boobs and belly wobble a bit.

Cooper jumps down and together we march around the side of the building, trying to move quickly but not run. It's harder than I thought it would be, keeping cool. I'm panicking on the inside, but must present as gala-serene on the outside. Look how I belong here! See how I glide in like this is just an everyday part of my charmed life! I glance over at Cooper and yelp at the sight of blood dripping thickly from his hand.

'Shit. Cooper!'

'What? Can you see someone? Have we been made?'

'No! You're bleeding!'

He looks down at his hand. 'So I am.'

'It's really, really bleeding. It must have been the glass on the window frame.'

'Delphie, reach into my inside pocket,' he instructs. 'There's a handkerchief in there but I don't want to get blood on my tux.'

I hurriedly open up his tuxedo jacket and root around the inside pocket, feeling a multitude of bits and pieces but no fabric.

'I can't find it,' I say, frantically wiggling my hand around his pocket.

'The other side. Try the other side.'

I do and I'm now so close to Cooper that I can see the outline of his chest against the white cotton of his shirt. I can smell his soap. My heart starts to pound. It must be the sight of blood. I've never been queasy about it before but this is already quite a high-octane situation for someone who, until last week, had only spoken to four people in the last year.

'There's no hanky in there either!'

'Christ. I must have forgotten it.' Cooper stumbles slightly, at the blood loss or his surprise at forgetting something? Could be either.

The cut is bleeding really badly now. Heavily enough that in another few minutes we're going to be in a serious pickle. The fire alarm stops and we hear the sound of guests exiting the front of the hall.

'Let's just go inside, okay? We need to get that seen to. It doesn't matter if they suss us out. We can't have the both of us die for this.'

'Die? What? No. It will stop any minute now.'

'Let's use your suit jacket to stem the bleeding.'

'Then my jacket will get covered in blood!'

'Who fucking cares right now? For someone who went to Oxford you can be a bit thick sometimes.'

I press Cooper down onto the grass. He doesn't look the type to pass out, but better to be safe than squished forever beneath his massive chest. Then I get a brainwave. I reach into his inside pocket once more, pulling out the Swiss Army knife. I lift up my dress, cut a slit into the shorts part of my shapewear, ripping right around the thigh until it's fully torn off. I step out of it, immediately kneeling down and wrapping it around Cooper's hand, squeezing it as tightly as I can.

'It's working,' I whisper. While Cooper's hand remains impressively steady, mine is trembling. 'Does it hurt?' I ask.

'No. We'll be late, though. The ruse will be ruined.'

'That's not important right now.'

I continue holding the fabric in place until the bleeding subsides. And then, grabbing the Swiss Army knife again, I rip off the other thigh. As I do, I notice that Cooper is looking right at my legs, his eyes almost black. 'Yes, some of us have meat on our bones,' I say in response to his weird expression. Then my heart starts to thud again. I ignore it and wrap the other piece of fabric around his hand, tying it at the bottom.

'There,' I say. 'Looks like a fancy black bandage.'

Cooper stands up, inspecting his hand before his eyes drop down to my thighs which now have two slight muffin top bulges spilling out of the remaining shapewear.

'*Jonah* appreciates them a little chunky,' I say, pulling my dress back down.

I hear the swell of voices softening from the front of the building. Cooper hears it too.

'They're going back in,' he says. 'Come on! Hurry.'

As we reach the front of the manor, the last of the couples are disappearing into the grand porticoed entrance of the building.

'Shit. Shit, nooooo,' I mutter as a guy with a walkie-talkie stands out at the front, eyeing us with suspicion as we approach.

'Keep cool,' Cooper says, striding purposefully towards the man.

'Do you have your tickets, mate?'

'Of course not,' Cooper immediately says, with the same imperious air I know him to be excellent at, since he's been using it with me pretty much since we met. 'Our phones are inside our coat pockets which, of course, are inside the manor, abandoned during the panic of the alarm. How irritating for the fire alarm to go off and stall the festivities.'

'Coats?' the man says. 'In a heatwave?'

Cooper realises his mistake, his eyes widening in panic. This is a man unfamiliar with failing. I need to distract the bouncer away from the coats line of questioning because it can only end badly. I know what to do. I've seen plenty of old movies in which women use their feminine wiles to disarm an enemy. I'll take a crack at that.

I step in front of Cooper and smile at the bouncer, knowing that right now is the best I've ever looked in my whole life. I bat my enhanced eyelashes, open my glossy mouth and swiftly remember that I have never, ever flirted before. Not ever. I have no fucking clue what I'm doing.

'You are . . . very handsome on your face . . .' I try, immediately flailing.

'Come again?'

'And I like your . . . buttons.' I trail my hand down the buttons of the man's black shirt. Wow. Some distant part of me knows this is bad, but somehow I cannot stop. 'They're shiny buttons. I like it shiny.'

I wink at the man.

I *wink*.

Cooper darts in front of me.

'Ha-ha. Forgive her, mate. We may have already had a little too much free champagne. You know how it is . . .'

'Too much free champagne? No, mate, funnily enough I don't know how that is.'

The bouncer narrows his eyes at us and I truly think we're about to be busted when suddenly he peers down towards my knees, his eyes sliding across to Cooper. I follow his gaze to Cooper, who's frantically trying to smooth back his curls which have returned to full wild disarray after the whole window-smashing thing. The bouncer nods slowly and gives a little chuckle. 'Ah, that's why you were around the corner, eh? A little hanky-panky? My wife likes it in the open air too.'

Huh? I look down at my knees and see the green grass stains from when I kneeled down to bandage Cooper's hand. He thinks we were doing it?

I lean in. 'Kindred spirits, your wife and I!' I giggle. 'But I am parched now. You know . . .'

'Of course, love,' the man says, waving us through. 'Go in and get yourself a drink – looks like you've earned it.'

Ew. Ewwwwwww.

I hook Cooper's arm and drag him along with me to the lobby of the manor where a waiter holds a tray filled with crystal champagne flutes. Cooper plucks two of them from the tray and hands one to me, clinking his glass against mine.

'You like it shiny?' he asks, amusement lifting the corner of his mouth. 'That's a new one.'

I down my champagne and immediately grab another.

'We will never speak of it again.'

Chapter Twenty-Eight

Derwent Manor is astonishing and intimidating. As Cooper and I walk into the ballroom I can't help but gasp at the opulence. There are chandeliers that are bigger than my bathroom, the walls are painted a dark blue so inky that it could be black. Hundreds of gold gilt frames display stunning oil paintings. Holy shit, is that a Titian?

On a wide platform a pianist and accompanying swing band play Rosemary Clooney's 'Mambo Italiano' as guests twirl and sway about the room, sipping champagne and chatting like this isn't the most ridiculously luxurious thing to ever happen to them. I scan the room but I don't see any professional dancers. Perhaps they're still getting ready, warming up somewhere? Then it occurs to me that if there are guests already dancing here, why would the event planners hire professionals to do it too?

Cooper nudges me and points in the direction of another Gatsby and Daisy. I spot two more talking to each other by a table with an ice sculpture of a chubby cherub reading a thick storybook. Amongst the Daisys and Gatsbys there's an Adam and Eve, a Justin and Britney, an Elton John and David Furnish, and a Julia Child and Paul Cushing Child.

'Where is he?' I mutter as I stand on my tiptoes and search

for Jonah. 'I should go and, you know, circulate. Try to find him. The longer we're here, the more chance we have of getting thrown out. He might be in a back room or something.'

Cooper sips his champagne, appearing fully at home in this environment. A woman dressed as Elizabeth Taylor walks past, looking Cooper up and down. She gives him a coquettish little grin. Cooper holds his glass up to her, his eyes glinting like a wolf.

'I said I'm going,' I repeat. 'To find Jonah.'

He's still got his eyes on Elizabeth Taylor as he nods. 'Happy hunting,' he says distractedly.

I'm immediately pissed off.

'I'm not hunting,' I tut, wiggling uncomfortably because the torn spandex has rolled up and is now really digging into the tops of my thighs. 'I'm doing my duty to a poor man with venereal disease! Has it ever occurred to you that some of us want more than a string of bodies to fuck without ever knowing their names.'

Cooper blinks and glares down at me, the tips of his ears turning red. His eyes fix onto mine. 'I'm sure Jonah will be very pleased to see you looking so . . . good, Delphie. Very good.'

I press my hands to my chest and fake a swoon. 'Good! Very good! What a wonderful compliment, Cooper. Thank you for boosting my confidence. No wonder these women find you irresistible with flattery like that.'

God. I don't even care what he thinks anyway. He probably only agreed to help me so he could find some kinky costumed rich girl to bring home tonight.

I neck the rest of my champagne before taking Cooper's glass from his hand and draining what's left inside it. Then I hand him back both empty glasses and march off into the centre of the ballroom to find Jonah.

I have hovered around eight or nine little groups of people, trying to figure out if any one of them is Jonah. I'm having no luck at all. It doesn't help that a bunch of guests are wearing wigs, most of them actively in disguise. What if Jonah was hired to dance in costume? I'll have no chance of finding him!

No. Remain positive. You've come this far, Delphie. He's here. He has to be. And once you find him, everything is going to be okay.

I grab another flute of champagne for myself, and one to give to Jonah *when* I find him. I venture towards the hallway in search of a makeshift dressing room, but just as I'm about to leave the ballroom, the band stops playing. The tap of a microphone echoes, followed by the tinkly tones of a voice that makes my stomach drop to my knees. A voice I never, ever wanted to hear again.

I spin around, the room shuddering a little due to either the champagne or the shock, I don't know.

Standing on the stage, dressed, of course, as Marilyn Monroe in the pink dress from *Gentlemen Prefer Blondes*, is Gen Hartley. Beside her lumbers Ryan Sweeting, a little thicker-set than he used to be but still objectively handsome, especially dressed as Joe DiMaggio in full vintage baseball garb. Surprise, surprise: he's still a jock.

I take a deep breath and try to steady my heart, but the chime of her voice, so pretty and melodic, feels like someone has taken a ladle and is scooping out my insides bit by bit.

'And as you know, it's been an honour to host this event tonight on behalf of Lady Derwent, who is somewhere out there!' Gen shades her eyes from the glaring lights and gazes out over the crowd, waving as the audience clap for Lady Derwent, wherever she may be. 'And, as always, Lady Derwent and I have chosen the most deserving of causes for us all to lend our support to this evening. Ditch the Bullies helps provide training and support for school teachers so that they are better able to protect our children against bullying, which now, with the advent of social media, is as prevalent as it's ever been.'

An anti-bullying charity? My hunched shoulders soften a little. Is this Gen's way of trying to make amends somehow? Does she feel guilty for what she put me through?

'I myself was deeply affected by the trauma I endured at the hands of others during my time at high school in West London,' Gen continues. 'Pranks, exclusion, psychological warfare. So much so that I left the area. It was only recently – with the help of my husband and my own two precious little ones – that I had the courage to return when the opportunity to buy my beloved childhood home became available. It was challenging to come back. But I knew it was where I belonged.'

Beside her, Ryan rubs his wife's shoulder, nodding sympathetically.

Are you fucking kidding me? She's using my story as a

way to ingratiate herself with these people? To make them think she was ever some kind of victim? *She* was the bully. She was the one doing the excluding and playing the pranks. The room tips slightly. I cannot feel this way again. I look down at my hands and try to focus on my prettily painted nails. But, of course, I can still hear Gen speaking in the altruistic tones of someone who has never put a foot wrong.

'The entertainment will continue with performances from John the Magician and Elbow the Singing Dog. In the meantime, please do follow the links on your digital tickets to the donation site and give all you can. We'll do an announcement of the final tally in one hour. Esteemed guests, we'd love this to be our most successful gala yet. For the children. So if *you* hate bullying, prove it!'

The audience claps heartily and I don't know if it's the adrenaline or just the chaos of the last few days but I suddenly feel a bolt of energy through me. It's unlike anything I've ever felt before, making the hair on my arms prickle and my heart pound in my ears like an intense drumbeat pumping me up for battle. How dare she? How *dare* she? I march towards the stage. I *want* her to see me. To see that I know what a liar she is. That not everyone in here is taken in by her false sweetness and saccharine voice.

Gen spots me, her eyes widening. She nudges Ryan and when he catches sight of me, he narrows his eyes as if trying to place me.

How dare they stand up there and talk about being kind when they made my life hell on earth? How can they pretend so easily?

Fury worms its way through my body, so hot that I'm sure my eyes must be crackling with it like something out of a sci-fi movie. I walk up to the platform and face Gen.

'Delphie Bookham?' Her jaw drops as she looks me up and down. 'I can't believe—'

'Oh, fuck off, Gen.' My heart surges. The energy running through my limbs makes me feel like I could lift a truck. My head is filled with flashes from school – a grim montage like the one from Merritt's video.

'Delphie!' Gen hisses. 'What are you—'

'I thought I told you to fuck off,' I blurt out, the nearby microphone making my words reverberate around the ball-room. My voice, combined with a spine-tingling shriek of feedback means that the bubbling chatter of the gala immediately stops, an uncomfortable hush settling over the room. My eyes mist with tears. I squeeze them away. I will not fucking cry in front of them.

'You say bullying ruins lives?' My voice is trembling despite the champagne that has dulled my nerves. 'You bullied me! You ruined *my* life. My crime?' I shake my head. 'I still don't fucking know.' I step closer to Gen and lower my voice. 'What did I do to you? I was your best friend. And you treated me like you hated me. Why?'

Gen steps towards me to move the microphone that's catching our entire conversation. But for a brief, terrifying moment I think she's going to push me or trip me or stick something in my hair. Instinctively, I lift one of the full glasses of champagne and swish it in her face. It's a pre-emptive act of self-defence, one that I immediately realise was not necessary. Gen just stands there blinking, liquid sliding down her face, marking her dress. Her lips curl with fury. I place the glass on the floor, open my mouth to say something else, but the angry, alcohol-boosted adrenaline that filled my veins just a moment ago has trickled away, all used up. I have nothing else to say.

I turn to see that every person in the room is watching us. Cooper is right there in the middle standing next to the Elizabeth Taylor woman. His lips are pressed together in a gloomy line.

And then, behind him, I see the dazzling blue eyes I've been thinking about since the day I first saw them. He's dressed in a black-and-white-checked flannel shirt and khaki chinos. It's clearly a costume, but I don't know who he's supposed to be. Even in such an ugly outfit he's still ridiculously handsome, hair perfectly neat, shoulders pleasingly broad. He's peering at me curiously, head tilted to the side. Merritt said that memories are wiped when accidental visitors arrive at Evermore. I need to tell him who I am.

I go to him.

Chapter Twenty-Nine

I'm with him. Standing in front of him. The two of us in a small storeroom, just off the main ballroom. He looked surprised when I asked him to come with me but did it anyway. To his mind, I'm a complete stranger. My stomach sinks.

He looks around the room; I do the same. It's lined with shelves stocked with candles and candlesticks, lightbulbs of every size and shape, and a couple of chandelier pieces in need of repair.

'A whole room just for light-related paraphernalia,' I remark, my voice a little shaky.

'How the other half live,' he adds, resting his attention on me.

'My name is Delphie,' I say.

'Jonah.' He holds out his hand to shake mine. I do and a swoosh of heat warms my stomach as I recall the first time he touched me, how we just stood there holding hands like it was the most natural thing in the world. He smiles. He doesn't much seem to mind that I've dragged him away from the party. I wonder what he thinks is happening right now. I should probably explain myself.

'Are you here tonight to dance?' I ask instead, putting off the conversation I actually need to have. 'For a gig?'

KIRSTY GREENWOOD

He frowns slightly. 'How did you know I was a dancer?'

'Oh! Yes, so . . . Someone mentioned it out in the ballroom. Some guy? He said you shared an agent . . .'

'There's another Alabaster Disaster here tonight, is there?' He laughs. 'Sorry. In-joke – my agent's a little less than effective these days. No. I'm here off the clock. As a plus-one.'

Oh! Maurice must have had the Post-it note not because Jonah was hired here tonight, but because he wasn't available to be hired anywhere else. 'Who are you supposed to be?' I ask.

Jonah laughs and brushes a tiny bit of lint from the chest of his flannel shirt. 'It's a bit of a niche reference, to be honest. Have you seen the film *Beetlejuice*?'

I shake my head.

'It's this Tim Burton movie from the eighties. I love it. When the girl I'm seeing invited me to accompany her here tonight, I wanted us to dress as Adam and Barbara from the film. Like I said, niche.'

'The . . . the girl you're seeing?'

'Yeah. It's pretty new, but going well, I think! I . . . Why did you want to speak to me? I'm intrigued. It's not every day a mysterious Daisy Buchanan hurries me away to a light-related paraphernalia room.'

'Yeah, I'm sorry for dragging you in here like a total weirdo. It's so busy out there, though. You must think this is all very strange.'

He laughs lightly. 'You seemed pretty angry back there. I wasn't about to say no to you. Although I am, you know,

228

curious.' He leans back against the wall. 'Why did you want to talk to me?'

Because he is perfect. Perfect and gentle and soulmate-y. I take a deep breath, opening my mouth to explain why I need to speak to him. But then I halt. Despite thinking about it nonstop I actually have no clue where to begin explaining any of this. How the buggering hell do you start a conversation so big? So earth-shaking? I can't exactly tell him that we've already met but he doesn't remember because we were both dead at the time. But I can't start off too slowly either because it's taken me this long to find him and I no longer have the time to get to know him a little better first. I just need him to kiss me. As soon as possible. Then later down the line I can explain things at a pace that won't potentially melt his brain – maybe even go on a first date . . .

I lift my chin and stare Jonah right in the eye. I look more than 'good, very good' tonight. I look pretty. Maybe even beautiful. And if Jonah was attracted to me in my nightie and pickle-green socks, freshly dead, then surely, *surely* he won't mind if I just, you know, kiss him. And if it's a good kiss, which, despite my lack of experience, it has to be because *soulmates*, he will kiss me back. It will be *instinctive*, nothing at all like the terrible kiss I had with Jonny Terry when I was eighteen. And . . . well, I don't need to think further along than that. I just need him to kiss me *back*. That's what Merritt wanted. For him to kiss me. There's nothing else as important as that.

Okay. I've made my decision. There's no point in waiting any longer. I reach out my hands to take his, just like we did in Evermore. I frown as the spark that ignited my body the first time I touched him is absent. Then I look into his eyes, and my stomach dips as I realise they are not interested and a little horny like they were when we met in the waiting room, but flicking from left to right as if looking for help. I peer down at our hands and find that his are just hanging limply in mine. I drop them.

'Um . . . I'm sorry,' I say quickly. 'I thought . . . I thought we had . . . And I just wanted to . . .' I trail off.

Jonah starts to fidget with the collar of his flannel shirt. 'You're very pretty. Incredibly so. But as I said, I'm seeing someone. She's just out in the ballroom—' He cuts himself off and looks towards the door awkwardly. My heart starts to judder with panic. He can't go! If he goes then it will all be over!

'No! Stay! Your date will wait, this is important!'

'Excuse me?' his voice is now openly sharp.

Why did I say that? And why is my voice now coming out as a squeak? I sound absolutely batshit.

Jonah's eyes widen. He looks scared? Shit. No. I don't want to scare him. I need to start over again. Try a different tack. A gentler, less crazy, less tipsy approach. But he's now backing away from me.

I need more time with him. He needs to get to know me. But I won't get more time unless he . . .

'Just kiss me!' I shout in a panic, leaning forward again. He sidesteps so that my lips hit nothing but air.

Jonah looks around in dread, reaching behind him for

the door handle, jerking it open and running backwards out into the corridor and down towards the ballroom.

'Jonah, no!' I call out. 'You don't understand! Let me explain!'

I follow him out of the room, stumbling on these stupid shoes. I kick them off and start to run after him. I can't lose him. Not again. Not after everything. I don't have time!

I chase him into the ballroom where the band are now playing some swoony Harry Connick Jr song, the beautiful guests whirling elegantly about the ballroom floor. Jonah disappears into the crowd. No, no, no. I can't lose him again! It's been so hard to find him. This is my only chance!

'Jonah!' I cry out, my voice emerging as a screech. It's a noise so blood-curdling it makes the band stop playing.

'Not this lass again,' someone mutters beside me. The crowd clears and there's Jonah, right in the middle of the dancefloor. I scurry over to him. The other guests are watching us.

'I . . . I don't know what you want, but whatever it is I'm not interested.' He holds up his palms like he's trying to calm me down.

'You are interested, though,' I say. 'Just let me explain . . .'

'Yeah, maybe another time.' He takes another step backwards.

'There isn't time for another time!' I throw my arms up in frustration. 'You're never where you're supposed to be! You didn't show up at the life-drawing and then by the time I got to the Shard—'

I cut myself off as Jonah's mouth drops open. He looks genuinely terrified. Beside him, a pretty dark-haired woman in a floral dress grabs his hand, looking at me curiously.

'Nooooo,' I murmur, except it's not so much a murmur as a whine.

Shit. I am making this much, much worse.

'What's going on here?' It's Gen. Her dress is still stained but dry, hair perfect as ever. 'Are you okay, Jonah?' she asks. She knows him?

'How do you two know each other?' I frown between the two of them.

Gen frowns at me. 'Jonah is my dear friend. He's danced at many of my events.'

'I've double-checked and she's definitely not on the list.' Ryan lumbers up, pointing at an iPad. 'She's an interlooper,' he adds. 'Is that how you say it, babe? Interlooper? Or is it interloperer?'

Gen ignores him. She smoothly signals for the band to start playing again and gently shoos the crowd away from us. Jonah is staring at me, complete confusion crumpling his beautiful face. Beside him, his companion squeezes his hand.

My eyes fill with tears again. I wipe them away furiously. On the periphery of my vision, I see Cooper approaching.

'Have you come here for some sort of revenge?' Gen asks with a frown. 'Just move on and forgive me already! I was an idiot in school. And so was Ryan. We were lost. Trying to find our way. Secondary school is a jungle, you know?'

'You've literally just used what you did to me and twisted

it on stage so that *you* were a victim! Take some responsibility, Gen.'

'I'm supporting Ditch the Bullies! I *am* taking responsibility!'

'You never reached out to me. All these years you could have got in touch. Apologised.' My voice breaks. 'Why didn't you?'

She looks tired. For a moment my defences weaken and I see the girl I used to play with. The one who let me use her roller-skates when mine broke. The one who I giggled with until two in the morning when she slept over at my house. And that makes me remember the girl I used to be. Unafraid and open.

She blows the air out from her cheeks. 'I had totally forgotten you even existed, to be honest, Delphie. And anyway, I was a total shit to everyone back then, not just to you.'

'Babe, we weren't that bad,' Ryan pipes up, adjusting his tight baseball trousers. 'At least, not from what I remember. I don't fully remember. You're Delphie, right? Red hair? You're the one that did that drawing?' He sniggers and Gen elbows him.

'You'd forgotten?' I stutter. 'You had forgotten I existed?' A punch to the gut.

I have thought about Gen and Ryan every single day since I walked out of school for the last time.

I look between the two of them. Gen's phone buzzes and she pulls it out of her tiny silver bag, glancing at it briefly before looking back at me.

'I have to announce the next act. So will you forgive us?'

I open my mouth but once again nothing comes out. I'm empty. I'm done. I turn to apologise to Jonah, to try and fix things, but he's disappeared once more. Probably run for safety, or gone to kiss that other woman instead of me.

'Are you ready to leave, Delphie?' Cooper says airily from beside me. He takes my arm. 'I'm bored.'

Gen gasps. 'Oh, wow, you're R. L. Cooper?' She smiles widely, as if our own interaction is now a distant memory. 'I'm Gen – Gen Hartley. We met at Harrogate Festival two years ago: I was running a charity event with the author Peter Johnson, for the Royal Literary Fund.'

'I have zero recollection,' Cooper says, giving her the smile that seems to make all other women swoon. It does the same with Gen. She glows pink, her tongue poking out a bit.

'Of course, you must have had so many people fawning over you that day.' She bites her lip. 'Ooh, could I quickly take a pic for my Instagram?' she hands her phone to Ryan and hisses at him to take a picture. He nods dumbly, ready to obey without question, just like he always did.

Cooper shakes his head, his smile even wider, as he lowers his voice and leans in close to Gen. 'Gosh, I'm so flattered, Gemma, but I'm afraid I'd rather scoop out my own eyeballs than spend another moment talking to you. Do have a wonderful evening, both of you.' He nods to Ryan, who gives a thumbs-up back. 'Come on, Delphie. Let's go.'

Chapter Thirty

It's only when we get outside that I realise I've abandoned my shoes inside Derwent Manor. Luckily, we're in the middle of a heatwave and the grassy country lanes are as dry as dust. It is, however, disconcerting now that the sun has set into pitch black. I could step in anything.

Cooper uses his phone torch to light the way.

'Are you okay?' he asks as we pass by the field that is now empty of sheep.

I don't think I am.

Not because of seeing Gen and Ryan, which would have been bad enough on its own, but because I can now firmly surmise that I have unequivocally failed at this chance Merritt gave me. I lost him. I lost Jonah. He looked at me like I was someone to be afraid of. He didn't kiss me. He's never going to kiss me. Which means not only have I lost the potential love of my life but I'm going to die again in three days. And while I never thought my life was particularly special, these past few days have turned everything I thought I knew on its head. Things have been stressful and weird and scary and overwhelming. Yet, somehow, I've felt more alive than I ever thought possible.

'I'm fine,' I say, although I can feel the tears that seem to come so easily now popping up to say hello. God knows what will happen to Mr Yoon.

'I'm starting to think that finding this Jonah was about more than informing him of an STD?'

'There never was an STD!' I snap as a soft twig breaks beneath my bare foot. 'I've never even . . . I just . . . I said that in the moment because I didn't know you. I did think there was something real between Jonah and me . . . and I needed there to be . . . I *needed* him to be . . .' I trail off. It's too difficult to explain, and especially to someone like Cooper. I sigh heavily. 'I've just fucked it up, like everything else.'

'I'm sure it's not so bad.'

'Cooper, I just chased after a man and humiliated the pair of us in front of a room full of people.'

'I'm sure he was flattered by your determination.'

'Oh, please.'

Cooper's voice softens. 'Sometimes, when people want to go, it's easier to just let them.'

'I don't want to talk about it,' I say, wiping away another uninvited tear. 'And especially not with you. I just want to go home.'

'I understand.'

We continue trundling along the country lane in miserable silence when suddenly there's a weird rustling sound from above. Both of us stop walking and look skywards. We are rewarded for our curiosity with a massive splatter of rain bucketing all over us. An abrupt crackle of lightning illuminates the shock on our faces, immediately backed up by a rollicking clap of thunder. Now? It's going to rain and thunder and lightning fucking *now*? It's been the hottest summer since records began, it hasn't rained in a whole month. But it suddenly decides to when I'm stuck on a country lane, barefoot, crestfallen, embarrassed and marked by death?

I laugh. I laugh and I cry and I shake my head. 'Perfect!' I yell at the sky over the roar of the thunder. 'Genuinely. Your timing is fucking sublime!'

'Delphie, come on!' Cooper shouts, his hair already drenched. 'Don't just bloody stand there!'

I look down at my feet, the rain already softening the previously dry ground beneath me. I lift up my foot. There's a squelch.

'Come on, we'll get soaked.'

I can't seem to take my eyes off my feet. I'm going to die in three days anyway. What does it matter if I get soaked? If I drown in this rainfall? Literally nothing matters anymore.

Cooper approaches me. 'I'm gonna carry you back to the car, okay?'

I shrug half-heartedly, sort of expecting him to swoop me up into a cradle and carry me like I weigh nothing at all. But no. He does not do that. He scoops me up – yes, without any effort – but he throws me over his shoulder like I'm a sack of potatoes, which, frankly, after this shitshow, I might as well be. My head dangles down his back and when Cooper runs along the country lane my head starts to bounce against his butt.

'Cooper! Put me back down!' I yell because this is just too much humiliation even for me. But the rain and the thunder is so resounding that he doesn't hear me. I wonder briefly if I will get a bruise because while Cooper's bottom is a little rounder than average it is still pure solid muscle. It's like my head is bopping against a basketball.

I give in, deciding to just dangle, and soon enough we're back in the car park, where Cooper places me on my feet outside the car. He reaches into his inside pocket for the keys, and then into his other inside pocket. He pulls out the Swiss Army knife and the architectural plans and a wallet. Then he takes off his tuxedo jacket and dives into his trouser pockets.

'Fuck,' he barks. 'My car keys. They must have fallen out when you were looking for my handkerchief. Did you not hear them fall?'

'Of course you're blaming me,' I shout, rain sweeping my mascara right into my eyeball. I lift my hands and try to shield my face. 'You could have lost them at any time. Just use the Swiss Army knife to unlock the car door. It worked on the gates!'

Cooper glares at me, a wet lock of hair falling into his eye. He swipes it away. 'It won't work. This is a special lock. It's made so that it can't possibly be picked.'

His jacket is slung over his shoulder and his tuxedo shirt is so wet it has become see-through and plastered onto a torso which looks to be as solid as his bum. I can't seem to take my eyes away. My mouth feels dry. I feel the rain on my lips and catch some with my tongue. Cooper stares at me for a moment, panting, the rain dripping from his eyelashes.

'The pub,' he says suddenly, pointing at the warm yellow

lights of the Bee and Bonnet. Without asking he scoops me up again, flinging me over his shoulder and running towards the pub, my head once again bouncing against his thoroughly soaked bum. For fuck's sake.

Cooper flings open the pub door and plops me onto my feet inside.

'Fucking hell!' I cry out dramatically. Only we're now out of the rain and this pub is very, very quiet. There's the gentle sound of a radio playing Adele, and only three other customers – a slightly damp grey-haired couple and their grey-haired pug – in the whole place.

The bartender looks down at the puddle we're making on the stone floor and sighs. He disappears into the back, returning with a slightly damp towel that looks like it might have already been used on the grey-haired couple and their dog. Cooper grabs it and rubs his hair and face before handing it to me. I do the same and then place the towel on the floor to simultaneously wipe my feet and soak up our rain puddle. I hand it back to the bartender, who hangs it back on the hook, ready for the next wet customers, I assume.

'Do you have rooms available?' Cooper asks the bartender.

'Rooms?' I pull a face. 'I can't stay here. Just call the AA or something? They'll fix your car. Or let's get a taxi? I really do just want to go home.'

Cooper huffs. 'I wouldn't feel great about asking anyone to drive out to us in these terrible conditions. Would you?' He looks at me like I've just suggested he shit in a Jiffy bag and post it to his mum.

He's right, though. It's apocalyptic out there. I definitely don't want anyone driving in that. I shake my head.

'Look,' Cooper says his eyes softening a smidge. 'We'll wait it out and I'll call my friend in the morning. He has a spare set of keys to the car.'

What other choice do we have?

I look up at the bartender. 'What he said. We need a couple of rooms.'

'That won't be a problem,' the barman says, indicating the empty pub. 'Now what do you two want to drink?'

'Alcohol,' Cooper says bluntly.

'And plenty of it,' I add, burying my wet head in my hands.

As pubs go, it's not the worst one to be stuck in – it's cosy, the chairs are soft, and the alcohol in Duckett's Edge is half as expensive as it is in London. Cooper and I have settled ourselves into a corner by a crammed gallery wall filled with oil paintings of women, each one in a different artistic style – an abstract nude, an impressionist woman in a wild garden, a full-on portrait in a classical Renaissance sort of style. Cooper is drinking whisky neat because of course he is, and I am having vodka martinis, sans olives. The drinks have been made with a very old, very sweet, possibly out-of-date vermouth because – as the barman said – 'this is not Chiltern bloody Firehouse'.

I reach into my bag for some bobby pins and braid my wet hair into its usual style until it's safe and secure.

A young, extremely pretty woman in denim shorts walks

by our table. I wait for Cooper to meet her gaze with that flirty look he's always dishing out, but he doesn't. He just plays with a beer mat, brows furrowed.

'Are you okay?' I ask. 'Only a very hot woman just walked past and you didn't notice.'

'I'm not some sort of Casanova, you know.'

I raise an eyebrow. 'Tell that to the queue of women outside your flat.'

Cooper shakes his head. 'Humans need company.'

'Sure.' I say with an eye-roll. '*Company*.'

He looks at me then, serious. 'I assume you've never felt lonely then. If you had you wouldn't be so judgy about people doing whatever they can to avoid that particular feeling.' He sighs lightly. 'Even if it doesn't work.'

'I'm sorry.' I say, my gaze flicking up to meet his. 'I didn't know.'

He tears a bit of cardboard from the corner of the beer mat. I watch him fiddle with it, feeling ignorant for making such assumptions. Surely I know him better than that now.

'So, then . . .' I start to ask, and then clamp my mouth shut.

'What? Go on?'

'Why not one woman? If you're lonely, surely sticking with one person – regularly – would be better?'

Cooper puts down his scrap of beer mat. 'I don't date because I've never met anyone that made me feel like—'

'Oh, fuck!' I yell, my heart suddenly lurching as I remember. 'I won't be there tonight to check on Mr Yoon.'

'Why do you need to check on Mr Yoon?'

I shrug. 'I check he's put his cigarettes out at night and turns off his gas – you know.'

'Has he left his cigarettes lit before?'

'Well, no. But his memory is foggy. He's become pretty forgetful this past year.'

'Mr Yoon will be fine,' Cooper says, taking a sip of his drink. 'He might be getting older but that man is sharper than the pair of us.'

'How would you know?'

'Because I've yet to beat him at a game of poker.'

I frown. 'You play cards with Mr Yoon?'

Cooper nods, flipping his beer mat between his hands. 'Three weekday afternoons a week. We have lunch and a game.'

'You make him lunch?'

'I *buy* him lunch. He would not like my cooking.'

'Wait, are you the one who got him hooked on those fizzy cola-bottle sweets?'

Cooper laughs. 'I brought them once. He wolfed them down, so I brought them again.'

I exhale. 'You can't keep buying them. They're not good for him.'

'Delphie, he's eighty-something. Let him have some joy.'

'I just want him to be okay,' I say. I bite my lip as I think about what the hell is going to happen to him when I'm gone.

'Listen,' I lean closer to Cooper. 'Mr Yoon is waiting for a council assessment. He needs extra care. But the waiting list is long.'

'Oh. I didn't know that.'

'Yeah. And I was going to take over his care until they sorted it, but . . . If for some reason I'm, you know . . .'

'What?'

'Like, incapacitated or something, would—'

Cooper leans back, an amused twitch lifting the corner of his mouth. 'Why on earth would you be incapacitated, Delphie?'

I tut. 'It's hypothetical, okay? I just want to know that if anything should happen to me then someone will take care of Mr Yoon.'

Cooper fixes his gaze onto mine as if he's trying to get a peek inside my brain. 'You really care about him, don't you?'

I look away and take a large sip of my martini. 'I just want him to be, you know, looked after.'

'Okay. In the unlikely event of your incapacitation, I solemnly swear to make sure Mr Yoon is taken care of. Of course.'

I meet Cooper's eyes again, relief and vodka warming my limbs. 'Really? You will? I mean . . . you would? In the, uh, unlikely event of my—'

'Mr Yoon will be fine,' he cuts in. 'It's cool that he has you to look out for him.'

My shoulders unclench, although not as much as I might hope they would, given Cooper's promise that Mr Yoon will be looked after without me. The simple fact is that I've got three days left on earth and I'm stuck with my admittedly not-quite-so-despicable neighbour instead of kissing my literal soulmate who has the power to save my life.

But then what would I being doing on my last three days alive if I *wasn't* in this situation? If I hadn't been sent on this ridiculous mission by Merritt? I'd probably be at home in the flat I was born in. Staring at my latest sketchbook and pencils purchase, inventing any reason to avoid actually using them. I'd be watching true crime documentaries about innocent women being taken in by those they loved – a genre of which there is a depressing amount of content to choose from. I'd be seeing Mr Yoon, of course. I'd go to work, probably still avoiding talking to Leanne and Jan beyond surface-level work bullshit. But mostly, I'd be on my own. Hiding. And my life would just roll on in a series of 'typical days', just like on Merritt's DVD. There'd probably not be many more worst moments. But there definitely wouldn't be any best moments either.

It hits me like a kick to the stomach.

I've wasted it.

I've wasted my life.

I excuse myself and take my phone to the ladies' room to call Mum.

There's no answer.

Chapter Thirty-One

'No, no, nope. Absolutely not.'

The bartender looks around the pub, helpless. I follow his gaze, astonished that it seems to have filled up with people while me and Cooper were drinking in the corner. 'I didn't expect it to get so busy,' he says. 'An oddly large amount of people got caught in the rain and nearly all of them wanted rooms. Are you two not a couple?'

'No,' Cooper declares.

'Absolutely not,' I say at the same time. 'Hence why we asked for two rooms.'

The barman shrugs. 'You'll just have to share. The others have already paid now.'

'Dammit.'

Cooper suddenly chuckles.

'You think this is funny?' I cross my arms.

'This reminds me of—' He catches my fury and doesn't finish. 'Nothing. Don't worry. It's a double bed. We'll top and tail.'

This situation could not get any worse.

'It's a small double, yes,' the barman says with an apologetic cringe.

I stare hard at Cooper. 'I'm not about to be that cowbag

who makes you sleep on the floor but you better not touch me, pal.'

Cooper takes a step forward so that his chest is almost touching mine. His gaze travels across my hair, then my eyes and nose, resting on my lips for a moment, before he meets my eyes again, a slight smile briefly crossing his face. 'Not even if you begged me to, Delphie.'

The barman is grinning, looking between us, but stops when I give him my iciest glare. I hold my hand out for the key, which he plonks into my palm.

Inside the room I immediately see that 'small double' was a generous description. This bed is barely bigger than a single. The decor is nice at least – fresh white cotton sheets and pretty silvery damask wallpaper. If I was alone I'd be quite pleased at the thought of spending an evening in here. But I'm not alone.

'Shall I shower first or you?' I ask, grimacing at my dirty feet and the still-wet dress which, while perfect for a fancy party, is going to be hellish to try to sleep in. I open the wardrobe, pleased to see a few extra sheets in there. I'll just wrap myself up in one of those as a makeshift nightie and then I won't be in danger of scratching my eye out with an errant feather.

'Actually, you go first,' I say. 'I need to take my braids out.'

Without a word, Cooper disappears into the bathroom. I hear the hiss of the shower, clouds of fragrant steam billowing out from under the door. I get an unsolicited image of him in there. Ugh. The steam is making the room even warmer. I open the window. It takes three yanks to get the stiff handle to loosen.

I organise the pillows so that there's one at each end of the bed and then perch gingerly on the edge and wait impatiently for him to finish so I can wash this whole day off. When Cooper eventually emerges in a haze of steam, a towel slung around his hips, I gulp like a nervous cartoon character. His arms are huge and strong-looking; his torso is as muscled as I suspected, still glistening with water droplets from the shower. I've never seen a naked man up close and – oh, holy heck – it's disorientating. How can someone with the face of a surly English professor casually have the body of a Dothraki? I wonder what it must be like to wander through life knowing you had all that beneath your clothes. It's probably why he has so many women buzzing around his place – he wants someone to show off to, probably. I tut.

Cooper stands completely still and watches me watching him, a surprised grin on his face. He raises an eyebrow.

'It's purely scientific interest,' I blurt out. 'I've never seen a naked man up close and so naturally I am a little curious.'

'What about Jonah? He remained clothed while you hooked up all over town?'

Shit. My brain is malfunctioning. 'Hot water is for me!' I inexplicably say, disappearing into the bathroom and leaning back against the doorframe to catch my breath.

Out of the shower, I take the earrings over to Cooper. He's already lying in the bed, propped up at the opposite end to the headboard.

The extra sheet has worked well as a nightie – I've managed to wrap it around myself twice, tucking it in at the top so it's as secure as if I had been sewn into it.

'Here you go,' I say, pressing the jewels into his hands. 'Thank you for letting me use them.' I massage my earlobes, which I believe the earrings have now lengthened by at least a couple of millimetres.

Cooper slips the earrings into the inside pocket of his jacket which is hanging off the bedpost beside him.

'I'm sorry about Jonah,' he says, resting his hands behind his head. His makeshift shapewear bandage has gone, replaced with a plaster he must have got from the first aid kit in the bathroom cabinet.

I head over to the window to close the blind, only to find that it's somehow jammed at the top. I pull hard and a bunch of dust flies into the air. I decide to just leave it alone; while the rainfall has cooled the air a little, it's still boiling hot, and the room isn't overlooked by anything other than the tall trees of the countryside.

'His costume was a bit obscure.'

'I liked it,' I say in a small voice.

I liked everything about Jonah. Or at least, I thought I did. But then at the gala, the sparkling, magical connection I felt with him in Evermore had changed.

I switch off the bedside lamp and the full moon shines brightly into the room, casting a silvery glow over everything, including Cooper, who looks like he's been sculpted from platinum.

I avert my eyes and climb into bed, scooching myself as close to the edge as I can without falling out.

A breeze rustles outside the window, bringing the scent of wet leaves and fresh, clean, post-rain air. I'm struck by how beautiful it smells – like open space and honeysuckle and soil. I've never smelt anything like that before in London. They might have a Diptyque shop at Evermore, but surely only earth could smell like this. I take in a lungful of air and try to commit the exact scent to memory.

'Are you crying?' Cooper asks, grazing the silence.

'No. Not at all.'

Cooper shuffles and then, from the opposite end of the bed, his hand grabs mine. I gasp with the shock of it. But I don't pull away. I can't seem to.

My tears stop.

We stay there in the silence for around five minutes just holding each other's hand. I'm starting to wonder if Cooper has fallen asleep when he slowly begins to circle his thumb across the base of my thumb. It must take him a whole fifteen seconds to complete one circle. A bolt of desire kicks right in the pit of my stomach, which shocks me enough that I jolt, my foot making contact with some part of Cooper's face.

'Fuck!' Cooper growls, sitting up in bed, his hand no longer holding mine. I bolt upright to see him covering his nose with both hands.

'You did that on purpose.'

'I didn't!'

He drops his hands, eyes locking onto mine. 'You absolutely did.'

The look of shock on his face sends a bubble of laughter into my throat. 'It was an accident,' I hoot. I lean forward for a closer look. 'You're not even bleeding!'

'Hmmm. I suppose you did warn me not to touch you,' he murmurs, his voice suddenly light.

'Not even if I begged you to,' I reply. My voice has gone all croaky.

I notice then that his eyes look completely black. Like his pupils have swallowed his irises whole. My breath quickens.

'We have fun, don't we?' he murmurs. 'Me and you.'

I think of how annoying he is. How frustrated I get when he's near. How, before I fall asleep, I've started thinking of comebacks to use on him, things that might make his lip twitch in amusement.

'Yes,' I whisper, my heartbeat quickening.

Cooper tilts his head to the side, reaches out a hand, and gently wraps the ends of my hair around his fist.

'Jonah is a fucking idiot,' he says, voice low.

I blow out the air from my cheeks, feeling suddenly hot at the soft pull of my hair in his hand. 'I mean, I came on a little strong to Jonah. Sort of locked him in a room with me? Idiot. Very dumb of me. I should have taken it slowly. But alas, time has not been on my side.'

Why am I talking so quickly? Why am I using the word 'alas'?

Cooper's eyes mellow. He removes his hand from my hair and uses it to hold my chin between finger and thumb, lifting it so that my face is half in the moonlight. Then, just as I had started to hope he would, he leans forward and presses his lips cautiously against mine.

That felt . . . Oh, no. That was not supposed to feel like *that*.

He pulls away and stares at me hard, his own breath hastening. Then he kneels up on the bed, hooks an arm around me and roughly scoops me upwards so that I'm also on my knees, my torso pressed completely against his.

I gulp. 'Are . . . Is this because you're lonely?' I say, my cheeks reddening. 'Because I—'

'No, Delphie. This is because today is the first day in five years that I haven't felt lonely. Not one bit.'

He grabs my face with both hands then and kisses me again, his tongue dipping softly against mine. I melt and my entire body starts to pulse in time with my heart, the beat of which has accelerated to a hum. I kiss him back, swinging my arms around his neck, one hand running up into his dark curls, the other trailing down to his arm, which feels solid and sure beneath my fingers. I squeeze and make a noise I don't think I've ever made before – a sort of half-gasp, half-squeak.

'I thought you hated me,' Cooper murmurs, trailing his mouth across my throat, his bottom lip like velvet against my neck.

'I do,' I breathe, tilting my head back because whatever he is doing feels like magic on my skin. 'But you hate me too, so . . .'

'I despise you, Delphie,' Cooper groans into my mouth.

My body takes over and I kiss him harder, my tongue exploring his. I feel how hard he is and go dizzy with the pull of it, the anticipation.

I pull back, breathing heavily. 'I . . . I . . .'

'What is it?' Cooper asks, leaning in to kiss my shoulder and then my earlobe and then my mouth again.

'I'veneverdonethisbefore,' I blurt out.

Cooper leans back, his chest rising and falling quickly. 'Never done what?'

'I'm a virgin,' I say. And then I start to laugh because it sounds so unlikely but also because I'm a little embarrassed. Which I know I shouldn't be because past Delphie was certain that it was the right thing. But now everything has changed. And I'm going to die in three days. And if this is what it feels like to be wantonly kissing an objectively hot yet despicable man in the moonlight, I suspect I might have been a fucking idiot to have avoided it for so long. And yes, sleeping with your neighbour is probably a terrible idea, but what does it matter? In three days I won't ever see him again. It's not like he will care. He's used to one-night stands. He's probably an expert in them.

Cooper doesn't question me. He doesn't ask about Jonah and the hooking up all over town. Instead, he looks me right in the eye. 'Would you like me to stop? Just say the words.'

'Do . . . do *you* want to stop?' I ask, fiddling with the edge of the sheet I'm wrapped in. 'Because I, well, I really don't have very much idea what I'm doing. How to do it. I mean, technically I, you know, *know*. But there's a lack of field research. So we can stop now. You know. If you want to.'

Cooper swallows, his gaze locked on mine. 'I'd rather scoop out my own eyeballs than stop whatever this is,' he says, which elicits another laugh. 'But it's in your control. Whatever you want, Delphie. Seriously.'

I examine his face in the silver light. I think about the way he just wrapped my hair around his fist and how it was the sexiest thing that has ever happened to me.

I literally have nothing to lose – this is the only time in my life when there won't ever be consequences for my behaviour.

Despite everything, my shoulders soften. I trust Cooper. I'm safe with him and, to my surprise, I don't feel awkward or embarrassed. I feel excited.

'Yes. I want this,' I say firmly, my breath catching with anticipation. 'I really . . . I really just want to know what it's like.'

'Then let me show you,' Cooper whispers into my ear, drawing me back to him.

Chapter Thirty-Two

The first time doesn't hurt like I thought it might. It feels enveloping and unusual but good. Really fucking good. Cooper explores my body and it transforms from something that holds nothing but fear and anxiety into a conduit for electricity. As he pushes into me, I rise my hips up to meet him, feeling more comfortable with every thrust until I'm the one who quickens the pace.

When Cooper comes, he presses me so tightly against him that I feel his heartbeat reverberate through my entire chest.

We lie back together on the bed, breathless and dazed.

Cooper leans up on his elbow and grins at me. 'Woah.'

I nod, waiting for the stars in my eyes to abate. 'Woah.' I laugh out loud.

Cooper chuckles. 'Why are you laughing?'

'I never thought the first person I slept with would be the downstairs neighbour who told me to fuck off because I asked him to turn down his music at six in the morning.'

Cooper frowns. 'Huh? I didn't do that?'

I nudge him lazily with my shoulder. 'You did. It was five years ago. The morning after Halloween. I remember because you had pumpkins lit in your window. You'd had a party, I think?'

Cooper inhales. 'I don't remember saying that to you.'

'Still drunk?'

He shakes his head. 'No. That was actually the morning Em died. My head was . . . *I* was somewhere else.' He strokes my shoulder and it brings my whole arm out in goosebumps. 'Your skin is porcelain.'

'Like a plate?'

'Like a figurine. But sexy. A hot figurine.'

I shrug. 'I'm an indoor cat.'

'I didn't think this would ever happen either,' he says. 'Although I *do* know you thought I was handsome.'

'Oh, really? How's that?'

He laughs. 'That Christmas Eve after I first moved in. I accidentally opened one of your packages – a box of paints, I think. I brought them up to your flat and you were clearly pissed, open bottle of sherry on the table.'

The old bottle of Christmas sherry I found in the cupboard. I had been sad that night. Lonely.

'Shit. What did I say to you?'

Cooper's eyes glint. 'You told me I was handsome on my face. I hadn't remembered the exact expression until you said it to that bouncer earlier.'

I bury my head in my hands. 'Wow.'

'I liked it,' he laughs. 'I told you that I thought you were pretty on your face. But then you told me to get out because you were a lone wolf, unable to love or be loved. Something like that. You told me to leave, so I did.'

'Mortifying.'

'I thought you didn't care what people thought of you.'

'Most people. Not all people.'

He smiles at this.

I sit up. 'I don't think I'm gonna be able to get to sleep.'

'Me neither. Do you want a drink?' Cooper stretches up like a meerkat and looks over towards the kettle. 'There's . . . tea. Only tea.'

'Tea is perfect.'

As Cooper stands up and wraps the other bed sheet around him. I push the pillows against the headboard and sit up too, watching as he boils the kettle and dunks teabags into the big yellow mugs.

'Sugar?'

'What am I? Twelve years old?' I say, mimicking him. 'I'll take two, please.' I won't be needing healthy teeth anymore so what does it matter?

Cooper hands me the mug and I take a sip, exhaling contentedly. 'It's a good brew.'

'Like I said, being an author is a lot of making hot drinks while you panic about what to write next. I'm well practised.'

Cooper climbs over to the opposite side of the bed and leans his pillow up against the endboard so that we're facing each other. I flip the bedside lamp on, his face lit into full colour. His cheeks are pink, his lips redder than usual like all the blood has rushed into them.

'Why are you not a writer anymore? Did you get bored of it?'

Cooper looks down into his mug and bunches up his nose. 'No, I stopped writing after Em died. It's like my brain just forgot how.' He gives a small mirthless laugh. 'No

256

amount of hot drinks helped. Every time I sat in front of the computer my heart just felt empty. Like nothing mattered unless Em was there to talk to about it.'

'Did she read your books?'

He nods. 'She'd read all my first drafts. Crime wasn't her kind of thing but she was the first one to take me seriously. Before I got an agent or a deal. She'd read everything and send me notes. Good notes. Sometimes harsh, but good. She was so much more insightful than anyone gave her credit for. She's the reason there's a love story in my first book. Said no one would give a shit about a bank robber unless he had something real to lose. Unless he had love.'

'She sounds smart.'

Cooper smiles sadly. 'She was brilliant. You'd have liked her, I think.'

'How did she . . . ?'

'A blood clot on her lung. She'd just flown back from LA, she'd been to a convention there. And apparently she'd developed a DVT. The doctors said it was quick and painless. That's good, I guess.'

I shake my head. 'I don't know how you'd ever get over something like that.'

'You don't. Or at least, I haven't. I never will. I was with Em from the moment of my birth and she was with me. Even when we weren't together we were, you know? I always sensed her. When she was excited, or sad or angry. She was the same way with me.'

'Did you . . . did you know when she had died? Like, did you feel it?'

He nods. 'I'd been having a party. The Halloween party. At about six in the morning I got this feeling. Like my heart sort of fluttered and a surge of sadness just swarmed through my entire body. It was so strong it woke me up. I tried ringing Em immediately but, of course, there was no answer. I knew it was crazy for me to think that something had happened to her but I couldn't get back to sleep. So I turned on my record player as loud as I could, trying to distract the terrifying thoughts. I think that's when you knocked on the door? I can't fully remember. But I knew. I knew something was missing.'

I put down my mug and take his hand into both of mine. 'I bet wherever she is she's doing alright.'

Cooper laughs sadly. 'For about a year after Em died I would see her everywhere – in the street, in the background of a movie I was watching, in my dreams. And every time I realised it was just my mind playing tricks on me it was like the shock of it hit me all over again. Mum wanted us to get a psychic, can you believe it? People truly lose their minds when their hearts get broken.'

'So you definitely don't believe in an afterlife then?'

'Ha! No. No, I do not.'

'I never used to believe either,' I murmur.

He turns to me. 'So what changed?'

I open my mouth to speak. He'll think I'm crazy. It is objectively crazy. I clamp my lips together. 'I, uh, I watched this incredible show called *Ghost Whisperer*?' I say, deadpan. 'Convinced me.'

Cooper laughs out loud and shakes his head. 'Dark, Delphie. Very dark.'

'Can I have another cup of tea?' I say, handing my mug to him. 'This time with three sugars?'

We spend the next hour stretched out at opposite ends of the 'small double', talking about everything and nothing.

Cooper tells me about the time he did a reading at Waterstones and just one person turned up – a woman who had wandered in for a place to rest her bunioned feet. I tell him about the life-drawing class and the hilarious splits pose Kat did, and about how when I was ten I badly wanted to have a nickname so I told all the teachers to start referring to me as Lil D, and not understanding why they absolutely refused to allow it.

I tell him how I miss my mum. He tells me about how his heart feels cracked. Like he could plaster over it with friends and family and books and life and joy, but that he knew it would never really be mended as long as Em wasn't in the world.

When he asks me about Gen and Ryan I swiftly change the subject. I don't want them in my head anymore. Instead, I tell him about my top five TV shows and how the light outside my window at 8 p.m. during the final days of August is so perfectly lilac that it takes my breath away every single year. I ask him what the best thing that ever happened to him was and he tells me it was when he taught Em to ride a two-wheeler, and how they spent the whole summer of their tenth year wheeling around Hyde Park together with their grandparents, stopping to swim in the Serpentine, eating ice cream and reading paperbacks – *Goosebumps* for him, Judy Blumes for her.

In between the talking, we grin at each other, giggling because the sun is starting to come up and we shouldn't be awake. But we really don't want to sleep either.

'Come here,' Cooper commands.

I do as he says, crawling across the bed and yelping as he pulls me onto his lap, the sheet falling away from me, exposing my breasts in the brilliant golden light of the dawn.

Cooper's eyes feast on me. 'Fuck, you're beautiful.'

'Shuddup.'

'No.'

I narrow my eyes. 'Don't use your lines on me.'

He moves then, his hardness straining beneath me. Feeling bold, I reach my hand beneath his sheet and touch him, the hot smoothness making me bite my lip. I move my hand and he pulses thickly beneath my palm in response.

Cooper leans his head back against the endboard. '*Christ.*' His voice is all raspy and so deep that I swear I can feel the vibration of it in my belly.

He grabs a condom from his wallet and rolls it on. I straddle him and slip down onto his dick, gasping as he fills me.

I tentatively start to rock, slowly at first and then quicker as I get into a rhythm. Cooper watches me, his green eyes as dark as coal. I watch him watching me and the intensity of it, the sun bright on both of our faces, our bodies, makes my heart pound, adrenaline enveloping me.

His fingers dance lightly across my ribcage. Then he presses his palm against my breast, softly flicking his middle finger over my nipple. He raises his head and takes me ever so lightly between his teeth.

'Oh my God.' The most gorgeous ripple of sensation starts to spark in my gut.

Cooper responds to my exclamation by flipping me over and pinning my arms above my head, pushing into me so deeply that it makes me gasp. We find a rhythm and move against each other as Cooper growls 'Fuck' over and over with each new drive into me.

'*Oh my God*,' I cry out again as the spark in my belly ignites across my whole body, flames of pleasure licking at every limb. I am only flesh and wetness and pure electric energy.

Cooper groans, his forehead pressed against mine, eyes looking right into me. Seeing me.

We catch our breath. Cooper licks his plump bottom lip. I stare at him and conclude it's the sexiest bottom lip I've ever encountered. How had I never noticed that before?

Cooper gazes at me like I'm the first woman he's ever had and there's a slightly puzzled flicker behind his eyes. Of course I know I'm one of many. But I can't help but like the way it feels when he looks at me like that.

Shit.

Things have gone wildly off course.

Chapter Thirty-Three

It turns out that all these years I might actually have been a latent slut, just waiting for the opportunity to bloom. Because once Cooper's friend has dropped off his keys and we're driving back to London, I can think of nothing else except for having sex again. Specifically with Cooper. At the very least it's the only thing that feels like it will take my mind off a) impending death in two days, and b) the pervading sense of regret that I didn't try this out sooner.

Cooper stops the car behind a hedge on a silent country lane, pushes the car seat back and uses his tongue to make me come again. But I need more and as we near our building I ask him if we can try the doggy-style position, to which he says that we certainly can, but we should probably shower first. To which I ask if we can shower together. To which he answers that we can do whatever I want. I feel bold and unconcerned about any consequences. Having a death sentence will do that to you.

We turn onto Westbourne Hyde Road and our giggles stop short when we notice there's an ambulance parked outside the building. Two paramedics wheel someone out of the front door. I see immediately that it's Mr Yoon, an oxygen mask on his face. Was there a fire? Did he leave his cigarette lit? I open the car door before the car has fully stopped moving and run over to Mr Yoon who is being loaded quickly into the back of the ambulance.

'Mr Yoon!' I cry. 'What happened? Are you okay?'

'Are you a family member?' the paramedic asks, barely making eye contact.

'I . . . No. I'm his neighbour. His friend.' I step up to get into the ambulance but the paramedic stops me.

'Only family members can travel in the ambulance. We'll be at UCLH, okay?'

Mr Yoon lifts his hand and reaches towards me.

'I'll be there soon!' I call over to him as another paramedic presses wired stickers over his chest. Mr Yoon's face is wet. I think he's crying. No!

'Cooper!' I spin around. Cooper is looking into the ambulance, his face pale. 'Come on,' he says. 'Get back in the car.'

At the hospital we dash to the reception desk and ask for information on Mr Yoon who came by ambulance. The woman taps on her computer and asks for his first name.

'I don't know,' I say. 'How do I not know?' I turn to Cooper. 'Do you know his full name?'

He shakes his head. 'He's just always been Mr Yoon, for as long as I've known him.'

'Y-O-O-N,' I spell out to the receptionist. 'He was born in Korea and now lives in Bayswater if that helps?'

'Yoon. Got him,' the receptionist says. 'Someone will be out to update you soon.'

'Oh, God.' I turn to Cooper. 'I can't bear this.'

'It's going to be okay,' he says, giving the receptionist my name, then taking my arm and leading me to the waiting area where we find two free seats beside a lad with a bleeding forehead and a woman with a horribly quiet toddler.

We sit there in silence until a tall woman in green scrubs with a stethoscope round her neck calls my name. Cooper grabs my hand as we walk through, but it doesn't feel right so I let go. The woman pulls us into a side-bay.

'You're Mr Yoon's neighbour, yes?'

'Yes,' I say, the anticipation of her words making my voice shake.

'I'm Dr Chizimu. We're running tests because it seemed that Mr Yoon was having a cardiac event.'

'Oh, God. Oh, no. Can I see him?'

The woman holds her hands up. 'But it appears that he has had a very painful gastritis episode, which then set off a rather extreme panic attack.'

A panic attack? And he was all alone. My God. 'Please let me see him.'

'We usually only allow family members to see patients.'

'She is his family,' Cooper interrupts. 'She sees him every morning, makes him breakfast, checks he's got everything he needs.'

I nod. I do that. 'Please let me see him.'

The doctor nods her assent. 'Okay. But no excitement. He needs calm. So just you.' She points at me.

'I'll wait out here,' Cooper says, thumbing back to the A&E reception.

I follow the doctor to a private glass-walled room and

there, half sitting, half lying, and covered in wires is Mr Yoon. He looks tired, but other that than, pretty much like he always does.

'Mr Yoon!' I cry, before lowering my voice so that it sounds less frantic and more calm. I take a seat by his bed and grab his thumb, because the rest of his hand is taken up with a cannula. Mr Yoon smiles at me and rolls his eyes as if to apologise.

'I'm so sorry I wasn't there last night. I got stuck in Duckett's Edge with Cooper and—'

Mr Yoon chuckles silently, his shoulders jiggling.

'You're *chuckling* right now?' I goggle. 'Okay. That's a very good sign, actually. Good. Chuckle away. But calmly. The doctor said you need to stay calm. Stop jiggling your shoulders like that.'

Mr Yoon lifts up his other hand and clenches his fist – the sign he used to make when he was looking for a pencil, before I bought him a box of 100.

'You want to write something?' I ask. 'Now?'

He nods. I go out to the nurses' bay and ask for a pen and paper. I expect the nurse to grumble because she's busy doing other important things, but she smiles at me, leans over one of the desks and hands me a biro and a fresh ring-bound notebook as if people ask for pens and paper all the time.

I take the writing instruments back to Mr Yoon who tries to pull himself up in bed. I help him and rearrange the pillows so that he has more support around his creaky back. He blinks slowly and it occurs to me that he's probably been given sedatives.

He grabs the pen and starts to scrawl over the page, the letters neat and even but shaky.

You look alive.

I feel myself go red in the cheeks. I probably look like I've had a lot of sex in a short space of time.

'I'll take that as a compliment?' I say. 'Hadn't realised I was looking not-alive but . . . thanks.'

Mr Yoon smiles and writes on the page again.

It's nice to see you looking happy.

My chest aches at the notion that any happiness I might be feeling is temporary. Jonah will never kiss me of his own free will and Merritt has all but disappeared. My fate is set.

Mr Yoon soon falls into a soft sleep, his monitors beating steadily. I swallow hard, sorrow submerging me as I think about the fact that Mr Yoon has no family. No friends. Just me. And when I'm gone, who will be there for him besides Cooper? Who will have been a witness to his life, so that he is truly remembered after he's gone?

I gently take the pen and paper out of Mr Yoon's hand. I look outside for the doctor. No one is telling me to get out yet. I hunch over and, without being forced to by anyone, just because I want to, I start to sketch the outline of Mr Yoon's face. My shoulders relax with the feeling of it and I soon lose myself in the lines and crevices, the long earlobes, his thin smiling lips and the small shaving cut on his friendly round jaw.

I peek at the clock and realise that a whole forty minutes has passed by the time the doctor reappears.

'Ms Bookham, we have to run some more tests on Mr Yoon just to make sure we've covered everything, but you can come by again in the morning, if you like? We will do more tests, as I said, but the likely outcome is that he'll be discharged tomorrow after a full review from a cardiothoracic specialist.'

Out tomorrow. I nod, expelling the air from my cheeks, placing the paper and pad at the side of Mr Yoon's bedside table.

'He'll write down answers to your questions if you need him to,' I tell her. 'Took me three years to figure that out.'

The doctor smiles, glancing down at my drawing. Her eyebrows shoot up. 'That is excellent. You're an artist?'

'God, no,' I say, immediately turning red. 'Ha!'

I reach down and turn the page onto the one where Mr Yoon has written that I look alive. The doctor reads it and gives me a curious look. There's a lurch in my stomach as I realise that not only am I going to snuff it in less than two days, but I have no idea how it will happen. I mean, there's no way I'll let myself choke on a burger again. How will I die? Will it be painful? Will I end up right here, where Mr Yoon is, being treated by a team of experts trying hard to save a life that has already been reserved for Evermore?

I shove the morose thoughts away. 'I will be here tomorrow!' I say brightly, backing out of the room. 'You have my number. Please call if anything changes.'

I race into the A&E waiting area to see that Cooper is

hunched over, quickly tapping his shiny-shoed foot and flipping his phone about in his hands. I race over to him. He jumps up as soon as he sees me. He still looks panicked.

'Did you not get my text?' I ask.

He looks down at his phone and shakes his head.

'I sent one. The signal must be bad here. Mr Yoon is okay. He's going to be just fine.'

Cooper exhales, his shoulders dropping in relief as he pulls me into a hug. He presses his hand against the back of my head. I close my eyes and feel a softness spread through my body, a calming of sorts. All this time, when my muscles were painfully tight, my jaw rigid and tense, was the key just another human body pressing itself against mine?

His human body.

I sigh, long and low. Everything would be so much easier if Cooper was my literal soulmate on earth, rather than just someone to have some fun with. I've already kissed him a gazillion times – my life would have been saved a gazillion times over.

Cooper's forefinger trails absently from my hair to my neck and I shiver.

I pull myself away from the hug and mentally slap some sense into myself because having an erotic thought about your downstairs neighbour in an Accident and Emergency department is wrong on so many levels.

'Let's go.'

When we reach our building we stand in the hallway like a couple of gawps, just staring at each other.

'I . . .' Cooper murmurs, looking back towards his door.

'Thanks for . . .' I trail off, shrugging so that a wayward shoulder feather pokes me in the cheek.

'I'm sorry that . . .'

Mrs Ernestine's door creaks open and she pokes her head round it. She takes a bite of a red apple and munches loudly before tutting.

'If neither of you are gonna finish a fucking sentence, will you bugger off and let me get back to *Better Call Saul*? Jesus!'

Cooper apologises and smiles his charming smile, but it has zero effect on Mrs Ernestine's glare. I see her NEVER AGAIN tattoo and I wonder if the thing she is reminding herself to never again do is murder someone.

I do not want to find out so I wave goodbye to Cooper and the pair of us do as she says and bugger off to our respective flats, a multitude of unfinished sentences hanging heavy in the air.

Chapter Thirty-Four

Hi darling! Sorry I missed your call. Things manic here. Hope you're well!

I hang up Leanne's dress before diving into the shower, where I find myself fixating on my previous realisation that while I know I will die again in two days, and I know that it will be at 6 p.m., I have zero clue how on earth it will happen.

It could come about under any circumstances. It won't be choking, because since the last time I have chewed and swallowed my food so slowly and thoughtfully that it's taken me twice as long to finish a meal (on the upside, my digestion has improved considerably). I could fall down the stairs. I could slip on a sneaky bathroom-floor shower spill. There could be a gas explosion. Or Mum might actually call me back and the shock of it would incite some sort of cardiac event. I'm basically living in *Final Destination* right now.

I step out of the shower with extra care and take tiny, vigilant steps into my bedroom. I could be walking down the street and have an air-conditioning unit crash onto my head. Or maybe I fall down a manhole because I'm too busy thinking about not dying to see that there is a manhole in my path. Fuck. I could get murdered. I could get murdered by Mrs

Ernestine. And then she could find all my library books about how to hide a body and no one would be any the wiser.

'Merritt!' I call out frantically, wrapping myself in my dressing gown. 'Merritt, I need some reassurance! Some sort of guarantee about the way this is gonna go down! What is death's design for me?'

A big gust of wind makes my curtains flap and then there she is, faint and iridescent at first and then fully solid, standing at the foot of my bed wearing a white flippy dress covered with cherries, her face glaring at mine.

'You actually answered me!' I exclaim.

'What did I tell you?'

I grit my teeth. 'I'm sorry, I know I'm not supposed to contact you, but I'm freaking out right now. Are you going to have me murdered? Is Mrs Ernestine gonna murder me? Because I'm telling you, she's got it in her.'

Merritt looks around her, eyes panicky. 'Every time you call out to me my phone beeps. One beep for every sentence! We don't have silent mode in Evermore so it's bringing me even more heat. You cannot do that. They think I'm in the loo right now. I'm pretty sure Eric is waiting for me outside, to catch me out, and if that happens then all bets are off, Delphie.'

'You still need the loo in Evermore?' I muse. 'Seems unfair.'

'So that's it?' she says, ignoring my question. 'You're just going to give up on Jonah? *Pas fantastique!*'

'What else am I supposed to do, Merritt? He was quite clear. He has a girlfriend. He was scared of me. I *chased* him.'

'In *Twilight*, Bella was literally in danger of her blood being guzzled not only by Edward but also by his whole family and his enemies too, of which there were an excessive amount! And she still found a way to make it work because *soulmates*. And here you are giving it one in-person meeting that didn't go the way you anticipated and then nothing? All done and dusted? Maybe you and Jonah are not instalove – more a slow burn like Josh and Lucy in *The Hating Game*? But there won't be anything to slow burn if you don't spark the initial flame.'

'This isn't a romance novel, Merritt. It's my life. And he straight-up doesn't like me. I know you said he's my soulmate, but . . .' I get a vision of Jonah, the dislike in his eyes as he ran away from me. Let's face it, the terror.

'That pesky fear of rejection. You would literally rather *die* than make yourself vulnerable even one more time? If you let that happen you're a hopeless eejit. Imagine if Bridget Jones had never let herself be vulnerable? She probably would have ended up in a toxic marriage with Daniel Cleaver! My God.'

I frown. 'I already did make myself vulnerable. I got on a podium and danced. I showed my labia majora outline to the entirety of Kensington Gardens. I auditioned for a role in *Murder in the Pretty Village*. I had to interact with the couple who made my school life an absolute nightmare and I continued to look like an idiot in front of them. It all failed, Merritt! If I have two days left on earth I don't want to spend them gambling on something that has almost zero chance of succeeding. And going back to Jonah? That's what it would be. Another humiliation. This week has been a full nightmare.'

Merritt shakes her head. 'A full nightmare? Has it? Has it really? The whole week. *Just* a nightmare? Think about it, babe.'

I blink. 'I . . .' I trail off, realising that while I've been frustrated and angry this week, I've also been nervous and excited and amused and full of anticipation. Perhaps in certain moments, something close to happy. 'Maybe not the whole week . . .'

She folds her arms. 'If you're going to give up on Jonah, why don't you just come back with me now then? Before Eric discovers what I've been up to and rats me out. At least that way you know you'll be in Evermore and not somewhere else.'

I think of Mr Yoon and how he'll need someone to settle him back in at home tomorrow. I have to write Cooper a list of dos and do-nots. I have to chase up the council and see about getting him an assessment.

'I . . . I can't. It's just two days. I've got things to do. I need to, you know, get my affairs in order. Please. Just hold them off for two more days. I promise not to call you again. And when I come back I'll be your guinea pig, like we agreed.'

'Great. That's great, Delphie, because this guy arrived yesterday and he's looking for love.' She flicks her fingers and a mirage pops up in front of my wardrobe. It's a hologram of a sweet-looking fifty-year-old man dressed in a woolly jumper.

'He's called Roger Pecker and he was a farmer back on earth. And he was mad into it, farming. Like, *obsessed* with farming. He especially likes explaining the benefits of using a chisel plough over a mouldboard plough. You would think he had nothing more left to say on the matter but he does. He has a lot more. He's been single for twenty years so he'll be keen to tell you all about himself, I expect. So that's what you can look forward to if you don't kiss Jonah and save your damn life.'

'You seem angry with me? I thought you *wanted* a guinea pig?'

Merritt looks at the floor. 'I wanted a happy ever after. I wanted . . .' She trails off and stamps her feet.

I shake my head. 'Happy ever afters don't happen in real life. You work solely with dead people. Surely you know that?'

Merritt's mouth sets in a grim line and she twists one of the many rings on her fingers, biting her lip.

There's a knock at my door. Merritt jumps. Wow, she really is on edge.

'Two days,' I say, putting my hands together. 'You can run circles around those guys I thought? Around Eric? You can hold him off. I've made peace with it. I'll even date Roger Pecker, no complaints.'

Merritt looks like she's about to say something else but then stops herself. Instead she throws her hands up in exasperation. She lifts her chin. 'Please just try, Delphie. And no. I can't promise that Mrs Ernestine won't murder you, so maybe watch out!'

She's kidding.

Right?

Before I can confirm she's kidding she has shimmered and popped off back to Evermore.

I open the door to find Cooper standing there, hair damp, wearing a black T-shirt with a photo of Jack Nicholson kissing Helen Hunt. Underneath it says GOOD TIMES, NOODLE SALAD.

'Nice,' I say pointing to it.

'It was a gift.'

'I like it. Are you . . . ?'

'Yeah, I was thinking . . . ?'

We laugh. I take a breath. 'How can I help you, Cooper?'

He laughs too. 'You could allow me to take you to dinner this evening.'

'Excuse me?'

'This evening. Dinner. With me.' He thumbs at his own chest.

I brush my hair back behind my ear. 'You mean . . . like a date?'

'I do.'

'I thought you didn't date?'

'I don't.'

I grin. I've never been on a date before. And the last time I went out to a restaurant in London was in 2015 and that restaurant was the Paddington branch of Chicken Cottage. I think of what Mr Yoon said: *It's nice to see you looking happy.*

I might not have much choice in how long I stay alive. But I do have some say in how much life I can pack into the days I have left. How much happiness I can experience. I have zero to lose now.

I nod. 'Okay, yes. You can take me to dinner.'

He smiles then, the tiny gap between his front teeth visible. It's a real smile. An excellent smile. A not at all despicable smile. I think about the first time I saw him downstairs after he moved in. When he bowed to me in the hall with those glittering eyes. How my stomach had flipped with distant, impossible-seeming possibility. And then, when he told me to fuck off that November morning, immediately feeling like an idiot for thinking of him at all. Now I know it was because his beloved twin sister had just died. Of course he told me, a grumpy woman at the door, complaining about his music, to fuck off. But I didn't think about that. All I thought was that this man was simply confirming everything I already knew about people. They were all terrible.

I wonder if I had tried again to make conversation, if we'd have found ourselves in the same scenario as this, only with more time to see what came of it.

'I'll see you at seven,' Cooper says, before turning on his heel and striding back down the hall.

I guess we'll never know.

Chapter Thirty-Five

A few years ago, in a rare burst of confidence and hope, I bought the sexiest, most beautiful dress I'd ever seen from a boutique on Westbourne Grove. It was only when I got back to my flat that I realised I actually had nowhere to wear it. And even if I did, it was way too glamorous and slinky for someone like me. It's been hanging unworn in my wardrobe ever since. I decide that I might as well wear the pale green dress with the slit tonight because I literally have nothing left to lose. If I'm going to dive into these last two days I might as well really dive in. While the heatwave has finally broken, it's still warm, so I tie my hair up with a black ribbon, brushing the hair so much that the waves sort of puff out, making the ponytail super voluminous. It looks cool, I think. My heel blisters mean that the only footwear I can conceivably wear without ripping my feet to shreds is a pair of silver flip-flops I picked up last summer. They might not exactly go with this dress but at least I can comfortably walk in them.

I opt for some tinted moisturiser and dab on more of the glossy lip balm that Leanne leant me for the gala.

Cooper has an appointment somewhere before our date

so the plan is to meet him outside the restaurant. I have no clue what to expect, this being my first date and everything, but as I shuffle down the street with the other summer revellers I am filled with nerves that feel very different to the nerves I'm used to. These nervous jangles are soft and bright and twinkling, not the heavy thunking darts of dread I've previously felt.

I've never been to Chelsea so I use the map app on my phone to find the way to the restaurant – a place called Concept and Caramel. As I reach the restaurant, a discreet-looking building with darkened windows, I see a group of teenagers sitting on a wall opposite. Two of the teenagers are laughing at one of the others, a younger-looking girl with buck teeth and acne-scarred skin.

I halt and watch as one of the older kids nudges the other as if to say *Watch this*, and then takes a huge wad of pink gum out of his mouth before splatting it onto the younger girl's head with a slap that is audible to me from across the street. I picture Gen and Ryan doing the same thing to me. You'd think teenagers would have thought up new, more interesting ways to harass each other. Some things just never change.

Before I can think about what I'm doing I march across the road. One of the girls is laughing at the 'joke' while the other teenager takes a pic on his phone. The younger girl has tears in her eyes. I can tell this is not her first rodeo with these goons.

'Hey, idiots,' I say to the two older kids. 'What the fuck is wrong with you?'

Their mouths drop open like I'm Beyoncé or something. I do look pretty good tonight, to be fair. 'Woah,' the boy says.

'Are you okay?' I say to the younger girl. She nods forcefully but it's clear that she's not.

'You're a loser,' I say pointing to the older girl. 'And you're a loser,' I say to the older boy. 'And you know what? You're always going to be losers. Making other people feel bad because of your own lack of talent or personality or charisma might feel good now, but it's a trap.'

The older girl sniggers.

'Oi!' the younger girl says, her voice shaking. 'They're my friends. They were just having a laugh.'

'They're not your friends,' I say to her, chest aching at her attempt to downplay what's going on, a move I'm horribly familiar with. 'They're a couple of lowlifes who are bullying you for kicks. Stand up for yourself, for fuck's sake!'

Her chin wobbles a bit. 'Don't shout at me.'

'Hey! Delphie! Hi!' I whirl around to see Cooper waving at me from outside the restaurant on the other side of the road. 'You okay?'

I blink and swallow down my anger. 'Just a sec,' I call back. 'I'm sorry for shouting,' I say to the girl, pointing to the gum in her hair. 'Olive oil will get it out. You don't have to cut it.'

My own chin wobbles.

The younger girl just stares at me, slightly horrified. The older two giggle, but they sound nervous.

'Try to be kinder,' I say to them with a sigh. 'Bullying people is just . . . It's pathetic.'

With one last hard stare, I turn on my heel and go to meet Cooper for our date.

Before I can even process what just happened and how I feel about it, Cooper and I are met at the restaurant front desk by a man with a curled-up moustache wearing a full velvet jumpsuit in neon green. He looks, somehow, glorious.

'Guys, I'm Sullivan and I'm the maître d' – welcome to Concept and Caramel: "The Experience".'

I side-eye Cooper, who does a sort of nervous gulp as we are lead through a corridor to a large white room where groups of cool-looking people sit at large white tables, some of them licking their plates, some of them eating with their fingers, most of them laughing and shrieking. The other waiters are all in velvet jumpsuits of varying neon colours. This is what restaurants are like these days? This is not the impression that TV and film has given me.

We are led to a table in the far left corner where the maître d' wishes us a magical evening before melting away into the fray. He is replaced by a waitress in pink who asks us what we would like to drink. She's wearing contact lenses that make her eyes look the same colour as her jumpsuit. I don't realise I'm staring until Cooper clears his throat. 'Delphie? Drink?'

'Hmm . . .' I say dazedly. 'Do you do Liza cocktails?'

The waitress screws up her face.

I think back to The Orchestra Pit and the sequinned barman. 'It's vodka, I think, with apple sours, and something else I can't remember.'

'We don't do that specifically, but I have something similar. It's vodka-and-apple-based.'

'Okay, yes. That would be lovely, thanks.'

'And you, my dude?' she asks Cooper, who I don't
believe has ever been referred to as 'my dude' in his life.

'Bourbon, rocks,' he says.

'We do a bourbon-based hard seltzer with a chocolate-
and-truffle-foam top?' she suggests.

He shakes his head. 'Just the bourbon, thank you.'

She nods, looking disappointed, before handing us two
menus and disappearing to the bar. I look around in astonishment, noticing that the couple at the next table appear
to be licking some sort of sugary goo off each other's
fingers.

'I'm so sorry,' Cooper says, in a strangled voice. 'I googled restaurants with an arty vibe and this came at the top.
When I saw it had "caramel" in the name I just reserved it
because I know how much you like sugar.'

'It's cool,' I say with a nonchalant shrug.

'It's kind of terrible, though . . .'

'Yeah. Truly awful.' I laugh, which makes Cooper laugh,
until we're both looking around us and laughing at how
weird this all is.

The waitress brings our drinks (mine incredibly delicious), and we order a couple of starters – Cooper miso cod
and me mushroom pâté.

'So,' Cooper says when the waitress has disappeared
again. 'What was that outside?'

My cheeks turn pink. 'Uh . . . I just saw this kid getting

bullied and . . . you know. It sort of set me off. At school, I . . .'

He grimaces. 'The woman from the gala.'

I meet his eye. 'Yeah. She made my life a misery. Her and her boyfriend. Husband now . . .'

'The idiot in the baseball kit?'

I nod.

'I'm sorry. Jesus. I got some ribbings at school but nothing so bad that I still remember it. I can't begin to imagine . . .'

I knock back my drink and signal to the staff for another. 'It's taken up a lot of my life. Too much of it, to be honest.'

Cooper bunches his mouth to the side and sips his drink. He looks brighter than usual – he's not wearing black today, but instead a light blue linen shirt. He looks . . . All this time I was living so close to him. And now . . . No. Don't think about that. Tonight is for fun only.

'Have you considered therapy?' he says. 'I don't want to be that guy, but Em swore by it and—'

I prickle, thinking about my GP. How she said she was convinced that I would benefit from counselling. How the very thought of telling a total stranger all of my feelings makes me want to throw up. 'Have *you* considered therapy?' I shoot back.

He surprises me by nodding, a small laugh escaping him. 'I . . . That was the appointment I just had. My first session. Figured it was about time to start dealing with Em and thinking how I might get back to writing at some point. I know she'd hate it that I'd stopped.'

My eyebrows shoot up. 'Oh. That's great, Cooper. Wow. Had that been on the cards for a while then?'

He shakes his head. 'I booked it after we went to see my parents.'

'Why then?'

He looks down at his glass. 'I think that's the first time I've properly laughed since Em died. It felt . . . like a relief. I wanted more of it.'

I catch my breath as it occurs to me that getting involved with Cooper – a man who is still dealing with the grief of losing his sister – may not be the most considerate idea I've ever had when I'm also going to expire in a couple of days. But then . . . we barely know each other. He'd probably be a bit sad, but he's dealt with far worse. And this is all still pretty casual, right? An entirely sex-based dalliance? He'll be alright. Won't he?

'I made you laugh that night!' I say proudly, trying to distract myself from my own dark thoughts.

'You did. I'm grateful for it.'

'Oh, it's nothing.' I shrug him off, blushing. 'Just a natural skill of mine.'

'One of many,' he says, in a voice low enough to send a shiver right through me. Yes. Definitely an entirely sex-based dalliance.

The waitress returns and places my starter in front of me, along with a pot of paint and a paintbrush.

'Now,' she says, 'this may *look* like paint, but it is an edible coulis, perfectly prepared to accompany your starter.'

She puts a square white plate down in front of me. 'You paint the sauce onto your plate, in any way you like. I'm a fan of thick, abstract splotches, some diners prefer a simple ground layer, others a pointillist application.'

I look at the plate, and at the paint pot, and then at the other plate that holds my pâté. I look over at Cooper and he has a similar set-up but with a piece of fish, his paint a dubious green colour that the waitress says is made from broccoli.

'But . . . why?' I ask, genuinely curious.

'Excuse me?' The waitress blinks.

'Why did you not pour the sauce on already?'

She gawps at us. 'Because the point is to paint it?'

'Yes, but why?' Cooper adds.

The woman shakes her head. 'Because the plate is the canvas,' she explains slowly, as if we are dumb.

'No one else has ever asked you why before?' I ask.

She shakes her head before backing away, eyeing us curiously.

'Again, sorry.' Cooper laughs. 'It had good ratings online so hopefully the food is actually delicious and we're just a pair of dickheads who don't quite get the concept bit of Concept and Caramel.'

'That's definitely it. I mean, I know for a fact you're a dickhead.'

I pick up the paint pot and dump its contents over my food. It splodges messily right out to the edges of the plate.

Cooper tuts. 'And you call yourself an artist.'

'I've never called myself an artist.'

'You should. Those drawings . . .'

I shake my head. 'I don't really do that anymore.'

'You don't like doing it?'

'I love doing it. I just . . .' I trail off awkwardly. I just what? I got burned in school and gave up? Gave up on the thing I loved more than anything else?

I grab my glass of water and down it.

Cooper smiles. 'Well, if you ever have an exhibition, I'll be first in line to buy a piece.'

He forks some miso cod into his mouth and swallows it. He waits for me to take a bite of my pâté, which is claggy, the sauce tasting like actual paint.

'McDonald's?' he whispers, a smile playing around his eyes.

I nod. 'Yes, please.'

Chapter Thirty-Six

We get out of the taxi at Paddington and walk past a pub where a group sitting at the tables outside are singing 'Happy Birthday' to one pink-cheeked man in the middle. His face glows over a little Victoria sponge stuffed with candles.

The man looks embarrassed to be the centre of attention, but also kind of overjoyed. All of those people there celebrating him. All of them looking at him with love or, at least, like. That must be a really nice feeling.

Once Cooper and I have our burgers we wander down Craven Road past the rows of white houses towards our building.

'I know how to show a woman a good time, right?' He waggles his eyebrows at me while biting into his quarter-pounder, almost demolishing the whole thing with one bite.

'I have zero comparisons!' I sip from my milkshake. 'That was my first date.'

Cooper stops walking. 'Seriously?'

I nod and pull a face. 'First date, only date.'

Last date.

'Well, let me assure you, this is romance at its finest!' He laughs and reaches into his paper bag, pulling out a couple of fries and handing one to me.

'I literally have no choice but to believe you.'

He stops outside our building, his eyes growing serious. 'I feel honoured to have been your first, Delphie. And I . . .'

He doesn't get to finish his sentence because there's a woman sitting on the front step of the house, watching us. I recognise instantly that it's one of the women I've seen exiting his flat before – an impossibly beautiful leggy brunette with a little hat that looks like a spider. 'Wednesday Addams walking for Chanel', as Cooper's sister would term her.

'Lara!' Cooper says. 'What are you doing here?'

Lara stands up and brushes off her long burgundy skirt. She bites her lip and gives Cooper a knowing smile. 'I was just in the neighbourhood and you popped into my head. Thought I'd see if you wanted to come out to play.'

The woman's eyes wash vaguely over me and I'm annoyed at myself for being offended that she hasn't even considered that Cooper and I are on a date. Of course, why would she?

I take another sip of my milkshake, the loud burpy sound of it alerting everyone in the vicinity that it's finished.

'I'm actually on a date right now, Lara,' Cooper says smoothly. I look at him in surprise. Lara does the same. 'You? A date? Ha!'

'It's true,' Cooper laughs. 'But it was nice to bump into you.'

I think of the last time I saw them together, a few months ago, kissing in the hallway; Cooper, wet-haired and sleepy, looking like a dirty dog – the kind of man who wouldn't dream of saying no to a woman like that asking if he wants to 'play'.

Cooper grabs my hand and leads me past an astonished-looking Lara.

As soon as we get into his flat, he drops the McDonald's bag on the table and pushes me up against the wall. He grabs my face and gives me the slowest, deepest kiss, his body pressed so close to mine there's barely room to exhale.

He pauses, running his teeth over his bottom lip. 'I've been wanting to do that since the moment I saw you harassing those teenagers outside Concept and Caramel.'

I kiss him back, using my tongue to explore his tongue and feeling my body melt with the sensation, like I'm a chocolate pudding in human form. I pull back. 'I've been wanting to do that since you told me you'd googled "restaurants with an arty vibe".'

He runs his hands over my shoulder, gasping as the silk strap of my dress falls down, exposing the top of my breast. He leans down and kisses it, then trails the kisses up the side of my neck before dragging his teeth across my jaw. Hungrily, I unbuckle his jeans and reach inside to feel the hotness of him in my hand.

'Christ, Delphie,' he breathes, running his hand up my thigh, lifting my dress and using his thumb to lightly stroke over my underwear in exactly the place I need him to. We touch each other, fully clothed, just standing there, eyes fixed on each other. Somehow, it's more unfiltered, sexier than anything else we could be doing in the moment.

'How does that feel?' he murmurs as he deftly slides my knickers to the side and slips a finger inside me. I respond by increasing the speed at which I'm stroking him. He matches my pace, both of us breathing hard. I lean my head back against the wall. His eyes don't leave mine except for a millisecond when they're on my mouth as I lick my lips. When we come within seconds of each other, my knees buckle. Cooper swings his arm around my waist so that I don't fall.

'My God.' He shakes his head.

'I know,' I say, my whole body sparkling.

Cooper leaves to go to the bathroom and when he returns a few minutes later, I'm sitting on the sofa still trying to catch my breath, holding on to the blissful sensations that cloak my body, a lazy smile on my face. My phone buzzes from across the room with the sound of 'Jump Around'.

'Love that song,' Cooper says as I hurry over to my bag, heart racing. I open the text.

Is this part of your game plan to kiss Jonah?

It shimmers and pops into nothing. I peer around. Is she watching me? I dip into the bathroom and close the door behind me so Cooper can't hear.

'Did you just see *that*?' I hiss into the air.

The phone sounds out again.

Ew, of course not. But I know a post-coital glow when I see one.

'Stop! Anyway. I'm not sure I should be listening to you anymore,' I whisper into the air. 'I'm pretty sure Jonah is not my soulmate.'

Soulmates is no longer the point here, Delphie! Shouldn't you be trying harder to save your own life?

I frown. I refuse to spend my last two days on earth gambling that precious time on something that is almost certain to end in more humiliation, sadness and awkwardness. I switch my phone off and return to the living room.

'Wanna shower?' Cooper asks, a wolfish grin on his face, holding out his hand for me to join him.

'Yes,' I say, slipping out of my dress. 'Very much yes.'

I'm lying in Cooper's bed, my head against his chest. He runs his forefinger up and down my arm. I sigh.

'What's up?'

I turn onto my side to face him, propping my head up with my hand. 'When we were walking back earlier, there was a group of people outside the pub. Singing "Happy Birthday" to their friend.'

'I saw them.'

'I usually find the idea of parties and the like a full nightmare.'

'You do? Why?'

I blink. 'Well . . .' *Because no one has ever thrown me a party and I knew that no one ever would throw me a party?* 'You know, all that performative jolliness. Yikes.'

'That's a dark perspective on parties, Delphie.'

'Maybe I'm a dark-hearted person.'

'I see you. You're not a dark-hearted person. God, no. If

your heart was a colour it'd be yellow. The colour of a sunflower.'

I laugh. 'That was so corny, Cooper. You sure you're a writer?'

Cooper does a mock-wounded face. 'I take it back. Your heart is hollow and grey like an old tin can.'

I laugh and sit up in the bed. 'What I'm saying is that tonight I saw those people singing "Happy Birthday" and I got it. Those guests, friends, family, whatever. They were witnesses to that guy's life. The fact that they were there to see him change age – some arbitrary occasion – it marked it. It meant that it was remembered. That *he* will be remembered. Even when he's gone. Because he had, you know, witnesses.'

'I'm not sure I understand.'

I sigh again. 'Mr Yoon is fine, yes. But he's old. And he might not be fine for much longer. For whatever reason, he's shut himself inside that flat for as long as I've known him – over twenty years. If he had died this morning, then who were his witnesses? Who would have been at his funeral? Me and you. And we don't even really know him that well. And Jesus, soon I'll be . . .'

'You'll be what?'

I turn to Cooper. His dark green eyes are twinkling and there's a lazy half-grin on his face. He actually seems to like me. Beyond the sex. I wonder once more how bothered he'd be if I was gone. Would he miss me? Surely not enough for me to halt all this for the next two days? I mean, maybe he'll think about me for a week or so. But it wouldn't be like when he lost Em – someone he actually knew and cared deeply about. I expect he'd get over me pretty quickly with the help of Lara and all the other women I've seen visiting him over the years.

'Mr Yoon needs more witnesses,' I say eventually. 'More people to know him. People who will remember him. Who will check in on him.'

'He has us.'

'It's not enough.' I bite my lip. 'There need to be, like, contingency people.'

I tap my hand against my knee and narrow my eyes as a plan starts to form.

'Contingency people?'

'Yeah . . .' I nod my head firmly and sit up straighter. 'That's it. I'm going to throw a party for Mr Yoon. Nothing big. Nothing overwhelming. But just something to, you know, introduce him about a bit. To people.'

'Introduce him about a bit? He's eighty-eight years old, and he seems to like being alone.'

'Eighty-six. And does he? Do we know that? I mean, I've pushed people away my whole life. I made that choice and now I . . .' My voice wobbles but I swallow it down. 'Mr Yoon, even if he wanted to have witnesses to his life, people to remember the important occasions, it's got to be near impossible when you're getting forgetful and you don't speak and your body's all creaky. He's missed out on so much.'

'He's always seemed pretty content to me.'

'I'm going to do it on Sunday.'

My last day on earth.

Cooper laughs in disbelief. 'You're going to throw a party for our eighty-six-year-old neighbour the day after *tomorrow*. Why the rush?'

I take a deep breath. 'Because life is too short to wait around on a good idea.'

Chapter Thirty-Seven

The next morning, the doctor confirms that Mr Yoon can come home, which is the very best news. I ask her if a gathering would be out of the question, and she tells me that if he is willing, it would be a nice thing – something to distract and uplift him. She warns me that in addition to taking a new medication to settle his stomach Mr Yoon must absolutely avoid any spicy or acidic food.

'No more giant fizzy cola bottles!' I chastise Mr Yoon as I help him into the taxi. 'And the smoking really needs to stop.'

He snorts in response, shaking my shoulders a little as if I'm the one who needs to relax.

'I'm serious,' I say sternly. 'I won't always be here to look after you.'

After that Mr Yoon stops chuckling, and though the ride continues in silence, we lean against each other the whole way home.

I enter the library to see Aled arranging a table in the middle of the room. I head over and look down to see that it's a table full of Cooper's books, with a hand-drawn sign above it saying LOCAL AUTHOR. Wow. There are ten books there, including the one I ordered and never had a chance to read.

'Delphie! My short-lived best friend!' Aled smiles when he sees me. He's wearing a purple jacquard waistcoat over a brown shirt today. He looks like a snooker player. 'Did you find your missing body, love?' he asks, in a more excitable tone than that particular set of words should allow. Another library member side-eyes me with horror.

'My missing *alive* person. Yes. I found them.'

'Ah, jolly good. So, you are ready to read for pleasure then? I've actually made a list of recommendations for you—'

'No . . . No, I mean, that's lovely of you Aled, but I came to ask for another favour. It's quite an ask, though.'

'Ooh,' Aled says. 'Go ahead.'

'Well. I have a friend, Mr Yoon. Super-cool guy. He's just been in hospital. He's fine, thank God, but he's old. He's lived around here for a very long time, but he doesn't know many people.'

'No friends? How very sad. Poor him.'

'Some people are lone wolves,' I say, prickling at the overt pity in Aled's voice.

'Ah, not me. I like there to be as many people in my life as possible. I collect people, like ornaments. I have different people for different things.'

I pull a face because collecting friends like ornaments is one of the creepier concepts I have encountered recently. 'What am I for, then?' I ask, curiosity getting the better of me. 'How do I add to your collection.'

'Well, we are at the start of our relationship so I don't have it figured all the way out yet. Although I suspect you may have come into my life as my grumpy friend. The one I have to work hard to soften, but can never quite manage to. We've already made great progress – the first day I met you you scowled the whole time. Today you have only scowled once! You will teach me the art of perseverance, I expect.'

I laugh at his blatant main character energy and continue with my request. '*Anyway*. I want to hold a little party for Mr Yoon. Something to celebrate him and to also introduce him to some of the neighbourhood locals.'

'My grumpy friend with a centre as soft as honey, it seems,' Aled says thoughtfully. 'I'll be there. Just let me know where and when.'

'Well, no, that's the thing. I was hoping we could hold it here . . . In the music room specifically. Mr Yoon used to play the violin so I know he likes music. And it's such a beautiful space.'

'Hmm. I mean, we would have to put in a formal request. Luckily for you I am the one who decides and I can tell you right now that it's going to be a yes from me. When are you thinking? September? October? December is tricky because of Christmas bookings, but perhaps on a weekday?'

'Actually, I was thinking tomorrow. Which I know is ridiculously short notice, but I'm going away for a bit, and I don't know when I'll be back. So I'm in somewhat of a rush.'

Aled grimaces. 'Holding such a short-notice party here at the library would be against all of the rules. And libraries mean nothing without rules.'

'It wouldn't be for long,' I plead. 'A couple of hours at most. And not more than ten people, probably. It would be super low-key. And tomorrow is Sunday – the rest of the library will be closed so we could keep it a secret.' I press my hands together. 'Please?' I ask, my voice cracking. 'The music room is so beautiful and you *are* the mighty keeper of the keys.'

Aled presses a hand to his chest and looks around before leaning towards me and whispering. 'I am indeed the mighty keeper of the keys and while technically this is against all the rules and I could possibly get fired, I do owe you.'

'You owe me?' My eyebrows shoot up.

'Frida,' he says. 'We've been texting nonstop. She is a delight. Did you know she can speak four different languages? And that she has a qualification in dog grooming?'

'Um, no,' I say, impressed. 'I haven't known her very long. We only hung out briefly.'

'Delphie, she is wonderful. It's early days but I have a feeling she may turn out to be more than my most beautiful new friend. I mean, not that you aren't beautiful. But . . .' He turns red.

'Chill.' I pat his arm lightly. 'Frida is gorgeous, I know. And genuinely lovely.'

'She truly is, right? When you come back from wherever you're going we must all do something together! Oh, we could invite R. L. Cooper, too! Wouldn't that be fun?'

I swallow down a lump in my throat as I realise that the thought of doing something like that doesn't fill me with horror the way it certainly would have done last week. It actually sounds like it would be fun. Nope. Not helpful to even consider that.

'Is three p.m. tomorrow okay?' I say. 'No more than ten to fifteen people?'

Aled nods and clasps my hands. 'I have never broken the rules before,' he says in a giddy voice.

I clasp his hands back and give them a squeeze. 'Well, Aled, maybe it's time we live a little.'

Chapter Thirty-Eight

On the way back from the library I call Mr Yoon's GP, Dr Garden, who tells me that it's completely inappropriate to ask him to socialise with patients. Then I dip into the dry cleaners, where the couple who run the place look at me like I'm an idiot when I invite them to a last-minute party for a stranger. While their rejection prickles a little bit, it's cushioned by an eager acceptance from the sequinned barman from The Orchestra Pit who – when I call the bar – tells me his name is Flashy Tom.

I head to the pharmacy where Leanne and Jan are immediately well up for the idea of a party. They've never met Mr Yoon, but according to Leanne, although I rarely talk at work, when I do, it's 'Mr Yoon this' and 'Mr Yoon that': 'Mr Yoon needs some decent-quality bananas so I'll take an extra five minutes on lunch to get them from the farmers' market.' 'Mr Yoon has a vinyl record of Kylie Minogue and I keep wondering how it got there because when I put it on he put his hands over his ears.' So they're excited to meet him because – as Jan puts it – he feels like a local celebrity to them.

As I return her costume from the gala, Leanne asks about the dress code. I tell her that it's smart casual, to which she gives a disappointed grunt. 'You don't want a theme?' she asks. 'Another costume party? Maybe . . . Disney? You could have a Disney theme?'

I picture Mr Yoon's face seeing a room full of strangers dressed up as cartoon characters. The face is disdainful.

'We're keeping it low-key,' I say, before asking if they can recommend any other people who might be interested in attending a party for someone who they don't know but if they met would surely like. Jan mentions Deli Dan at Baba's Deli down the road. She goes to the deli every lunchtime to get our sandwiches and it's clear she has a little crush on him. I, however, have never met him. I feel the usual nerves at the thought of going to talk to someone completely new, but I haven't got any option except to get on with it – the more locals I can get to come, the more potential people Mr Yoon can rely on in my absence. Plus, I've been through way scarier things this past week.

On the way to Baba's Deli at the end of the road, I decide to nip into the other shops on the row in the hopes that some of those people might be interested in the party. First up is the corner shop. The surly teenage girl with her nose ring and thick black eyeliner is the model of my perfect shop assistant, because she never, ever tries to make conversation with me. She audibly gasps when I march up to the counter and invite her to a party. She stutters and looks around.

'Are you talking to me?' she says, looking behind her in confusion.

'I am,' I say. 'Do you know Mr Yoon?'

She shakes her head no. I suppose she wouldn't. She

must have been a baby when Mr Yoon was still out and about around these parts.

'Well, he's a lovely old man who could do with a few friends. He's been a little unwell and I thought it might cheer him up to have a few local people round to the library to, you know, celebrate him. I know it's a weird ask.'

The girl narrows her eyes. 'Yeah. That is a bit weird. Will there be free booze there?'

'Well, yes,' I say adding *Buy booze* to my mental to-do list. 'Of course! That's customary for a party, right? Definitely.'

'Nice. I'll be there then!' she says, eyes suddenly alight. 'Can my sister come?'

'Wait . . . How old are you?'

She pauses for a moment. 'Eighteen.'

'And your sister?'

'Like . . . eighteen also?'

She's definitely lying. 'Maybe you could bring your dad as well,' I say.

'Maybeeee . . .'

'Great! I'll see you at three tomorrow. Tyburnia Library music room. I'm Delphie, by the way.'

'I'm Shelley.'

'Nice to meet you, Shelley.'

As I walk down to Baba's it occurs to me that I've probably been served by Shelley 500 times and never known her name until now. How did that not seem weird to me all this time?

In Baba's Deli, there's a crowd of women all shouting over each other to get the attention of a handsome grey-haired man with bright ice-grey eyes that could rival Paul Hollywood or a goat. His name tag says DAN BABA. That's Deli Dan, and he clearly loves the attention, occasionally winking at the customers as he serves them. I wait patiently in the queue while the women ahead of me flirt and buy pork pies and cheese. When I get to the front Deli Dan fixes me with his eyes and I can see why Jan has a crush on him, as does, it seems, every other woman of a certain age in the neighbourhood.

'Hi, Deli Dan,' I say. 'My name's Delphie and I've come to invite you to a party tomorrow. It's a bit last-minute, I know, but I only decided to hold it last night.'

Unlike Shelley, Deli Dan acts like party invitations fly at him every day and that a strange woman wandering in to ask him to one is entirely expected.

The queue continues to grow behind me as Deli Dan shrugs and says, 'No can do, love. Very busy. What can I get ya?' His accent is pure Cockney.

'Oh,' I say, my shoulders sinking a little. 'Jan said you'd definitely say yes.'

He puts down the turkey sandwich he is wrapping up in wax paper. 'Jan Meyer? From the pharmacy?'

'The one and only,' I say.

Deli Dan bunches his mouth to the side. 'Nice lady, Jan. Very nice lady. And she'll be there?'

'Yes! She will one hundred per cent be there.'

He nods, a small glint in his eye. 'You got catering sorted?'

Catering? How had I not considered catering? Is catering even necessary, though?

'No,' I say. 'The party will only be for a couple of hours.'

'You can't not feed your guests, dear,' whispers an older woman in a headscarf behind me. 'It would be terribly rude.'

'Oh,' I reply. 'Right, yes.'

Deli Dan rolls his eyes good humouredly. 'I s'pose I could help you out. A few pies, sarnies, cakes.'

I nod. 'How much would that cost?'

Deli Dan responds with a figure that seems in line with general West London prices, in that it is eye-wateringly expensive. I couldn't afford it unless I dipped into my rainy-day savings. The money I've been putting away in case of some unknown emergency.

But if this isn't a rainy-day emergency then I don't know what is. I could spend the whole lot of it. Fuck. It literally doesn't matter. In fact, that's what I'm going to do.

'It's a deal!' I say, taking my phone out of my bag, transferring my entire life savings into my current account, and handing my debit card to Deli Dan.

'Would you bring some of that cheese?' I ask before he swipes my card. I point at a big block of something extra smelly-looking. 'Actually, can you sort out booze too, please? Or do you know somewhere I can get it wholesale?'

Deli Dan nods. 'How many guests you got coming?'

I grimace. 'At the moment around nine, including you. But I'm hoping it will be more like fifteen max.'

'Yeah, that's doable. I'll sort you out, love. Beer? Wine? Champagne?'

'Champagne,' I say with a firm nod. Why not go all out? 'Thank you so much!'

He shrugs. 'Do what I can for the locals. And Jan will definitely be there?'

'One hundred per cent.'

'Can you please hurry it along?' the woman behind me says. Another woman behind her discreetly reapplies her lipstick.

'Tyburnia Library music room,' I tell Deli Dan. 'Two-fifteen for a three p.m. start.'

I breeze past the queue of women and out onto the street, adrenaline pumping.

I'm doing it! Me, Delphie Denise Bookham! I'm throwing a party!

Chapter Thirty-Nine

It's Sunday. I wake up with an immediate ache in my heart.

My last day on earth.

Everything that's happening and everything that might happen floods into my brain: asking questions, second-guessing, wondering about alternatives. I swipe it all away. Today is my last day on earth before I return to Evermore, according to the rules of a deal I *chose* to make. I have made my decision. And part of the decision was to be at peace with the decision because the truth is – there is no alternative. It's all way too overwhelming to fully contemplate and I'm scared that if I really, truly think about it I will crumble. And I have things to do today so crumbling is not a possibility. I'm holding a party for Mr Yoon. I can't imagine a better way to spend this day.

I busy the morning away, writing out various bits and pieces of Mr Yoon's routine, his likes and dislikes that I know of, and the exact way he likes his coffee, into a notebook I picked up from the stationers yesterday. I'll leave this for Cooper, who will be able to hand it over to the council whenever they arrive for their assessment. Hopefully it won't be too long now, seeing as I've sent them around five emails expressing the importance of a speedy visit.

I get dressed in the pale green dress again, because it was expensive as hell and because the way the dress made me feel the other day has solidified the notion that I should have been wearing lovely dresses every single day while I had the chance – what the hell was I waiting for? Even if I was just lounging around the house in them it would have made me feel a least a percentage better. I add some sparkly little drop earrings I found in my mum's bag of stuff, and brush my hair until it shines and falls neatly over my shoulders. Then I go next door to collect the man of the hour.

Mr Yoon is admiring himself in his bedroom mirror. I look on with approval at the sharp navy shirt and grey trousers he's picked out for today. I ask if I can comb his hair at the back, to which he agrees. I stand next to him in the mirror and we smile at each other.

'We look good!' I say, posing with my hands on my hips.

He leans his shoulder into mine and gives me a thumbs-up.

'Are you sure this isn't too much?' I ask. 'I'm not, like, an absolute tit for throwing you a party the day after you got out of hospital?'

He grabs his pencil and pad from the table.

I'm delighted. My first party in thirty years.

I think back to the photo of him collecting the award for playing the violin. How he reacted when I brought it up. I wonder once more what led him to hide away from the

306

world? From people? What made him leave the things he loved behind? The last week seems to have brought us closer. If I'd had more time I think he might have opened up to me eventually. Perhaps, when I'm gone, he will open up to Cooper. Or to one of the new friends I hope he makes at his 'meet new people' party.

Mr Yoon blows out the air from his cheeks.

'Are you nervous?' I ask. 'About meeting new people?'

He shakes his head no and rolls his eyes at the question.

'Me neither,' I lie. He chuckles, seeing right through me.

We're on the way out of the door when Mr Yoon holds his hand up for me to stop. He spins and lopes back into the flat. I wonder if he's changed his mind about doing this, but instead he grabs his crossword puzzle book from the kitchen table.

'Oh, you won't need that!' I say. 'It's a party. You can't do crosswords there.'

He clasps it to his chest and meets me back in the doorway. I try to take the crossword book off him because the last thing we need is Mr Yoon ignoring everyone in favour of his puzzle book, but he clings on to the book with a grip so strong it is very clear that I am not to attempt to take it from him again. I hold my hands up. 'Fine! Jeez. We can take your crosswords.' It must be a comfort thing. Emotional support puzzle book. I get it. 'But I bet when we get there it'll be so much fun that you forget all about it.'

In response Mr Yoon opens the puzzle book a millimetre,

gives a quick nod and then pats the book twice as he holds it to his chest.

'Whatever gets you through, I guess.'

I gasp as Mr Yoon and I enter the library music room arm-in-arm. Beside me I hear Mr Yoon gasp too.

'Woah.'

It looks beautiful. It was already a beautiful room with the domed ceiling, the tall circular shelves of books and the instruments. But Aled has strung the shelves with hundreds of tiny warm twinkle lights and laid a folded white sheet on top of the grand piano, atop which there are five crystal vases filled with yellow roses. I spot Deli Dan at the far end of the room. He's pushed together two study desks and is laying out foil trays of sandwiches and cakes.

'Everyone loves a fairy light, eh?' Aled says, popping out from behind a double bass, carrying some sort of little machine in his hand.

'It looks incredible!' I say. 'Thank you so much! Mr Yoon, this is Aled. He works at the library.'

'Yes. I run this magnificent ship. It's cracking to meet you.' Aled shakes Mr Yoon's hand, beaming at the possibility of a new friend to add to his collection. 'Delphie told me you don't speak.'

'Rude, Aled!'

Mr Yoon waves me away, grinning. I can tell that he immediately likes Aled's forthrightness.

'No offense intended,' Aled says. 'It's just that I was curious if you had ever seen one of these.' Aled holds up the little machine and switches it on so it lights up with a keyboard screen. 'It's a VOCA – a Voice Output Communication Aid. We have one here at the library for our non-verbal visitors to use. You'd be surprised how many of them didn't know it existed. Anyway, Delphie told me you were a recluse these days and—'

'Aled!'

Mr Yoon shakes with silent laughter, the sight of it a balm. He is clearly on board with Aled's straight talking.

'And,' Aled says giving me a pointed glance, 'I thought you might not have heard of them either. You basically type in what you want to say and the machine speaks it for you.'

Aled types in Hello, hello and a jolly good day to all, and a man's voice – which sounds an awful lot like Louis Theroux – speaks the words loudly into the room.

'How cool!' I gasp.

Mr Yoon reaches out for the machine, inspecting it, a stunned grin on his face.

'You can pre-load it with other phrases too,' Aled says handing the device to Mr Yoon and then swiping onto a new screen that has boxes filled with phrases such as THANK YOU SO MUCH, IT'S GREAT TO MEET YOU and, curiously, GET AWAY FROM ME!

Mr Yoon presses the THANK YOU SO MUCH button and nods, impressed when the Louis Theroux voice pipes up again. He swipes straight onto the previous screen and types out This is very good.

'It's great!' I say, beaming at the excited flush on Mr Yoon's face.

Mr Yoon types again: 'My name is Yoon Jung-won.'

My heart lifts. 'Yoon Jung-won!' I hold my hand out to shake his. 'It's good to know you, Yoon Jung-won.'

Mr Yoon gives my hand a firm squeeze.

'The VOCA has so many useful elements,' Aled says excitedly. 'Shall I show you? We have a few minutes until the party officially begins.'

Mr Yoon swipes onto the next screen, already an expert, and presses the YES button.

Aled escorts him to a velvet two-seater on the other side of the room, where they sit down together, both of their faces animated as Aled chatters away and Mr Yoon replies on the VOCA.

I grin at the pair of them, already feeling quite sure that they will get along very well. A speaking device. How brilliant.

'Firm friends already, I see.'

I turn around to see Cooper looking perfect in a black T-shirt and grey slim-fitting trousers, resembling a curly-haired Gene Kelly. He's wearing a large backpack and I'm about to ask what on earth is in it and why he needed to bring it to a party when his eyes travel down my body and I'm immediately swept back to the other day, when those same eyes blazed onyx while he watched me come. A shiver runs through me. He must see it because he does that grin that I used to find so cocky and arrogant and which now makes me want to test how quickly I can remove my clothes and his.

My horn is dampened when it occurs to me that there's

someone close behind Cooper, looking around the music room, an impressed expression on a usually very unim-pressed face.

'Mrs Ernestine!' I trill side-eyeing Cooper. 'Uh, welcome.'

'Mrs Ernestine has never met Mr Yoon, can you believe it?' Cooper explains. 'She asked what I was doing "all dolled up", so I thought I'd bring her along for the fun.'

'You've never met Mr Yoon? I thought you'd lived in the building for over five years now?'

'He lives on the floor above, don't he?' she says, as if this perfectly explains their lack of interaction. 'I only ever talk to this one here.' She points to Cooper.

'Well, the more the merrier!'

'Fancy room, ain't it? Didn't know this was here, to be honest. Thought it was just a normal library.'

'Me neither,' I say, noticing that she's wearing a fresh pink rose behind her ear. 'I only came in here for the first-time last week. It looks like such a boring building from the outside. You wouldn't have a clue.'

'I said I'd help Dan Baba carry in the barrel and the ice for the champagne,' Cooper tells me, backing away.

I throw him a *Please don't leave me alone with Mrs Ernestine* look, which I can tell from his face he totally sees but chooses to ignore, because even though I now fancy him, he still has many despicable qualities, one of which is finding my dis-comfort amusing.

He strides away with a chuckle. Mrs Ernestine and I stand there in supreme awkwardness. I glance at the clock on the wall. There are now three hours until I go back to

Evermore. I think about what Merritt said about not promising that Mrs Ernestine won't murder me.

'I . . . I like your tattoos,' I say, like an absolute moron, pointing at NEVER AGAIN on her knuckles.

She looks down at them and rolls her eyes. 'Oh, they're bloody daft. Got it done in the nick, to make myself look 'ard. Embarrassin' or what?'

'The nick? Like, prison?'

'Of course prison. What else does "the nick" mean, you thicko?'

'Were you . . . Did you . . . What was your crime?'

I just about manage to stop myself from asking if she partook in any murders.

Mrs Ernestine turns a little pink in the cheeks. 'Got caught up with the wrong people. Drugs. Dealing. It was the nineties and I was a fucking idiot.'

'Wow,' I say. 'So . . . What does "Never again" mean?'

Mrs Ernestine looks down at her trainers. 'The way my daughter looked at me, getting dragged away by the police. I was ashamed. I promised myself I'd never again have her look at me like that.'

'And did she?'

Mrs Ernestine's eyes meet mine. 'No. I've turned my life around. It's not big, it's not flashy, but it's honest. My daughter is a doctor now. Chloe.' She smiles proudly and it transforms her usually scowling face into one full of love and experience.

'You can get tattoos removed now,' I say. 'You know, if you're embarrassed by them.'

Mrs Ernestine shakes her head. 'Oh, never. I don't like them but my past is what makes me me. And all of it, good and bad, has led me here today. On a sunny day in August, in this fancy room, about to drink a shit-load of free champagne.'

I think about my past and how it has led me here too, talking to my 'scary' downstairs neighbour. If I hadn't choked on that burger I might have gone my whole life never realising that Mrs Ernestine was a secret badass. Never meeting Aled, or Frida, or finding out for myself that sex is basically the most fun you can have on earth.

'Speaking of which.' Mrs Ernestine points over to the buffet table where Deli Dan and Cooper are dunking champagne bottles into a barrel full of ice. Beside it there's another desk filled with plastic flutes and cans of pop for anyone not drinking alcohol. I wouldn't even have considered that. Deli Dan has done me such a huge favour. If I wasn't so lusty for Cooper I would have a crush on him for sure.

I laugh as Mrs Ernestine takes off, grabbing an entire bottle of champagne out of the barrel. She pops it open before wandering away – without a flute – to sit near Aled and Mr Yoon, who seem to be deep into a conversation about Bach via the VOCA device.

I look around me. While I was talking to Mrs Ernestine the room has filled up, not only with the people I've invited but more than a few who I haven't, including two of the women who were behind me in the queue at Deli Dan's. I spot Cooper's parents heading over to greet him, Amy immediately fluttering her eyelashes at Deli Dan. Cooper must have invited them to make up the numbers in case other people didn't show. I grin at him, but he's too busy nattering away to his mum to spot me. There's Shelley from the corner shop and someone who I take to be her sister, also making a beeline for the champagne. I see no sign of their dad, but I don't have time to worry about it too much because there's a tap on my shoulder.

'Frida!' I say as she gives me a huge hug. She smells like roses and lemons.

'I'm pleased as punch to be invited,' she tells me. 'Aled says we'll go on a date together, me and you and Aled and R. L. Cooper.' Her face drops for a moment. 'Well, I think he meant date. We're texting so much but he hasn't made a romantic move yet.'

'Oh, he's well into you,' I say.

'You think so?'

'It's obvious.' We look over to where Aled is showing Mr Yoon and Mrs Ernestine a glass case filled with wind instruments. Cooper approaches them with a bottle of champagne, a bunch of flutes and a huge smile.

'He is so hot,' Frida breathes, her eyes flashing.

'He really is,' I say, eyeing Cooper as he pops the cork on the bottle of fizz.

'Ooh, English sandwiches!' Frida cries, scurrying off towards the buffet table. 'I hope there will be eggy mayonnaise.'

I wave at Leanne and Jan who appear to have brought

three other unknowns with them. I'm about to go and introduce them all to Mr Yoon when Cooper's mum, Amy,
approaches me. She hands me a glass of champagne.

'Thought you'd like this.'

'You thought right,' I say, taking a sip and enjoying the
feel of the bubbles on my tongue. 'Thank you. It's getting
busy. I hope Aled doesn't mind.'

'Which one is Aled?' Amy asks.

'Purple waistcoat, looks like a snooker-player-slash-
science-teacher.'

'He looks very happy to me.'

She's right. Frida has joined him and his face has gone red
with delight. Behind him I see Cooper opening up his giant
rucksack and pulling out a set of small Bluetooth speakers.
He fiddles with his phone and within a few seconds the
sounds of Charlie Parker's saxophone blares out. I laugh.
Cooper looks around the room until his eyes meet mine and
he gives me and his mum an over-the-top thumbs-up.

'He really loves Charlie Parker,' I snort. 'Look at his
dumb face!'

'I do love that smile.'

I laugh as I remember how his mum demanded that he
smile for her at the family games night. How different his
smile is now, reaching his eyes and igniting them.

'It's a great smile,' I say quietly.

'I've never seen him in love before,' Amy says casually,
putting a hand on my arm. 'It's fascinating. Like he is lit up
from the inside.'

I blink. Cooper's in love? Hold up. She means . . . ?

'Oh . . . Cooper and I . . . It's totally casual.' I remember the deal I made with him to pretend to be dating and quickly correct myself. 'I mean, we're dating, definitely. But it's, you know, casual.'

Because it is. Cooper and I are definitely lusty for each other, there's no denying it. And the past couple of days have been an incredible distraction from the overwhelm of what is actually happening – what is actually about to happen. But love? I snort. 'Not love.' I chuckle at the prospect.

Amy's kind eyes meet mine. 'You might want to tell him that.'

I shake my head. 'But . . .'

'I know my boy,' she says. 'He's not smiled like that in a long time. Since we lost Em I didn't think we'd ever get him back – the bright, easy comfortable man we all knew and loved. And then you. It's like magic. Look at him. He's fallen. All the way. Don't tell him I told you,' she adds, her tone softening. 'He'd be very cross with me, I imagine.'

I follow her gaze. Cooper struts over to us, hamming up playing the air-saxophone as he does so. He grins at me, eyes full of warmth before leaning in and pressing his lips softly against my cheek, his bottom lip catching the edge of my earlobe. My arms goosepimple in reaction. I catch his eye. Is what Amy said true? Does Cooper love me? And if he does, what's going to happen when I'm gone? Will this destroy him all over again? When I thought that sleeping with Cooper was just a little fun it didn't seem so bad that I wouldn't be around. Why would he care? Especially when he has a line of other much more impressive women literally waiting outside his door. But if there are real feelings ... Love feelings ...

My phone blasts out loudly with 'Jump Around', to which Cooper's mum says, 'Ooh, I do like that song!'

It's a Merritt message! Fuck. Do I have to go to Evermore right now? Have we been found out by Eric or one of the Higher-Ups? My heart starts to race. I press my empty champagne glass into Cooper's hands and dart out of the room towards the toilet. I push open the door and check there's no one in either of the two cubicles. Sitting myself down on a toilet lid, I open the text.

> Great news! Eric was not suspicious of anything at all. He was hanging around because – get this – he fancies the fuck out of me. He's into me bad. Should have known, but I've been so distracted with YOU that my usually perfect romantic intuition is wonky.

And then another ...

> Jonah is still out there, you know.

I blink at the message as I realise I haven't thought of Jonah in almost two days.

> Whether you want him or not, surely it's worth one last push before you just ... give up? Kissing Jonah will save your life. It seems to me that you're having too much fun to just leave

it all behind . . . Come on, Delphie. Isn't this all worth fighting for? xoxo

The message disappears and I exhale, trying to slow down the furious pounding of my heart.

I open the cubicle door and walk over to the big mirror on the wall. My cheeks are red and my eyes are wide with terror.

I bite my lip and try to reconnect with the me of a few days ago. The one who was sure that not pursuing Jonah was the exact right thing to do. The one who made the choice not to spend her final days chasing after something already proven to be futile. Because it was absolutely, definitely impossible. Right? Jonah was never going to kiss me. Not after the total shitshow at the gala. It was impossible. I would fight if I thought it was going to work. I've *been* fighting. But I can't waste these last hours on a wild goose chase that will almost certainly lead to nothing.

Can I?

Chapter Forty

I walk back to the music room to find that everyone is gathered in a circle.

'She is here!' comes an electronic voice from the middle. I see that it's Mr Yoon on the VOCA.

'What's happening?' I ask, as Aled sets up a silver music stand and Cooper reaches into his rucksack, pulling out a hard black violin case.

Mr Yoon places the VOCA on the table behind him. He opens up his crossword puzzle book and carefully leans it against the music stand. Has he lost his marbles? Why is he putting his puzzle book on the music stand?

Cooper hushes the other guests. I'm about to ask what the heck is going on, when Mr Yoon draws his bow across the strings of the violin and begins to play.

Gosh.

I expected that he would be good because there's a literal picture in his cupboard of him winning some kind of award. But that picture was taken years ago and I've never seen or heard Mr Yoon play an instrument in the whole time I've lived next door. And after his anger at me finding the picture I never thought I would.

I don't recognise the music but it is slow, winsome and yearning in a way that makes my heart fill up with melancholy anticipation. Mr Yoon closes his eyes and starts to relax into it as the piece becomes louder and full of longing. Around me I hear gasps and murmurs from the other party guests and as I watch my grumpy old neighbour play it occurs to me that this is the most beautiful thing I've ever heard. The most beautiful thing I've ever seen. The most beautiful thing I've ever felt. The notes transform into a quicker, more cheerful crescendo and I don't realise that I'm crying until Mr Yoon plays the last note, his trembling hand creating a vibrato that oscillates around the airy room. He opens his eyes and I see that they are filled with tears too.

The applause is loud and enthusiastic and I'm clapping harder than anyone.

'Bravo!' Frida shouts from behind me.

'A star in our midst!' Jan cheers.

The other guests eventually return to milling about, getting to know each other in that stilted, awkward way that I now realise is the way that pretty much all new relationships start out. Mr Yoon points at the violin and then beckons me over.

When I reach him, he taps the crossword book on the music stand and I see that resting on the pages of a puzzle are two sheets of paper covered with bars of music. They've been neatly written onto the paper in pencil.

'You composed this yourself?' I gasp. 'Mr Yoon!'

He points to the corner of the paper and I see there in his

small neat print: 'Delphie From Next Door. A Sonata'. The date at the top is from two years ago. In fact, I remember it's the day after my birthday. The morning I took him a slice of my cake for breakfast.

My eyes fill with tears again. My throat is so thick with emotion I can't say anything. I just catch my breath and smile as I look at the paper full of shaky scratches that just produced the most beautiful music I've ever heard. A piece of music named for me.

Mr Yoon picks up the VOCA from the edge of the table behind him and types into it, his eyes squinting at the letters. I make a mental note to ask Cooper to arrange an optician's appointment.

Mr Yoon presses enter on the machine.

'Started writing this a long time ago but I never finished it. I was too afraid to play.'

'Why?' I ask. 'Why were you afraid to play? Is that why you got angry with me for finding the picture?'

Mr Yoon types again. 'Long story. Another time. When you came to me at the hospital I knew how to finish it.'

'Wait . . . Is that why you were scribbling away all last night?'

Mr Yoon nods and chuckles.

'He forced me to sneak in his violin,' Cooper says, appearing at my side. He fiddles with his phone, jazz tinkling out into the room once more.

'May I . . . may I hug you, Mr Yoon?' I ask.

He shrugs and then smiles and nods.

We hold each other in the middle of the Tyburnia Library music room and he smells just like his house. Like cigarette smoke and coffee and woolly jumpers, even though it's summer and he's wearing a shirt.

'May I cut in?' Cooper says, after a few moments.

Mr Yoon nods before picking up the VOCA machine and wandering over to where Jan and Leanne are chatting to Deli Dan.

Cooper shoves his phone in his pocket. 'At the gala . . . You know, before you . . .'

'Threw champagne in someone's face and then propositioned an innocent man in front of everyone?'

'Yes. Before that. I wanted so much to dance with you.'

'Why didn't you ask?' I murmur.

'You would have said no.'

He's right. I would have. How have things changed so much in just a few days?

'Ask me now.'

'Would you dance with me, Delphie?'

I take his hand in mine. He puts his other hand on the small of my back and presses me to him, guiding me in time with the music, the beat of which I can't quite grasp hold of but he seems to know by heart.

Beside us Frida and Aled also start to dance, Frida's cheeks pink with joy, Aled swaying awkwardly from side to side.

Cooper leans his head back, eyes travelling across my face. 'Honey,' he says, 'you really do sparkle and shine.'

I can't help but laugh as Cooper raises an eyebrow

cornily, referring to the slogan on my terrible nightie. He grins and pulls me even closer.

I think about his mum's excited words. Cooper is in love with me. He is in love. With me? How can that be when we don't even really know each other yet? It can't be. I don't know about love but I get the sense that the way I feel right now, dancing with him, is the way humans are supposed to feel. Anticipation. Hope. An excitement about the days to come. And if I disappear back to Evermore, the emotional fallout for a man in love would be . . . It doesn't bear thinking about.

Behind me Jan and Leanne laugh out loud at something Mr Yoon has typed into the machine. Aled has just kissed Frida on the cheek. She gives me a thumbs-up behind his back. Shelley from the corner shop and her sister are chugging champagne in the corner, and Flashy Tom from The Orchestra Pit is talking to Mrs Ernestine, his mouth full of a Baba sandwich from Deli Dan.

My heart lifts and my stomach churns.

How am I supposed to leave this? This . . . life. Because what I was living ten days ago wasn't a life at all. But this? This noise and laughter and mess and fear and . . . people. Friends. Possible love.

I can't lose this.

There are people in this room who wouldn't want to lose me either. I make a difference to them.

I can't leave. Evermore is too far away. I don't want to die. Fuck.

I want to live.

I glance up at the clock on the wall.

I have two hours until Merritt takes me.

I need to find Jonah. Now.

And for the first time in the last ten days, I know exactly where to go.

Chapter Forty-One

The party is becoming more raucous as I quietly slip away and hail a taxi to Ladbroke Grove. When I reach the house, my throat tightens as a montage of memories come tumbling back. Not the awful memories, but the earlier, happier ones. The ones of sitting on the grass in this front garden playing with Barbies, making up dance routines, talking about what we would be when we grew up (me an artist, her Rihanna). As soon as she answers the door, the happy thoughts are replaced by nerves and anger and fear. Everything in my body wants to turn around and run away. But I stand firm. I'm not at school anymore. I'm a grown woman. With friends. I have friends now. New friends, starter friends, but still. People who like me. Who like what is good and right and funny and true, not what is loudest or scariest or prettiest or meanest.

It's four-fifteen in the afternoon but Gen is dressed in a fleecy dressing gown.

'What do you want?' she asks, her voice flat.

'Can I come in?' I say. 'I'll be quick, I promise.'

She hesitates before rolling her eyes and inviting me in. While the interior design of the place has been updated in what is clearly a tasteful way, there are kids' toys and stacks of bills and piles of clothes strewn everywhere.

'Where are your children?' I ask curiously.

'Park. With Ryan,' she says, plonking down onto her cream sofa and vaguely indicating that I should sit. 'He's just always *around* . . . you know? Since school he's just always been there. A girl needs a little break sometimes is all.'

She picks up an almost empty glass of wine from the coffee table in front of her and takes a sip. 'You want some?'

I shake my head no.

She gives a mirthless laugh.

Gen takes a sip of her drink. 'So, have you come to apologise? You threw champagne at me? You ruined my gown, you know. Cost four hundred pounds, that did.' She chuckles. 'Didn't think you had it in you, I'll be honest.'

I tamp down the anger that starts to crowd my chest. 'You deserved it,' I say evenly. 'Using my experiences – trauma *you* caused – to lie for your own gain? That was really fucking horrible. I thought maybe you'd have grown up.'

Gen shrugs and finishes her wine before pouring herself another glass.

I open my mouth to ask her what I came here to ask her, but a different question pops out.

'Did you really forget about me?' I ask. Because after everything, that's what I can't get my head around. Even if she hadn't made my life a misery, we were so tight as kids.

Gen meets my eyes and shakes her head. 'No. I didn't forget. When you wouldn't accept my apology I wanted to make you feel bad.'

I nod. 'You're very good at it.'

Gen sits forward. 'Do you remember when you cut the hair off my Barbie because we didn't have a Ken and your mum went mad?'

I instinctively laugh at the memory before clamping my hand over my mouth.

'Why did you hate me?' I ask, the question blurting out of my mouth more desperately than I intended. 'We used to have so much fun.'

Gen bites her lip, a little hiccup escaping her. 'I hated you because you hated me first.'

'What? Why on earth do you think that?'

'You just stopped inviting me round to yours. You knew my parents were always at work. How I had no one at home. I practically lived with you and you just cut it off because you were jealous.'

'Jealous? Of what?'

'How close I was to your mum.'

I think of back then. Of me, Gen and Mum singing and playing and cooking and gossiping together. How Mum and Gen did seem to get along so easily. Like a couple of grown-ups.

I look down at my feet. 'Maybe I was a little jealous. But that wasn't the reason I stopped inviting you over. My mum was . . .'

'What?'

'My dad left and then my mum fully lost it. She was drinking and crying all the time. I didn't want you to witness that. I was embarrassed.'

Gen shakes her head. 'Jesus, Delphie. I would have helped you! You didn't tell me.'

'I . . . I . . . didn't. You're right. But you were . . . You fucking took me out, Gen.'

Gen sighs and runs a hand through her hair before making eye contact with me. 'I'm sorry, okay?'

A tear spills over onto my cheek. I wipe it away with my fist.

'I need to find Jonah,' I say, glancing at the clock on her wall. 'As soon as possible. I need you to give me his address.'

Gen's face screws up. 'What is that all about? Jonah said he'd never met you before. But you were acting so weird around him. Was he lying? Do you know him?'

I nod. 'Yeah, but not in the way you think. I . . . I can't explain why I need to see him because, well, it's ridiculous. But I need you to give me his details. His number, his address. You owe me.'

'Are you going to try to kiss him again?' Gen asks with a grimace. 'Because – no offence – you scared the shit out of him. He's usually such a cool customer.'

She stares at me for a moment longer before getting up and padding over to a large mahogany dresser. She opens a drawer and pulls out a piece of paper and a pen, scribbling on it before handing it to me. 'It's Jonah's number and his address. Don't tell him I gave it to you.'

I exhale. Finally. I'm gonna do this.

As I leave down the garden path, Gen calls after me. 'Hey, Delph?'

I spin around. 'What?'

'Are you fucking R. L. Cooper?'

I nod. 'All the time.'

'Nice.' She leans against the doorway and shrugs a shoulder. 'Do you . . . do you want to hang out sometime? Grab a drink?'

I look down at my feet before meeting her eyes. A flicker of understanding passes between us. But it's not enough. 'Absolutely not,' I say. I hold the piece of paper aloft. 'Thanks for this, though!' I add, before breaking into a run.

Chapter Forty-Two

With less than an hour left on earth, I return to my building and immediately hear rowdy laughter coming from Cooper's flat. What's going on? Who's in there?

His door is ajar. I peek my head around it to find that most of the guests from the library party are inside, sitting on the sofas and on the big windowsill. Jan is in the kitchen, head very close to Deli Dan, while Leanne chats to Cooper and Mr Yoon. She laughs at whatever they're saying, her head tipped back gleefully.

Aled spots me first and hurries over. 'Delphie! We got busted!'

'What?'

'My colleague Laurel came into the library to pick up her forgotten umbrella and discovered us! I didn't realise we'd been playing the music so loudly but R. L. Cooper's little Bluetooth speakers pack a real punch. Anyway, in she storms saying that we immediately needed to vacate or else she would call the police.'

Frida joins him, in a much more sober state. 'He shouted, "Leg iiiiiiitttt!" Which in the UK means, "Run!" So we ran. Most of us anyway. Mrs Ernestine told Laurel she was a miserable cow and should fuck off or else.'

'Cooper invited us all here,' Aled tells me, his cheeks red with booze. 'We missed you – get yourself a drink.'

I nod and hurry over to Cooper whose face breaks into a huge grin when he sees me.

Mr Yoon types quickly into his VOCA. 'We got busted,' says the Louis Theroux voice.

'I heard!' I say, thrilled that I can communicate with him so quickly but somewhat distracted by my impending death. 'Cooper, I need a word.'

His eyebrows dip at the urgency in my voice. I grab his hand and pull him into the bedroom, closing the door behind us, shutting out the happy noises of the party.

'Are you okay, Delphie?' he asks, pressing his warm hand immediately to my cheek. I wish more than anything that I could just close my eyes, nestle into him like a cat, and ignore the reality of what's actually going on right now. 'Where did you go? I texted you, thought maybe you'd gone home for a bit of a breather. Wait . . . Have you been crying?'

I catch a glimpse of myself in his wall mirror. Mascara streaked down my face, hair mussed up and sweaty from the run back. I look insane.

'I need a favour,' I tell him, my words tripping over themselves. 'Can you drive me somewhere? You've not been drinking, have you?'

He shakes his head. 'Just club soda. I laid off, in case Mr Yoon felt ill again – it's been a huge day for him. Are you alright? Where do you want to go?'

My heart lifts at Cooper's innate thoughtfulness towards Mr Yoon. I take a deep, steadying breath. 'I need to get to

Mayfair. Like, right now, right this second. I'd get a taxi but the wait is too long and it only takes about fifteen minutes in the car. I don't have much time.'

I'm trying to sound reasonable, but my voice comes out low and shaky and desperate.

'Mayfair?' Cooper glances at his wristwatch. 'Right now? Is everything okay?'

I bury my head in my hands, letting out a groan of frustration at the questions, his lack of panic. Although, of course, why would he be panicking when he's completely in the dark about what's been going on? 'No. No, it's really not okay. It's the furthest from okay it could possibly be. And I *wish* I could explain it properly, Cooper, but, God, even if I did you wouldn't believe me. You *couldn't* believe me. Just . . . Come on, let's go. We need to go right now! It's literally life or death!'

Cooper pulls a face and sits down on the edge of his bed. No. I don't need him to sit down. I need him to get in the car and drive me to Mayfair, to Jonah who, somehow, I have to get to kiss me without any preamble. I think of the remainder of my savings in the bank. 'Maybe I could pay him to kiss me?' I mutter to myself. He would still be kissing me of his own free will, right? Would that work? Would Merritt allow it? Christ, my head is spinning.

'Maybe we should just sit down for a moment,' Cooper says gently, as if we have all the time in the world. He pats the bed beside him, his expression concerned. 'Would you . . . would you like a cup of tea? Shall I telephone a doctor?'

I get a flashback to the last time he offered to telephone a doctor for me. When he found me on my living-room floor in my nightie, confused and muttering about a missing burger. Fuck. He thinks I'm having some sort of episode. With trembling hands, I check the waiting time on my ride-sharing app – it's now thirty minutes. Way too long.

'We need to go!' I shout, sheer panic making my heart pound so hard in my skull that I can feel it in my nose. I grab Cooper's hands and despite my best attempts not to lose my shit any more than I already am doing, I start to fully sob. 'Please. If I don't kiss Jonah then Merritt will send me back to Evermore and I don't want to go there, not yet. I want to stay here. Alive. *Please!*'

Cooper inhales sharply, eyes flashing. 'What did you just say?'

Shit. I've made it worse. I really do sound like I'm unwell. Cooper stands up from the bed. 'Who . . . who is Merritt, Delphie?' he asks, his voice quiet and even.

I throw my hands up in the air. I give up. 'Merritt is my Afterlife Therapist.' Cooper opens his mouth to say something but nothing comes out. I realise that I'm making absolutely no sense to him, I'm barely making sense to myself. 'I know it sounds crazy,' I plead. 'But . . . I died. Okay? I fucking *died* ten days ago. And I . . . I met this crazy woman in the afterlife who is obsessed with romance novels and she' – Cooper suddenly looks like all the air has been taken from him. He drops back down onto the bed as if his knees have stopped working – 'she wanted me to kiss Jonah – that's why I've been trying to find him – not because

333

he's the love of my life but because it's a deal I made with Merritt. She wanted me to give her a real-life happy ending, like in her romances, otherwise I would have to die all over again. Which I thought I was okay with. But then, today . . . the last few days, being with *you*. It's made me realise that I'm not okay with it. I don't want to die. Not at all. So please, please, please. Let's go. Even if you don't believe me and I completely understand why you wouldn't, please just take me to Mayfair. I need to at least try! I know it makes no sense but I need you to please just help me.'

I'm properly crying now, panicked little breaths escaping me. How could I have played so fast and loose with this?

'Obsessed with romance novels?'

This is what he got from what I just told him?

'Look I *know* it sounds like something I've invented but I promise it's real.'

Cooper stands up again and stares at me, his mouth set into a grim line. He trails the heel of his hand over his jaw, up to his forehead. His eyes are shining with tears. 'Are you telling me the truth right now, Delphie? Because if this is some kind of sick joke about—'

'Why would this be a joke?' I run my fingers through my already messed up hair. 'It's not in the least bit funny.'

Cooper swallows hard, shaking his head slightly. He bites the corner of his lip, his eyebrows dropped low.

'Please,' I whisper. 'Please drive me to Mayfair – I'm all out of options.'

Cooper's eyes flick from side to side, like he's weighing up his choices, which I'm pretty sure are a) do as I ask, or

b) telephone for medical attention. He eventually lets out a sharp breath before grabbing my hand and leading me out of his bedroom, through the happy fracas in the living room and out to his car.

He doesn't say a word as he screeches away with such urgency that it slams me against the window. I feel like he doesn't believe me as much as he wants to see where this is going. If he has somehow gotten himself involved with a psychopath. Either way, we're finally on the way to Jonah. There's still a chance.

'Address,' Cooper barks, tapping his hands against the steering wheel, impatient or irritated, I can't tell.

I fumble with the paper in my hands. 'Ten Berkeley Street . . . I have his number, too. I should call him. Fuck.'

I stab the digits into my phone, hands trembling, tears obscuring my vision. I eventually get the right combination but the phone rings out.

Cooper turns onto Edgware Road and puts his foot down so that the cars and the trees lining the road flick past with increasing speed. He glances across at me, eyes narrowed, and even when he's looking at me like he doesn't know me at all, my heart lurches with the depth of what I've grown to feel for him in such a short time.

Cooper. Always there, downstairs. My dickhead neighbour who turned out to be the sweetest, funniest, sexiest, most interesting man I've ever known. And I think even if I'd met every man on this earth and every man in the afterlife I'd still feel that way about Cooper . . . Cooper. Wait . . . I don't actually know his full name . . .

'I . . . I need to know something,' I blurt out as we drive around Berkeley Square.

Cooper's eyes are back on the road, his front teeth rubbing back and forth over his bottom lip. 'What? What is it?'

'What's the R. L. stand for? What's your first name? I need to know.'

'Are you serious right now?'

'I . . . just want to know your name. Your proper name.'

Cooper's nostrils flare. 'Fuck's sake . . . Fine. It's Remington Leopold. My name is Remington Leopold Cooper.'

'REMINGTON LEOPOLD?' I repeat at full blast, before bursting into shocked laughter. This cool, clever, sexy, despicable man is called *Remington fucking Leopold*.

It must be the nerves and the terror and the general batshitness of this whole thing but once I start laughing I can't stop. It takes over my whole body until I'm convulsing with it. I feel like I'm going to throw up.

I manage to stop for a moment to see Cooper looking at me, a surprised laugh bursting out of him. And then, just as we turn onto Jonah's street, there's the sound of a car horn, so loud it hurts my ears. I turn to Cooper who is frantically turning the steering wheel to the left, a look of horror darkening his face.

Then there's a loud bang, and the force of being thrown forward, my body straining against the seatbelt of the car in a way that steals my breath. My head cracks against something. There's a yell in the distance. A sharp surge of pain.

And then nothing.

Chapter Forty-Three

'Open your eyes . . . That's it. Time to come to . . . Time to awaken . . . Aha, there you are! Hey, darling girl.'

I open my eyes to see Merritt in front of me, hands on her hips. She's standing beside a washing machine, dressed in a navy-blue boiler suit. There are pink plastic chopsticks holding her hair up in a messy bun. Beside her stands a man so ridiculously good-looking he looks computer-generated. He is tall and blond with pale green eyes and long dark eyelashes that soften the effect of a jaw so sharp it could cut glass.

Merritt turns to the man 'Well, here she is. The bane of my existence, Delphie Denise Bookham.'

The man waves, giving me a grin that looks like it ought to be photographically captured for a *Vogue* spread. 'I'm Eric. It's nice to meet you.'

'Eric? The man who . . .'

Merritt leans her head on Eric's crisp white-shirted shoulder. 'As it turns out, ours looks to be a classic tale of "rivals to lovers" – honestly, you couldn't write it. Well, Lucy Score probably could.'

I shake my head, trying to process what is happening right now. A car crash? That's how I died the second time? I was so busy worrying about manholes and murder by Mrs Ernestine that I didn't imagine it would be something as plebeian as a car accident. My stomach twists and clenches as I realise that I didn't even make it to Jonah. No. Oh, no. And then I cry out as I remember that Cooper was in the car beside me.

'Cooper! What about Cooper?!' I scramble up from the chair. 'Is he okay? My God, was he injured?'

'He's right there, Delph,' Merritt grins, pointing at one of the plastic chairs behind me. 'Such a sleepy thing, isn't he? Arrivals have usually woken by now. I can't wait any longer. I'm going to wake him!'

Oh, no. God, no. Cooper is here? Cooper doesn't belong here. What have I done?

'No. Please.' I dart over to where Cooper lies in the chair, head resting on his shoulder, looking for all the world like he's having a peaceful afternoon snooze. I . . . Cooper's *dead*? I did this? NO. This was not meant to happen. Oh my God.

'Wake up!' I put my hands on both of his shoulders and shake frantically. 'Cooper, wake up.' I turn to Merritt. 'Send him back. You have to send him back right now. He doesn't belong here! Not him. Cooper, wake up right now. Cooper, please.'

'Hey, go easy,' Merritt scolds. 'Don't scare him!'

Cooper cannot be here. He can't be dead. I plead with Merritt. 'You have to send him back. His mum will be . . . They already lost their . . . He can't. He belongs on earth! He has so much left to do . . . Books to write, joy to bring, joy to *have*. He's already been through too much!'

I must be getting through because Merritt's eyes glitter with tears at my desperation. She leans down and whispers something into Cooper's ear.

I watch as his eyes slowly open, a brief flash of panic before they come to rest on Merritt crouching in front of him. The fear in his eyes transforms into confusion and then shock and then . . . delight? *What?*

He exhales shakily and whispers, 'Oh my God.' My jaw drops as Cooper jumps up from his seat and immediately, fiercely pulls Merritt to him. He wraps his arms around her, one shaking hand pressed to the back of her head. 'It's you,' he murmurs, voice rasping. 'You're here. I . . . You're *here*?'

Merritt rests her cheek on his chest, eyes squeezed shut, the corners of her mouth lifted. Cooper pulls away and holds her face in his hands, using the crook of his forefinger to tenderly wipe away the tears that have begun streaming down her face. His shoulders, always so hunched and stiff, lower, sinking into something resembling relief. He starts to speak, but whatever he's about to say turns into a deep sob as he pulls Merritt back to him. Merritt laughs, right from her belly and then Cooper laughs too, a quick bark of a laugh. The two of them are just desperately clutching each other, laughing and sobbing at something only they are privy to.

'Is this real?' Cooper says eventually. 'Are you real? Is this a dream?'

Merritt takes a deep breath and exhales slowly as if she's trying to steady herself. 'It's real, Coop. Not in any way the kind of real that you're used to. But I'm here. And you're

339

here.' She clasps his hands in her own. 'And my God, I missed you.'

Eric watches on, an indulgent smile on his face as Cooper shakes his head, looking around the room in astonishment. His eyes are wide, and though he looks confused and light-headed he doesn't look frightened at all. He looks almost *happy*. I don't understand.

'Wait . . .' he says, taking in the decor of the room. 'What the fuck is this? Is this Franny's Launderette in Barnet? You absolute weirdo.'

'You know I loved hanging out there,' Merritt says with a shrug. 'But I've been getting some less than stellar client feedback about it. Apparently, what might be a calming environment to me could come off as creepy to other people. Should probably change it to something super basic that everyone gets. The apartment from *Friends*, maybe. Or just something generic and beige like a hotel lobby. What do you reckon?'

'Stop!' I choke out, utterly confused. Fuck. What if this is not Evermore? What if it's some weird alternate reality? What if the Higher-Ups caught on to the plan and now they've sent me to some place where my destiny is just to be perplexed for the rest of forever? 'Why are you all acting like this is normal?'

'Delphie?' Cooper finally realises that I'm standing right there at the back of the waiting room. He hurries over to me, his face crumpling into a dark frown, like he's finally cot-toned on. 'Fuck, are you okay?' He tilts my chin up with his hand, inspecting my face, then running his eyes across my body. 'Are you hurt?' He pushes a hand through his hair causing the curls to stick up at odd angles. He glances at Merritt. 'How long can we stay here with you for? When can we go back? Is Delphie safe?' He turns back to me, eyes staring deep into mine. 'As soon as you said "Merritt", I knew you were telling the truth. I thought it was some sort of cruel trick at first, but you're not the cruel trick type. And then when you said about the romance novels, I knew it was my Merritt.'

'Your Merritt? Wait, are . . . are you in on this whole thing?'

Tears of frustration threaten to spill.

Cooper grabs Merritt's hand and pulls her over. Eric is holding Merritt's other hand so he gets yanked over too. A chain of very attractive people who are all acting very, very strangely indeed.

'Delphie, this is Em! It's *Em*. My sister.'

I look between them, and it suddenly occurs to me that their eyes are not only the exact same shade of dark emerald green, the exact same big almond shape, but that they are tilting their respective heads at the exact same angle.

'But . . . but this is Merritt? I thought your sister was called Emily?'

'Her name is M,' Cooper explains. 'As in the letter M. Not E-M.'

It dawns on me like a drizzle at first. And then a cloudburst. Em is *M*. For Merritt. Not Emily. Cooper's bookish twin sister is . . . Merritt? I notice then that she's wearing the earrings that Cooper leant me for the gala. She must have

341

swiped them from his flat the day we got back! Merritt sees me looking and touches her hand to her ear.

'I missed them.'

'The Irish accent,' I mutter with a frown.

'I went to Trinity College. Lived in Dublin for ten years.'

I had assumed she had gone to Trinity College Cambridge. Cooper stares at his sister in wonderment. Now it makes sense why he's not more scared, why he seems elated, why he doesn't seem to have fully caught on to the ramifications of what all this means. I know how much his heart broke when he lost his sister. How did he describe it that night? Like his heart had cracked and while he could find ways to plaster over those cracks, he knew they'd never truly mend. And now . . .

Merritt looks back and forth between us. I feel a weird surge of anger on behalf of Cooper. Because while he's still in the midst of shock and delight at seeing his dead sister again, it doesn't change the fact that she willingly brought him here. Away from his life for her own benefit. Was this the plan all along? Was I part of some sick ruse?

Merritt shakes her head as if she's reading my mind.

'I was never planning on Cooper coming here!' she protests. 'Of course I wasn't, I'm not a total monster. I was initially planning to just have you, Delphie. But fate intervened and, as we know, fate is bigger than anything at Evermore.'

'You're saying the crash . . . That wasn't you?'

'No!' Merritt presses a hand to her chest, offended. 'A crash? I would never. So prosaic. Crashes are dark. I was planning to have you fall into an open manhole for the comedy of it. That crash was fate. Cooper being here is *fate*. And human will? That's even more powerful than anything we can conjure up here.'

Cooper looks like reality is starting to dawn on him. 'So we can't actually go back to earth, Merritt? Ever?'

Merritt's face falls, her eyes filling with tears. 'You're not glad to be here? With me? It's pretty cool, once you get used to things.'

A question begins to form at the edge of my consciousness, but it doesn't get a chance to fully realise because my vision starts to go hazy, the lights in this weird launderette flickering, a buzzing sound and then a siren.

'Oh!' Merritt gasps. 'Are you kidding me? Well, well, well, Delphie. This is a turn-up for the books! Looks like you're getting that kiss after all . . .'

I sway slightly. Before I know it, Cooper has me in his arms.

'Delphie? Are you okay? What's happening, M? What's happening to her? Shit, is she fainting? Delphie, can you hear me? Delphie! No. Come back to me. M, help me! Do something! I can't lose . . .'

Sounds start to fade away. I put my hand to Cooper's face but the hot sensation of his skin disappears beneath my fingertips into nothing.

I disappear into nothing.

Chapter Forty-Four

I awaken again, a forehead touching my forehead, my nostrils pinched closed by a finger and thumb, lips pressed against my lips. I feel the whoosh of Listerine-flavoured air filling up my lungs and start to cough, spluttering and spitting. The owner of the forehead yells, 'She's alive! She . . . I saved her! I saved her life, oh my God!'

Pain immediately envelops me, my shoulders throbbing, the evening air stinging a small patch on my cheek, the taste of blood in my mouth. My knee. My knee feels like someone has taken a hammer to it.

I try my best to concentrate on the face above me, the big earnest blue eyes looking imploringly into mine.

Jonah.

'Hi,' he says softly, brow furrowed. He touches my hand and I flinch.

I open my mouth to say something but he shakes his head.

'Hush. Just stay still, okay?' He looks up, nodding at something or someone I can't see. 'The paramedics are here now. You're okay.'

My head feels thick and heavy, my heart skittering out of rhythm. A mad burst of activity beside me as a mask is placed over my face and I am lifted by two paramedics onto a trolley. They're talking to me. I know because I see their mouths moving, but the words seem all jumbled because my brain is filled with only one thought.

Where's Cooper?

I lift my head and a kind-faced paramedic gently pushes it back down onto the trolley. But not before I see Cooper's car crashed up against a Land Rover, and there on the ground in front of the cars, is Cooper himself.

He's lying straight, arms at his side, eyes closed – he looks like he's playing pretend. Surrounding him are four or five paramedics. One of them is pressing on his chest over and over, his face red with the effort.

'No,' I manage to whisper before I'm wheeled up a ramp and into the ambulance. It takes off, sirens blaring mournfully.

'You're okay,' Jonah says from my side. *What is he doing here? Why is he in here with me?* 'You're going to be okay. You crashed your car down the road from my house. I heard the bang from inside and ran out to find you lying on the road. You must have crawled out. You're safe now, though. You're okay.'

I'm not okay. Nothing is okay.

My heart punches in my chest, the force of it making my whole body ache. A machine starts to beep and suddenly the paramedic with the kind eyes is above me brandishing a needle. I don't feel it go in. I don't feel anything.

I wake up God knows how many hours later, in a room with walls made of glass. The pain in my knee is unbearable. I sit up and my whole body feels like it's been chucked down a full flight of stairs. I'm dressed in a hospital gown and my leg is wrapped in bandages. My head feels foggy and my mouth is as dry as dust.

'Oh! You're awake! Do you want some water?'

It's Jonah again.

He's sitting on a plastic chair beside my bed. He pushes a bottle of water towards me, but then, realising I could probably do with some help, he unscrews the cap and holds the bottle to my lips. I gulp down the liquid. It dribbles on my chin and plops onto my chest.

'You had surgery,' Jonah says. 'On your knee. You have bruised ribs and a cut near your ear. But they gave you stitches. There will barely be a scar.'

'Cooper. Where's Cooper? Is he— Is he . . . ?'

'The man you came in with – Cooper – is there.' Jonah points to the left of me.

I look through the glass window and there he is. Lying in a bed, sleeping soundly. The relief that he's not dead bursts out of me in the form of a noisy sob, mixed with a yelp of pain because the movement makes my ribs feel like they've been squeezed in a brutal mechanical contraption.

'He . . . uh . . . he's in a coma, I think,' Jonah says.

'A coma. People wake up from comas. He's not dead. He's going to wake up.'

Jonah doesn't say anything, just sets his mouth into a stoic line. The stubble is thick on his jaw. His eyes are red and his linen shirt is crumpled.

'Have you been here all night?'

'Yeah. I wanted to know you were okay.'

'I am,' I say, looking over at Cooper. 'Thank you so much for staying with me. But I'm okay now. You should go. Get some sleep.'

Jonah nods, but seems reluctant to go. He scooches his chair closer and picks up my hand. 'I . . . I'm really glad you're alright,' he says.

I laugh mirthlessly. 'I've terrified you twice in one week.'

He half smiles. 'Yeah. You're kind of extreme.'

I nod. 'Honestly, you can go. I promise not to chase you.'

Jonah takes a deep breath and stands up, stretching his arms upwards so that his shirt rises and I can see the bronze hairs of his lower belly. I think about how I felt when I first met him in Evermore. I mean . . . I get it. But that spark that tickled me the first time he touched me? It's fully done a runner.

'Feel better soon, I guess,' Jonah says, hesitating at the door.

'Thanks, Jonah,' I mutter, turning my head so that I'm watching Cooper.

He'll wake up soon. And I want mine to be the first face he sees.

The doctor tells me pretty much the same as Jonah did – gnarly broken knee, bruised ribs, general bashed-up body, extremely lucky to be alive at all. When I ask about Cooper and when he will wake up, she grimaces which I'm pretty sure is not in the manual for how doctors should respond when someone asks when a patient will awaken from a coma. The doctor explains that Cooper's injuries were very serious. She says words that no one should ever have to hear in normal life: intercranial pressure, mechanical ventilation, *fluid*. When I ask her the average amount of time that patients are in comas for following an injury like Cooper's she replies with an unhelpful: 'Every patient is different.'

I can't leave my bed yet, so I just stare across at him, lit up beneath the harsh ceiling lights. His body is right there. But *him?* He's in Evermore. And the thought of anyone being stuck with Merritt would make me worried, but as it turns out, she's his sister. And they clearly adore each other. So he's okay. I know that much. But he doesn't belong there. He belongs in this world. Listening to Charlie Parker. Drinking delicious wine. Planning fictional heists. Being despicable. Kissing me.

I press the buzzer for the nurse, asking if she'll help me into a wheelchair so that I can go sit with him.

'Oh . . . you came in together, right? Is he a loved one?' she asks, glancing down at her notes.

'Yes,' I say, the words coming out of my mouth with absolute certainty. 'Yes, he is. He's a loved one.'

Once I'm at his bedside I take hold of his hand, marked with the bruise of a failed cannula insertion. I run my thumb over his palm. He looks so calm. So *empty*.

I look around to make sure there are no medical staff in the near vicinity.

'Merritt,' I hiss angrily. 'Merritt, you need to send him back home now.'

I know it will be difficult for her to just wisp into a busy hospital so I check my phone, waiting hopefully for the sound of 'Jump Around'.

But there is nothing.

I try to reason with her, muttering into the air that I know she's missed her brother, that I know she is sometimes bored in Evermore, but that she has Eric now. Why does she need Cooper? Cooper belongs here. And why would she do this to her own parents? Put them through this?

Still no response. Apart from the regular beeps and the whooshing sound of the machine that is helping Cooper to breathe, the room is silent. And while Merritt has disappeared on me before, I start to get the sinking feeling that Merritt won't ever be getting in touch again. I've fulfilled the deal I made in Evermore. Jonah literally gave me the kiss of life. It might technically have been emergency mouth-to-mouth, but his lips touched mine of their own free will. The contract is over. I have my life back.

But as I look down at Cooper's pale face and slightly clammy forehead, I realise that I'm not ready to know what that life looks like without him.

349

Chapter Forty-Five

Despite my protestations, I am moved to a less intensive ward, no longer in a private room but surrounded by other patients, some of them groaning in pain, most of them quiet. I've given the hospital staff Cooper's parents' contact details and they're on their way. He needs people at his side. I also managed to call Aled who, to my great relief, stayed with Mr Yoon last night (albeit passed out drunkenly on his sofa) and reassures me that he will have no shortness of people to pop in and make sure that he's okay. When he asks after Cooper, I burst into tears.

'He's . . . he's . . .'

'He's dead?' Aled screeches. 'R. L. Cooper is dead? No!'

'He's not dead, Aled!' I say sharply. 'He's in a coma. And he's going to wake up.'

Aled goes quiet on the other end of the line. I can picture his face. The same awkward grimace as the doctor when I asked how long it'd be until Cooper would wake up.

'I hope he does. But perhaps you need to be prepared for—'

With trembling fingers I press end on the call. I don't want to hear the rest of that sentence.

My knee starts to throb again, the machine at my side starting to beep quickly. My chest feels tight. I can't breathe.

A nurse arrives and, after checking my vitals, sits beside me and rubs my back in slow steady circles, telling me that I need to calm down. She talks me through breathing in and out until the beeping slows to a steady pace once more.

'Are you in pain?' she asks.

I nod.

'On a scale of one to ten?'

I remember that when Jonah accidentally visited Evermore, he was having dental surgery. He had been knocked out. An 'unconscious visitor', Merritt had called him.

'Ten,' I say immediately. 'I need the strongest thing you have.'

Well, that didn't work. To my great disappointment I wake, not in Evermore, but three hours later still in the hospital. My head is throbbing and Cooper's Uncle Lester is staring down at me. Behind him are Amy and Malcolm. Amy's eyes and nose are red. Malcolm is just pale, his lips almost the same colour as his skin. They're a mess. They've already lost Merritt and now this. And it's my fault.

I sit up, the room tilting slightly as I do so, a sharp bolt of pain surging through my knee.

'Well, at least someone's awake,' Uncle Lester says, to which Amy gives him a hard glare and Malcolm tells him to pipe down. Uncle Lester presses his mouth together and becomes immediately enamoured with a sign on the wall detailing the hospital's fire safety policy. I notice that his eyes are shining with tears too. My stomach dips. Fuck. Fuck, fuck, fuck.

'How are you feeling, love?' Amy says, pulling up a chair at my shoulder, while Malcolm remains standing at the end of my bed, hands in his trouser pockets, looking almost as if he's in a trance. I swallow down the bile that rises into my throat.

I did this. I did this to them.

'I'm so sorry,' I say. 'I . . . Cooper was driving me and I think I distracted him. We were laughing and . . .'

'He was laughing?' Amy says, a slight smile glinting in her eyes before it's quickly replaced with worry.

I nod, about to tell them that I had just found out his real name and then deciding against it, because, after all, they were the ones who saddled him with it.

'How long will you be here for, do you expect?' Malcolm asks, his voice weak, like he's got nothing left to give. 'The doctor told us you had surgery?'

'Yeah. My knee is . . . I won't be walking for a while. And my ribs . . . Well, I'm fine. They say I'll be here for another week, at least. I didn't want them to move me away from Cooper. If it was up to me, I'd be down there with him right now.'

'Do you need anything?' Amy says, taking hold of my hand like she's not met me only three times before. I bite the inside of my cheek to hold back the sob that swells in my chest.

I shake my head no, although I haven't even considered the fact that I don't have anything here with me beyond the handbag that I took to Mr Yoon's party. I have no change of clothes, no toothbrush, none of my medication.

'I have everything I need,' I say, as brightly as I can manage. 'Honestly, I appreciate you coming to see me, but I'm okay. You go, be with Cooper.'

Malcolm takes a deep breath. 'Cooper mentioned you didn't have family here in London. If you need some help when you leave – you're more than welcome to stay with us. We have room.'

'That's kind, but you really don't need to . . . We've not been dating for very long and—'

'Long enough for Cooper to be the happiest he's been in a long time,' Uncle Lester says, his bottom lip wobbling. 'And that's all we need to know.'

I nod my thanks, knowing that I won't take them up on the offer. I couldn't cause them more hassle than I already have.

'I've been chatting away to him for the past hour and a half. I wonder if he can hear me . . .' Amy mutters, almost to herself. 'I hope he at least knows he's not alone'

I desperately want to tell her that he's with Merritt. But I know it would complicate things even more. Bring up further pain and questions I wouldn't know how to begin to answer.

'I think he can hear you,' I say. 'I think wherever he is he's okay.'

Amy starts to cry then, loudly, right from her belly. Her whole body crumples. Uncle Lester and Malcolm rush to her, helping her up.

As they leave the ward I start to shake. I press the buzzer for the nurse and this time a different one arrives. I tell them I'm in pain. A ten, I say again. And soon enough they inject me with something that sends me right back to the warm nothingness. I drift off, hoping desperately that by the time I wake, Cooper will be back in the land of the living.

Chapter Forty-Six

The next three days bring nothing more than sporadic waves of consciousness. I wake in the morning and am wheeled down to see Cooper while my brain is still fresh from sleep. I spend half an hour talking to him, pleading with him to come back.

In between waking and sleeping various people come to visit me, though I'm mostly hazy and not much use to anyone. I vaguely remember Mr Yoon popping in, speaking to me through the VOCA. And Frida brings me a packet of Marks & Spencer nightdresses and a box of black thongs because they had no full briefs available. I think I have conversations with people, but the only ones that seem to remain in my memory are the guttingly one-sided ones I have every morning with Cooper.

After day four of this routine, I press my buzzer for my usual eleven o'clock fix of mind-softening drugs. Manny, the head nurse of the ward, turns up and perches on the edge of my bed.

'We're cutting you off,' he says plainly.

'What?'

'No more morphine. No more sedatives. The doctor said you shouldn't need them at this point.'

I tut. 'But I do! I really need them.'

'I know your beloved is down in the ICU. And that is troubling, for sure. But drugs are not gonna fix the pain, believe me.'

'That is literally what drugs do.'

'No more.' He throws me a smile, full of pity. 'Your knee is improving. I'm sorry, Delphie. The doctor says it's time to start reducing the meds.'

When he's hurried off to help another patient, I huff and grab my phone for distraction. There's a text from Mum. I squint my eyes and scroll up, realising that I appear to have texted her yesterday. I don't remember doing that – I must have been drugged up.

My text to her says:

Mum I'm in hospital. Car accident. Knee, ribs. Ward 8 UCLH.
I miss you x

I scan her reply.

Darling, oh no! Sorry to hear it! Get well soon!

I stare at the message for several seconds. Then I scroll upwards and upwards and upwards. All the messages from me, all the brush-offs from her. My chest aches. I think of what Cooper said the night of the gala after Jonah ran away from me. If people want to go, sometimes it's easier to just let them.

I tap into my contacts and delete her number.

*

The next afternoon I am in possibly the worst mood I've ever been in in my entire life. This morning the doctor told me they were having trouble understanding why Cooper had not yet woken up and that I needed to be prepared for the prospect of it never happening.

I'm having a little cry when Leanne shows up. She's dressed in a jumpsuit made of yellow and green pineapple fabric that looks lit up amongst the muted pale blues of ward 8. Her eyelashes are somehow even longer than they have ever been, and so heavy it looks like they're slightly weighing down her eyelids. She's holding a carton in her hands and is approaching me gently, eyes wide, like I'm a lion in a cage and she's a kid tempted to stick her finger between the bars but is too scared to do it. My face must be an exact reflection of my mood right now.

'You look like you used to,' she says.

'What?'

'Grumpy. Like you don't want anyone to talk to you.'

'Yet here you are.'

'I brought you soup,' Leanne says softly, waving the carton at me.

'Why?' I lean forward and sniff the carton. It smells good.

'That's what you're supposed to do when people are sad,' Leanne says.

'That's what who does?'

'People. Pals.'

'Okay, but why?'

She blinks and stares into the distance for a moment.

'I actually don't know. It's just . . . that's what they always do in books and films. I think it's a comfort thing.'

We ponder this for a moment.

'When I had endometriosis surgery the food was horrid,' she continues. 'The peas were mashed into a single ball. Like one giant soft pea. It makes me want to chuck up just thinking about it. Anyway, this soup is from Baba's so it'll be delicious.'

She reaches into her bag and pulls out a paper napkin, unwrapping it to reveal a silver spoon. My bottom lip begins to wobble at her kindness and I feel immediately guilty for my shortness with her. I hadn't really thought about the hospital food being gross because I've mostly not been hungry. But now that the soup is in front of me my stomach growls.

'I didn't know you had endometriosis. That's rubbish.'

'You never asked.'

'I'm sorry for that,' I say with a wince. 'All these years I thought I was protecting myself by keeping my distance from people. But I'm starting to think that maybe I was—'

'A massive fucking bitch?'

I laugh out loud, immediately yelping as it pulls my ribs into a direction they're not ready for.

'Yeah,' I grin. 'A massive fucking bitch. Why did you even want to be friends with me?'

'Because it would be a terrible reflection on my personality if my only work mate was my own mum.'

I laugh.

Leanne shrugs. 'Seriously, though. I like you. And that night we drank wine after work? You told me about your mum leaving.'

'I did?'

'Yeah. And you were so funny too, when you didn't have that guard all the way up. I knew I'd break through eventually. I mean, I thought it might take another year or two but here we are. Sharing soup.'

'Sharing?'

'Yeah, I was actually hoping you'd dish it up now.' Leanne pulls out another napkin and spoon from her handbag. 'I've not had any lunch yet because Mum brought in a tuna sarnie, which, absolutely no thank you.'

'You don't like tuna?'

'God, you really haven't been listening to me for all these years, eh? I once had someone come into the pharmacy with persistent bacterial vaginosis. Haven't been able to stomach the scent of fish since. Mum loves tuna, though, so whenever she has it, I bail.'

I laugh again, clutching my ribs. 'You need to stop making me laugh.'

'I can't promise anything,' Leanne says, lifting her chin, a proud smile on her face. 'But I'll try to hold off until we finally go for our drink.'

'What drink?'

'The one you agreed to join me and Mum for in return for giving you late-notice time off.'

Ah, yes. That. God. It seems so long ago now.

It's odd. When I'd agreed to that I'd immediately started to think of ways I could renege. But now, in the midst of everything being terrible, I can see how it might just be a salve.

Chapter Forty-Seven

My procession of visitors continues a couple of hours later with Jan. When she shows up, I'm crying again, because that's now all I am able to do.

Mostly I'm crying for Cooper. Because as each day goes by that he doesn't wake up, the more likely it seems that he won't wake up at all. And when Amy told me that Cooper was in love with me, I didn't really stop to think about how I felt about him.

Yes, I knew I fancied him. I knew he made me laugh in a way that felt like freedom. I knew that behind the surliness was a tender and generous heart. I knew that he had shown me how to use my body as an instrument for joy instead of fear. But I assumed that was just lust. Now I'm facing the prospect of not getting to see what comes after lust.

I wanted to know him. Really know him in a way that takes longer than ten days. To listen to him brushing his teeth, to hear what he thought of the TV shows we watched, to find out his favourite colour, breakfast cereal, poet, side of the bed, toe. To sit up all night again, like the night of the gala. Talking about everything and nothing – all of the inconsequential things that add up to mean that you almost know what the person's going to say before they say it.

What if I never again get to feel that fizz in my stomach, the one that tickled and sparked with pride when I made him laugh or come or shake his head like he couldn't believe I was real.

'I made a batch,' Jan says, handing me two tuna sandwiches wrapped in clingfilm, along with a bottle of Lucozade and a bunch of green grapes.

'Thanks so much.' I already know that I will not eat the sandwiches based on Leanne's earlier tale. I grab a fresh tissue from the box on my bedside cabinet and blow my nose before dropping it onto the large disgusting pile of snotty tissues I've been constructing like some pathetic game of Jenga. 'Sorry, Jan. I never used to cry at all, you know. Was hard as steel.'

Jan tuts. 'Well, that's nothing to be proud of.'

I think of my mum always telling me that only wimps cried: 'Bookhams are made of sterner stuff. '

'Crying means you're feeling,' Jan muses. 'That you're living. That you're loving.'

'That you're laughing?'

She ignores me. 'It means that you care.'

'It sucks, though. Now there are all these people around. And I like them. And I miss them. And I can't stop crying. That objectively sucks.'

Jan laughs. 'No! No, it doesn't. Well, it does, but God, wouldn't it be a dull old life if you never had anything to cry about?'

I think about the last twelve years of my life. How I absolutely ensured that I had nothing to cry about.

'Were you aware that emotional tears have a higher protein concentration than tears that come from irritation?' Jan asks, as if this is something that the everyday person would know. 'I read online that the higher protein content makes them fall down your cheeks more slowly – increasing the chance they'll be seen by people and attract help. Your body is literally built for community. Tears literally attract people. So cry away!'

'That's beautiful,' I say, despite myself.

'I think so too.'

'I never wanted people, though. They make everything messy.'

'That's a good thing, love. The thing about people is you have to let them drag you to places you don't want to go. Let them tell you things you don't want to hear. Let them break you and put you back together. Like my beloved Stephen Sondheim wrote, "Somebody hold me too close, somebody hurt me too deep." That's what being alive is.'

'I don't know what to do, Jan.'

Jan grabs my hand. 'What you do is you focus on getting better. You get back to life as best you can. And you keep hoping. You keep hoping that life will turn out the way it's supposed to.'

The kindness in her eyes, the genuine care, makes me feel like I'm going to burst into sobs all over again. I steady myself.

'Did you kiss Deli Dan?' I ask, remembering the way they were flirting at the party.

Jan raises an eyebrow and gives an unusually throaty

laugh. 'We did more than kiss, Delphie love. I've had a crush on that fella for years. Never thought he'd look twice at someone like me. But that's what I'm saying. Fate has a way of giving you exactly what you need, when you need it.'

I look out of the window, out into the distance to wherever Merritt and Cooper may be right now.

I sigh, long and low. 'I really hope you're right.'

It's something Aled says on one of his visits that gets my brain cogs whirring. He asks me how on earth Cooper and I got to dating after living in the same building for so long with nothing more than the odd snipe between us. When I tell him about Cooper needing me to pretend to be his girlfriend so that his parents wouldn't set him up with their next-door neighbour, Aled cries, 'Fake dating! My favourite of all the romance tropes. You were *destined* to fall in love.'

When he leaves, I start thinking about romance tropes. Merritt is clearly obsessed with them and the more I consider it, the more suspicious it seems that my Afterlife Therapist is the sister of my downstairs neighbour. That couldn't possibly be a coincidence. And why didn't Merritt ever mention it?

I grab my phone off my bedside table and google Romance novel tropes.

The top website tells me that the most popular romance trope is something called 'enemies to lovers'. I read on.

The line between love and hate is gossamer-thin, and nothing gets readers going like the bristling tension

between enemies who you just know would have mind-
blowing sex if they would only get out of their own way.
The banter! The conflict! The angst! The lust!

I bite the inside of my cheek. Weird. That sounds a *lot* like
me and Cooper. I continue reading the list, terms like 'forced
proximity', 'sharing a bed', 'love triangle', 'fake dating' and
'taming the womaniser' popping out at me.

I throw my phone down onto the blanket, my eyebrows
squishing together. Cooper and I were forced to share a bed.
And with Jonah we were in a love triangle of sorts. Hmmm.
Before me Cooper had a different woman visiting his flat
every night. Did I 'tame the womaniser'?

I bite my lip, my mind turning corners, scrabbling about
for the pieces of a puzzle that don't quite fit together. Was
this whole thing . . . Was this all a plan by Merritt to get me
to date her *brother*? Is that the happy ever after she actually
wanted? Surely not. Wouldn't she have just sent me back
with instructions to kiss Cooper? Why would she have me
chase Jonah all over London? And why would she now keep
Cooper in Evermore? What was it all for?

Wait . . .

Unless . . .

I gasp, my body straightening, my heart starting to gallop
at the notion. Is . . . is she actively planning on sending him
back?

That's *got* to be it! Merritt is nuts but she's smart. There's
no way she'd go to all of this trouble, risk her job even, just
to separate me and Cooper after we'd finally found each

other. I mean, why would she be that cruel to her own twin brother? She wouldn't. Probably her plan was always to send him back here. The likelihood is she just wants to spend a little more time with him before she has to say goodbye again.

'I know you can hear me,' I cry into the air. 'I know your game!'

The elderly woman in the bed next to me leans forward, peering at me through thick glasses. 'Why, yes, it's gin rummy, dear. Do you have cards? Shall we play?'

'Maybe later.' I smile, leaning back on my pillow and shaking my head, a small, relieved chuckle escaping me. I can wait. I've waited this long to feel anything other than rubbish. If waiting another week or two is all that I need to do to get Cooper back then I will happily do it.

It takes another three days of treatment and monitoring before I'm given permission to return home. Now that I'm certain it's only a matter of time until Cooper returns, my mood has lifted. Well, as much as one's mood can when they've recently died twice and their new favourite person is in a coma.

Leanne has generously promised me that she will drive me back to the hospital every morning so that I can continue to visit Cooper, hold his hand, and keep him up to date on everything that's been going on. I don't know if he can hear me. I expect he's gallivanting around Evermore with Merritt before he returns back to earth. But I talk anyway.

I'm wheeled down to the front entrance of the hospital by a kindly porter. Outside I spot Aled and Frida and Leanne and Jan and, weirdly, Flashy Tom from The Orchestra Pit. They're standing in a little group arguing with each other.

Thanking the porter, I take my crutches and hop over to them.

'Hiya,' I say, noticing that even in the one week that I've been stuck inside the hospital the air has cooled into a far more comfortable temperature. 'Why are there so many of you?'

Aled turns to me, teeth gritted. 'I said on the WhatsApp group that *I* was coming, but it turns out that Leanne didn't check her notifications.'

'I'm busy!' Leanne says. 'And I don't see you scolding Frida or Flashy Tom. They're also here because they didn't see your WhatsApp message in time.'

'A WhatsApp group? What are you talking about?' I ask, wobbling on my crutches before Leanne takes one arm and Frida the other.

'Our Delphie group,' Jan says, as if the fact that there is a WhatsApp group named after me is entirely normal. 'We've been using it to co-ordinate visits. But it turns out there was a mix-up this morning about who was supposed to pick you up.'

'A mix-up? Or a lack of attention?' Aled mutters, his cheeks pinkening.

Leanne snipes back at him to which Frida calmly tells her not to speak to him that way. Jan rolls her eyes at me.

'You have too many friends,' she says, patting me on the shoulder before leading me and my crutches to her own car while the rest of them continue to bicker.

I smile, a gratifying sensation blooming in my chest and warming my whole body.

Too many friends.

What a concept.

When we reach my building I'm startled by a figure in a black shirt and baseball cap facing my front door.

'Cooper? I gasp, my breath catching with delight.

But then the person turns around and my heart wrenches.

Jonah. It's just Jonah. I'm an idiot. Cooper is much taller and broader and comatose.

When he sees me, Jonah breaks into a wide smile and I notice that his teeth are perhaps a little too perfect – like gleaming little Tic Tacs all in a neat row. I wonder if the dental surgery was maybe veneers?

'Delphie! You're here. I called the hospital and they told me you'd just left.'

'I'm sorry but now's not the best time,' I say, eyes flicking to my crutches. I have no clue what to say to him.

Jonah's face falls. 'Oh. I just wanted to talk to you.'

'Is that the lad that saved your life?' Jan hisses beside me. 'Be nice.'

It is the lad that saved my life. I owe him everything.

'I have to be off, but maybe you can help her up the stairs? Save us waiting for the others to get here,' Jan says, much to my annoyance.

'Of course. Yes. I can help!' Jonah responds eagerly.

I shoot daggers at Jan while she gets back in her car.

Jonah unlocks my door for me, picking up my bag and holding the door open so I can hop in.

He looks up towards the stairs. 'Do you want me to carry you?'

I get an immediate memory of Cooper scooping me up in the rain not so long ago. My head bouncing against his backside while he jogged with me towards the Bee and Bonnet.

'No, thanks,' I say. 'I'll scooch up on my bum. By the time we get to the top you'll have said what you wanted to say?'

Jonah's mouth sets into a grim line and I remember what Jan said about being nice.

'Sorry,' I say. 'I really don't mean to be rude. I'm . . . Life is tricky at the moment.'

He nods and follows me up one excruciating step at a time while I lift myself up by my bottom.

'So . . .' he looks down at his trainers for a second and then laughs. 'I'll just cut right to it. The thing is . . . I can't stop thinking about you.'

I pause on the stairs, my eyes widening. 'You what?'

Jonah takes off his baseball cap and runs his hand through his hair. 'I mean, you scared the shit out of me at the gala. Obviously.'

'Obviously.'

'But then . . . when I . . . when I gave you mouth-to-mouth. I felt this feeling. This sort of thump in my stomach. Like a connection.'

I almost want to laugh at the irony.

'I thought it was the adrenaline – you know, from the panic. But then every night before I go to sleep, all I can think of is . . . well, you. I called it off with Lulu this morning.'

'Lulu?'

'The woman I was seeing.'

Oh, yes. The dark-haired woman at the gala. He broke it off with her?

'She didn't make me feel like . . . And I suppose I just came to ask if you were involved with the man you were with at the accident . . . It wasn't clear because at the gala you said you felt like we had a connection. And I . . . I think you might be right. I feel like I know you somehow. Like we've met before. Before the gala of course. Why were you outside my house that night?' He crouches down on the step in front of me. His face is so close that I see the dark golden bristles of fresh stubble glittering across his perfect jawline. 'It can't have been a coincidence, that you were there, out of all the streets in London.'

'I . . .'

Telling the truth to Cooper got him stuck in the hospital. Maybe Merritt was right and Jonah is one of my five soul-mates. But . . . it doesn't matter. I'm pretty sure I'm in love with someone else. I'm in love with Cooper. Even if Amy was wrong and Cooper doesn't feel that way about me, I know that I do feel that way about him. And I'm convinced it's only a matter of time until I'll get to ask him in person. Could be days, could be a couple of weeks. But Merritt has this all planned. Cooper will come back.

I smile grimly. This Adonis-like man with the blue eyes and the easy smile is not for me. I want the scruffy-haired, green-eyed, despicable jazz fan in a coma. And as long as the machine is still beeping, I'll be waiting for him.

Jonah is gazing at me like I'm the greatest woman on earth.

I need to do him a big favour and end this right here and now, in case he ends up in a batshit obsession that can only end in disappointment. I take a deep breath.

'I'm so sorry, Jonah. You deserve someone wonderful. But that's not me.'

'But . . . but I saved your life.'

I take his hand in mine. No leftover spark whatsoever. 'And I'll always be so grateful. Truly. But . . . nothing is going to happen between us. I know I said we had a connection. But, God, that was a whole lifetime ago.'

'It was just over a week ago.'

'I was a different person then,' I tell him. Which I know sounds ridiculous because how much can a person really change in ten days?

As it turns out, the answer is almost completely.

Chapter Forty-Eight

Twelve Weeks Later

As I walk towards the library – still hobbling a little but finally without crutches – I smile, enjoying the scatter of copper-coloured leaves that blanket the pavement and crunch under my boots. I shove my hands into my coat pockets as I stride by Baba's, nodding my hello to Deli Dan inside as he chops up a cucumber at lightning speed. It's four o'clock in the afternoon and already the sky has greyed, the orange lights of the lampposts fluttering on one by one as I pass.

Since I've got home I've been following Jan's advice to remain hopeful. To expect the best from life, from people. For the most part it's working, especially with the help of the new therapist I've been seeing who is doing her best to help me figure out my messy brain and how I can work with it to stop myself from spiralling into isolation again.

I've been to see Cooper every single day at 10 a.m. on the dot. Every morning I desperately hope that this is the day he will wake up. And every day, nothing. Just the steady beep and whir of the machines keeping him alive. There are murmurs at the hospital about the possibility that Cooper will never wake up, and what decisions Amy and Malcolm may want to make about his care. But I can't face thinking about that. So when I'm with him I give him lengthy recaps about life at number 14 Westbourne Hyde Road.

I tell him about Mr Yoon, who has now bought his own VOCA and is such a whizz on the keyboard that Aled (his *actual* new best friend) says he thinks he has the best word-per-minute rate of anyone he's ever met. I tell him how the council have approved the need for additional home care and that he now has a lovely helper called Claire who makes sure that he has everything he needs to be clean and comfortable and cared for. I tell him how the VOCA has meant that my continuing breakfasts with Mr Yoon have led to a now-encyclopaedic knowledge of his life – I know now that Mr Yoon grew up in a small Korean village with his sister. They had a serious falling out after he had an affair with the wife of his conductor and got kicked out of the orchestra where he was working, blackballed from joining any other orchestra in the country.

I hold Cooper's hand as I regale him with stories of Mrs Ernestine, who has taken to joining me and Mr Yoon every morning for breakfast before she sits for me. In my head I imagine Cooper asking me why Mrs Ernestine is sitting for me. And so I tell him that I've been drawing her. In fact, I've been drawing every visitor I've had. There wasn't much else to do stuck in bed with a broken knee, and everyone who turned up at my house was happy to be drawn while we chatted.

It's funny the things people talk about when they think

you're not really listening. I've gotten to know this community of people around my building more than I ever thought I would. More than I thought I ever wanted to. Now, I can't imagine not knowing the glee that comes with being privy to Leanne's weird phobia of lizards that once made her pass out on a school trip to a reptile sanctuary. Or that Mrs Ernestine was once a contestant on *Catchphrase* and had an on-screen argument with the eventual winner because she thought they were cheating, leading to the episode getting cut.

I see Aled's collecting of friends as something deeper and more heartfelt than a slight desperation, after he revealed to me that he too had been bullied, but at university rather than at secondary school. His reaction to that trauma was the opposite to mine. While I shut myself off from anyone and anything that could hurt me, he actively searched for people to love and love him in return. Frida told me yesterday that she is falling in love with him.

I even love knowing that Deli Dan has, according to Jan, 'the straightest most proud-looking penis she ever saw, and she has seen her fair share of penii'. The very knowledge of it makes me feel pleased for her on a daily basis – Jan deserves all the good things. We're even going to visit The Orchestra Pit together next week, which I will endure because she's quickly becoming one of my favourite people.

I push open the door to the library and pass the display table filled with the books of R. L. Cooper. I swallow down the despair that darts through my chest as sharply as if it were still those lost hours immediately after the accident.

When I visited him yesterday I begged him once again to please come back. I had been so certain that Merritt was planning to make it happen, but as the weeks have drifted by with zero change in circumstances, I'm starting to lose faith.

I drop the books I've been reading – a selection of excellent romance novels Merritt had mentioned and the first two of the R. L. Cooper series I've been hooked on – into the returns box and head down the long back corridor, past the huge stained-glass windows and into the large, bright reading room where my exhibition is being held today.

An exhibition. Me! It's sort of ridiculous, really. I've only just started to go back to the weekly life-drawing classes with Frida and I'm very much still an amateur, but everyone I drew thought it would be a nice idea to display my work for an afternoon so that we could celebrate. I refused at first, on account of acute embarrassment. And then I remembered what Jan said at the hospital – that being alive is about experiencing the full gamut of emotions. If you're not feeling pushed and pulled and scared and delighted instead of just safe, then you're not doing it right. So I decided to just go for it. The exhibition is called 'My People – the Characters of Westbourne Hyde Road'.

Most of the invitees are already here. Mr Yoon, with Aled and Frida at his side, the three of them pointing at my framed ink drawing of Mrs Ernestine on my sofa, head resting lightly on her hands, before moving on to the nude I did of Leanne, who was thankfully a little more discreet in her poses than Kat was at the life-drawing class. Jan and Leanne and Jan's mum, Diane, are chatting by a series of portraits of Mr Yoon, all of his most used expressions apparent in the series: Mr Yoon grumpy, Mr Yoon laughing, Mr Yoon blissfully playing his violin, and Mr Yoon sneering because I made him listen to the excellent new Doja Cat album. Flashy Tom holds up his camera and takes a selfie with my drawing of him dressed up as Bernadette Peters in *Annie*.

I circulate the room, thanking everyone for coming, unable to quite believe that these people have turned up for me. Unable to quite believe I am willingly and happily conversing with each and every one of them in talk both big and small.

I glance over to the section of the wall that holds my portrait of Cooper. Of course, he was unable to sit for me, so it's mostly been done from memory and the visits at his bedside. In the drawing he's doing that cocky smile. The one that simultaneously makes me want to snipe at him, stroke his face and climb into his lap. His eyes are twinkling, chin lifted, as if he's on the edge of breaking into a laugh. I think about the way he laughs with his whole body, like every limb wants in on the fun. The thought of it brings a sting to my throat, the space behind my eyes aching with yet another round of tears.

I step out into the musty hallway of the library, taking a few deep lungfuls of air to steady myself. The people in that room have seen enough of me crying to last a lifetime. The worst thing I could do is invite them to an event to witness more of it, only this time in more salubrious surroundings.

I'm about to go back in to join the others when I hear someone clear their throat behind me.

'The exhibition's just through there,' I say absently, thumbing in the direction of the reading room.

'What, no cutting remark for the most obnoxious man you've ever encountered? That's a first.'

I whirl around. And there, in a wheelchair, in front of the blazing stained-glass windows, is Cooper. He's dressed in a pristine white shirt, his grey cargo pants a little baggy on his legs. His dark curls are past chin length, his eyes glinting and intense. They drink me in thirstily.

His lips lift into a full, wholehearted smile. 'You know, I had this really strange dream about a girl who looked just like you.'

I start to laugh.

He's back. Cooper came back.

Chapter Forty-Nine

I fling myself at him, pressing my hands all over his face to make absolutely sure he's real.

'Are you a ghost?'

I grab hold of his arms and squeeze gently. They feel real and solid and definitely strong enough to squeeze a little harder.

'Not a ghost.' His voice is extra raspy. He rubs his throat. 'I woke up this morning. Still a human. A little skinnier. Unsteady on my feet. A bit battered, but nothing some physical therapy won't help. But yeah. I'm right here.'

'Right here,' I repeat, the tears behind my eyes finally giving up the battle to remain there. He hooks his arm around my waist and pulls me onto his lap. 'Wait . . . I don't want to hurt you. Shouldn't you be in hospital?' I scan his entire body, inspecting him for injuries, signs that he is actually well enough to be here in the library.

Cooper shakes his head and laughs. 'I'm completely fine. Sat up this morning and felt like I'd had a long lie-in. The doctors said it sometimes happens like that. People just wake up. It'll take a while to build my strength back to where it was but I'm honestly good.'

'I can't believe it.'

'They spent most of the day giving me every test imaginable before they deemed me fit enough to go home. I have to go back for a check-up in two days, but otherwise they seemed happy enough to free up bed space.'

'Do you feel well?'

'I do now.' Cooper eyes me and grins.

'Your parents! Do they know?'

'They dropped me off here. They're going to grab a coffee somewhere and then come to meet us inside. They told me you were having an exhibition.' His eyes glitter. 'Heard you did a drawing of some super popular author guy.'

I grab his hands. 'Merritt . . . Is she . . . ? Did she make this happen?'

'Like any of those other gobshites could have pulled it off.'

I gasp as Merritt shimmers into focus at the end of the hallway. She's wearing a hot-pink suit, a pair of green winged glasses perched on her little nose.

I jump off Cooper's lap, running over and immediately pulling her into a tight hug. 'Thank you,' I whisper. 'Thank you for bringing him back to me. I convinced myself you would, but then the longer time went on, I thought . . .' I trail off, unable to finish the sentence.

Merritt gently shrugs me off. 'Looks like someone got hella comfortable with physical contact! Good for you, Delph.'

I step back and shake my head in amazement as Cooper wheels over to us. Merritt hugs him and he ruffles her curls.

Merritt looks between me and Cooper. 'God, you are cute

together. I should have known right away that you were meant to be. I was fooled by all the sniping.'

'Hang on . . . So you didn't send me back *for* Cooper? It wasn't all part of a grand plan from the very beginning?'

Merritt scoffs. 'God, no! I recognised you as his neighbour but it never occurred to me to set you up. Wouldn't ever intentionally inflict him on anyone, TBH.'

'Oi,' Cooper warns, giving her an over-the-top glare.

I bite my lip. 'So why Jonah? Why did you say he was my soulmate?' I look at Cooper. 'When he clearly wasn't?'

Merritt shrugs. 'It was a compelling catalyst, was it not? A fine inciting incident, as authors put it.'

'But why him specifically?'

Merritt steeples her hands together, placing them beneath her chin. 'I suppose I just selected someone you'd fancy – the same physical type as your old art teacher – and brought them for an unconscious visit. I mean, I knew he'd fancy you because you're gorgeous and one of his ex-girlfriends looked a bit like you, but it definitely helped that he was high on pain medication. Made him all dreamy.'

I frown, remembering how Jonah looked at me like I was the most charming woman he had ever met. But he was just high on painkillers that whole time?

I shake my head. 'I thought his pupils were so dilated because . . . Oh my God. He was high. You're a terrible person!'

'Yes, but also clever, right?' Merritt laughs.

'Or just deeply intrusive,' Cooper retorts.

Ignoring Cooper's comment, Merritt clasps her hands to her chest gleefully. 'I originally thought I'd just get some high-quality entertainment, help you to get laid and maybe figure your shit out along the way and assuage my boredom. But then we had a twist in the plot – you went to games night with Cooper and made him *laugh*! I hadn't seen him laugh in five years.' She throws him a tender glance. 'And then I saw how he looked at you when you returned from the Shard that night. The way he plucked that petal out of your hair and how pink your cheeks were when he did it. You both seemed to light up. Like someone had finally pressed your 'on' buttons. Imagine my delight when I realised I'd found myself a beautiful little love triangle.

'A classic romance trope,' I nod, remembering the article I read in hospital.

'Absolute classic. So, once I realised that maybe you and Cooper could be something special, but that the pair of you were too stubborn to see it, I knew I had to help before time ran out.' Merritt crosses her arms smugly.

Everything starts to connect in my mind, 'Oh my God . . . Wait . . . You pushed us together? Did you . . .'

'Make it rain the night of the gala? Yes. Steal the car keys? You bet. Cause an influx of people in the Bee and Bonnet so that you had to share a bed? Affirmative. "Shared bed" is my very favourite trope of all the tropes. Not that I stayed around to witness any activity – gross.' She holds her hands up. 'But yes. *C'était moi!*'

'Her plan worked a little too well,' Cooper adds leaning back in his wheelchair and giving me the grin that makes my insides flip-flop.

'Did it ever! I thought falling for Cooper would make

you try even harder to find Jonah – to save your own life so you could be with him. But then to my dismay you totally gave up,' Merritt cries. 'On the only person who could actually keep you on earth. You just flailed and accepted your fate like a . . . like, well . . . *not* like the heroine in a romance novel!' Merritt flings her arms in the air and shakes her head. 'And I couldn't change the contract you'd signed. I couldn't help you any more than a little nudge here and there without over-riding free will. I was terrified you wouldn't kiss Jonah, and that when you inevitably came back to Evermore Cooper's heart would break again. But to my surprise, right at the last minute you got your fight back. You got Jonah's address and got in the car—'

'But then the crash,' I murmur.

'I'd missed Cooper so much,' Merritt says, her eyes shining with tears. 'I knew that keeping him at Evermore wasn't the right thing, but I had no way to send him back. The Franklin Bellamy Clause wouldn't work because Cooper wasn't actually dead. After week eleven, Eric and I were starting to get truly sick of watching Cooper moon around after you. Eventually Eric organised a huge meeting with the Higher-Ups. Made a case for allowing Cooper to return to his body because technically he was actually an unconscious visitor, just a little longer term than the norm. He made a PowerPoint presentation, wore a suit and everything. Isn't that the most romantic thing you've ever heard?'

'Like something out of a romance novel.' I grin.

'So romantic – Nicholas Sparks could never.'

Merritt gazes at me for a moment, her teeth running across her bottom lip, dragging off a bunch of ~~orange lip~~stick in the process. She peers behind her out of the window on the landing. 'I should probably get going . . .' She turns back to us, the tears in her eyes brimming over. 'We got a fresh Dead in yesterday, this woman called Lindy. She is going to make the perfect guinea pig for Eternity 4U. I can't wait to get going. Eric is now project assistant. Office romance incoming! Like a Sally Thorne but without the hate. Well, unless we're role-playing of course.'

'Zero boundaries!' Cooper throws his hands in the air.

I pull Merritt into another hug. She rests her chin on my shoulder. 'I'll miss you,' I say.

'No, you won't,' she replies, pushing her glasses up her nose and looking me right in the eyes. 'You'll be too busy having the time of your life with this loser.' She tilts her head towards Cooper. 'And when you're not hanging out with him, you're going to draw and paint and be there for your friends and have breakfast with Mr Yoon, and go on adventures and marvel at the beauty of being alive. Which is exactly as it should be.'

Cooper wheels forward to hug her but she waves him away 'Nope. Not again, Coop. We've done our goodbyes three times already. I can't take it.' She immediately relents though, flinging her arms around her brother and lightly kissing his cheek.

'Thank you, sis,' he says, his voice cracking. 'For everything.'

'Goodbye Merritt,' I say, a lump in my throat.

'Goodbye, both of you.' Her voice wobbles. 'Hope I don't see you for a long time.'

Cooper and I can only stare as she fades into a glimmering mirage before eventually disappearing into nothing, as if she'd never been there at all.

I snuggle into Cooper's lap once more. Cooper takes my hand and leans in close, nose nudging mine. 'So, Eric said that if I could find you and kiss you within ten days, then I could stay.'

'I see,' I murmur.

'Ergo, I would very much like to . . .' He trails off, glancing hungrily down at my lips.

'To what?' I whisper.

'Kiss you, Delphie. If you want me to, of course.'

'I've never wanted anything more.'

His lips graze mine immediately, the pair of us smiling madly. We kiss softly at first, tentatively and then harder and more passionately until we're pressed so close together I can feel the beat of his heart as if it's my own.

'I think that should do it,' I eventually laugh, head thrown back. I look at him through eyes blurry with tears. 'God, I can't believe you're actually here. I was starting to think you'd decided to stay in Evermore.'

Cooper shakes his head. 'Being with M again was . . . It was everything I've been thinking about for so long. And if this had all happened when we first lost her, I would have stayed there without any hesitation. But . . . *you*. You, Delphie Bookham. I can't be without you. I don't *ever* want to be without you.' He strokes his thumb across my cheekbone. 'You make me laugh and you infuriate me. You make me want to be completely myself and to learn how to do that from you. You make it fun to be me. I love you, Delphie.'

'I'm so in love with you,' I whisper back immediately, pressing my forehead against his. The words are brand new and exciting on my tongue. I get the feeling I'll be saying them a lot.

I wheel him into the reading room where, one by one, the other attendees race over, laughing and crying and rubbing Cooper on the shoulder. Mrs Ernestine gives a nonchalant shrug before turning back to inspect my nude of Leanne.

Amy and Malcolm arrive and I laugh out loud as a crowd forms around us.

I'm holding hands with the love of my life.

I'm surrounded by people.

My people.

The ones I love and who love me back. The ones who will be at my side during the peaks and the dips and all the precious bits in between. Those who will be a part of those small everyday moments that might not make it into the poems and the grand paintings and the history books, but all together add up to something more precious than anything.

A life, witnessed. A life, *lived*.

There's so much to see, so much to do, so much to *feel*.

Cooper interlinks his fingers with mine and squeezes tight. I squeeze back, my heart bursting with the anticipation of all that's to come.

I'm so ready.

Acknowledgements

It takes a whole bunch of people to create a book and bring it into the lives of readers, and I have been so lucky to have the very best bunch of people on board to help with *The Love of My Afterlife*.

Thank you from the bottom of my heart to Hannah Todd – my exceptional agent who championed this book before the first line was even written. Your editorial know-how, smart and steady guidance, generosity, and the ambition you have for yourself and for me are responsible for so many of the incredible things that have happened. You are a force to be reckoned with and I wouldn't want to be without you, summer fruits squash and all.

Thanks also to the magnificent wider team at Madeleine Milburn Literary Agency, particularly Valentina Paulmichl, Hannah Ladds, Amanda Carungi, Elinor Davies, Liane-Louise Smith, Casey Dexter, Madeleine Milburn and Hayley Steed. It is a genuine pleasure to work with you. Thank you for changing my life!

Huge thanks to my wonderful and clever editors: Katie Loughnane in the UK, Jen Monroe in the US, and Deborah Sun de la Cruz in Canada. Not only has your collective expertise transformed this novel into something so much better than I ever could have hoped for, but your warmth, thoughtfulness and passion have made the whole process so enjoyable and seamless. I'm endlessly grateful to you.

ACKNOWLEDGEMENTS

Big thanks also to the incredible publishing teams at Century, Berkley and Penguin Canada who have already blown my mind with their dynamism, mad skills and general coolness. In the UK, special thanks to Jess Muscio, Hope Butler, Rachel Kennedy, Katya Browne and Issie Levin, and to Alice Brett and Georgie Polhill. In the US, special thanks to Claire Zion, Candice Coote, Christine Ball, Craig Burke, Jeanne-Marie Hudson, Erin Galloway, Jessica Mangicaro, Loren Jaggers, Jin Yu, Kaila Mundell-Hill, Kim-Salina I, and Kiera Bertrand. How lucky I am to get to work with you.

I would also like to send my sincere thanks to the wonderful publishing teams at Sperling & Kupfer, Droemer Knaur, Anaya, General Press, Editura Trei, Kobiece, Znanje, Euromedia, Companhia das Letras, Leya, Leduc, Laguna, Tchelet Books, Bazar and Bard.

Thank you to Ceara Elliot and Vi-An Nguyen for creating the most stunning book covers.

Thank you to Antalya von Preussen for the gorgeous author photos!

I wouldn't have been able to write this book without the help of my author friends. Special thanks must go to Cathy Bramley for the actually life-changing Zooming, and for dancing with me the whole way through the first draft. Big thank you to Caroline Hogg, Cressida McLaughlin and Cesca Major for the cheerleading, draft notes, support and giggles. Thanks also to the wonderful Isabelle Broom, Keris Stainton, Katy Colins, Katie Marsh, Josie Silver, Sophie Cousens, Mhairi McFarlane, Penny Reid and Lia Louis. You are all gems.

The Love of My Afterlife

Thank you to the friends and family who inspire and bring joy into my life in so many different ways: Elizabeth Keach and Ophelia Maleki Rae, Will Bex and Grace Bex, Dawn Dacombe, Angie Jordan, Andy Jordan, the Walshes and Greenwoods, Naomi Johnson, Nicky Allpress, Michael Roulston, the BML crew, Oya Alpar and darling Tupi.

I would not be here without my magical, noisy, unwavering family, who taught me everything I know about love. Thank you Mum, Dad, Net, Nic, Tony, Mary, Will and C. I love you and am grateful for you every single day.

Edd – the love of my life. You make the ordinary extraordinary.

Finally, thank you to my readers, old and new. I hope this book brings you joy.

389

Turn the page for bonus content from
Kirsty Greenwood . . .

Kirsty Greenwood on the inspiration behind
The Love of My Afterlife

1. Page 1 – *A Humbling Death*

I used to have this weird obsession with dying in a mortifying way. At the pool, I'd avoid any novelty floaties, because what if it tipped over and I got stuck underwater and I drowned and then I'm forever that girl who passed away via inflatable iced doughnut?

I would only ever wear Very Sensible Underwear so that, should I happen to get mowed down by a bus, the paramedics wouldn't judge my unmentionables. My gym playlist was curated so that if I had a massive heart attack on the treadmill, I wouldn't have been listening to 'My Humps' by the Black Eyed Peas at the time of my death.

I know now that all this obsession was a manifestation of my general anxiety at the time. I'm much better these days. And yet . . . you will not find hide nor hair of 'My Humps' on any playlist of mine. Not now, not ever.

I used this fear to inspire Delphie's death. I wanted it to be something pitiful, anti-climactic and, well, humbling. Not only to show that this is a woman who doesn't think enough of herself to care how she's living, but also to give her the catalysing kick up the bottom she needs – *this* is the culmination of her life? Choking on the sort of burger that has no expiration date, totally and utterly alone? *No!*

2. Page 74 – *The Inspiration Behind The Orchestra Pit*

I once read a writing tip which said that while in first draft mode, an author should give themselves 'cookie scenes' throughout the book. Cookie scenes are those scenes you just kind of frolic in as a writer. It could be a juicy moment of tension, or a setting you adore, or even something as simple as describing the exact light of an early April morning. The cookie scenes might not make it into the final book, but the theory is that when you find yourself flagging during the drafting process, you march towards your cookie scenes to keep your energy and creativity up.

This entire scene was a cookie scene for me. I am a massive musical theatre fan. When I moved to London, I joined a workshop for musical theatre writers and one of our first trips out as a group was to a place called Overtures – a musical theatre piano bar in the basement of a casino. It was modelled after Marie's Crisis in New York. Basically, everyone gathers around the piano and belts out their favourite showtunes, regardless of talent or ability. I loved it so much, but I also knew that for some people it would be an absolute nightmare. Delphie is one of those people. When the time came for Delphie to get out into the world and make her first steps towards finding Jonah, I wanted it to be as alien and uncomfortable for her as possible. At the same time, I also really, really wanted to write a cookie scene in a mad musical theatre bar! And so that's how this chapter was born!

3. Page 102 – *Buddying Up*

When I moved to Paddington myself, I realised I needed to make some new friends. I had been in London for a year but found myself getting lonely in the city. How to make new friends as an adult? Terrifying, not least to an introvert. When we were kids, we could just go up to someone and bluntly ask them to be our friend, like Frida does in this scene, asking Delphie to 'buddy up' – but that's much trickier to do in real life!

I once read an article in which Nora Ephron said that she made new friends as an adult by simply asking them to have dinner with her. That sounds lovely and all, but she was Nora Ephron! Who would decline that invite? No one in their right mind.

While I didn't yet have the guts to straight-up ask strangers out for dinner, I made a concerted effort to keep my eyes and heart open to people who seemed like they were also looking to connect with others. I was surprised to learn that pretty much everyone is. Once you push past the awkwardness, people are surprisingly willing to chat in the supermarket queue for a little longer, or give you recommendations for their favourite places in the city, or invite you to a glamorous midnight art exhibition at the Tate (something cool that came out of one of my interactions with a stranger).

Yes, the risk of being more open about buddying up is that you may get rejected, or thrown an annoyed glance or possibly scammed out of all your life savings. But the rewards, should it go well? Untold. Your next favourite person is going about their life right now, right this minute, maybe feeling a little lonely, possibly wishing that they had someone new to go for dinner with. Go find them. Go buddy up!

4. Page 201 – *Time for a Makeover*

When I was a child I would write my own stories for fun. They almost always included a makeover scene. As an eleven-year-old dweeb with frizzy hair, thick pink-and-blue patterned glasses, double braces and a chronic nail-biting habit, I used to fantasise about somehow, suddenly, emerging from my cocoon as a butterfly.

Many years later, I still love watching, reading and writing makeover scenes. Not only are they just unabashed fun and fantasy, but thematically they're a great way of getting a character to see themselves in a way they never have before. Delphie's internal makeover has already begun, but this external one will give her the burst of confidence she is going to need for what happens next . . .

5. Page 220 – *My Favourite Scene*

This whole gala scene was my absolute favourite to write. Going into it, I didn't *fully* know what was going to play out for Delphie at Derwent Manor. I just knew that I wanted her to have this little unexpected adventure, something completely different from anything she had ever experienced. I was also excited for us to see a more fun side to Cooper and how seeing that would affect and complicate Delphie's feelings for him.

I've created a playlist for the gala for you – these are all the swishy, elegant songs that the band are playing inside Derwent Manor for this scene! I'd recommend listening with a glass of something fizzy.

Playlist songs:

'Mambo Italiano' by Rosemary Clooney
'The Way You Look Tonight' by Doris Day
'Cheek to Cheek' by Ella Fitzgerald
'Alright, Okay, You Win' by Peggy Lee
'L-O-V-E' by Natalie Cole
'Till There Was You' by Etta Jones
'Let's Call the Whole Thing Off' by Fred Astaire
'That's All' by Mel Tormé
'September in the Rain' by Dinah Washington
'A Wink and a Smile' by Harry Connick, Jr.
'*C'est si bon*' by Louis Armstrong
'Trust in Me' by Etta James
'There Will Never Be Another You' by Chet Baker
'I'm in the Mood for Love' by Julie London
'I Wish You Love' by Nancy Wilson

6. Page 275 – *Good Times, Noodle Salad*

In this scene Cooper is wearing a T-shirt emblazoned with a scene from the movie *As Good as It Gets*. I wanted to pay a little tribute to the movie which is not only my favourite film of all time, ever, but also a huge inspiration for *The Love of My*

Afterlife. Melvin the misanthrope finding an unlikely love and community in New York makes my heart dance every time I see it. I so wanted to imbue that sense of hope, transformation and human connection in my own work. I hope I did!

7. Page 341 – *Surprise!*

Did you guess? Did you see this coming? There are clues all the way through the book – some I planned and others I didn't. Here are some of them . . .

- Cooper and Merritt both have curly hair and green eyes.
- Cooper's sister was the one who read all his first drafts and told him to include a love story in his first crime novel.
- Cooper's *As Good as It Gets* T-shirt was a gift (from Merritt!).
- Cooper refers to his sister as being the only one who could ever outpush Aunt Beverley, which makes sense when you think of how pushy Merritt is!
- The earrings that Cooper lends Delphie are from an estate sale. When we first meet Merritt she is wearing a ring on every single finger – a fan of any and all unusual jewellery.
- Cooper's sister was a book nerd who loved reading Judy Blume novels at the park.

Kirsty Greenwood
March 2024

Keep in touch with

KIRSTY GREENWOOD

Be the first to hear Kirsty's latest publishing news, and discover exclusive competitions and behind-the-scenes content by signing up to Kirsty's newsletter at:

www.kirstygreenwood.com/newsletter

You can also follow Kirsty on X and Instagram or visit her dedicated Facebook page.

𝕏 @KirstyStories

⟳ @kirsty_greenwood

f /KirstyGreenwoodBooks

Discover the new novel from

KIRSTY GREENWOOD

SEXY SPOOKY LOVE STORY

Pre-order now